His Last Name

A Tale of Espar

His Last Name

D. Lambert

4 Horsemen
Publications, Inc.

4 Horsemen
Publications, Inc.

Published By: 4 Horsemen Publications, Inc.

4 Horsemen Publications, Inc.
PO Box 417
Sylva, NC 28779
4horsemenpublications.com
info@4horsemenpublications.com

Cover by J. Kotick
Typesetting by Autumn Skye
Edited by Jen Paquette

Library of Congress Control Number: 2024944397

Paperback ISBN-13: 979-8-8232-0632-7
Hardcover ISBN-13: 979-8-8232-0633-4
Audiobook ISBN-13: 979-8-8232-0635-8
Ebook ISBN-13: 979-8-8232-0634-1

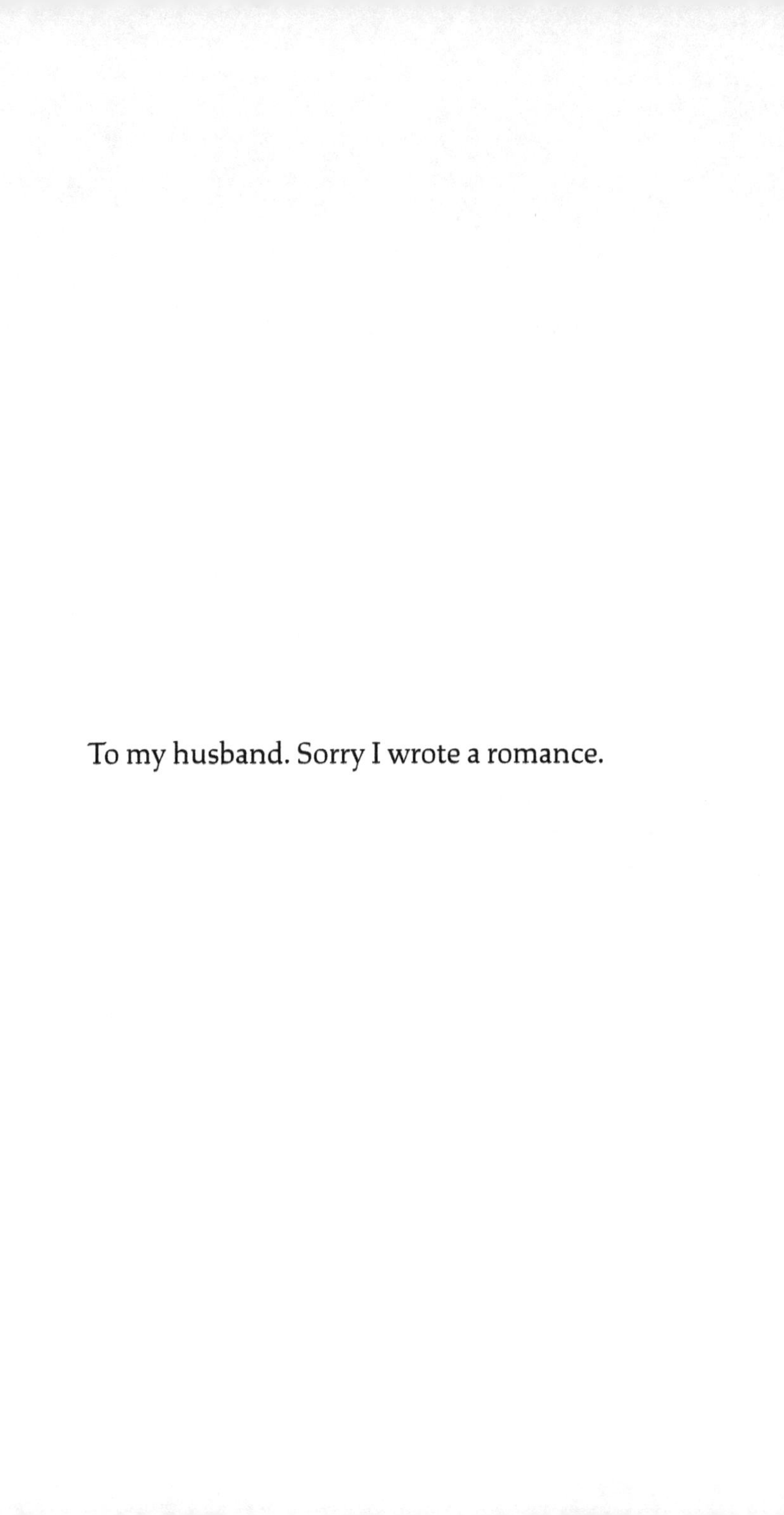

To my husband. Sorry I wrote a romance.

Table of Contents

K itable crossed off the charcoal writing, discouraged. The code line broke the flow of the spell and would sour it beyond use. He would have to start again.

He tossed the useless vellum onto the stack that had formed on the table before him, burying the various broken or half-finished enchanted trinkets. Somewhere near the other edge of the table, a cup of tea was getting cold.

Shimmer was reading yet another ancient book in the other room, seeking a reference to focuses. It seemed a waste; her energy would be better put toward honing her skills and reducing the words of a spell as he was doing. Although much of their magic was arranged in pre-casted hovering spells, efficiently casting a spell from scratch was invaluable under duress. Shortening one word out of a dozen could save time and, possibly, their lives.

He had put distance between them deliberately. Something about Shimmer seemed off this morning, and he did not want her apparent distraction throwing off his work. She was still determined to find the secret behind the focus, claiming it could be a vital tool in defensive situations, but her efforts led to constant dead ends, and he was too discouraged to keep at it. All he knew about a focus was that it was not something made of wizard magic. That made it uninteresting.

There was a knock on his door, and preoccupied, Kitable did not even consider his response. "Go away!" he snapped.

"Tough," the deep voice replied from the other side of the door. "You have to open the door for me, Kit."

Had he failed to recognize the voice, Kitable would have known the speaker by the nickname. Only one man alive called him "Kit."

Leaving his work, Kitable opened the door to admit King Tohmas.

"Unexpected visit, my King," he said. He saw Prime Protector Carsh in the hallway but gave the tough Rydan a look that prompted him to stay outside. Kitable closed the door quickly. Carsh hated magic anyway. He'd be glad for the excuse to stay in the hallway.

"Being unexpected," the king replied, "is why my enemies hate me."

Although the King of Espar visited about every mooncycle, he always paused within the entrance to Kitable's chambers, claiming to be checking if anything had changed. The chambers, although spacious, were sparsely decorated and jumbled. Bookcases filled with either magical trinkets or books lined all walls but one, and their contents varied depending on the research whims of Kitable and Shimmer's recent projects. The smooth white wizard-stone of the ceiling was marred by various stains, splatters, and two curious green lines that had appeared after a confrontation with an old curse; they had faded to a blue lately. The one bare wall bore windows that looked over an elaborate garden in late summer. He'd adjusted that enchantment last quartercycle to better bring in the light during the afternoon. The chambers were underground in truth, but it would be hard to tell.

Finishing his assessment, the king found a seat at the cluttered table. King Tohmas had instigated the custom of offering drinks during meetings, making it expected for Kitable to immediately offer his patron the only beverage he had available: the tea Shimmer had made that morning. He quickly dug out the tea cup and topped it off from the ever-warm tea pot. The king accepted it as smoothly as any drink, although the small cup looked like a toy in his large, rough hands.

Shimmer stuck her head into the room to investigate. She should have been able to guess the identity of their visitor. King Tohmas was the only person Kitable could be convinced to let in.

Her face brightened to see their patron sitting his bulk on a rickety chair. She had been pestering him to get the seat fixed, or at least reinforce it magically, for almost a year. Her grin now suggested she wondered if it would collapse under the king and prove her right.

But then, Shimmer was always smiling. Kitable could scarcely remember half a dozen moments lacking her grin since he had met her three years ago. Since becoming his apprentice, Shimmer had shed her colorful clothing and jewelry. Now, she was typically found in plain ankle-length dresses and shawls, her crimson hair tucked away under cowls and wimples. She looked nothing like the performer and apothecary who had traveled Espar, except for her persistent apothecary bag. He spotted it over her shoulder even now.

"So," the king said, "how are you and Shimmer getting along?"

Every mooncycle, Kitable would be accosted to provide an update for his patron. It had never been so direct before, but assuming the king's purpose was the same, Kitable asked Shimmer to clean the world's mobile.

"It's not dirty," she replied.

"You are assuming I want you to clean it because it is dirty."

Her smile grew, warning him he would not like her next sentence. "No, I'm pointing out I know you are not asking me to clean it because it's dirty." She skipped back into the side room, allowing Kitable to sit across from his patron in temporary peace.

"You two doing all right?" the king asked.

"She is disobedient, headstrong, and useless," Kitable said. After letting the words settle, he added, "She's also eavesdropping."

"Oie!" Shimmer's voice came from the side room.

"Eavesdropping is unbecoming of a lady!" he shouted.

"Whoever said I was a lady?" she shouted back.

Instead of getting into yet another debate, Kitable said a single word. One of the many pre-casted spells hovering around him answered by sealing the side room with a Wind Barrier.

"That will hold her for a short while," Kitable explained. "Not long." He'd spent the last two years cultivating her talent in magic. He could not be upset by her adeptness.

"So, how is she really doing?" the king asked.

With his apprentice no doubt already working through the spell's defenses, Kitable did not have time to be ambiguous. "She is brilliant," he admitted. "She has the most critical, beautiful way of thinking. These days, our work has us both making discoveries. I am not sure there is anything else

I can teach her." The admission caught him by surprise. If he had nothing left to teach her, Shimmer's apprenticeship was ending. He did not like the thought.

"Are you two available?"

His response was as reflexive as his earlier dismissal of the knock. "I hate missions."

The king chuckled into his cup. "No, you like missions. They give you something to work on. You hate missions that make you leave your room." With a mischievous smile, he added, "You are not going to like this one."

"So where are we going?"

"Lour."

Kitable's stomach sank. He did not like traveling anywhere in Espar, but the Province of Lour in the west was his least favorite destination. In the last twenty years since he had left it, he had visited exactly once and still thought that one time too many.

Proving further that he was losing the shrewdness they had come to love, the king did not seem to notice Kitable's discomfort.

"Digging?" Kitable wondered. If he was going to clean out more collapsed tunnels, he would be annoyed but not concerned. He could finish that kind of job quickly and be out before anyone thought too hard about it.

"More complicated," the king said. "The problem was in StonePeak for a while; it appears to have moved."

"What exactly is the problem?"

The king shrugged his massive shoulders. "I do not know."

"So why does this involve me?"

"Because it is probably magic."

"Probably?"

"'Probably' is why I appreciate you, Kitable. One way or another, you will know."

Unable to argue the point, the master wizard asked, "If it is no longer in StonePeak, where is it?"

Putting down the teacup gently, the king leaned forward. "A small village east of StonePeak called Woodcutter's Retreat. It's—"

"I know it."

Kitable's unease was too obvious this time for the king to miss.

"You've lived in Galanth for your entire life except for our move here to Trulin's border, to my knowledge. You going to explain how you know such an insignificant corner of Lour?"

Kitable shook his head. There was no point.

"Right..." The king shrugged. "They have been getting some odd activities, like thefts with no trace, strange lights, noises. No one can figure it out, so Kingsman Loritat came to me. You up for it?"

He wished he could say "no," but Kitable had never been able to refuse Tohmas, and problems in Woodcutter's Retreat already made him nervous. He would investigate regardless. It would be easier if he did so officially.

"I will check it out and travel up if necessary. Is that satisfactory?"

The king grinned and finished his tea in a single swallow like shooting spirits. "I never expect less of you."

"You should, you know," he reminded the king, but Tohmas did not seem to hear him.

Shimmer broke down the Wind Barrier in time to hear the king's farewell.

She looked like she had something to say, but Kitable's frown discouraged her. Instead, she went back to disassembling the world's mobile for cleaning.

Long after the sun had drifted under the horizon, Shimmer found her way to her room in the Manor of Trulinar. Needing to earn her keep if she wanted to have money for food later, she'd finished her work with Kitable and then worked in the kitchens. She was exhausted, yet her mind continued to turn over the research. Mysteries were her favorite pastime, at least until they interfered with her sleep.

She could hear her bed calling by her full name by the time she finally returned to her room.

To her surprise, Prime Protector Carsh met her in the hallway, his tattooed chest bare and his wrists wrapped in dried grasses traditional to the Rydans of the Outlands.

He was not her favorite person, although they had come to an understanding at some point. The prime protector's mission in life was to kill wizards whenever he was not occupied defending the king and queen, and his skill made Shimmer's skin prickle with sweat whenever someone mentioned his name. The multitude of knives he carried and his proficiency with them made her fear well founded.

He had not threatened her recently out of respect for Kitable, but that relationship was at risk of changing in a blink if Carsh ever believed Shimmer meant King Tohmas harm.

Thankfully, another voice called her away from the prime protector. "Miss Weaver," King Tohmas greeted her, "a word?"

King Tohmas and Queen Arnika advanced down the corridor, the larger group of protectors at their backs keeping a respectful distance. The king dwarfed his petite wife, standing taller than any other man Shimmer knew. As far as Shimmer was concerned, he had one supernatural power: he could ask a question and make someone want to obey. Although he paused to let her reply, the answer was already decided.

"Any time, my King," she said, eyeing the Rydan prime protector who lounged against her door. She met his toothy grin with a smirk, recognizing the game. Rydans understood only one thing: strength. She could not show hesitation.

Her greatest strength was her magic. She whispered a word to activate one of her hovering—ready but inactive—spells. The new shield, designed to stop any physical contact from the front, appeared between them. It was not visible, but the prime protector was one of the few in the world who could detect magic without being a wizard, and he recognized the demonstration of power. Chuckling in satisfaction, he moved aside.

She had to disarm three wards before she touched the handle to her room.

Dumping her bag by the door by habit, Shimmer left the door open for her guests. She rummaged for cups, knowing etiquette demanded she serve drink as a hostess, but the queen stopped her.

"We appreciate it, Shimmer, but it's approaching midnight. We won't be long," Queen Arnika said softly. The little woman's voice had gained strength as the years went by, and she fell into her position as ruler of Espar. With her son nearing his second birthday, the queen was again pregnant, although it was hard to tell on her tiny frame. She had given birth without difficulty, a contradiction to her build, much like her strength and her quiet demeanor.

The couple left the protectors in the hallway and wandered into Shimmer's mess. The king seemed instantly fascinated by her cluttered room. Even the bed hid under broken trinkets and half-finished items. There never seemed to be time left for tidying; Shimmer's mind was continuously occupied by the next project.

"You're in late," King Tohmas said absently, watching one of her glass shard mobiles built to demonstrate light refractions with wonder.

"I work evenings," she said.

"Kitchen?"

She nodded.

"And with your father?" Queen Arnika prompted, making Shimmer bite her lip in reluctance. Match and Mixer, the moving show and apothecary shop, had a reputation she kept unconnected to her work with Master Kitable.

Seeing her hesitation, the queen frowned. "I would hate to think you had given up your dancing!" When the king glanced at his wife with one eyebrow raised, the queen laughed. "Well, someone had to say it, and if you did, people might start terrible rumors. I, on the other hand, can compliment Shimmer on her dancing with complete impunity."

"I still dance," Shimmer confessed. "I Relocate to Wayburn." The casual mention of such a potent spell was wasted on the king and queen; they had no idea how complicated it was to cast the spell that accurately moved an entire person to a prescribed location. It had taken her a year under Kitable's tutelage to master it, but with Master Kitable as the only other caster they knew, it was no wonder they thought such advanced magic commonplace. "I go at least once a quartercycle. I use a disguise and..." She trailed off, thinking that was a lie. She didn't wear a disguise at Match and Mixer. She wore one here.

"We did not come here to protect our reputations," Queen Arnika consoled.

The king nodded. "I wanted to ask you about..." The sentence fell off when he caught sight of a spinning orb, part of a trinket she was working on. Like an unfocused child, the man's eyes fixed on the orb with complete absorption.

Into the subsequent silence, the queen finished, "Kitable, Shimmer. We wanted to ask you about Wisavi Kitable. How is he?" Shimmer hadn't heard anyone call him "wisavi" for a while. It was a formal title of advisor to the king, but when they worked together, Kitable was "master," the title he had earned by being a wizard.

A little baffled by the king's distraction, Shimmer answered without censoring her reply. "Grouchy as ever." She smiled apologetically at the queen's bemused expression. "He is Master Kitable, my Queen. He hates that Rydan title, by the way."

"We had noticed he was acting strange these last mooncycles. A little shorter in temper?" the queen said.

The use of the word "we" felt out of place. The king was not noticing much of anything.

"I guess I agree he's bristling more than usual," Shimmer answered. "I've asked him about it, but he'll not talk about it, at least not to—"

"If not you, then no one, Shimmer," Arnika insisted.

"Good to hear he is doing well," King Tohmas said, his smile surprisingly sincere. "We should let this poor girl sleep, my lady."

Knowing her words had never implied "well," Shimmer looked at the queen for an explanation. King Tohmas was known for having a good sense of humor, but she heard no jesting in his voice. What had they discussed earlier in the day?

"Can you give us a moment, my love?" Arnika said. "I think we might have some womanly things to discuss."

Dismissed like a servant, the king complimented Shimmer on her room, wished her and her father well, and left.

Shimmer waited until he had closed the door. "Did I say—?"

"Not you, Shimmer. It's him. It gets worse when he is tired. It's been a long day."

"It?" she asked. "I look at him and do not see the man who conquered Espar, my Queen. He seemed like a child! Like…" Knowing finishing the thought would insult the king further, Shimmer let it drop.

Releasing a long sigh, the queen nodded grimly and finished, "Like his mind cannot see what is in front of him. Yes. I am sorry to bring this to you. Kitable already knows, but I wanted to tell you as well. Tohmas is unwell." Her longing eyes went to the recently closed door. "Every mooncycle, he worsens. His ears hear one thing, but his mind another. As much as suggesting it would be seen as blasphemy, I believe it is SoulBurner's doing."

Shimmer shook her head, knowing the reputation of the sword as a gift from the Goddess Inac, Tohmas' patron goddess, but she stopped when she remembered the day he had accepted the blade from a red-haired woman.

The legend claimed the Goddess Inac had presented the sword. Still, Shimmer had recognized all the fires as apothecary ploys and the presenter as Celebrant Loni FireDancer, a whore and holy woman who had been with the armies.

No goddess had been involved. To reveal as much to the people of Espar would undermine Tohmas' claim to Espar, but it made it likely the queen was right to suspect the enchanted weapon. Although the sword's powers had been unexplained initially, they had found a source: untouchable powers. These strange powers were known to dispel wizard magic, but beyond that, their origins and uses were a mystery. Occasionally, people, usually celebrants to the gods, could manifest the power, but no one knew how to teach the ability.

That was for the best, in Shimmer's opinion. She didn't want anyone using untouchable powers around her; beyond merely being immune to magic, a touch from an untouchable would destroy her magic trinkets and hovering spells too. They were a thing of nightmares for wizards.

The queen smiled weakly. "He snuck away from me to give Kitable a mission, and while I agree with the mission, I needed you to know about the situation before you left. I wanted to ask if you might find something to help him. Kitable has already said it is of a different kind of magic than yours, the untouchable kind. It affects Tohmas the most when he is tired, so maybe something could help him stay aware longer? Anything that will help him keep up appearances."

"We will try," Shimmer promised readily, knowing that her master would not object to such an oath. Tohmas had been Kitable's patron for years, and she had no doubt the wizard was fond of his king.

The king's wife nodded in thanks. As she turned to go, she added, "I believe he was right to assign Kitable the task, so I will let it remain. Please keep me apprised."

Shimmer immediately bowed her head in obedience. The idea that the queen was dictating to her husband should have upset Shimmer, but if the king's weakening mental capacity became widely known, the consequences would be far worse. They needed the king to hold the unity he had forced upon the land. Without him, Espar would revert to bickering princedoms and ancient feuds. The new kingdom was too young to be left on its own. They needed their king.

Her fatigue had left entirely, and she doubted she could sleep with the new mystery to occupy her. A cursed sword?

And how could they stop the sword if their magic was use-less against it?

Too agitated, she decided against sleep.

The night felt darker than usual, and even the magic light of the wizard-stone manor could not lift the feeling. Desperate for relief, she took a long walk outside the Manor of Trulinar. Every time she left, she had to walk farther to leave the growing settlement and get beyond the cut trees. But once she was surrounded by old cedars and oaks, she cast her Relocation spell.

In a blink, she was at Match and Mixer, which had set up a permanent place in Wayburn far in Espar's south. Close enough to the southern borders, the apothecary shop attracted visitors from the Outlands as well as the regulars from Galanth's capital, keeping her father's apothecary business brisk. When the lamps on the street corners were going out, Match and Mixer closed its sides and put out the benches for the shows. Her father had his minor castings and juggling, but the show truly filled to capacity when Shimmer joined.

Under the light of torches, finally allowed to dress com-fortably and wear her jewelry, Shimmer found what she had come for—she danced.

Her heart settled with the movement, her mind clearing. Along with cheers, coins, shouts and propositions, she drew a huge crowd. Here, she was not a practicing wizard; she was a dancer and apothecary.

She was home.

For the first time in years, Shimmer dreamed. In her dream, Shimmer danced on a raised stage in her ribbons and bangles. Kitable watched but turned away when she tried to bring him to the stage with her. New hands reached out to her, inviting her to dance, and all the while, Kitable walked away, unwilling to dance.

When she woke, her spells were gone, as sure as a kiss from an untouchable. She rolled out of bed feeling cold, naked, and annoyed. At least here, in her chambers within the Manor of Trulinar, she was protected. She relied on the other defenses as she rebuilt her hovering and defensive spells.

She'd been due to replenish the spells regardless. Over a brief breakfast, she checked the tarot cards, something she knew Kitable would have scoffed at. It only confirmed something was afoot, but she was no closer to knowing what by the time she returned to Kitable's room at her customary predawn hour.

Kitable waited for her at the table.

"You've been up all night, then?" she asked.

Disgruntled, he shifted in his seat, then stood and moved to the shutters. His rooms were underground, but the windows still showed a view of the nearby gardens and the early sunrise when he pulled the shutters away. "What makes you say that?" he asked.

There was no sign of fatigue in him, but he was prone to putting illusions over himself when showing weakness, making it possible what she saw was incorrect.

"You made tea," she pointed out, pouring herself a cup. "Means you have been up for a while." The teapot was still hot, but Kitable's cup was cold behind the stacks of books they had left there the night before.

"I was Scrying."

"Without me?" she said. "I'm offended! Secrecy does not suit you!"

"The king has asked us to look into a problem in Lour, so I was Scrying to determine if it merited our attention, Miss Weaver."

Shimmer's heart skipped a beat, but she only raised an eyebrow outwardly. "Bad news?" she guessed. It wouldn't be about her, she assumed. Queen Arnika would have mentioned if the quest involved Shimmer's previous life with Match and Mixer. And it wasn't that anyone in Lour knew her well. She and her father avoided it.

She wished Kitable had, after opening the shutters, kept looking out the enchanted wall and into the barely lit greenery outside. Instead, he turned, and his frown was prominent.

"Have you been casting divinations, Miss Weaver?" Divinations were not as bad as thought magic, but they were a close second. He spoke as if implying she had been gambling.

So it wasn't to do with her; he was annoyed by her accuracy.

"You called me 'Miss Weaver,'" Shimmer answered with a smirk.

"That is your name, Shimmer Weaver, or so you—"

"You only call me 'Miss Weaver' when you're upset," Shimmer explained, finding her way to the table. "I get demoted to plain 'WEAVER!'" she said, mimicking of his irritated shout, "when you're mad at me, but 'Miss Weaver' is for when someone else is the source of your frustration. I am called Shimmer, remember? It took me a year to get you to use my name!"

When he had no response, she chuckled, pleased to have rendered him speechless, and added, "So I conclude that you have come to an unpleasant decision. Since I know how much you love traveling, I supposed that means we must go somewhere. You mentioned Lour." She tossed her hair, beaming at him. "So, how good are my mundane divinations doing?"

He sat at the table with a grumble, trying, but not quite succeeding, to smother a small smile. "We are going to be traveling to Lour," he confirmed. "Some problems, petty thefts, and whatnot."

Definitely, she decided, nothing to do with the blank section on her official papers under "mother's name." That was good. She had been nervous enough about putting her history on one of King Tohmas' new identification papers, finding it all too permanent once it was spelled out.

She dropped her ever-present sack on the floor beside him and dumped his cup back into the pot to be heated. She took to tidying the room since they had left out all the scrolls and ink from the day before. "Sounds far beneath the Wisavi of Espar," she commented, pushing the worry out of her voice. She hoped their destination was not going to be the capital of Lour. Setting foot in StonePeak would probably not be a problem, but if they had to talk to the kingsman or his ilk, Shimmer worried she might upset a few things if she or, more importantly, her pedigree, was recognized.

As predicted, Kitable snorted at the title, but her baiting look, tossed over her shoulder at him, at least made him smile again. He knew she'd goaded him. It seemed to lighten his mood.

"It would be," he confirmed, "but I cannot Scry on the problem, and my Reflections are coming up empty." His pause was deliberate.

Shimmer finished the thought. "Which means either a wizard blocking divination and alteration or an untouchable."

"Two years ago, I would have bet on wizards," Kitable admitted, "but I have accidentally reduced the number of casters in Espar recently. It could be untouchable."

Putting away the books from the table, Shimmer grimaced. "If it's an untouchable," she said, "it shouldn't be our problem. Why should wizards chase something that can't be affected by magic?"

"Because we can hit back if we're smart about how, Shimmer. Tohmas' men would be absolutely helpless against an untouchable manifesting power. Besides, untouchable powers work similarly to ours. We have a better understanding of them."

She blew a sigh at a loose strand of her hair in disbelief. "So, we're going to Lour?" she asked, facing him squarely, hands on her hips. She had changed back into clothing more suited to living in the home of the King of Espar: a modest blouse and skirt with basic pouches and no jewelry. It was uncomfortable.

Kitable nodded.

"Just because the kingsman has a series of unexplained events that may or may not involve magic, which might be wizard or untouchable?" she pressed.

Another nod.

"No other reason?"

The nodding stopped, and he narrowed his smoke-gray blue eyes on her. Her heart fluttered. "No other reason," he repeated.

"You're hiding something. Something about Lour? Something..."

"Gather your traveling supplies, Weaver."

There it was: "Weaver."

Her suspicions confirmed, she raised an eyebrow at him.

Recognizing the slip, he put his head in his hand in frustration.

Forgiving his refusal to elaborate, Shimmer kicked her bag. "I'm always ready to go. Just tell me when." That was a part of her life: a quick escape. Her father had taught her that lesson repeatedly in her youth.

"I need to speak to your father first," he told her, visibly relieved that she had not pursued her questions. "I would rather not be recognized as we travel; his clothes should fit me. Faster to do that than try to arrange something locally."

Still in its infancy, the Manor of Trulinar housed only essential staff. The nearest towns were all small enough to be inconsequential, which had been the point. It was a retreat, not meant to host large gatherings or attract political attention. The kingsmen knew its location, but few others did.

Finding a tailor locally would be impossible, but the mental image of her master, who was now in his mid-thirties, wearing her father's flamboyantly colorful garb, made Shimmer giggle despite herself.

"He's at the shop, as always," she said. "Will we need the cart horses?"

The master wizard stood and sorted through his wardrobe. He picked out a traveling cloak and pouch. "No point. We'll walk until we're out of the area. Then we can Relocate closer."

"Closer?" she asked. "Not there?"

Kitable shook his head. "If it's a magic user, they may track the spell. I'm not ready to let the manor here become widely known. And I'd rather not arrive with a powerful spell advertising our involvement."

Traveling was familiar. She felt a twinge of excitement. "Should I be changing?" Shimmer asked.

When Kitable looked at Shimmer, she blushed. For once, he seemed to be considering her appearance, her costume of bland colors and unassuming styles.

"You should probably switch back to your old clothing," he surprised and delighted her by saying. "We will go as merchants, so you should look the part."

He never concerned himself much with housekeeping, not even when leaving for long periods. Hurrying to follow, she failed to put away the cups and tea.

"So am I wrong about this being more than just about some petty thefts?" she called, grabbing her bag and skipping after him as he left.

"You are wrong, Miss Weaver," he replied.

She smirked. "You are so bad at lying."

She pretended she didn't see his partially concealed defeated smile.

They were on the road by midday. Kitable had swapped into one of Dust's colorful shirts and baggy trousers and wore a diklo around his throat because Shimmer's father had insisted "the outfit isn't complete without it." The short scarf—a radiant maroon at odds, in Kitable's opinion, with the purple and black shirt—itched. At quiet times, he forgot it was there, then suddenly felt like someone was trying to strangle him.

The jewelry was mostly plain, but several magic trinkets, basic ones that could justifiably be in the hands of a merchant such as Dust Weaver, were interspersed. His belt was the type used by tinkers or cutters, holding a dozen small pouches of various sizes and descriptions.

Shimmer matched him in style, although that meant every garment was from a different source, and none matched in color. Her blouse was cut short, reaching the bottom of her ribcage, and hung off a shoulder most of the time. Her skirts were layered heavily from hip to ankle yet did not impede her movement. She wore a thin vest, and her jewelry was far more ostentatious than his, yet flattering. Her brilliant red hair had been partially tied instead of hidden under a hood or bandanna. Beads and bangles danced in the thick locks, at least two of the beads enchanted.

He did not blame her. He had taught her those enchantments and the paranoia that made them both expect to need the defensive magic.

Once out of the manor, she all but glowed in excitement, a fact Kitable expected to resent. Instead, he found himself catching some of her enthusiasm. He had not seen her so relaxed since they had first agreed to an apprenticeship. He knew the politics of the king stifled her. She had worked to overcome the confines of the stationary life, yet he had seen some of her shimmering dim.

The roads nearest the Manor of Trulinar were packed earth. Once on the main road, the trail grew wide enough to allow waggons. Since Prince Tohmas' conquest of the lands, the roads had become the responsibility of the kingsmen. Seemingly terrified King Tohmas might find their efforts inadequate, each kingsman competed for the prestige of the best paths. In Solta, they were well maintained.

Had they been planning to walk or ride the distance to Woodcutter's Retreat, they could have expected nearly a mooncycle of travel, including a stretch through mountains. Instead, only the first and last day of the journey would be on foot. It was a perk to being a caster, Kitable had to admit. That long in the saddle would have left him very sore.

They followed along treed paths, standing aside for waggons or riders, nodding to fellow travelers on the road. They could not easily discuss magic like they usually did without revealing themselves; wizards were too few. Instead, Shimmer filled the time with stories about her travels and her father's adventures, some of which Kitable doubted he believed.

But as evening fell and they set a basic camp, she surprised him by saying, "So, your patron's wife came to talk to me."

She had timed the conversation carefully. They were alone, and it was unlikely anyone would be moving about in the shadows, risking losing the road or coming across a predator. These roads were wide but not well frequented. Still, avoiding the names was good practice, even if it seemed unnecessary.

"Did she?"

"She wanted me to know about her husband's condition," Shimmer said.

His suspicion confirmed, Kitable frowned. "Good to know."

"Have you looked into it? It is truly untouchable?"

"Without a doubt," he confirmed, "which is why we suspect the source we do."

"Have you spoken to the celebrants about it?"

He could not help but smile. Shimmer had been presented with a problem and would seek the answer until the world ceased to be. Solving problems filled her with a contagious enthusiasm Kitable enjoyed.

"Calanor is difficult to track down these days," he admitted, "and Celebrant Sedgan is inconsistently manifesting, depending on his degree of faith. Of course, the real source, the one person I could expect to be able to do something about it, is dead."

He did not say Celebrant Loni's name. Tohmas insisted it was severe bad luck to mention the name of an angry spirit out loud. Kitable suspected the concept came from Tohmas' mixed upbringing, but he had never gotten around to asking a Rydan if it was a commonly held belief of their people.

Shimmer considered the information for a long while, her eyes on a spot in their small campfire. Like her, his mind went to the troubles of the king's sword, SoulBurner, and the difficulty manipulating it.

The sword was legendary now, embedded in the myth of King Tohmas' conquest of Espar. Kitable and Shimmer had witnessed its arrival, but Shimmer had easily explained every one of the "miracles" performed by the "goddess" who had briefly walked among them. Kitable knew he was one of the few who believed that the goddess thought to be Inac had been nothing more than the mad Celebrant Loni in disguise. Her tricks had fooled the masses efficiently, and

Kitable had never seen cause to disrupt the devotion the event had brought to King Tohmas.

"I wish you had told me sooner," Shimmer said.

"It was a delicate matter," he apologized. "I was not permitted to tell you; otherwise, I would have. I find your assistance with such things useful."

When she adjusted her seat on the stone, it was by shifting her shoulders. They were bare again, the way he remembered her throughout the Northlander war and the conquest of Espar. It suited her so much better than the conservative attire she had worn lately.

"Was that a compliment?" She laughed, and the sound of it made him smile. "Am I ill? Dying?"

"Is it unreasonable to assume I find you an acceptable travel companion?"

"Two compliments!" she exclaimed, feigning shock. "Wait, are *you* dying?"

Her joyful jibe made him laugh aloud. It felt strange, and he sharply realized he had not laughed in some time. Perhaps she was not the only one stifled by the politics of Espar of late.

"Not that I am aware of," Kitable said. "But I admit, I have little to add to your musing right now." He felt a yawn sneaking in. "I... I also am beginning to suspect that may be the case in general."

She cocked her head, her smile unwavering. Knowing him well, she was waiting for the rest of the thought. In the campfire light, she glowed.

Since mentioning it to the king, the idea had been nagging Kitable. "It..." Kitable began, hating the way he hesitated. Finding words had never been so difficult. "It seems to me you no longer require my guidance."

He thought her smile waned a touch, but she stubbornly kept it in place. "Am I being too obstinate?" she joked, tossing her head. "Not that I'm apologizing or suggesting I will change. I gave up on that after the first cycle!"

Their first cycle together had been filled with a profound awkwardness. She had been one part apologetic and one part deferential, which had been maddening. After enough time, Kitable had told her he had no patience for simpering people, and she had shocked him by dropping the charade. With her seeking to challenge him as much as he challenged her, the apprenticeship had thrived.

But it will end, Kitable reminded himself. Two years was a short apprenticeship, but she had not come into it as a child. She had already known much. He had helped her grow her power. Her brilliance made him superfluous now.

Kitable cleared his throat and pulled his traveling cloak around him. "It's nothing," he said, yawning. "But it has been a few years since I have been on my feet for such a long day. Sleep beckons."

A bedroll had never been his choice, but there were no shelters on hand, and conjuring something would leave a large aura to be noticed. He'd selected a roughly flat region, bunching his hood as a pillow.

She paused, reconsidered her following sentence, then said, "Do you have an anchor for tomorrow?" She mirrored him by sliding into a well-used bedroll she had selected as supplies from Match and Mixer.

Kitable shook his head. "We can Scry to get one tomorrow, then share it."

He considered making it into a lesson on the Two-Person Relocation spell but decided against it. He was going to be tired enough. The familiar Relocation spell was straightforward, and they both had plenty of practice with it. He could trust Shimmer to manage her own. A Two-Person Relocation, using a single spell to move them both, was far more complicated and better suited to anchors they knew well.

"Sounds good," she said, nestling down. Her red hair formed a pillow around her, framing her face. She closed her eyes and seemed to drift off immediately.

Kitable watched her for a few moments over the fading fire. When he realized he was staring, he rolled over, determined to keep whatever was stirring in his thoughts from rising.

After this mission, he decided, he would let her go. She deserved a title and a chance at making her own way in the world. Anything less was him being selfish.

He found it hard to sleep.

In their travels the next day, they were at risk of getting burned by the summer sun. Kitable surrendered, finally wearing the hat Dust had lent him. It was wide-brimmed and rode uncomfortably low on his brow, and it made Shimmer reminisce about other misadventures she and her father had shared.

Shimmer put on a bandanna and adjusted her collar strings to protect her shoulders. Her skin had become pale during their time together.

The Relocation spells were flawless. Kitable did not have to prompt Shimmer at all. Once he had located their target, he passed her the anchor and spent another candle searching the area for any hints of magic surveillance. She joined him, holding the anchor at the ready while managing the other spells, a feat only a handful in the world could achieve. Once their inspection of the area yielded no hidden threats, they each cast their Relocation spells along the anchor.

The woods he had chosen were on the Lour side of the border, making it unnecessary to deal with guards. Since King Tohmas' reign had begun, the borders had become more tightly controlled, a necessity for properly applying taxes for the king and his kingsmen. They even had official documents prepared, although Kitable knew both of their personal versions were poor representations of the documentation the king was making more widespread. Shimmer's listed no mother, something he had not asked her about. Doing so seemed hypocritical, as Kitable's had no last name or parentage.

Besides, not knowing her history was vital to preserving his respect for her, he was certain.

Still, Kitable knew her previous life had forced her and her father to travel extensively, giving her a story for every bend in the road. He had to remind himself that her father was a traveling showman, making it unlikely that most of the stories were hers or even true, but they were still amusing.

As they moved out of the forest and onto a well-traveled road, Shimmer returned to her stories of adventure, thievery, and love.

The day passed with little of interest. While they sought a campsite, Shimmer went into telling a story about the first three founders of Clandac's fishing trade: the man, the fish, and the worm.

When Shimmer abruptly stopped her story, Kitable brought his attention to the road. In the late afternoon, there were no travelers. Instead, three men stood on the path, having hidden behind a bend. Two were on horseback, but the tallest man, who towered as tall as Carsh, stood with his arms across his chest at the center of the road.

To avoid drawing attention to themselves, Kitable had ordered Shimmer to avoid using magic. They each wore basic hovering spells, hidden carefully from most divinations, and had an assortment of enchanted items. If someone were keeping Woodcutter's Retreat out of Scrys, they would likely expect him to take notice. Overt spell casting could betray them.

"There's a toll," one of the men on horseback insisted. "Hand over your pouch."

Apparently "toll" meant "thief."

With Shimmer looking to him for the reply, Kitable pulled the pouch from his belt and tossed it to the horse rider. It was easier than…

"Radiance!" the standing man shouted, his beady eyes on Shimmer. "Hello, gorgeous! Bet you don't remember me!"

Standing tall, which invariably stuck out her chest and drew attention to the blouse slipping off her shoulders, Shimmer gave the man a twinkling smile.

"Do I get the pouch back if I win?" she asked, laughing lightly. Before the man could answer, she said, "Black Wall tavern, south Clandac, four and a half years ago. You were so drunk, you never did tell me your name."

The man's two companions chuckled when the thief blushed. "Hell of a night, too! What you doing with this peacock?" the man asked.

Shimmer is an actress, Kitable reminded himself. The look of scorn she gave him, her master, had to be false.

"Life got rough. I took a patron. This is Ren, boys," his apprentice said in a fake Southern accent.

Gritting his teeth, Kitable said nothing as they all smirked at him, assuming things he didn't want to consider. Had they known they were wizards, "patron" would mean master. But without knowing that, any older man taking in a young, attractive woman was more likely to be looking for company after sunset.

"A girl like you doesn't need a patron, Radiance. You must still be making good money."

Complimented, Shimmer's smile was no longer sweet. Even the way she sat had become deliberately captivating. *Playing along*, Kitable told himself. She was trying to keep the three armed men happy so they would let them pass.

Hefting the pouch, the rider gave Shimmer a suggestively raised eyebrow. "I think we can pay your next month's wages now," the man declared. "You two are now our guests. For tonight, you're staying with us."

There was a finality to the statement that made Kitable cringe. *Time for a spell?* He had at least two that could deal with all three men simultaneously. One was fatal too, and it was tempting in light of their disrespect of his apprentice.

Shimmer laughed and started toward the thieves before Kitable could decide. "Can't say I'd mind spicing things up! Tell me you've got some strong ale and consider me in!"

Following Shimmer's lead, Kitable did not activate his spells, knowing she was right. There would be another way.

By the time they found the campsite in the woods, an obvious hideaway from the king's soldiers, Kitable was reconsidering.

There were, in fact, five of them. Whether Shimmer had known about the two behind them during her conversation, Kitable did not know. Still, her decision to join the men instead of fight seemed all the more practical when he spotted the highwaymen's assorted weapons. All five were burly enough to have made their weapons effective. Trying to kill them all would have been tricky and risked injury. He was without many of his most critical defenses. A knife could kill a wizard, after all.

Shimmer's performance promised to be the safer, if more uncomfortable, solution.

They made a show of sitting Kitable on a rock by the fire. Then, keeping all the gold spokes for themselves, they ostensibly gifted Shimmer one of the silver disc coins from Kitable's purse. With the next gesture, they presented Shimmer with a wineskin of drink, and she, still the actress, took a quick gulp in preparation.

Being the "peacock" kept him out of most of the festivities and so kept him sober. He wished he had been much less clear of mind.

Shimmer danced.

Her skirts were already cut to allow for dancing, and her blouse lay flatteringly low off her shoulders. Sensual and suggestive, she moved around the fire in time with the pound of a makeshift drum one of the men had made out of a pot. Despite the limitations, she was skilled enough to be on Leviathan's grand stages, her movements graceful. She had the wineskin and its potent contents in hand as she moved, yet never spilled. At various intervals, she swept a leg over the lap of one of the onlookers and joined them in drinking.

As she got progressively unstable, her face reddened, and her words became sloppy. The men matched her drink for drink, each growing louder and stupider. Eventually, one decided Kitable too should drink and prompted Shimmer to force some repulsive firedrink down his throat.

Drunk as she was, she landed in his lap, hooked her legs around him, and guided the wineskin to his mouth. He had not quite figured out what to do—the sight of her legs up to the hip had a numbing effect on his mind—when she, under the guise of nibbling on his ear, whispered, "Whatever you do, don't swallow."

Kitable spat a mouthful of mealy spirits to one side and choked on the rest, to the delight of the highwaymen. Surprised by her perfectly sober directions, the coughing was authentic.

It took another quartercandle to understand fully.

The thieves slowed down. With Shimmer still prancing between them, tipping more drink down any throat opening for it, the thieves became drowsy. One slipped off a log backward and did not sit back up. Soon, the man was snoring on the far side of the log, and while still snickering at their friend's sudden slumber, two more toppled over themselves.

Shimmer was sitting on the fifth one when he finally went down, a smile on his face. Gingerly, Kitable's apprentice pulled the man's unconscious head from her bosom where it had fallen and placed the man on the ground.

She dusted herself off as she rose.

With a finger to her lips, she gathered her bag, and together, they loosed all the horses. Despite the sun's absence, they found their way back to the road and went on their way.

When the morning dawn arrived, Kitable finally felt they had put enough distance between the attackers and themselves to allow conversation.

She pre-empted him by a breath.

"Heavy dose of old lady's slippers flower and a touch of frozen freedom extract," she said. "The old lady's slippers knocks them out, but the freedom makes them happy about it. It also prevents them from noticing they're being drugged, which is nice. I'm glad I remembered it."

Kitable glanced at her canvas side bag, wondering what else was hiding in its depths. Dust Weaver was known as a juggler, a bard, and an apothecary. Shimmer Weaver was a match for her father with herbs and potions. Although it

had been a long time, Kitable had seen her use her knowledge before.

He decided he would have to take over making the tea in the morning. If she could knock out five full-grown men, he did not want her messing with anything he drank.

"I couldn't get the rest of the coins back," she said with a frown. "I'm not as good as my papa when it comes to picking pockets but..." She held out the single disc they had given her, the silver flash muted in the dawning light. "Should be enough to get accommodations for a few nights, less though if we have to buy food too often. I can dance for dinner anyway, so you can..." When she trailed off, he realized she was looking at him. "You're not mad at me, are you? I never wanted—"

"You did well, Radiance." He used her fake name to get around the more revealing use of her real name. "I forgot how varied your skills were."

He meant it as a compliment, but she bit her lip in the sunrise and turned her eyes back to the road. He had the distinct impression he had said something wrong.

With an inn ahead and a sleepless night behind, they stopped to rest instead of speaking further.

Knowing the common spaces would be busy in the morning, they shared a single room, where Shimmer curled up in her bedroll and slept on the floor.

Shimmer slept well in the familiar bedroll, dozing until midday. She woke when Kitable stirred, and still without much conversation, they hiked out once more to catch up on lost time. With their money limited, Shimmer handed the remaining funds from their room rental to Kitable and went to talk to the innkeeper of their next stop. Given permission, she adjusted her clothes and earned her dinner.

At least one man recognized her, calling her Seraph, so she became Seraph for a night.

Kitable sat at the bar, looking like a puppy stuck in a snowstorm. She had convinced another man to buy her a drink with dinner when Kitable finally left to go to his room.

It was harmless flirting, but she feared he was misunderstanding. She could get free food by pulling her top that much lower over her breasts and her skirt farther down her hips. By dancing, she could earn a handful of coins, coins which they would need to buy food and shelter until they reached their destination. Once in Woodcutter's Retreat, Kitable could reveal himself as the wisavi and expect the king's name would provide everything they needed. Until then, they had to survive. It was not as if she was going to sleep with any of her would-be suitors.

She had been fed nicely by the time she excused herself from her captive audience, pleading a place at her patron's side, and found the room.

He was on the bed, sitting cross-legged as he always did when Scrying, and had placed a Scry detecting stone on the bedside table. A spell word seemed on his lips, but he paused upon her arrival, disapproval seeping from his expression.

Her heart dropped.

"Nothing from Woodcutter's Retreat," he reported in a painfully bland voice.

Shimmer checked, but the stone on the bedside table—enchanted to go red if Scrys were watching—remained a pleasant gray color. "Are you at least going to ask me about—"

His raised hand stopped her cold. "I do not care," Kitable insisted. "When I took you on, I told you your previous life did not matter. I hold to that." His voice grew heavier. "I do not want to know."

"Why can you not—" Shimmer tried.

"Enough, Weaver," he threatened, untangling his legs and standing. "I do not care to know about your nightly misadventures. I have no interest in what happened between you and those men or any other random meetings you might have—"

"You do not even give me a chance—"

"Because I do not want to know!" he snapped with finality.

She threw her hands in the air. "How could I forget!? You have always hated my dancing!"

"Hate your dancing?" He stalked forward. "Any man still breathing adores your dancing! What I hate is how those drooling imps stare at you like you are a piece of meat dressed in bangles for their enjoyment! But far be it from me to interfere with a long-standing tradition! Shimmer, Seraph, Radiance... Do you even *have* a real name?"

"My name?" she shot back. "What about you? Do you have a *last* name?"

He froze a single pace from her, still pointing an accusatory finger.

Master Kitable was only ever Kitable. No relations, no history, no name. Until he had been "discovered" by the previous Prince of Galanth, no one had known anything about him. There was still a deep mystery around his training and upbringing. After two years, Shimmer knew that his apprenticeship had been a disaster, but only because he had laughed when she suggested he train her as he had been taught.

If he could not trust her with even that...

Straightening, he let fall the finger. He drew back to the bed and sat, folding his legs under him in a silence that hurt more than any of his accusations could have.

"Master—"

Shimmer stopped abruptly when she felt the wash of magic over the room. On the table, the stone they set out at every camp went red.

Kitable tensed but calmly said, "We should be getting some sleep."

The intruding Scry was a weak spell. The caster would have to make it stronger before they could channel any other spells through it, assuming they could even do so. For now, it felt more like a passing survey. So long as they gave the observer no reason to take an interest in them, they should be safe. Kitable was playing a part.

Neither of them were public figures. Would the scryer know Kitable's face enough to recognize him without the green and silver of the king? Shimmer had done her best to disguise his blond beard with a reddish tinge, and he had allowed it to grow ragged. Would it be enough?

Kitable lay down, and Shimmer remained by the door for a moment longer, uncertain. It would be strange for a woman who had identified him as her patron to be allocated the floor for sleeping. The reason to keep someone like her around was to share the bed. But she had no idea how to communicate any of that to him.

He saw her hesitation and gestured for her to join him. Her heart in her throat, Shimmer complacently crossed the room and lay down beside him. She went through the motions of putting out the light and pulling the single cover over them. Neither of them, she suspected, closed their eyes in the darkness. He gently adjusted behind her to better share the small space, placing a hand on her waist.

Shimmer could not track her thoughts. She was trying to watch the magic in the room to detect if it was becoming more than a Scry, but the press of Kitable numbed her. Trying to chastise herself for such a juvenile reaction, Shimmer swallowed hard and reached out her senses to the magic, which lingered but did not intensify.

He was right there, warm against her back.

After another dozen flickers, the magic faded away. The stone beside them returned to a neutral gray in the dim window light.

Kitable cast, and Shimmer did not stir, not wanting to disturb him and, in the same breath, not wishing to move.

"Blocked," he mumbled, his mouth so close to her ear she felt his breath. "Quickly blocked too, but I don't think I was seen. At least we know they are still around."

When he moved to withdraw his hand, Shimmer caught it where he had placed it on her waist. "You should stay there. They might come back," she said, her voice tight.

"Shim..." he said, but the argument was weak.

"Trust me," she pleaded.

He paused for an eternity. Then his hand slowly went back to her hip. "You're the only one I *do* trust," he muttered.

Silence took the room, not to be broken until morning. Shimmer lay awake for a candle more, her heart still pounding as his breathing settled to regular behind her. The fear of attack slowly wore off, replaced by a new excitement as she suddenly recognized something he had said in his anger.

He liked her dancing.

When she finally fell asleep, she was grinning.

It was heaven. For one night, Shimmer was euphoric. It might have only been for appearances, but she could ignore that fact in her giddiness. For one night, she had lived in a dream, Kitable's arm around her.

In the morning, the world interrupted. Kitable carried on as if everything was the same. Their casting, concealed well, was done before the innkeeper had even emerged to make breakfasts. Like a few other early-morning travelers, they had to wait in the main room.

The man from the night before was there, calling her Seraph, but Shimmer was in no mood for the game. Her head was too crowded with thoughts of Kitable. He had spoken about her apprenticeship ending and then admitted to enjoying both her company and her dancing. Had the night before indeed been only a show? She doubted so much.

"I'm sure I could pay you better," the man was saying when she paid attention. He had approached close enough she could smell his rotten teeth. "How could a stuffed pig like that satisfy a girl like you?" Surprising her, especially since she usually had magical defenses to prevent it, he grabbed her arm and pulled her in.

Misdirection and deflection were her usual strategies when physical force would draw attention. But before she could shrug the man off, Kitable grabbed her other arm and pulled her from the stranger's grip.

Shimmer was so surprised, she stared at her master mutely.

"Lay another hand on her, and I'll break your jaw," the Wisavi of Espar stated, as calm as she had ever seen him. She did not know how he would follow through on such a threat unless he meant using a spell, which seemed unlikely. Kitable was a caster. He never had to resort to physical attacks. He was fit—casters had to be to resist the pain of casting— but she wasn't sure he even knew how to throw a punch.

The man seemed to consider her master to be as little of a threat as Shimmer did, if for different reasons. He puffed himself up. "I'll buy her from you! She's got to be worth—"

Kitable punched the man squarely in the jaw, knocking him off his feet.

In the moment of shock following, Shimmer recognized magic was in the room. It was the same as the night before: a faint tickle to her sense that warned weak magic was nearby, not powerful enough to act as a window for other spells.

Distracted as she had been, she did not know when it had arrived, but someone was watching.

The spell was gone by the time Kitable was shaking the effects of the impact from his fist, looking down at the unconscious man.

Catching her eye, he flushed as if embarrassed. "He was..." Seeing the man on the floor seemed to confuse her master further. "I just..." Giving up, Kitable sighed and quickly sat at a table. "Keep the locals off my back for a moment. I'm going to follow that Scry."

She had still not found words. Turning her attention to the innkeeper and the laughing guests was a blessing.

Defending me? she wondered. Perhaps ... perhaps all the bluster had not been disapproval of her after all. Was it possible he'd been jealous?

"Got it," Kitable said abruptly. "Come on. I've got an anchor. After a quick view of the area, let's pay a visit."

"See!" Cole shouted victoriously. "Cannot be him! You think a powerful wizard goes around decking people? Heck, even I can do spells strong enough to make that oaf regret playing with any girl of mine. Your wizard could have turned him into ash! That's not him!"

Cole checked over his shoulder, confirming that his mother was still within earshot. Sure enough, she stood by the campfire, doling out oatmeal. After completing the dozens of long overcoats for the acolytes that milled around the camp, Marionna had kept herself busy with cooking for the group. The acolytes were all boys under fifteen, who seemed to eat twice that of a grown man, forcing her to cook a large pot for every meal, from oatmeal to stews. But being busy didn't mean she wasn't listening.

He removed the next set of curses from his commentary about the Scry he had performed on the inn in Woodcutter's Retreat.

"Besides, you said it might take a while to get attention. StonePeak is one thing, but no one gives a rat's—" He cut himself off. Adult or not, one did not swear in front of one's mother. "No one gives a hoot about a little town like this.

If you want to attract the right people, I say we go back to StonePeak. At least there, Black can…"

The man he was speaking to was not listening, so Cole stopped. It did not matter what he said. Celebrant Tamort was going to do whatever he wanted anyway. Cole was on hire to him as an assistant in magical things only, meant to fill in Tamort's understanding of wizardry and provide Scrys. For some reason, although Tamort's powers were varied, the celebrant could not perform a basic Scry. Cole had seen the man start a fire without flint and lift objects three times his weight, but the ability to move his senses to a distant location evaded him.

"Black may yet be useful," the celebrant mumbled in the half-whisper Cole often had trouble understanding. It did not help that Tamort was from south Galanth, a long way from Lour, and sported a thick Galanth accent. When he was not making an effort, the Celebrant of Inac was about as coherent as a drunken Rydan warrior with a four-word vocabulary.

"Good!" Cole, thinking he had gotten agreement from the celebrant, clapped the man on the shoulder and regretted the gesture immediately. All four of his hovering pre-casted spells were instantly destroyed.

In consideration of his mother, he did not curse out loud. *Damned Untouchable!*

"So can we go?" he said instead. He'd recast the spells later. It wasn't like they were too taxing; he knew only basic spells. They didn't take too much effort. "Mother's duties are done here so—"

"No," the celebrant interrupted, his face brightening slightly. "No. He is coming. He followed you."

"No way!" Cole objected. "I tell you, those were not casters! No hovering spells on them, and powerful casters don't... Demon shit!"

Forgetting the proximity of his mother, he let loose the swear. He could hear magic coming, and it was potent by its sound. Tamort was right! His Scry had been followed.

Ruining his image further, Cole's mother chose that moment to stand up. "I know you said—"

"Not now, Mother," Cole said. "Someone is coming. Please sit down."

Despite a pout he knew would become a scolding later, she settled beside the fire and stirred the oatmeal again. She shouldn't have been here anyway, he thought. Her job was done.

Tracking the magic, Cole heard the singing note of magic go sharp and start to circle the clearing. Cole suspected Tamort could sense magic, for he too followed the spell. He wondered if the celebrant heard it, although that seemed unlikely. *Probably senses it like most magically inclined people.* The acolytes, finishing breakfast, tilted their heads, but none of them rose or investigated. They were watching Tamort, not the spell that circled them. They were blind to the magic.

Cole gave them no warning. It was Tamort's duty to control his acolytes, not Cole's.

Both Cole and Tamort were staring at the place when the magic went into a crescendo, and the casters Cole had been observing appeared.

The pair that appeared were strange, both dressed in colorful, if unmatched clothing. She was cute enough to deserve all the attention she had attracted at the inn, and her bare midriff implied she liked being stared at. Her hair, bright red, had just the right amount of curl, and her eyes were a lovely, mischievous green. She looked like someone he would have liked to run into in a bar, especially if he could get her drunk.

The man was considerably more serious, despite his equally colorful clothing. His beard had been dyed, Cole could tell, and his expression was sour. The look changed to mild confusion, more like perplexion if such a word existed, when he saw Tamort.

The acolytes froze in their seats, all eyes on Tamort for instructions. *Kids,* Cole thought. He'd certainly never been that dependent on anyone, at least not that he'd admit to. Acolytes started young and were stuck catering to their celebrant until they were at least twenty. Most of these boys were ten to fourteen, Cole guessed. They must have had some bad luck to get Tamort as their celebrant.

Celebrant Tamort, who spent most of his time serving the Warrior Queen and Bitch Goddess version of his goddess, did not often smile, although Cole was glad for that fact. Now that the man had his quarry in sight, the smile was dark enough to be an outright leer.

"I saw the other camp fellows," the arriving caster said, "but you did not happen to see the celebrant in the Scry, did you, Shim?" The redhead shook her pretty little head, making the beads in her hair shimmer. "Demons," the man finished with a disappointed but unconcerned sigh. "Untouchable after all."

"Well, well," Tamort declared, "about time. Hello, Wisavi."

Cole's heart stopped. *Wisavi?* He knew the wisavi, the only wisavi in all the world, was the most powerful wizard in Espar and a political disaster to be around. The man was ruthless when offended, and he was well beyond what Cole could handle. Black had sent him with Tamort as magical backup, but no one had said the wisavi would be involved.

Tangling with Wisavi Kitable was suicide. And he wasn't even alone; the woman was his apprentice.

As Cole floundered, Tamort raised his voice and commanded, "Grab her, boys."

The acolytes rose from their seats, hastily putting away their cups of oatmeal and surrounding Cole's mother aggressively. His mother offered little protest as two of the acolytes held her arms and the rest formed a ring around her.

Cole's voice croaked when he forced out words. "Now wait a—"

"Quiet, boy," Tamort snapped, stopping Cole short. Before Cole could reorganize his thoughts, the celebrant faced the two casters again.

"Now, Wisavi," he said with a sneer, "look what I have—"

The disguised wisavi had an expression of disgust on his face when he lifted his hand. With a shriek of magic only Cole could hear, the entire circle of acolytes was thrown from Cole's mother, their black robes flapping around them and revealing the red and gold formal garb beneath. With a word from the girl caster, the robes tangled down and seemed to grab the ground, keeping each acolyte pinned no matter how they struggled.

"Pathetic," the wisavi said dismissively. He then turned his steely stare onto Tamort. "Now, who by the hells are you, and what are you trying to accomplish?"

Cole thought it unlikely that Celebrant Tamort would give the strangers his name, but before the celebrant could answer, the apprentice did it for him. "Celebrant Tamort."

The wisavi looked at her in surprise. "Is there anyone in Espar you do *not* know, Shimmer?" he exclaimed. "Who is that anyway?"

Evidently tired of being discussed without being addressed, Tamort squared his shoulders and declared in a bizarrely loud voice, "I am Tamort Firewalker of Galanth, Celebrant to Inac, the Goddess of Vengeance." His fluster at having his acolytes so handily dismissed began to resolve as he announced himself. He held himself high, proudly baring his chest to show the double undulating lines of his goddess's mark.

The wisavi stared at Tamort, his sneer unchanged and unimpressed.

In a much smaller voice, the apprentice supplemented, "He was Celebrant Sedgan's acolyte but one of the first to accept Celebrant Loni during the Northlander War."

At the mention of the other celebrant, one Cole had never heard of, the wisavi started as if having been pricked by a pin. Cole was the son of a seamstress; he knew exactly what that looked like.

The wisavi's voice was more cautious but remained formal. "You have caused disturbances in both StonePeak and Woodcutter's Retreat, Celebrant Tamort. You will—"

Cole jumped back when he felt the manifestation of Tamort's magic. While he heard wizard magic—one of the more unusual means of detecting magic, he was proud to say—he felt Tamort's powers like the flow of oil on his skin. Since Cole was already dispelled, the forces did no damage, but he still brushed his arms off once it had passed.

Cole had wondered if other people could sense untouchable powers. Not knowing another wizard, he'd had no one to ask. But the wisavi and his apprentice reacted; the wisavi threw a spell in the path of Tamort's powers. An earthen wall shot up out of the ground. Tamort's magic toppled the spell, but the untouchable powers were used up in the process. When the cloud of particles cleared, the two casters had vanished.

"Very funny, Wisavi!" Tamort laughed, a sinister sound that made even the celebrant's previous sneers seem friendly. "Come now. I know you've not gone far! You wouldn't dare!"

A new song reached Cole's ears, a spell cascading across the clearing at his mother, and he forgot entirely about Tamort. He didn't know what the spell was, but he had to stop them!

Cole ran at her, lagging behind as the powers raced ahead of him like a screeching eagle.

"Oh no, you don't!" Tamort called, throwing his arm out.

The wave of greasy untouchable powers passed over Cole, slapping aside the wisavi's magic. Marionna was unharmed.

Cole's mother remained where she was, her eyes wide and frightened. Cole skidded to a stop and put a protective arm around her, wishing he could cast a Relocate spell like the two intruders had. Things were out of hand. He now understood why Tamort had hired Marionna to make robes and hide their identity, but she should have been returned to Woodcutter's Retreat. Having her as a hostage against the Wisavi of Espar, who was renowned for being pitiless, made Cole's stomach crawl up his throat. If Wisavi Kitable did not do as Tamort said, what would happen to Marionna? And why would anyone expect the wisavi to fold to that threat?

The acolytes were beginning to get clear of their various spells, pulling at their robes until they tore or twisted out of them. One acolyte came to his feet entirely nude, yet proud of his accomplishment and looking to his master for the next instruction.

"Come along, Wisavi!" Tamort shouted at the empty clearing, ignoring his acolyte.

Cole heard magic come at Tamort from one side, but some manifestation from the celebrant stopped the spell before it could have any effect. There was a long silence.

"You know I know! You cannot possibly be thinking I will not use my advantage!" Tamort cried, his voice tightening as frustration slipped in.

"Use what advan—?" Cole began to ask, interrupted when the oily feeling of powers from Tamort slid between him and his mother, pulling them apart. He tried to yank back, but his hands slipped over the surface of magic he could not counter.

It *was* about Marionna. His mother was the target.

He wanted to be angry, but Cole only had room for confusion and fear. He was dispelled, but he wasn't disarmed. He had to find a way, yet only curses came to mind. "Tamort, you double-crossing—"

The oily film went over Cole's mouth, and his insult was cut short. Vindictively, Cole laughed when another tune of magic shot at Tamort from the side, the intruders attacking from an invisible location. But Tamort was too fast; he tossed untouchable powers in the path of the spell and it fell short.

Even their most powerful spell would fail against an untouchable's tiniest touch. It was not a duel he expected them to win.

Across from him, powers held his mother fixed in the standing position, her hands stuck to her sides, tears pooling in the corner of her eyes. Cole struggled, but he could not break the powers that held him. The magic over his mouth kept him from even screaming in frustration.

"I have them, Wisavi!" Tamort shouted, rotating to view the forest edges around the clearing. "Show yourself or one of them—"

The ground under Tamort's foot vanished. He caught himself with his powers before falling flat on his face, but Cole still smiled to see the bastard stumble. As much as he did not understand what was going on, Tamort was using him and his mother as leverage. His contract was void. He'd kill the celebrant if he could.

His face nearly as crimson as the robes he wore, the celebrant shrieked, "If you do not show yourself and surrender, one of them dies!"

Cole's smile vanished. He thought of his knives, ready on his belt. He needed line of sight. Dead was dead, untouchable or not. If Tamort didn't expect it…

But the powers did not stretch or break no matter how much he strained against them.

Bushes nearby rustled. The wisavi stepped out of the forest, his steps sure. To one side, the wisavi's colorful companion stood by, looking confused, magic circling her like fireflies but held in check.

Tamort leered again. "See now? Not so bad, is it? Dispel yourself, Wisavi. No more spells for you."

"What on earth makes you think—" the wisavi began, but Tamort, already short on patience, tightened the magic around Cole's mother in answer, and she squeaked. Her mouth opened, choked by the grip of the powers on her.

"Now, or I will choke the life out of her!" Tamort threatened.

To Cole's shock, the merciless Wisavi of Espar noticeably flinched. Then, his eyes fixed on Tamort, and his jaw clenched visibly. He uttered a word. All the tittering spells hovering around him vanished. Where Cole had heard a tinkling of chiming spells, there was only silence.

His companion went pale and reached for him, but the master wizard waved her off.

"Over here," Tamort demanded.

With Cole's mother going blue, the wisavi obeyed. Wisavi Kitable allowed Tamort to lay a hand on him to confirm the dispel. Even if he had hidden magic, none would remain now, not under Tamort's callous hand.

The hand on the wisavi's shoulder to dispel him became a fierce grip. Tamort dug his fingers under the wisavi's clavicle, making the wizard wince and drop to his knees. The apprentice peeped and stepped forward. When Wisavi Kitable slowly and deliberately shook his head, she stopped, one hand partially extended and terror plain on her face. The magic around her trilled louder to Cole, but none of the magic advanced.

"Well done, everyone," Tamort declared, dropping his magic and releasing Cole and Marionna. Marionna fell to her knees, gasping, yet Tamort did not seem to notice. "Perfectly acted. Cole, our contract is done."

Cole knelt beside his mother to check her but caught the bag of coins Tamort tossed at them awkwardly, hardly registering it. Marionna breathed better with every gasp, her color returning to flushed pink instead of pale blue. "On your way. Take your mother home," Tamort said with a chuckle.

The adrenaline was still pulsing in Cole, and he gripped one of his knives. He could throw it. His aim was good.

But they were free. He had the coin even. Black would be expecting him. This contract was ended. His mother was safe.

"Oh, and Shimmer," Tamort told the apprentice, "go tell your king of his wisavi's capture. If you try to interfere, I will slay him outright."

With the wisavi under his hand and no spells available to assist, it would take barely more than a thought from the celebrant to kill the wisavi now. The apprentice seemed to know as much, for her expression was one of strictly controlled fury, her face flushed and her expression seething.

Cole put his arm around his mother's shoulders and turned away. If he missed a throw with the knife now, he may damn them both. As much as he hated the celebrant, caution won out. The farther away they got, the better.

Behind him, Tamort addressed the girl again. "Go away, dancer and harlot! You remain, and I will—"

"Go back to your father, Shim," Wisavi Kitable interrupted in a pained voice. "Please."

Further words were cut off when Tamort tightened his grip again.

Cole pulled his mother back from turning around and kept walking. He assumed that the apprentice had done the same.

He was no closer to understanding by the time he made a campfire, too shaken to make it to Woodcutter's Retreat by the time night fell.

● ● ● ● ● ● ● ● ● ● ● ●

Having found the magic to follow from the Scry, Kitable had dismissed the notion of untouchables. With his apprentice at his side, he feared no wizard, regardless of the dozen thugs seen within the Scry. Tracking the Scry proved to be child's play. Soon they were in a clearing deep in the forest.

But then there was the celebrant, and the man was manifesting untouchable magic with better control than any Kitable had met before.

Each word from the celebrant made Kitable's heart sink further. Tamort knew. He had captured Marionna Granger deliberately. Kitable had to give himself up.

Shimmer objected in confusion but, for once, did not argue when he commanded her to go. He did not yet know why Celebrant Tamort was after him, but it was almost certainly not Shimmer's problem. More than anything, he did not want her to get involved.

The grip on his shoulder tightened painfully enough to make him suspect older injuries had failed to heal. The oily untouchable powers wrapped around him, holding him tight. He shivered, the chill shooting through him as the warmth of magic was stripped to a level he'd not experienced in years.

With his heart aching, Kitable saw Shimmer leave.

Once alone, Tamort brought Kitable to his feet and marched through the small campfire to face a pre-built cross. The acolytes took positions around the edges, freeing up leather straps to bind him. They had discarded their black robes and boasted their alliance to Inac in bright gold-and-red robes.

Tamort threw Kitable onto his knees before the cross. Perhaps he expected Kitable to grovel, but that was not who Kitable was.

Without the celebrant's active contact, the oil left Kitable's skin. His first thought was for his crystal pendant. A powerful spell lay in the crystal around his throat. When mixed with blood, the crystal could activate a Relocation spell that would take him to a safe location, and crushing the pendant had become a reflex for dangerous situations. His hand had already wrapped around the crystal by the time he realized it was useless.

Tamort's hand had touched the chain around his neck. He had dispelled the item. The Relocation spell was gone.

Kitable reviewed the other trinkets he had on him, seeking one that could assist.

Two acolytes came to lift him, presumably onto the cross.

Kitable threw the first off his feet with a punch. With his left hand, Kitable grasped a wand on his belt, pointed it sideways, and activated it. The second acolyte dropped to his knees, clutching his throat where the targeted force spell had taken effect.

Kitable lunged, taking the next acolyte by surprise. At first, the boy defended—they were, after all, followers of a Goddess of War—but Kitable's seemingly unarmed punches became stronger and faster with each blow, fed by another item hidden in his many-pocketed robes. He used his improved speed to launch himself from the enclosing circle of acolytes.

Once he was in the shadows of the trees, Kitable activated yet another item, this one providing a Concealment spell. He did not doubt Tamort would see through it, being untouchable, but he hoped it would buy him time from the acolytes who lacked Tamort's gifts.

Kitable dove behind a tree when he felt the untouchable powers reach out after him. The tree deflected the powers, and Kitable froze on the cold ground behind the trunk, counting on the magic and the tree to provide hiding. He started casting the Relocation spell, although he had yet to decide on an anchor for it. He had safe anchors in Wayburn or the Manor of Trulinar, but those were far, and his delay might endanger his mother or Shimmer. Did he know the inn where they had stayed well enough to use it?

There was a house in the north of Woodcutter's Retreat that he knew. How much had it changed in the two decades since he had last seen it? And how well did he remember it? Enough to define it and use it as an anchor?

"Impressive, Wisavi, but it will not save you," Tamort called. "Spread out! Find him! I will not let him leave."

An acolyte stepped up beside Kitable as he debated whether to run farther before finishing casting. It had certainly been a while since he had been forced to flee anything, but he was not above running if it meant surviving. Of course, he thought, if he escaped, Tamort would likely seek out his mother again. Kitable would have to get to her first.

But the Concealment spell was less effective when it had to deal with movement, and the acolytes were searching for him. The one nearest him might call an alarm if he moved. Words were needed to cast, but speaking would reveal him now. He held his spell.

The nearest acolyte stepped closer, narrowly missing Kitable's concealed leg. Pausing there, the man sniffed the wind. Kitable shuffled his leg back slightly when the acolyte wandered forward another step.

Another wave of untouchable powers, like a winter's wind, washed around the tree and him, reminding him that even a Relocation might be blocked. He had no idea what effect dispelling a Relocation mid-spell would have.

"I'll hunt her down, Wisavi! You know I will! I will have my revenge!" Tamort shouted.

Kitable did not bother to wonder which "her" the man meant. He made up his mind.

Activating the wand, he targeted the nearby acolyte, and the boy went down. Kitable bolted into the trees, counting on the visual obstruction of the many trunks to further confound those trying to spot him through the imperfect Concealment. When he felt the approach of the oily untouchable powers, like a flash fire coming up behind him, he ducked behind another tree. As he ran, he continued casting the Relocation, defining the old house with the short stone wall outside and the rosemary hanging from the eaves...

To his dismay, the untouchable powers passed through the tree, striking him as he hid on the sheltered side. His spell was instantly lost, as were his Concealment and speed.

He reactivated the alteration item that lent him speed and took off, skidding to a stop when untouchable powers manifested before him.

He spun to one side, restarting the escape spell, only to find his way blocked. It felt like a cage. He had been trapped.

It would not stop Relocation, but...

The untouchable power crashed into his side, and the new Relocation spell vanished, dispelled. The walls of untouchable powers moved in, and before he could breathe another word to cast, the sides had pinned Kitable. In finality, the power wrapped around his mouth.

Tamort arrived before Kitable, his grin broad enough to swallow melons whole. With his touch, all items were silenced, all spells gone. But this time, Tamort held a jeweled knife, which he put to Kitable's throat. Bound by untouchable powers, Kitable could not retreat.

The acolytes congregated around them, a perverted audience with wide, strangely innocent eyes.

"Strip him," Tamort commanded. "Everything must be taken. I will not have him escaping."

With a knife at his throat, Kitable dared not fight.

The acolytes removed Dust's colorful robes, dutifully passing each item to Tamort for dispelling. Kitable watched a hundred hours of spell-casting vanish in moments. As they finished their task, leaving him naked down to his toes, the powers slowly released him, although if that was voluntary or just the product of inattention from Tamort, Kitable did not know. At the least, it meant Kitable could speak.

"Will you explain why?" he asked.

The acolytes glanced at their celebrant, looking surprised by the simple question. Tamort, on the other hand, sharply flushed. "Why?" he shouted. He struck Kitable across the

face, making the wizard bite his tongue. "Why? You know damn well! Loni's death must be avenged!"

For a moment, Kitable could only stare at the man blankly, the taste of blood in his mouth.

He'd had no role in Celebrant Loni's death. He had hated the woman for being an untouchable, but he had never raised a hand against her, except in defense of his own life once, and even then, he had spared her.

He opened his mouth to correct Tamort but stopped when he realized where professing his innocence would lead.

He knew who had been responsible for Loni's death. He dared not direct Tamort's attention along that track.

Kitable said nothing further, allowing them to tie him to the post to be punished for his king's crime.

5

Shimmer could not follow. Knowing Kitable's life was threatened, and that her spells were ill-equipped to deal with an untouchable, she walked away.

She cursed him a dozen times for giving himself up and a dozen more for not telling her why he was doing so. She had some guesses, but why had he not taken a moment to explain? Did he know why Tamort was after him? Did he have a plan?

Walking helped her think, and so she walked without destination. Would she return to the Manor of Trulinar, as Tamort had said, and bring King Tohmas the news? SoulBurner, the king's blade and supposed source of his madness, was untouchable powers and had been made to combat wizard magic. Could it block Tamort's powers as it did hers and Kitable's? And would Kitable even be alive by the time she went to the manor and brought Tohmas back? Although she could do a Two-Person Relocation, she was reasonably certain she could not move SoulBurner magically. Did Kitable even have time?

That, she knew, depended on why Tamort was after him. And for that, she had no answers.

Her thoughts wandered in circles as she walked, distracted and unable to choose a course of action until she spotted a campfire.

With her bag, she had enough food to last a few days and the flint and tinder to make her fire, but she was not keen to spend a night sitting alone in the woods awaiting Tamort's decision on her fate. Company, whatever the form, would help camouflage her.

Surprisingly, she found the two people Tamort had been threatening. They looked even more confused than she felt.

The woman was the age of a young grandmother or an old mother and had a comely, good-natured face. The boy was darker in many ways, including a streak of black he had somehow stained into his dirty-blond hair. He wore shades of gray and black over an otherwise fit form. He was about her age, making her consider him young, but he had the same gray-blue eyes as Kitable.

Seeing her, the boy staggered to his feet and put up a magical defense. Bored, Shimmer shook her head. Compared to the elaborate constructions she had been trained to use, the boy's magic wall looked like a propped wood plank against Northlander invaders.

"I could break that into at least six pieces," she informed him curtly, "and I could break you into six pieces as an afterthought."

The boy, his knife out, stood in a practiced fighting stance, like someone accustomed to alley fights. Her defenses, still in place, would not allow a knife through. That threat was empty too. She was briefly fascinated by the combination.

She'd never seen a caster use a knife as a secondary weapon with any degree of skill.

"We're victims too!" the boy squealed.

"Demon shit," Shimmer flatly answered, "but I know Tamort used you, so I will not hurt you. I just want to share your fire. You can help me figure this out."

The boy checked over his shoulder and, seeing his mother move over in invitation, returned to his seat on the far side. He still kept an obvious eye on Shimmer, his knife in hand.

Shimmer pulled tea from her bag and offered it for the boiling pot of water. The boy wisely refused, leaving Shimmer to mix her cup. She chose her mind-sharpening green tea, hoping something would inspire her toward a course of action.

"He was very brave," the mother said, breaking the long silence as the tea brewed. "He knew what the celebrant was capable of, yet he still came."

"I call that stupid," the boy said. He extended his hand in cautious greeting, his expression changing from fear to curiosity. "I'm Cole Granger," he said. "This is my mother."

"Marionna," the woman introduced, accepting the tea once Shimmer had sipped her own.

"I'm Shimmer," Shimmer said, settling on her usual pseudonym, "and he didn't know Tamort was there. We had Scryed, but untouchables are invisible to Scrys. Since we were chasing a wizard, the untouchable was a surprise." She gave the boy, who was staring at the ribbons hanging off her blouse, a long look. "We never expected it to be both."

"I ain't a wizard," the boy said. "I cast a little, that's all. No master. No training. My father, now he was a real wizard, a master wizard, but he died when I was little."

"Shimmer," the mother asked, "what was his name, that man? Tamort called him 'Wisavi.'"

Having kept her emotions distant, Shimmer found she could not answer. Thinking about Kitable, knowing he was gone, made a lump form in her throat that threatened to choke her.

Cole indignantly threw his hands wide. His knife was still in one hand, a habit similar to Carsh's in Shimmer's eyes. "Mother! That was Kitable! Wisavi Kitable! We are lucky to be alive!"

"I thought as much," Marionna said with a nod, but Shimmer spotted how the hand shook on the teacup.

"Do you know him?" Shimmer asked.

Marionna shook her head, but it was hesitant. "I don't think so."

"Think so?" Shimmer echoed.

"Not if his name is Kitable. I don't know a Kitable."

Shimmer frowned. "So why did he give himself up for you? You have to understand: Kitable is practical. Bringing Tamort down would have protected hundreds more, but he gave up the opportunity for two people. His willingness to surrender himself for you was unprecedented. Did he know you?"

"I don't know a Kitable," the woman repeated resolutely.

"But do you know a thirty-five-year-old man with gray eyes and no last name?" Shimmer asked instead.

There was a long pause, confirming Shimmer's suspicion.

Marionna lowered her head, her mouth a thin line.

"Marionna," Shimmer insisted, "you must know something. He would not give himself up like that, not without a reason."

"It is possible..." The woman paused again, forcing Shimmer to breathe carefully. She was desperate for an answer, and the dithering wore down her patience. But shaking the woman would probably not help. "It is possible that he may be my son."

"Son?" Cole shouted, dropping the knife he had been absently playing with. "Son? I have a brother?"

"Half-brother," Marionna confirmed. "He would be thirty-five this month."

Shimmer sat back, nodding to herself. "That explains it."

There was no plan, no deception. Kitable had turned himself over to protect the two strangers because they were his family.

"You did not recognize him?" she wondered to the crestfallen mother, who held her face in her hands.

"I've not seen him since he was ten," Marionna admitted, tears filling her eyes. "I knew he must have been doing well because he sent money."

"I didn't know!" Cole tossed pebbles at the logs. "You never told me I had a brother! And the wisavi!"

Shimmer had her answer. Someone had figured it out first, despite every effort the wisavi had made to deny any family connections. Tamort had used his family against him, and now he was too far away for her to help. Besides, he had told her to...

She sat up straighter. Cole lifted an eyebrow questioningly.

"I have to go get him," Shimmer declared, grabbing her bag and doing a quick inventory. Drugs? How would she get Tamort to take one, and would any act fast enough to keep the man from curing himself with untouchable powers? Was that even possible? Magic could remove a drug, but it was not a simple thing. Would untouchables be the same?

She had some snap-bangs from her father's show, but those were only a distraction and not a long-lasting distraction at that.

"Go get him?" Cole echoed in disbelief. "Tamort is nasty up close, and Kitable is, well, he is Kitable. Maybe he's just playing. I mean, he *is* the best wizard in Espar. It's not your problem."

"He told me to go to my father," Shimmer answered, pulling out perfume and a handful of fake and real jewelry. Some were enchanted, and she went through their powers. One illusion, two dispels, two thought spells...

Cole glanced between her and his mother in befuddlement. "And that means...?"

"I call my father 'Papa,'" she explained. "I only use 'Father' when I need help. Kitable knows that, yet he said 'Father'! He was asking for help. I didn't notice it at first." She took a deep breath. "I'm going after him."

"It's still suicide." The boy shook his head, throwing another handful of stone into the fire and making sparks. "He's untouchable, and you're a wizard."

"That's it!" she shouted, and the boy dropped the remaining pebbles. In her excitement, she failed to stop herself from grabbing the boy's knee. "Perfect!" She left him stunned when she let go.

She had the jewelry for it: they had been carrying enough as part of their disguise. Her black blouse could be trimmed, and the laces from her spare sandals could make the lacings to turn it into a bodice. She would have to remove the sleeves and re-cut the collar to make it revealing enough.

"You have got to be the most bewildering woman I have ever met, and I've known some crazies!" Cole exclaimed.

"I'm not a wizard, Cole," she corrected, pulling out her gold powder makeup and the bright red paints she used for Dust's juggling outfit. It didn't match the shade, but... "I am a lot of other things, though. I'm an apothecary," she told him, tossing aside three vials of alchemist powders. "I am a dancer, and I am an actress."

"Meaning..." he prompted.

"Meaning I can become anyone I need to be. Today, that means Loni."

"I thought she was dead."

"Oh, she is, but Tamort believes he is doing Inac's work. He wouldn't be surprised if the goddess sent an emissary. Marionna..."

"I can adjust anything you require, dear. I am a seamstress, after all."

Shimmer startled. "I was going to ask you to swap skirts with me—yours is a wonderful red, and Loni was a follower of Inac—but if you are good with a needle and thread, I will take that too!"

It took almost a candle of time, but soon the costume was complete. She had Cole assembling fire bombs as she got dressed. Done, she took the four little explosives bags from him.

He was strangely silent, but as she turned, her costume complete and her plan ready, he called, "Look, if you get him but don't..." He trailed off, glancing at his mother. Pressing his lips for a moment, he finished, "If you don't kill Tamort, the way I see it, he's going to come for me and my mom again."

"Remember those six pieces?" Shimmer answered. "You get in my way and..."

He laughed, a warm sound very unlike Kitable. "Wouldn't dream of it! I was thinking that if this works and you bring back my brother, then Tamort will need dealing with. I want to help." She gave him a skeptical glare, and he quickly added, "I know I was working with him a little while ago, but he threatened me and my mom, and he'll do it again if he has to. I don't want that. Honestly, I don't think you'll free the wisavi anyway, but if you do, I'll help you bring Tamort down if you need me."

He avoided looking back at his mother as he spoke, shame filling his voice. Shimmer wondered if she had sounded like that before. Unlike Kitable, Shimmer had been forced to kill rarely, but she remembered it well and would not hesitate to do it again if it was for the right reasons.

"See you in about a candle, Cole, and I will take you up on that promise when I return," she replied.

The show was on.

• • • • • • • • • • • • • •

Kitable was an expert at taking his consciousness from his body to the black expanse on the verge of another dimension, where the spiral of magic, the source of all wizard power, drifted silently in the distant sky. When Tamort moved from threats to physical torture, that was where Kitable went.

It did not take long for Tamort to realize there would be no response from the body when Kitable's mind was absent and only a moment longer to figure out how to prevent Kitable's escape with a touch.

The spiral was wizard magic, and Tamort's touch was its antithesis. So long as the celebrant had a hand on Kitable, he could not keep his mind away.

Consciousness came in fits and starts, giving Kitable nightmares whenever he slipped into sleep. He so rarely dreamt, it took him far too long to reorientate when he woke.

"Do you regret it?"

Kitable opened his eyes, feeling the grip of the untouchable on his sore shoulder. The empty space where he had been hiding snapped away, replaced by the clearing and

campfire where Tamort had bound him. When Kitable tried to pull away, he remembered he was tied.

"Do you regret it?" Tamort repeated.

Tamort stood before him, one hand on Kitable's shoulder and the other holding a horse-tail whip. Kitable spotted blood on the tips of the whip already, but he was unsure which of his wounds had been the source.

"Do you regret killing her?" the celebrant demanded, emphasizing each word now.

Coughing to clear blood and phlegm from his parched throat, Kitable choked out a laugh. "I regret many things," he told the Celebrant of Inac, "but I do not regret Loni's death. She was a whore and a thief and a manipulative—"

The whip drew lines across his chest, and his words cut off. Vaguely, he thought he recognized the feeling. Had the whip already been used against his chest? Was he now crisscrossed?

He found it did not matter.

"You hated her because she was beyond your magic and control! But I will make you regret your—"

The man let go of Kitable's shoulder to swing the whip. The blackness by the spiral awaited. Kitable mentally withdrew, and the pain was momentarily too far away to be felt.

When Tamort struck him, Kitable's mind returned to his body. "No!" the man insisted once Kitable focused on him. "You will learn to regret your sin! Bring torches!"

The line of flames approached at the celebrant's instructions, but Kitable did not care. There had been several days during his life when his body had seemed to exist solely to ache. Whips and burnings were nothing new.

He chuckled at the sight of the flames, knowingly frustrating his captor. With no other hope, his only pleasure, no matter how minor, was in tormenting the celebrant.

"You ever hear of Spell Burn?" Kitable said, amazed at how hoarse he sounded. "Happens to every wizard every time he casts. Happens bad when things go wrong."

"You will know the fire that you—"

"Spell Burn," Kitable pressed, ignoring the celebrant's threats, "burns from the inside, from the bones. I've been burned worse than any man alive. Your torches are nothing."

Unable to retreat entirely to the black space because of the celebrant's grip, Kitable mentally withdrew as much as he could as they placed the fire against his arm. He knew it burned but could convince himself he didn't care.

The black of the space with the spiral beckoned until he heard a new voice.

"TAMORT!"

Kitable's stomach sank.

The low female voice spoke even that single word with a south-Esparan accent. He had trouble, through the water in his eyes, which had sprung spontaneously, seeing her at first. But as the distinctive style of dress resolved in his line of sight, his fears were confirmed.

Loni never walked: she slithered. She had a way of moving that accentuated every curve of her thin body. Her clothing, never modest, was a black bodice with gold trim and a red two-layered skirt this day. The inner layer was cut revealingly short while the outer layer had been left long along the sides, leaving her legs visible from the front suggestively high.

Even if Loni had not been a known untouchable, Kitable would never have found her attractive. Her hair was red like Shimmer's, but Celebrant Loni left it in a tangled hive, and it often looked darker because of the effect. Her face was painted with thick black around her green-tinged eyes and orange-gold on her eyelids. Her lips, her trademark, were painted bright red. Her skin, from her forehead to her bare feet, complete with painted nails and anklet, was pale and mildly gold-tinged.

That makes sense, Kitable thought. *She is, after all, dead.*

Tamort's hand dropped from Kitable's arm, but Kitable did not hide his mind. If Loni was appearing, she was a ghost. He had heard of such things occurring but never with enough evidence to believe it. Every sighting of a "spirit" he had investigated had been tricks, delusions, or illusions. This, however, looked far too real.

Bringing his attention forward made him again aware of how much his body hurt. His eyes wept, and muscles he did not remember being damaged were shaking. He was no longer standing but relying on the ties around his wrists to keep him upright. The bindings burned where they cut into his skin.

A minor fire had caught the hem of Loni's dress but did not seem to be spreading or bothering her. One of Tamort's less intelligent acolytes moved to intercept Loni as she descended from the nearby tree line, tracking smoke with every step.

The acolyte said something, presumably to stop her. When she ignored him, the acolyte tried to grab her physically.

"You dare!" Loni shrieked. A knife appeared in her hand as she spun at him. "You vile heretic! Non-believer! Traitor!"

She was so quick; she had the poor acolyte by the throat before anyone could move. She plucked him up, showing uncommon strength for a woman her size, and threw him off his feet. It could have been worse. At least her knife did not draw blood.

In the midst of the throw, Kitable's weary eyes caught sight of something on her back below the bodice. A scar was visible beneath the shoulder blade.

He recognized it.

The acolyte on the ground began to squirm and cry out, clawing at his throat. The acolyte's throat blistered. She had burned him with a touch. Ignoring this, the woman demonstrated one of Loni's legendary mood swings and smiled seductively at Tamort.

"Tamort," Loni cooed, sliding forward on gold-tinged legs, "oh, Tamort. Why do you surround yourself with such fools?"

Tamort ordered the acolytes away immediately. Rigidly formal, the celebrant knelt to the woman.

She reached out a bejeweled hand and ran her finger over the bowed celebrant's shoulder, around the back of his neck, and down his front, giving a sigh.

"Up, Tamort," she told him in Loni's low voice. "You should only bow for the goddess. I am merely a messenger."

When the man stood up, he looked like he had swallowed a bug. "My lady, Celebrant... I am honored. I am..."

"Surprised, I know," Loni finished. "But you are doing the goddess's work. She is pleased with you."

Kitable had to squint through the colored paint and the mild changes she seemed to have made to her face to make the disguise, but he was certain he was not being optimistically delusional. The scar on her back had come from a stab wound that had nearly killed her two years before.

It was Shimmer.

Tamort seemed to stand a hand taller with the compliment. "Without you, Celebrant," he said, trembling in his excitement, "it has been difficult to protect the faith. Without you..."

She circled him, close enough for the cloth of her skirt to brush his hand. "Oh, Tamort, I am here now. Do not fear."

Without willing it, Kitable's head lowered. He was suspicious of untouchable powers—was Tamort making him bow his head?—until he saw the blood at his feet. The blood had to be his. Just how badly had he been wounded?

"We have sought your killer!" Tamort said, stepping aside grandly to clear the path to Kitable.

Kitable heard her praising Tamort for his work and watched her feet circling him. As she had for Tamort, she ran a finger along Kitable's shoulders and down his arm. She brushed against more than one bruise or cut, each eliciting a spike of pain, but the touch was still soft.

He felt himself going cold. Although he knew his wrists were tied out to the sides, he could not feel his fingers.

He tried, but failed, to nod to himself when he realized the pool at his feet was growing. *I'm still bleeding.*

Kitable's visions faded as she finished inspecting him and moved back to the celebrant, who was watching with pride.

How she slipped her way into Tamort's arms, Kitable did not know, but when he managed to lift his head, Tamort had a hand on Shimmer's waist. Shimmer had her hand tucked between them suggestively.

Jealousy flared, and Kitable felt sick. Loni had been a whore, he reminded himself, and Inac could also be the Goddess of Lust. Shimmer was playing a role. She was just acting.

The excuses sounded hollower than ever when Shimmer passionately kissed the celebrant full on the mouth.

Kitable's visions blanked for a moment. Concerned cries brought his consciousness back.

Tamort was on the ground, his acolytes rushing to tend to him. Suddenly Shimmer was in front of Kitable, placing protective arms around him. A force spell spread from an item she had hidden from Tamort to encompass them both.

"Shimmer..." he heard his voice say, but he could not raise his stare again.

She was there. She had come back for him. He had not expected it, he realized as his consciousness slipped away.

He had always been alone before.

Pretending to be Loni was sickening. Shimmer had to pretend she enjoyed the sight of Kitable's flayed, beaten body hung by his wrists on a cross of wood. She had to resist the urge to put her hand on Tamort's throat and squeeze, knowing he could defeat her if his suspicion were aroused. She had to smile and saunter and lie with every breath until she finally managed to kiss the man.

He seemed to be expecting it, but Shimmer knew Loni had undoubtedly taken the man to her bed more than once. Bringing herself to kiss him, and trying to kiss like Loni, was disgusting.

Shimmer held on to Tamort, running her hands over him suggestively, trying to distract him from the fog coming over his mind. If he knew he was drugged, he might counter. If he was unaware...

He collapsed, and she let him fall.

Concerned for Kitable, Shimmer threw up a Force Cage out of an item. The acolytes ran to collect Tamort and drag him away, but she paid them no mind. Even if there were a dozen, she could handle them now.

"Kit!" Shimmer could not feel his pulse or temperature. Her one hand was still coated by the thin wax protecting her skin from the caustic gel that had scalded one of the acolyte's throats. But Kitable looked cold, and seeing the blood at his feet, she understood why.

He whispered her name, and the sound made her smile. At least he was conscious enough to recognize her voice.

"Defiler! Traitor!" the acolytes accused her.

She cut the ropes holding her master. "You get in my way," she threatened the cursing acolytes absently, "and I will happily castrate you." She glared at them as she took Kitable's limp body onto her shoulders. "Get me his clothes and things, and I'll let you live."

Crowded around the unconscious celebrant, the idiots sneered at her. "You will pay for this! Inac will..."

She activated Spell Sight off an item. It was a perfectly harmless spell, but it made her eyes shimmer like a smoky rainbow when she turned to them again. "Inac hates me about as much as I hate her. His things, now, or someone gets hurt."

Seeing the shifting colors of her eyes made them pause. One, a broad-shouldered boy, tried to move toward a pile of clothes, but another stopped him.

Already dispelled because of her contact with Tamort, Shimmer had to cast the spell fully. It took sixteen words, but it struck the obstructive acolyte perfectly. The minor destructive spell knocked him out.

The acolyte who had been pulled back ran to the pile of things and presented them to her. He would be quite the brute, she assumed, when he was done growing in earnest. By his big ears and feet, he still had lots of growing to do.

She had him put the clothes down outside the Force Cage and back away. He was surprisingly obedient.

She had to drop the Force Cage to gather his things, but lacking her enchanted vision, the acolytes had no way of knowing that the spell had been there or that it had been lowered. Kitable remained hunched on his knees beside her as she collected the belongings. His clothing was unimportant, but several of his items were magic and valuable. His crystal pendant, his final emergency escape route, felt dispelled when she examined it.

She threw his robe over his back to cover him.

Kneeling and facing forward, Kitable lifted his head, contemplating Tamort's prone body among the acolytes. Slowly, understanding came to his hazy eyes.

"Good night kiss," he whispered.

"You recognize it," Shimmer confirmed, collecting his things and stuffing them in her bag. She took the dispelled trinkets as well, knowing they could be re-enchanted. "Yeah, that one got you once, remember? I never understood why you let Maybel kiss you."

It took great concentration for him to remain conscious, and his attention was failing. Kitable slumped forward, his voice muffled as he muttered, "I thought she was you."

He lost consciousness in the next breath.

Shimmer's heart stopped, and she failed to catch him as he crumpled entirely. When the acolytes moved, she pulled one more item and sent a heat wave over them to keep them back, too distracted to be more creative.

Me? You thought...

Clutching her master, Shimmer pushed her amazement aside and sought an anchor for her next spell. The Two-Person Relocation was more complicated than the single-person version that normally hid in his pendant, but it whisked them both away safely when completed.

The words *"I thought she was you"* repeatedly spun in her mind.

When they appeared in the warm room, she was shaking, and it had nothing to do with fear.

6

"**H**ey!" Cole shouted long before he registered more than Shimmer's arrival. "I never said you could use me as an anchor!"

He regretted the outburst instantly. Shimmer had Wisavi Kitable slung over her shoulder and sagged under the weight. Her costume was covered in blood, as was Kitable.

"Then you should improve your defenses!" she snapped. Cole's mother, who had been sitting in the nearby rocking chair sewing, sprang from her seat and helped Shimmer lift the master wizard. Before Cole could join them, they had placed Kitable in the bed nearby. A torn curtain sheltered the space from the rest of the single-room home.

"Besides," the beautiful girl informed Cole roughly as she laid his half-brother in the bed, "you should make yourself less definable!"

He knew being unique in some way made it easier for magic to identify someone for targeting, but there were

thousands and thousands of people around. He wasn't that different.

"Definable? I am a perfect shadow! I am the face people forget before I've even left the room! I am—"

"Firstly," she interrupted, pointing, "you've got a scar under your right ear."

His hand went over where a brawler had almost removed his ear more than six years before.

"Secondly, you wear a unique necklace. Good luck charm?" A flick of her finger pulled on the leather tie to his rabbit's foot. "Wizards know better than to be so describable!"

"That's a lot of lashes," Cole heard his mother say in a choked voice. Shimmer spun back around, and Cole dismissed the argument to peer over Shimmer's shoulder.

Tamort had been efficient in the brief time. Kitable was all but flayed. His arms were sliced up by what Cole suspected was a skinning knife, and his chest was covered with multiple long lash marks that left his skin lying in broken strips, likely a whip's work. Burns made an undulating pattern on both of Kitable's legs, pink and red in a wave shape. The edges of the torn skin were gray in the firelight. Under the blood were patches of black and blue bruises and pale white scars, making him too like a poorly done tapestry.

He trembled despite his unconsciousness and shone with sweat.

Cole considered himself familiar with blood. He preferred not getting any on himself, especially his own, but the sight of blood was somewhat commonplace in his work. Still, in seeing his half-brother now, Cole's stomach tossed. It had also never occurred to him that the most powerful wizard in Espar would have scars. Who had wounded him? How?

"I was hoping you could stitch him, Marionna," Shimmer said, rummaging in her bag and sorting her findings in front of her as she knelt by the low bed.

"I have treated horse hair for that," Marionna agreed. "Going to be the most stitches I ever did on a person, but—"

The man on the bed said something inaudible, making them all pause. Despite his injuries, including a cut lip and massively swollen right cheek, the wisavi seemed to be trying to speak.

"Don't you dare start any of this 'last words' nonsense," Shimmer informed the wisavi without looking up from the poultice she was mixing.

Although it was a croak, the wisavi's following sentence was considerably stronger. "I am not going to die."

"Not if I have anything to say about it," Shimmer told her master. She handed Cole's mother a cloth soaked in something and crushed more leaves into a powder.

"I still have to kill Tamort," the wisavi muttered.

He passed out.

"Start stitching," Shimmer told Marionna before forcing something down the wisavi's throat with shocking proficiency. Once done, she took a new scrap of cloth, possibly made from the wisavi's discarded stained robes, and started cleaning his many injuries.

There was not enough room for Cole to stand beside his brother, and Cole did not feel right doing so. His experience with causing wounds was more extensive than healing, so he moved away and left the women to their work. They occasionally asked him for an extra hand, but ultimately, he was only good for fetching water.

But it was fun to watch Shimmer work.

Kitable awoke in a vaguely familiar room, staring up at rotten rafters and dried hanging rosemary.

He heard voices in the room. Shimmer was talking. Turning his head slightly, Kitable saw three people; the man he assumed was his half-brother sat between the two women by the low-burning fireplace. While they spoke, Shimmer worked on re-enchanting his damaged trinkets, absently casting between sentences flawlessly. She glanced over at him, met his eyes, and then continued.

She was giving him time to rest if he needed it.

Once confident in his legs, Kitable cast a simple spell, satisfied that he could manage it. Then, he slowly sat up. He ached everywhere as he moved, but he pushed it aside. They were not out of danger. He had to act, or else he would soon be back on the cross. That was motivation enough to get him to his feet.

Shimmer paused, cocking her head at him. He could sense that she had already replaced her spells and assumed she was fully defended with her usual complement of hovering spells. He could not be sure how long it had been, but she still wore remnants of the makeup from her disguise on her lips, so he expected it had not been long.

"I have overdone your pain pills," his apprentice said. "You should be too sore to be walking around."

Not acknowledging her chastisement, Kitable sat gingerly on the stool his half-brother vacated for him. The floor seemed too far away.

Outside, the day was bright. On the outskirts of the village, little stirred beyond the thin walls of the cottage. He could feel the spells Shimmer had erected, preventing entrance and keeping any sound from getting out. It was the same spell permanently surrounding Match and Mixer and worked well to keep conversations from being overheard without interfering with noises coming from outside.

"You heal fast!" Cole said in awe.

Shimmer would not let Kitable get away with it. "It's an illusion," she corrected. "He still looks like a demon sat on him, and he should—"

"Tamort," Kitable interrupted, trying to make his voice firm, "will no doubt be seeking us. We must be ready."

Shimmer was rummaging in her bag as she said, "Tamort should be waking up now. Good night kiss lasts about eight candles."

"Mine didn't last that long," Kitable pointed out, confused. He had never been certain exactly how long he'd been unconscious, but the time between Maybel's kiss and Kitable waking on the floor of his patron's tent had not been that long, he was confident.

"I countered yours," Shimmer told him, her voice gentle. "You showed up on Tohmas' floor. Who do you think he called?"

He faced the cooking fire. It was bad enough that she knew he had allowed a woman close enough to kiss him with poisoned lips. Appearing in King Tohmas' tent would have prompted the king to call for healers. No one knew poisons like Shimmer and her father did. "You never mentioned that before," Kitable said.

"You? You were knocked out by a—" Kitable's brother babbled.

"Hush, Cole," Marionna interrupted. "None of your business."

Shimmer, ignoring the other people in the room, placed two pills in Kitable's hand, her smile shy and only for him.

Kitable skeptically shook his head. "I do not—"

"They are more pain pills," she told him. "I know you will not be talked out of this, master. You will do better without being in agony."

She was a good enough actress to make him wonder how good she would be at lying to him, but he trusted her. He was aching with every breath. Alleviating some of the discomforts would make this easier.

He swallowed both. "Now, we set plans."

They gathered around the cooking fire. The warmth of the low flames, although it was little, helped keep the chill from Kitable's bones. He suspected that was the blood loss and was irritated that it was so persistent.

Shimmer left her chair and settled at Kitable's feet while Cole filled a cup from a kettle on the fire. When Shimmer nodded at him, Kitable accepted the cup from his brother.

My half-*brother*, Kitable corrected himself. It was unlikely the two shared a father. Marionna did not even know who Kitable's was. Besides, it seemed likely Cole had been named for his father.

"Cole, right?" Kitable asked.

The boy, a few years older than Shimmer, perched forward on the seat he had taken beside Kitable, wearing an annoying smile. "That's me."

"You're a caster," Kitable prompted.

"Marginal one. I'm good in a fight but no expert in magic."

"He promised to help if I rescued you," Shimmer pointed out.

Kitable sighed. She knew what he'd been thinking; he'd been about to tell the boy and his mother to go somewhere safe. The boy seemed to sense it too.

"I won't let anyone threaten Mom. Sounds like she needs defending right now, so I'm in," Cole insisted.

Two wizards, a caster, and a seamstress.

"Alright," Kitable surrendered, "but do as I say. I will not always have time to explain, and I do not want to be pestered with—"

"Dear, stop lecturing. Your brother and I want to help. Do not discourage us," Marionna said.

It had been so long since he had heard her voice, Kitable took a moment to recognize it. He managed to smile despite himself. Over two decades since he had seen her last, and she still sounded like his mother.

"Very well," he said with a nod, no longer the timid child. "Shimmer, you know Tamort's history. Cole, you know his current mindset, and you know the area. What we don't know is what Tamort will do now."

"That would depend," Shimmer said, "as Tohmas would say, on his goals. Exactly what did the Grangers do to offend Tamort anyway?"

"He thinks I killed Loni," Kitable admitted.

Shimmer nodded, understanding.

Cole frowned, which made him look like his father. But then, Cole's father had always been frowning in Kitable's memory. "Did you?" Cole asked.

"No."

"So..." The dabbler checked with the others. "So why don't you tell him you didn't do it?"

"Because I know who did."

"Who?" Cole demanded.

"Carsh."

"Who!?" his younger brother barked in frustration.

There was something profoundly satisfying about giving the boy only the truncated answers. Teasing a younger brother was a novelty fast becoming amusing enough to make Kitable wish he had known about the youth earlier.

Shimmer was more generous. "Prime Protector Carsh," she explained, clearly having heard the story. "Problem is, if Carsh did it, it was on Tohmas' orders. So if we tell Tamort who did it, he'll go after the king."

"I will not allow that." Kitable made sure there was no room for argument left in his voice.

The boy opened his mouth once more briefly, then reconsidered. "Well, he's offended the Grangers now. We have to go after him."

"Since he's untouchable, that means getting creative," Kitable replied.

Shimmer sat up and grinned. "We'll need to re-code the Contingency," she said. "We cannot be bound to a hovering spell, or he'll dispel us with his first manifestation."

"We can bind it to something else. Keep it physically stationary in the area. We'll have to stay in range," Kitable said.

"Most of his manifestations seem to be about thirty paces," she offered, and he nodded.

"Set it to fifty, then."

"At least. What about a barrier? Untouchable spells don't penetrate."

With the fading pain of his injuries easily forgotten, Kitable shook his head. "He can push magic through physical things, I assure you, if he wills it," he warned, remembering the tree he had hidden behind, but he already knew she would have a solution. She was too clever.

"So we bind it to something that goes underground. So long as it's down when the powers hit, it'll be protected. I doubt he'll think of going down. He doesn't know how magic works for us."

In contemplation, Kitable brought a hand to his chin but did not rub his face as he usually would have. At least two cuts and one burn had made his beard moth-eaten, and they were still sensitive.

"We can usually detect untouchable powers…"

"So it won't be hard," she finished, making him smile.

"What spells?" he challenged, already knowing the answers.

"Divination is a waste," she said. "From wizard magic's point of view, he doesn't exist."

"Alteration would be undone," Kitable said next.

"And he'll see through illusions." Having learned from her father before coming into his service, Shimmer's favorite magic was still illusions. The loss of the domain made her briefly pout.

"So creation and summoning and destruction…"

"And the destructions cannot be targeting him…"

He felt himself swell with pride. "Naturally."

As they paused, Kitable noticed Cole's mouth hanging open. The moment the boy saw Kitable looking at him, he closed it. "You two are scary," Cole said.

Shimmer, her eyes glowing with excitement, beamed at Kitable. "I learned from the best."

Without correcting her, Kitable cocked an eyebrow at his half-brother. "I presume you understood little of that."

"I know what a contingency is. That's where you lost me."

Shimmer laughed, but it was a joyful, not mocking, sound. "Don't worry," she told him, patting Cole's knee and making the boy blush. "I'll explain later."

"Cole," Kitable continued, "you must provide an anchor for us. I'm betting Tamort will seek you out a second time."

Cole cleared his throat noisily, looking like someone was slowly wrapping his hands around his neck. "But how will you kill Tamort if your magic can't affect him?"

He felt Shimmer's mood darken as she pulled knives from her bag and placed them on the floor. She had known the answer.

"Magic can still affect things around him," Kitable admitted. "Beyond that, we may have to do things old-fashioned."

He looked at Cole, then down at the three knives his half-brother wore on his belt. He had seen these knives before. Only one was a tool. The other two had curved handles for throwing.

Cole had said he was good in a fight. The way he was dressed, Kitable suspected he was a thug of some kind.

Shimmer handed Kitable a knife. He tied it to his belt.

"I assume you can help us with that part, Cole," Kitable said.

Cole glanced at their mother but nodded.

Marionna's face was impassive and set, but her eyes twinkled with tears. Although it pained her, she understood.

• • • • • • • • • • • • •

They parted to different corners of the house, each with chores. Cole, having none of his own, eavesdropped on the others. They still did not know where Tamort had gone, and he knew Kitable would be searching. Cole could contribute nothing.

The mother of the two casters resumed adjusting the clothing they had bought from the neighbors for Kitable. She kept her knife on a table beside her.

Once Cole saw Master Kitable was done casting, he decided to approach. The wisavi had enchanted several of his items but stacked them to the side where they would not rub on his injuries. He now sat on the floor, his expression pensive.

"Can I ask you some questions, Wisavi?" Cole cautiously asked. The man did not look tired yet, but the illusion over him continued to hide the blood and stitches. Logically, Wisavi Kitable could be expected to fall asleep at any time.

"If you want," the wisavi said, sitting back and closing his eyes as if meditating, "but drop that demon-cursed title."

Relieved that the formality could be excused, Cole sat beside his brother. "I don't even know what it means. Everyone says it like it's your first name."

"'Wisavi' is a Rydan word," Kitable said. "It means advisor or wise man. I got stuck with it to keep Rydans from trying to gut me."

"Advisor, eh? Perfect because I need some advice. Mom said you knew my dad. I was wondering what you remembered. You know, who he was, what he did. Mom doesn't talk about him much and…"

The eyes opened a crack. "I presume you were named after Master Sylas Colean of StonePeak."

Nodding eagerly, Cole sat up straighter. Everyone who spoke of his father used the title "Master." His father had been a wizard before Kitable had been the name to fear.

"I knew him," Kitable confessed. "I was apprenticed to him."

"Really?" Cole exclaimed. "He trained you!?"

"Sort of," the wisavi admitted.

"What was he like?"

Kitable dropped the meditative position and leaned forward. "I am not going to lie to you, Cole. You still want to know?"

Steeling himself, Cole forced himself to nod. He pulled a small knife and nonchalantly spun it on its tip on the floor. "I know he was involved with some less-than-noble types," he told his older brother. He glanced again at his mother to check if she was listening in, but she seemed engrossed in the sewing job. "I've met some of his old friends. Hells, I work with some of them. I know he wasn't exactly an avatar of goodness. But he was a real wizard?"

Content, the wisavi leaned back. His back pressed against the wall, holding him upright. "Yes, he was a wizard. He was the best wizard in StonePeak. He had dozens of apprentices, thousands of clients, and a reputation that kept most unfortunates from his door. He knew magic, but mostly he knew trinkets. He was brilliant at enchantments."

"What happened to him?" Cole had never meant to make his voice small, but he'd not planned his question. He'd never met his father and suddenly wanted to know why.

Without flinching, Kitable answered, "I was framed for his murder."

The spinning dagger clattered onto the ground, forgotten. "You?!"

"He fell out with a group of thugs," Kitable replied. "Something about him wanting to improve his position and oust the current leader. They sent two wizards to kill him. He killed them, but the other one killed him. The thugs assumed I had done it. I got chased all the way to Galanth, where I managed to disappear."

"But... then... YOU..."

"What's your version?"

"I was always told an enemy assassin had attacked the three wizards, killing them all. They said he was a mass murderer and..."

"I was thirteen. How did I have time to be a mass murderer?"

"Geez..."

"If you have no other questions, I should sleep."

It was possible the wisavi meant to do so sitting up, but Cole didn't dare ask. Instead, he pressed, "One more thing. Does Shimmer have anyone waiting for her? A husband? I didn't see a bracelet, but…"

The master wizard narrowed his eyes, and Cole could not tell if it was suspicion or irritation. Cole thought it was probably irritation. The wisavi must have heard the question all the time. Probably irritation. As Kitable was her patron, he was the one person who absolutely had to permit her to marry.

"No, there is no one. She doesn't have time. Plenty of people have tried, but she never bothers with any of them."

"So do you mind if I…?"

Kitable's voice sounded strained. "You can try," the wisavi allowed, "but she's been propositioned by everything from wandering drunks to kingsmen. Don't get your hopes up."

"Hey, just because she turned you down does not mean—"

His brother's calm was lost in an instant. "I am her patron! It would be completely inappropriate for me to even—"

"Boys!" their mother interrupted from across the room. "We're all tired and need sleep. Cole, stop bothering your brother."

Smirking at his brother's frown, Cole joined Shimmer, who had finished casting for the moment. She tossed her master a crystal pendant, which he examined for a long moment.

"Hey, Shimmer!" Cole said, squatting beside her as she replaced several trinkets into her bag.

"Not going to happen, Cole."

Dumbfounded, he sat back on his haunches. "How do you know what I was going to ask?"

"Your eyes give you away. And there are a few things that get Master Kitable annoyed. You're cute, kid, but not for me. Sorry."

Kid? She was younger than him, he was sure! And yet...

He consciously looked her in the eyes. Was it his fault his mother's blouses were big enough on her to drop the collar that low?

She shook her head.

Chased from two corners, he decided the safest place was to join his mother by the fire.

"I don't get it," Cole grumbled. "What's wrong with me?"

She did not even look up from her sewing. "It's not who you are, dear," she soothed as he sat at her feet and felt her ruffle his hair like he was ten again. "It's who you are not."

When he looked back at her, Shimmer had set herself against a wall facing Kitable and was smiling to herself as she closed her eyes. Both casters slept sitting up, leaning against the wall, facing the other.

Cole had been about to find a place to sleep when he felt the rabbit foot hanging around his neck buzz. He checked no one else had been awakened by the sound and crept out of the hut, leaving his mother to finish her work by the low fire.

Once beyond the short wall surrounding the cottage, Cole sat against a rock and pulled out his pendant.

"I'm here," he said aloud.

In the background, the item chirped like a confused hummingbird. The magic within came to life.

<Wanted an update,> Black's voice said, although Cole knew he, holding the pendant, would be the only person to hear the voice.

Cole let out a breath, trying to gather his thoughts. It had been a busy few days. "Contract's done and paid," he said.

<On your way, then?> Black asked, his voice tense.

"Delayed," Cole replied. "Family matters."

Cole thought he could hear concern in Black's voice when the old thief asked, *<Your mother all right?>*

"Fine," Cole comforted. "I just need to keep it that way." He took another deep breath, deciding where to stop in his explanations. The word "wisavi" would spook Black. Even if it had nothing to do with magic, Wisavi Kitable was the king's enforcer. Black dabbled in business on both sides of the law.

"That celebrant you assigned me to turned into a problem."

The silence between them hung heavily until, voice weighed with concern, Black asked, *<You need help?>*

Cole shook his head, then realized the man on the other end of the pendant would never see it. "I don't think you can help," Cole said. "The man's untouchable." Realizing the thief may not understand, he added, "Like a wizard, only a different kind of magic. This means he can kill your average person with a glance. So stay away. I'm dealing with it."

Another pause lingered between them. At length, Black said, *<Beat him at his own game, Cole. You've got skills he doesn't. He's just one more. Get into his head, figure out where he's going, and cut him off. Like always.>*

Cole again nodded uselessly.

<See you in a few days,> Black finished.

"Yeah," Cole answered, stowing the item around his neck. The noise stopped, indicating the end of the spell.

He crept into the cottage again, wondering if he wanted to get into Tamort's head at all. He didn't think he'd like the view.

Come morning, they were casting again. Shimmer let Cole help, wanting to avoid straining her master. She worked from early dawn through midday, layering spells onto the walking stick she had found and building a "bird" of magic that would stay above them, far from Tamort's reach. Kitable used a quill, ink, and some cheaper parchment from her bag to write the moving anchor point that would survive the loss of its connection to the caster. Cole knew enough to cast the spell while Shimmer did the majority of the casting of the hovering spells tied to the anchor.

Marionna kept them fed and warm, but Shimmer detected immense pride in the woman in seeing her younger son put to use.

As much as Shimmer felt attacking Tamort on their terms would favor them best, she dared not move Kitable more than necessary. At her master's request, she set defensive shields around the house. After a few candles of the work, she was exhausted and fell asleep beside the bed.

In the early evening, she awoke to the feeling of magic leaving her. One of her shields had been dispelled.

Rising gingerly, she found Kitable had placed a hand on her shoulder as she slept, although it rested against her Moulded Shield spell and did not touch her skin. He had also slept, taking a place on the bed above her. His hand hung off the edge as if to assure himself she would remain present.

When she moved, his eyes opened.

He was still weak, and his chest moved with deep, strained breaths. He had lost a lot of blood, and despite the herbs she gave him, it would take time for his strength to return. She could not judge the color of his skin as his illusion had not yet ended. He looked like a hale thirty-year-old, as if he had not aged a day since they had met.

"Something wrong?" he asked, withdrawing his hand from her shoulder.

Shimmer sat up fully. "A spell dropped."

"Good thing he can't Relocate," Kitable said. He rose slowly. The clothing they had found for him still did not fit well over his shoulders, but at least the trousers from the neighbor had been hemmed to not trip him. He did not look much like a wizard and certainly not like a master wizard.

He delicately put on his boots.

From what they knew, untouchable powers worked like wizard magic, so there was no reason that they would be able to perform a feat such as Relocation. But wizards had generations of shared wizard cant and catalogs of spells. Untouchable powers had never been so codified. It was a matter of time before the untouchables started pushing their capabilities beyond what they could see, but it had not happened yet.

Picking up her bag, Shimmer headed for the door, leaving the walking stick for Kitable. Marionna stood beside the fire, her eyes on Kitable's slow movements, but she did not speak. The mother could not see the wounds under the illusion, but she pressed her lips in uncertainty.

Pointing out his weakness was useless. They could not choose the time for this confrontation. It had found them. "Best we get out in the open," Shimmer said.

Still, Marionna stepped into Kitable's path as he made his way to the doorway. He still winced when she hugged him gently, but he did it without Marionna noticing. "Be safe," she said.

"Little of my life is safe, Mother," Kitable replied.

Her eyes twinkled. "Then you should try harder."

His smile made Shimmer breathe a little easier, pleased that some of his usual nature was coming through.

Once Kitable was outside, Cole made his way to the door from where he had been hovering in a corner. "Even if I'm only one more target, let's get this over with," he said.

Marionna gave him a more rib-crunching embrace and then tussled his hair. "You do what your brother says," she said. "He's your best chance of cleaning up this mess."

"Yes, Mom," Cole replied. He winked at Shimmer. "I've got some tricks of my own," he added.

They left into the evening, Shimmer pausing to meet Marionna's worried gaze.

"You'll take care of them both, won't you?" she asked.

"Kitable is the master here," Shimmer reminded her.

"But he's wounded. You're the one who saved him, Shimmer. Don't underplay your importance. Keep my boys safe."

Heavy responsibility settled onto Shimmer with the older woman's words. She had never been in charge, even in the days before her apprenticeship. Her father had decided where they would travel, when to leave, and where to go.

With Kitable, Shimmer was always second. Now, she was the strongest person in the fray.

And if they failed, it would be her fault.

"I'll do my best," Shimmer promised.

Marionna hugged her, although the woman's embrace never touched her skin through the defenses Shimmer had erected. "That's all I can ever ask."

Another spell dropped in the distance with a sudden release of pressure. Tamort wasn't hurrying; his approach was steady and slow. That was only the second ward disrupted so far.

"I've got to go," Shimmer warned when the woman's embrace lingered.

"Of course," Marionna said, pulling away. She spun, trying to hide the tears in her eyes.

Shimmer pretended she hadn't seen them and followed the men into the evening. Marionna took the opposite path from Shimmer, running toward the village and disappearing between the houses.

Outside the cottage were forest and fields. They had chosen the treed area as their battleground, knowing the trees would provide a visual barrier against the caster least able to use Scrys and anchors. While they knew his powers could pass through some surfaces, it seemed unlikely he could target them if he couldn't see them. The long evening shadows cast a gray light within the trees, the dark clouds above further deepening the gloom. They had agreed to cast no spells to assist their vision, knowing to lose such a spell at the wrong moment would all but blind them. They would rely on natural night vision and manage with shadows.

Shimmer found a place within the forest, her back to a tree, and waited. Cole set himself in the open by the trees, making a visible target for Tamort. He had volunteered to

draw the celebrant in since, as he had pointed out, Tamort did not want Cole dead, at least not yet. The same could not be said for Kitable or, considering her recent involvement, Shimmer.

Around them, the evening grew humid. Shimmer felt the energy in the air rising, a faint tingle of magic coming with the static. A storm was coming. Rain threatened in the haze.

Somewhere else in the shadows, Kitable was casting.

Shimmer felt her wards dispel one by one, each destroyed by contact with an untouchable as Tamort advanced toward them and the empty cottage. When the closest ward dropped, she spotted the celebrant walking alone along the road. Before reaching the low wall around the house, he paused, his head turned to where Cole stood on the forest's edge. Tamort left the road to face him, his long red robes undulating in the rising wind.

Standing in a cleared field, the two men stared at each other. There were no acolytes; had Tamort left them behind to deny the wizards leverage? Only Tamort himself was invulnerable to wizard magic, and based on his handling of Kitable earlier, he knew it. While Shimmer doubted the man had much love for his acolytes, it would have been unreasonable to believe he didn't care about them at all. The acolytes were under his care, tutored by him, and groomed to be the next generation of worshippers and leaders. In them, Tamort had a legacy.

Tamort stood before Cole, arms crossed over his scarred chest with confidence Shimmer thought arrogant. He was relying on his innate abilities to defend him from Kitable and her now, but that did not worry her. She and Kitable were ready this time.

"Cole," Tamort shouted as he halted under the first of the forest's branches, "your presence is an unexpected benefit."

Cole's voice was devoid of flippancy. "I want you to go, Tamort," he said. "Leave me and my family in peace."

Shimmer was impressed by his courage. She had expected a lack of composure, but Cole seemed determined to carry himself well.

"Turn over Kitable," Tamort said, "and you will have peace."

"Not going to happen," Cole answered.

"Then move aside."

"You take on the Grangers, and you take on all of us. You want him? You'll have to take him!"

To protect Cole as he turned and darted off into the woods, Shimmer shouted, and her distantly anchored spell answered. A bright flash of light lit the area. In the cover of the blinding light, Shimmer moved between the trees, not wanting Tamort to know where she was. She was used to casting subtly—Kitable had trained her that way—but that was not possible here. Her spells were tethered away from her, ready to answer only if her activation words reached them.

Tamort was still blinking away the spots in his eyes when Shimmer peeked out from behind a new tree. Above her, a burst of wizard magic streaked down from the clouds. She recognized the spell; Kitable had lashed out with a Force Spear.

Tamort threw up a hand to deflect the magic he felt approaching, but he was not the target. The force magic struck a nearby tree, cracking off a branch, which then dropped onto the celebrant. Tamort scrambled out of the way, his untouchable nature doing nothing to protect him from gravity.

Shimmer sent the next spell, trying to complement Kitable's attacks. Knowing she could not attack Tamort directly, she made the ground beneath him vanish, but he fell only briefly before his powers lifted him from the pit she had created. He was, without a doubt, the most skilled untouchable they had ever faced, so swiftly did his powers manifest.

"You'll have to do better than that!" Tamort shouted, throwing his arm wide. A powerful gust swept through the area, and Shimmer felt the greasy aura of the untouchable's powers run over her skin. To her dismay, the magic items she had concealed under her cloak and clothes were dispelled. Tamort had made the swell of powers cut through barriers this time; he was learning quickly.

But she had no connection to her main group of hovering spells; they were still tethered far above them.

As she planned her next attack, she noticed a buzz. It had to be a quiet spell, but she could not identify it. She only knew she was not the cause, which meant it had to be Kitable. He'd cut off other attacks, so what was he up to?

Shimmer shouted another command and was pleased when a large stone appeared above Tamort.

But the stone was blasted into pebbles before it landed. Shimmer tried again, this time sending a barrage of rocks, but the celebrant's powers effortlessly tossed them aside again. *He's too damn fast!* He was not tiring either, she noted. She would run out of spells long before the celebrant ran out of energy.

Before Shimmer could decide on a new spell to try, lightning crashed. She realized the buzzing noise had stopped. Thunder rumbled over the area, loud enough to deafen her. A second crash of lightning struck, this time the fork of light hitting the ground less than a stride from Tamort.

A third strike crashed down as the thunder of the second roared through the wind. The lightning burned into a tree, making it smoke.

Tamort snarled openly, the gray light throwing dark shadows over his glowering face. He screamed in incomprehensible frustration and threw untouchable powers around him without a target. Shimmer watched, but the attempt at dispelling something had no effect.

"Demon piss," Cole's voice suddenly said, Kitable's brother arriving at Shimmer's side out of the gloom. He fiddled with a knife as he waited for an opening. "The storm's a spell?"

Shimmer nodded. She had discussed the potential for altering weather patterns with Kitable as theoretically possible mooncycles ago. She knew Kitable had been working on the spells that could clear a storm or bring in fog for concealment, but he had never announced success. He *had* mentioned that summoning weather patterns was easier than creating them since weather had a surprising amount of variables.

If the lightning itself were magic, it would be dispelled when it struck Tamort, but if Kitable had succeeded in *summoning* a storm, then only its presence here was magical. If he knew, Tamort might send untouchable powers into the clouds and dispel the storm, sending it back to where it had come. But until he figured that out, the storm's lightning was real.

Tamort took cover among the trees. Shimmer sidled back, trying to conceal herself among the trees again, but she saw Tamort spot her. Having a clear path, Cole threw his knife as he darted away.

Although the knife was deflected with a thought from the celebrant, the distraction cost the celebrant the spell he had aimed at Shimmer, and she managed to get behind a new tree.

To her surprise, untouchable powers manifested around her. She threw herself from the affected area, sensing the forces tighten around her as she cleared it. She wasn't fast enough; her right ankle was caught. Pain shot up her leg, distracting her mind. She cried out despite herself as the bone in her ankle gave out and broke.

The clap of thunder sounded right on top of her, and the heavy air consolidated into dripping rain. Through the haze, Tamort advanced on her, untouchable powers again reaching out, making the air greasy as it ran along her like an abusive lover's touch. The pain in her foot was too much; she couldn't catch her breath enough to shout a command to activate a hovering spell.

Shimmer rattled off a Pain Destruction spell, unable to think of anything else. She was still a few words short of completion when Tamort paused his advance and pointed a damning finger at her in the thick gloom, his eyes glowing gold as he stared at her. Even if she'd had defenses, they were useless against his direct attack. Lying prone in the shadows of the storm, she had no escape.

This was not how she had expected to die.

Blinding light flashed. Shimmer squeezed her eyes shut reflexively. The wind smelled of something alchemical mixed with burnt wood as a crash of thunder shook the forest.

She waited, but only the rain struck her. After a dozen heartbeats, she opened her eyes.

Still seeing spots, she finished her spell, lacking anything better to do as she searched for Tamort and her imminent death. The pain from her ankle vanished upon completion. Confused, Shimmer brought herself to standing, keeping weight off her right leg. As another, more distant light flashed in the sky, she finally spotted the heap that was Celebrant Tamort between the trees. The nearby tree still glowed with embers, the smoke she smelled getting mixed into the mist of rain as she blinked through the damp. Tamort was down. He'd been struck by lightning. If Kitable had directed the bolt of lightning, she had no idea how.

Cole arrived at Shimmer's side, rushing toward Tamort with her, but Kitable stepped out from behind the burning tree and reached the downed celebrant first. He landed with his knee on Tamort's chest, a knife flashing in his grip as he dropped his staff beside them. It all seemed so unlike her master; Shimmer froze.

Her heart leaped into her throat as Kitable brought down his knife for a killing strike, and she approached again as quickly as she could. His reputation was of being ruthless when required, but she'd not seen it manifested with pure physical assault. Magic was clean and controlled. This was not him... or perhaps she was wrong. Perhaps this *was* Master Kitable, Wisavi of Espar. Perhaps she hadn't known him as well as she thought.

But Tamort coughed out something before the blade struck. Kitable's killing blow stopped.

Close enough now to look down on Tamort, Shimmer saw the celebrant's toothy grin as he sneered up at Kitable. "Hells," the wisavi grumbled. Then, in quick succession, Kitable dropped his knife, made fists, and jabbed one thumb into each of Tamort's temples expertly.

The celebrant lost consciousness instantly, his sick smile lost.

The roar of thunder crashed over them, lightning striking high in the trees. The rain was heavy enough now to soak through the canopy, not a downpour but a spattering of thick droplets cold and large enough to startle anyone they landed on.

Kitable stood up and stepped back, casting a quick light to illuminate the area as the darkness crept in. By his expression, Kitable wanted to kick the body, but he gritted his teeth instead. His chest was heaving, and Shimmer worried he was too weak to keep standing. It could have been enervation or his wounds. Neither was good.

Cole stepped between them, glancing from Kitable to Tamort. "Right, so he's still breathing. Shall I fix that?" Cole had a knife in hand that was surprisingly similar to Kitable's, but he had it up and ready while Kitable's lay in the dirt beside Tamort. Instead, Kitable picked up the walking stick he had been using.

"No," Kitable answered, his voice tense. "As much as I hate to say it, no." His eyes landed on Shimmer, and his expression of intense frustration softened. He cocked his head and, with a word to the staff he held, activated Spell Sight. His eyes glittered colorfully as he checked her over. "You are wearing a Pain Destruction. Are you hurt?"

Cole spun around, staring at Shimmer as if her hiding her injury was a direct insult to him. "Is that what the noise is? What happened?"

Shimmer blinked against a pair of big drops that hit her head and nose, feeling the cold wet seeping in as her heart rate settled, the threat passed, and the pain blocked. "Noise?" she asked Cole.

He shrugged awkwardly, a poor actor when it came to being nonchalant. "Magic. I hear magic."

"You are deflecting the question, Weaver," Kitable interrupted, although the look he gave his brother suggested there would be more to follow on that conversation later. Hearing magic was an uncommon natural talent.

"He broke my ankle. I couldn't function without the Pain Destruction," Shimmer admitted. She shrugged at Kitable, wanting to apologize and not knowing what words to use or why the desire to do so was so strong. She knew Kitable hated the spell, claiming that it was outright dangerous. Pain existed for a reason. Even now, she could be tearing more tissue or causing more bleeding internally, and she would have no pain to warn her. She could stand in a fire without noticing life-ending burns. But surely he would see that it had been a necessity.

He didn't scold her as she expected. Instead, he pointed to a nearby tree and said, "Sit down. I'll set it. The more unstable it is, the more damage it will cause. Then we can get back to the cottage and warm up." The rain was easing, but there wasn't much chill in the summer air, just the cold of being wet.

Shimmer, too surprised to object, lowered herself against the tree directly, causing a small rainfall over herself from the wet branches. She consciously extended the damaged leg, pulling the skirt out of the way to expose it for Kitable.

Placing his staff against the tree, Kitable knelt next to her.

Cole went to Tamort, hovering over him like a new storm cloud. He shouted to them, "So why am I not killing this man?"

"Because he claims to be able to help King Tohmas," Kitable replied, not looking up from Shimmer's leg where he had gently placed his hands. It occurred to her that they rarely touched since each of them preferred to use Moulded Shield spells that prevented anything but air from passing through. His hands were warm on her skin, yet goose-flesh rose.

Without looking up at her, he traced the bone down, found where it had shifted just above her ankle, and pulled it back into place. Shimmer felt no pain, just the pressure on her skin. He cast a quick pair of force spells to support the leg, then took a long, concentrating breath and began a far more complicated spell.

With him distracted, Shimmer looked at where Tamort lay in the forest's undergrowth. In her mind's eye, she saw Kitable again tied to a cross, his skin torn by the whip, and his face bruised almost beyond recognition. Hate filled her more profoundly than any she had known. She'd been in her share of battles and seen the disaster in its wake. She'd been subjected to physical and mental imprisonment, yet had never felt this caliber of pure hatred. She wanted Tamort dead.

She had had the opportunity and missed it when she had rescued Kitable, too intent on escape to give Tamort a more potent poison. Now, she had another chance. Dead, Tamort would not hurt Kitable again.

She had killed before. Those had been wizard duels to save her life, and it wasn't as though she'd wanted to kill her opponent. This was different.

She could cast subtly. Kitable was balancing a delicate spell with his enervation. His injuries were still healing, and the magic he had cast to strike Tamort down with lightning had been unprecedented. Would he notice?

"Demon shit," Shimmer mumbled, knowing she would not disobey Kitable. Tohmas was also her friend. If they could cure the king's insanity, it was worth the risk.

Looking up in the darkening light, she found Kitable's eyes now lifted and watching her. She regretted having cursed aloud.

He leaned back without a word and offered her a hand to bring her to her feet. Shimmer looked down at her leg, sensing the force spells still in place as a splint and lingering auras over the break. Gingerly, she took his hand and stood up. She tested, putting a bit of weight on her leg, then a bit more.

"Shimmer..." he prompted.

Shimmer dismissed her Pain Destruction spell.

Pain erupted, and she staggered, although the limb held. It ached as if she had been kicked by a horse, but at least she could use her leg, and it wasn't blinding her in agony. Her heart pounded again, and she was suddenly flushed when she had been chilled a moment before.

"I am going to be black-and-blue," she commented, looking at her puffy, red ankle. She let out a breath to reduce the pain and glared up at Kitable. "Since when do you know how to knit bones?"

"If you think I never broke a bone during my studies, you are deluding yourself," Kitable replied, retrieving his staff from where he had propped it and offering it to her. "And it's not fixed, just supported. I used the opposite limb as a guide, replaced the bones, and fixed them in position with force magic. You'll have to re-cast the spells for at least a cycle and avoid using the leg and..." He trailed off, squinting at her. "You know all this better than I do. I assume you have something in your bag that can help."

Shimmer nodded, accepting the staff and feeling the spells bound to it still present at the base.

"Right," she said, focusing on the ache of her leg. "Inside? Are we bringing him?" She pointed at Tamort.

Kitable's only real hatred was for other casters. Shimmer saw that venom in his eyes when he looked down at the celebrant.

"Unfortunately, yes," he said.

Knowing she could not lift the celebrant now that her leg was damaged and Kitable was in even worse shape, Shimmer looked at Cole.

Cole rolled his eyes. "I think it'd be safer if he weren't breathing anymore," he pointed out.

"This is bigger than our feud, boy," Kitable warned. "I can't move him with magic; he's still untouchable. Drag him if you have to but bring him along."

Cole shrugged, grabbed the celebrant by the legs, and marched off.

Shimmer hobbled after him, leaning on the staff but surprised by how strong her leg was. It was bruised and swollen but stable when it had no right to be.

By the time Cole flopped him down on the cottage floor, Tamort had a large clump of wet fallen leaves and pine needles caught in his robes. His entire back was smeared with mud, and Cole appeared pleased with himself.

Once she was inside, Shimmer made two quick mixtures. One was for her to stop swelling and promote healing. The other was to keep Tamort unconscious. She shoved that one down his throat.

She hoped it would give her and Kitable time to devise a solution.

The storm passed on the high winds, leaving the air warm and humid in its wake. As his mother threw open the shutters and let the fire burn low, Cole pulled out additional food and shared it with Shimmer. Like him, using magic seemed to leave her parched and hungry. He offered ale to both his brother and the apprentice, but neither accepted.

He made tea over the low fire as the night settled in out-side. It was strange to look out the window and see no evidence of the fight that had happened.

After shoving a pill down the celebrant's throat, Shimmer set at once to stripping the celebrant and wrapping him in blankets.

"He's sleeping under the effects of drugs," Shimmer told Cole when he asked why the tender care for the traitor. "He'll chill, possibly die, if we don't watch him." Shimmer glanced at her master sitting on the bed. He looked too tired to do more than scowl. "Apparently," she grumbled, "we don't want that."

Cole lowered his voice. "Don't want to get those doses wrong?" he asked, keeping a close watch on Kitable, but his brother looked to have heard him.

Shimmer smiled weakly. "Master Kitable has a purpose to this," she said, but Cole had succeeded: she had smiled. She accepted the cup of tea. "Here," she added, "let me show you and your mother how to check him. Then we can take shifts."

Cole and his mother listened intently as Shimmer went over monitoring breathing depth and pattern, checking the temperature on the back of the man's neck, and counting pulses using a sand glass. If the heart or the breathing slowed too much, they would have to adjust his drugs. If either became too fast, he may be waking. Shimmer then showed them how to check the depth of his sleeping. The first warning that the drugs needed to be topped up was his limbs becoming stronger.

Throughout the entire explanation, Master Kitable scowled at the celebrant. Cole was not sure the master wizard was seeing the man at all, but his gaze was intent yet infuriated.

Leaving Tamort with Marionna, Shimmer limped over to her master and slowly sat on the floor again by the bed. Cole joined them, leaning against the wall beside her. He could tell her leg was still tender, but she moved the short distance around the cottage without the staff. She seemed to hold her skirts tighter around her, preventing the leg from being exposed.

"I haven't enough drugs to keep him out for long," Shimmer told Kitable.

"Then find some," Cole's brother snapped. The illusion was still hiding his injuries, but his expression was weary. His voice sounded thin to Cole.

"These kinds of drugs attract attention. Unless you plan to have him awake within a day or two, a little town like this won't have enough," Shimmer said calmly.

Briefly, the master wizard's gaze focused on Shimmer. "I haven't a solution yet." His head nodded low, his eyes dropping, but he corrected it. "Whatever was in your pain pills is fogging my head," he accused.

Shimmer clenched her jaw, cutting short a reply. It was a habit Cole did too, but he thought she looked more calculated when she did it. She wasn't trying to avoid saying something stupid like Cole often had to. Shimmer was carefully altering her response.

"I expect the amount of blood you lost has more to do with that," she said, as calm and confident as before. "If not that, perhaps the fact that you summoned a demon-kissed thunderstorm, Master Kitable." The way Shimmer said his title made her words sound formal and less kind.

Kitable straightened, denying his fatigue in a manner that Cole thought instinctual. "I'm not enervated," he insisted. Enervation was a dangerous version of fatigue for wizards, as Cole understood it, and he assumed implying a wizard had exhausted himself to the level of enervation would be saying he lacked strength. That was likely to offend the master wizard.

"No, you're not, but you're physically exhausted," Shimmer replied, not cowering the way Cole thought he would have. Kitable had struck a man with lightning! The master wizard now ranked as the most terrifying person he knew, but Shimmer was not the slightest bit intimidated. "I'll go to StonePeak and get more of the drugs. Then we can take our time."

Kitable's head snapped around. "Stay away from—"

"Cole knows the place," Shimmer interrupted, setting her shoulders under his glare, "and there's nowhere closer that'll have what I need. Going there'll take less energy than any-where else, including Wayburn."

"I don't want—"

"But you need me to," Shimmer interrupted again. "If Tamort wakes up, we're beat again. If we're going to get infor-mation from him, we'll have to do it from within while he is still helpless. To do that, I need to keep him unconscious."

"Get into his head," Cole said, echoing Black's words.

Kitable's head dropped a finger's breadth, enough to make the master wizard startle up and shake his head.

Shimmer placed a hand on his knee, making Kitable wince. "Sleep, please, Master. I can handle this."

His eyes dropping even more upon the word "sleep," Kitable turned his bleary gaze to Cole. "This whelp doesn't know a Relocation, I assume," he said.

"Know it," Cole replied, "but can't cast it. Too much power." He shrugged, unashamed. He had never professed otherwise.

"I can do a Two-Person Relocation," Shimmer insisted.

Kitable turned his glare on her again. "Not going somewhere you don't know. Too dangerous, and too much energy is required. You'll enervate yourself."

The comment seemed to poke Shimmer. She sat tall and met the master wizard's glare with one of her own. "Don't be ridiculous. Cole knows the area. I am more—"

"You suggest thought magic?" Kitable replied, his voice gaining strength as his anger grew.

"Why not? I can do it, good as you."

Finally, Cole caught up. Without knowing StonePeak well enough to set an anchor by description, Shimmer would have to use a Scry to set an anchor, requiring her to mentally travel to the city first, set an anchor, then move the two of them along the same path physically. But Cole knew the city well. Shimmer could take the memory of a place from his mind and use that. That type of magic, while simple by way of energy, put both caster and target in a vulnerable state, at least to each other.

He was flattered by her trust in him but thought it unnecessary.

"I may not be able to cast a Relocation," Cole interrupted, "but I can set an anchor, and I know the place. All she needs to do is cast a Binding to share the anchor. And I know all the right people in StonePeak." His final sentence was for Shimmer alone. "I can get you what you need."

Cole thought her expression was one of satisfaction when she again faced her master.

"Go," Kitable said, defeated. He leaned back onto the bed, Shimmer rising to help him bring his feet up. "Wake me when you return." At once, his eyes were shut.

Shimmer seemed to consider placing a blanket over the man like tucking in a child, but she shook her head instead and collected her bag. She checked with Marionna again, providing a few pills in case the celebrant seemed to be waking, and headed out, staff in hand.

With the storm gone, the night was lit by stars but no moon. Cole followed her out and paused with her beyond the door. She took a long stabilizing sigh, tightening her posture. When she was ready, she turned to Cole.

Wishing to alleviate her tension, Cole tossed a small cantrip above his eyebrows, making them glow bright pink in the dark. He wiggled his eyebrows at her suggestively.

Shimmer cracked a beautiful smile in the starlight, chuckling despite her pain. He was unsure what she had taken by way of herbs, but it seemed to have taken much of the edge off. "You look like the waking fairy at the spring festival," she said. "Course, that particular fairy is supposedly prone to clumsiness. He's the one who gets caught in the honey pot."

Cole winked at her, confident she could see it with the pink lights above his eyes. He hooked her arm, pleased that the rigidity in her muscles had loosened. "Come, fair maiden!" he quoted. "The honey's fine this time of year, and the miller's pot is the place to find the sweetest kinds." He paused, then lowered his voice. "That line always confused me. Is there a type of honey that isn't sweet?"

Satisfied by her laughter, Cole formed an anchor to the central pillar of Thieves Hide Square within StonePeak. It was unique, making it easy to define. He let the cantrip drop, lacking the discipline to hold both spells.

With a word of activation, she bound him to share the spell.

Her next spell was longer and more complicated. Cole listened, holding his anchor, wondering what would happen if she made a mistake. Would they be split in half, their legs appearing in StonePeak and their torsos left in

Woodcutter's Retreat? Perhaps he would lose his right foot. He would have to replace it with a peg, which would make it hard to sneak around. Maybe he could put padding on the bottom of it should he need to move without sound.

By the time his attention returned to his surroundings, they were in StonePeak.

8

When they appeared in complete darkness, Shimmer activated a simple light creation spell and sent the magic out into the room. It soon reached a cavern ceiling, illuminating the only feature in the empty space: a pillar. The four holy symbols of the gods had a place of honor at the base of the black-stone structure. The carvings rose from there, following the themes of each god until they reached the ceiling. Pari's were trees and mountainscapes scattered with animals. Inac's was fire, the flames shaped like lovers and warriors as they rose. Totho's was covered with birds and clouds that soared ever higher. She could not see the far side to know what symbols represented Ocea here, although it would likely be children or themes of water.

"Where are we?" Shimmer asked. Tunnels led off from the small room, but they were unfamiliar.

"Thieves Hide Square," Cole replied.

Shimmer raised an eyebrow at him. "So named because thieves hide here, or because this is where they put the skins of thieves?"

Cole's smile was broad and genuine, unlike Kitable's. While she had managed to coax a smile from her master before, his smiles were always reserved. Cole was content enough to advertise his joy to the world while Kitable kept his confidential.

"Initially, the latter, but of late, the former. This way," Cole replied, offering her an arm and leading her toward one of the tunnels. She kept the staff in hand but leaned on Cole with her other. Between the two supports, her leg still throbbed, but it held her weight well. Cole did not appear to notice the gap between her skin and his, the Moulded Shield spell in place once more.

As they passed the mouth of the tunnel, Shimmer spotted dots and grooves on either wall. Cole ran a hand over one of them, nodded to himself, and led her on.

Despite the pain of her leg, Shimmer cast a binding tied to her light to follow them. Cole glanced back, then chuckled. "I usually do this in the dark," he said.

"Is there a problem with it being done in the light?" she asked.

"No problem," Cole replied. He reached an intersection and went left. Again, he ran his hand over an area of the wall markings.

"The markings guide you?" Shimmer asked.

"Everything in these tunnels has a symbol," Cole explained, "and they are carved into the walls pointing to them."

Releasing his hand, Shimmer ran her fingers over the same region Cole had and took note of the combination of grooves and dots. It was strange to touch through her Moulded Shield, the defense interfering a bit with the sensitivity of her fingers, but she thought it better to have the spell erected again. "Clever. Then you can find your way in the dark."

Cole flashed her a proud smile.

Following Cole, Shimmer juggled checking the symbols with using her staff as they traveled. The number of dots around the symbol seemed to represent distance, for they reduced with each intersection until none remained, and they came into a large cavern.

Shimmer dismissed her light. The lamps in the cavern were set in front of large mirrors, giving the space a dusky illumination. She assumed it would be brighter in the day, channeling in sunlight where it could.

A dozen people milled around this vast cavern. The carts stacked around the walls were flanked by sacks and barrels, each manned by a grungy person. It felt like a market but lacked signage or a sense of order. There were few displayed goods and no hawking cries. Each "merchant" sat among his things, glaring at the man or woman opposite him in uncanny silence.

Shimmer hardened herself, making an effort to hide her limp. She knew these sorts of people. It made sense. Where else would they find goods, let alone the herbs she required, at this late hour? Cole was showing off his contacts in StonePeak.

Kitable's half-brother chose a hawkish man on the opposite side of the cavern, walking past a half dozen others to reach him. The merchant had more wrinkles on his face than his age would have dictated, his hair a robust blond and his beard thick. He squinted from where he sat atop a sea crate, like a man with cataracts.

"Bale," Cole greeted, stopping before the man and releasing Shimmer's arm. Heeding the suggestion, Shimmer stood under her own power, holding the staff as if it was a walking stick, not a crutch.

"Cole," Bale answered. Bale squinted at Shimmer, his contemplation taking too long. He was drawing conclusions, complicated ones. She adjusted her stance to ensure he was drawing the correct ones: *do not mess with me.*

"Need some old lady's slipper," Cole said, "and ideally some fennal too. Where's Trank?"

"Taking tonight off," Bale replied, his eyes still on Shimmer. "You'll have to wait for another night."

Cole shrugged. "Don't have time to wait," he said, his voice apologetic. "If you show us what you've got, we can identify it."

"You don't have a clue what you're looking at, Cole," Bale replied, sneering. "Drugs ain't your style. Beyond you, I'd say."

Cole sighed. "Just tell me where Trank is, then."

"Why should I?" Bale replied. When Cole rolled his eyes and reached for his pouch, the man added quickly, "It'll cost you more than you've got, Cole. I ain't buggin' Trank for anything less than this fine lady's name." The man leered toward Shimmer, his squinting stare running up and down her.

She was dressed in dry traveling clothes, comfortable, flattering, and meant to draw eyes. Shimmer recognized the merchant's suggestive stare. This one was dominant. She assumed he had some experience with slave trading or pimping women. She was property, and she was the price he wanted for this favor.

Shimmer could play quiet and demure and then escape later. Or she could increase her value by flirting, but she was not in the mood.

She picked Bliss as her personality: bold and confident.

Shimmer met the man's stare square on and leaned in. She placed a hand beside him on the crate, giving him a close view of everything he could not have. "Clearly, the herbs ain't for him," she said, using her voice and body to speak to him. "I can save us all some time here. Firstly, I don't care how bad you make him look; I ain't interested in you. Secondly, he can't bargain using me because he doesn't have me. Thirdly, if you, or anyone else connected to you, try to lay a finger on me, I'll castrate you. Now that we've got that out of the way, I'll let you finish dealing with Cole here."

She leaned back but stayed beside the crate, close enough to keep her presence a bit uncomfortably close to the thief.

He reconsidered his assumptions, and it took him time. With a squinted stare, he visibly ran replies through his head, seeking one that would look good to Cole. Shimmer wondered if he believed her. It was not a bluff. Between the staff and her re-cast hovering spells, Shimmer had enough magic on her to obliterate the entire cavern. She was particularly fond of a simple reduction spell that could groin a man from a distance to get her point across. Playing this man's game damned her to play it forever. The game was over now.

"Better cooperate," a new voice said. "She means it."

Cole stood straighter in recognition. His smile was less joyful and more knowing. She saw confidence in him now. Bale shrank away from Shimmer as if caught by an angry husband.

"Hey, Black," Cole said without turning to look. "What brings you out so late?"

The man who stepped up beside Cole was as old as a kingsman but wore an attire of black cloth identical to Cole's. He even wore the same long knife Cole did, and it was one of several blades on his belt. He was clean-shaven, round-faced, and looked to Shimmer like the kind of uncle no one else in the family wanted to discuss. Shimmer detected magic on him, although he did not look much like a wizard. Without a doubt, several items he wore were magic, but she sensed there was something more.

"What? I can't be out to visit you. When did you get back from the job?"

"Just now," Cole replied. "Heading out again momentarily. I'll square up when I get back."

They had come directly via the Relocation spell. No one had seen them until they had reached this hall. Unless the man lived with a window overlooking the cavern, Shimmer thought, he could not be out solely to see Cole. This was idle chatting, she realized. They were making clear their relationship in front of Bale.

Shimmer tossed her head. Under the gesture, she activated a Spell Sight but chose one with Kitable's modifications on it; her eyes would not change, keeping hidden her assessment of the other wizard. She met the newcomer's stare, allowing her peripheral vision to assess his hovering spells and defenses.

He was strategically protected by magic, but every spell was concealed by another layer, safeguarding it from divinations, including Spell Sight. Unfortunately for him, Shimmer's version was modified and more powerful. Without it, all the spells except those on his trinkets would have been invisible. He seemed to have left his items—a knife, a brooch, and a ring—open for detection.

She memorized the spells for later assessment, then turned away. Her brief look determined his spells were subtle, mostly thought-based. But he still had a handful of what Kitable had called "deciding" spells. Those were the type of complicated, dangerous spells that could decide the outcome of a duel in a single strike. This was a potent caster.

"You need something, Black?" Bale asked, his voice a whine. "I'm sure I can get it, then Cole and I—"

"Apparently, we need some old lady's slipper," Black said, his smile broad, "and some fennal too."

"I could refill my supply of frozen freedom, if you have any," Shimmer added. She gave the newcomer a cursory smile. "I take it you are a friend of Cole's?"

"Black's the name," the man said, dipping into a short bow. "Cole's one of mine, and I assume Bale here knows it. You'll have to forgive Bale for his distraction. You, miss, do so light the room. Hard for any man to focus."

Shimmer wondered if he had said "light" in reference to her light spell earlier. Perhaps he *had* come out to see Cole, having detected their arrival. She had not attempted to conceal the Relocation spell. Another caster could have noticed it.

As Bliss, Shimmer did not allow the flattery to change her stance. Words did not sway Bliss.

"I'm sure *someone* around here can focus long enough to make themselves useful," she replied. She looked at Bale pointedly. "After all, finding what I need is how you get paid."

Bale checked with Black.

"Get a move on, Bale. I'll do it if you can't recognize the plants," Black replied. His voice darkened. "I doubt you want me going through your things. Better that I stay ignorant."

Bale nodded in a short, shaky fashion and slipped off the crate. He momentarily rummaged in the sacks, selecting one from the stack.

"I didn't catch your name, miss," Black said.

Before Cole could reply to offer introductions or apologize for the oversight, Shimmer interrupted, "Bliss is my name." She smiled at Cole. "No one around here is giving real names. Why should I?"

"Fair." Black's body language gave off calm confidence, but as he turned back to ostensibly check on Bale's progress,

Shimmer felt the push of a spell against one of her shields: thought magic-seeking anchor.

At the beginning of her apprenticeship, Shimmer had known little about thought magic. It was a complicated element, bending the rules of the domains in almost every casting. Kitable's training had improved her skills substantially, but in the process, she had also adopted her master's profound dislike for the element. Thought spells were often dominations, what she considered a form of torture. Kitable had always disapproved of them, and Shimmer had come to feel the same way.

She could stop him, even turn his spell against himself. She could attack back, strip a dozen defenses off him with a single word, but Kitable's teachings corrected her. Loud and flashy magic was sloppy. Big displays worked wonders on the uninitiated, but those who knew magic well enough to be using thought magic would be more intimidated by subtle power. She needed finesse, not bravado.

Shimmer met the man straight in the eye and smiled a little, the way Bliss did when she knew she had an advantage. Black's head tilted, sensing the threat. Then Shimmer activated an open alteration spell and bound it to the thought spell trying to work its way through her defenses.

With the open spell working, she could make the attack do whatever she wanted. Applying her magic, she pushed it aside. She made it circle Black, wondering how sensitive he was to magic. Did he recognize his spell was being manipulated? Could he sense it circling him? He wasn't giving anything away.

But when she pressed the spell against Black's shields, he flinched. Even if he had failed to recognize the manipulation of his spell, he had felt the push.

To her surprise, Black smiled again. "Well, well," he said.

"Just returning the favor," Shimmer replied coolly.

"Your Spell Sight doesn't show." Black's words sounded like a compliment.

"I don't give anything away for free."

Cole's jaw hung open during their exchange, making Shimmer believe Cole had been unaware of her remaining spells or that Black had used magic against her. That surprised her. She had gotten the impression he could detect magic.

"Me neither," Black replied.

There were layers of meaning in that sentence. He had concealed every spell from basic Spell Sights. But was he hiding more? Black wore magical items. If Spell Sight had failed to identify the hovering spells around him, Shimmer, like many people, may have assumed the magic she had sensed were his trinkets.

Had Cole been making that assumption? It was safe to assume his Spell Sight would not be as powerful as Shimmer's; he would not have seen.

"My dear lady," Black said, nodding his head toward Shimmer with reverence, "please do me the honor of being my guest when next you are in StonePeak. I have a feeling we would have a great deal in common."

She thought to answer, "I certainly hope not," but censored the reply. Bale had scrambled to appease this man, and Cole was using him as leverage. Black was powerful enough in this realm that Shimmer thought it unwise to antagonize him without cause.

"Perhaps," she said instead, seeing Bale approach with a sack. He folded it back and pulled out bundles of dried herbs, placing each on the sea crate in turn. Black stepped forward to watch but did not aid the man in sorting the plants. Instead, Bale looked at Shimmer for a decision.

Shimmer selected the three bunches of herbs she needed. She decided on an average but honest price and offered it to Bale.

The merchant checked with Black. She wasn't sure if he wanted to know to demand more or if he should discount it, but Black gave him no advice. Bale was stuck taking what Shimmer had offered. At the least, Shimmer thought, his partner would not be furious when he reappeared. It had been a fair price.

"Until next time, Cole," Black said once the deal was done. He patted Cole on the back.

"Sure thing, Black. Sorry for popping in unexpectedly."

"Never a problem," Black said, tossing his hand. "Glad you are keeping such fine company." Nodding to Shimmer one last time, Black added, "Fair lady," in farewell and headed down another tunnel.

She waited until Black was out of sight before retaking Cole's arm to leave the market. Their destination no longer mattered. She could cast the Relocation from anywhere, although she thought it prudent to avoid prying eyes. She would have to full-cast the spell and didn't want someone overhearing her code.

She let Cole conjure a light this time, wanting to conserve her energy. Even a tiny spell right now would have been taxing, and she still had to cast another Two-Person Relocation. In and of itself, that spell could flatten an amateur wizard, and this would be her second of the day.

"He seemed to know you well," Shimmer commented. She avoided the word "friendly." His behavior and words had been friendly, but Shimmer thought Black was anything but.

"Black's been around these parts for decades," Cole said. "He knows bloody everyone."

Shimmer cocked her head. Seeing no reason not to call Cole on his evasive reply, she pushed, "No, he knew *you*, and you knew his reputation enough to use it against Bale." Cole said nothing, instead checking down tunnels they passed as if inspecting the symbols. Since their direction did not matter, Shimmer asked, "What does he do around 'these parts'?"

Cole fumbled for words, leading to a pause. Into the silence, Shimmer added, "I assumed he was a thief, Cole."

With a relieved smile, Cole shrugged. "Sorry, we're not supposed to go giving people details," he said. "Black is the oldest thief in StonePeak. He survived the purge back in 185. Only one of the top echelons did. That gives his name a lot of weight."

"You dress like him," Shimmer noted.

Cole again shrugged, but he stopped fidgeting at last. He leaned against a wall, the light hovering between them. "Any member of his cadre does," he said.

"Hence why Bale panicked," Shimmer said, nodding. "And why you didn't expect me to hold my own against him and his spells."

Cole sprang off the wall. "*His* spells? I heard... I thought it was you!" he said, rambling. "Not you? Whose spells? Not Bale..." He trailed off, scrunching his face as he tried to read Shimmer's expression. "Black's?"

Shimmer smiled, knowing it looked cocky. "I guess he hasn't told you. Oh well," she said. She launched into the Relocation spell.

By the time she had finished the spell, Cole had calmed enough to quip, "He could've shared a code or two."

They reappeared in Marionna's cottage.

It took Shimmer until dawn to make more of the pills to keep the celebrant unconscious. Cole's mother watched until then, letting Cole catch a few hours of sleep. He had survived on less, so he traded off with his mother as the sun rose, sending Marionna to her bed. Kitable slept through everything, waking enough to moan and gingerly roll over. Cole suspected the man did not regain sufficient consciousness during those moments even to recognize the cottage.

Come morning, Shimmer found a place beside the bed. Amazing Cole, she dragged herself through more spells before wrapping her travel cloak around herself and falling asleep. He expected her to look bedraggled after so much casting, but the only hint of her fatigue was the bags under her eyes. She was no longer pristine, but she was still beautiful.

Kitable awoke as Cole found some leftover food in the mid-morning light. Cole had been watching the celebrant as Shimmer had instructed. He had finished checking the back of the man's neck and adjusting the man away from the fire when Kitable joined him.

Cole shared his food and helped his brother place the kettle in the cooking nook of the fireplace. Then Kitable sat back, pensive.

"Any ideas what to do with this one yet?" Cole asked, nudging the sleeping celebrant.

Kitable looked identical, but Cole recognized the illusion. The tinkling of the spell was present among the general buzz that followed the master wizard, although the noise was considerably less now. Only his movement, which was calculated and slow, betrayed the continuing pain the man was managing.

"One," Kitable replied. The master wizard settled into a place next to Cole and checked on Shimmer. Once he had seen whatever he had been looking for, he faced the fire again and sank deeper into his seat.

Cole waited for more from Kitable, but the wizard was casting. Eager to overhear any spells Kitable cast, Cole listened in. He found the wizard's open, vacant gaze disconcerting enough to move out of his immediate line of sight.

After two spells, Cole realized he was witnessing Kitable setting his hovering spells for the day.

If the legends were true, Kitable had invented the hovering spell. Before Kitable's innovation, spells had been full-cast, making duels a careful balance of complexity and speed. Short, weak spells could outdo more advanced spells by getting in first. The attacking wizard had been at an advantage; knowing they were attacking, they had the luxury of building defenses up in advance. Defenders had been left scrambling, often to their doom.

But then Kitable had shown the world how to tether a pre-casted spell and activate it with an assigned word. The world of wizards had become faster and more dangerous in a day. Massive spells could be set in advance, a word away at any moment. Anyone could be as fast as the best dueler, the time lost in their poorly designed spells already spent.

Now, the deciding factor of a duel was how well-prepared the wizard was. How many spells had he set? Were they the right ones? Could his combination circumvent those of his opponent?

Kitable had shared the hovering spell with the world, but he remained its master. The spells Cole overheard were complicated to a level well beyond Cole's ability. By the sound of the auras, he knew what domains and elements were involved but not how they came together or what they did.

Even once done casting, Kitable's magic sounded more subdued than it had on their first meeting. Cole doubted the man had the strength to cast his usual array of spells.

Focus returned to Kitable's eyes. Cole handed him the tea he had brewed and kept warm. His brother sipped it with deliberation, his hands shaking less than before.

Knowing it was due again, Cole checked Celebrant Tamort. The man was unchanged. "You setting up something with all those spells?" he asked.

"I like to be prepared," Kitable replied. He adjusted his shirt, looking uncomfortable.

"So what's the plan?" Cole asked. Kitable again checked on Shimmer, but the woman slept. "You can run it by me," Cole said, realizing what his brother was looking for: he wanted to talk to someone and was looking for Shimmer. "I ain't as good she is, but I can echo you fine. Keep it basic, though!"

Kitable sipped his tea again. He narrowed his eyes on the celebrant, but he said nothing.

"We don't have a lot of time. Try me," Cole offered. "Shimmer will be grateful for a plan formed by the time she wakes."

Kitable sighed and lowered his tea into his lap. "We can't move the celebrant," he said.

"Course not," Cole agreed, pleased that he understood this much. "He's untouchable. Relocations wouldn't work."

"We can't allow him to wake," Kitable added.

"He'd kick our asses."

"But he can't answer our questions if he's unconscious."

"Can't you read...?" Cole trailed off. "Course you can't read his thoughts. He's untouchable."

"He is also sleeping," Kitable pointed out. "He is dreaming. That's where untouchables go to sleep. We can't reach into dreams. No wizard can."

That was new information to Cole, but he saw no reason to refute it. "So what *can* we do?"

"We can get someone else who can read his mind, maybe even his dreams," Kitable replied. "As you said, get into his head."

Cole frowned, stuck on a significant flaw. "But he's untouchable."

"So is the person I want to have read his mind," Kitable said.

Cole sat up straighter in surprise. "There are more of them? I mean, I know there have been stories about these untouchables, but they're hard to find, and they don't go telling people, let alone wizards, what they are! Most don't know, ain't that right?"

"Yes," Kitable said with a frown, but Cole wasn't sure if it was the wordy ramble or the facts he agreed to. "That is correct. But I know two other untouchables."

"So can we get them out here?" Cole asked.

"We can't Relocate them," Shimmer interrupted, joining them by sitting beside her master.

The bags under her eyes were less, and the sound of her magic was a sweet warble. At least some of it was still focused around her leg, which she favored as she moved.

"Right," Cole replied. He smiled up at her. "Hey, I was doing pretty well!"

Her smile was as sweet as the sound of her. "I heard. He'll not even need me by this time tomorrow." She lost her smile. "You're thinking about recruiting Celebrant Sedgan," she wearily told her master.

"Tamort was his acolyte," Kitable said, "and Sedgan manifests his powers intermittently. We would not be able to Relocate him. Sedgan, if we catch him in a weak moment, would not be untouchable."

"You can stop being untouchable?" Cole asked. "Forget what I said, Shimmer. I'm lost again!"

Kitable fixed Cole with a patient expression. "Untouchable powers have historically been connected to religious fervor."

"So it's a god's power?!" Cole snapped. He moved back from the celebrant, nervous that the vengeful flames of Inac were about to strike him. Inac was the Goddess of Revenge, after all. "We're messing with a god's will?"

Shimmer had dressed up like a holy emissary. She had fooled the celebrant and poisoned him. Even now, they were keeping him unconscious against his will. How could the goddess *not* seek revenge?

Shimmer's smile was understanding, but Kitable rolled his eyes like a disapproving father. "Certainly not," Kitable said. "Gods are a thing of myth."

"This guy levitated out of a pit," Cole accused, pointing at Tamort. "I saw him smash a boulder before it hit him.

It took *lightning* to take him down. If they aren't wizards and get their powers from their *gods*..." He rose away from them. He would have to offer Inac more money than he could make in a lifetime to correct such a profound affront.

"I said it depended on their degree of faith, not the gods," Kitable corrected. "Gods don't exist, Cole. That's myth. People believe in them. That's fact. Certain people can turn belief into power. That's the power of an untouchable."

Seeing Shimmer continue to sit beside the untouchable without fear, Cole lowered himself back to the ground beside her.

"You summarized an entire book into half a dozen sentences," Cole said.

"I have researched this a great deal," Kitable said. "The point is, we can use a Relocate spell on Sedgan. Also, if what I have learned about the Dreamworld is true, he can enter Tamort's mind for a conversation. He's the man we need."

"Dreamworld?" Cole asked. He had not meant to speak, too confused, but the single word jumped at him.

"The source of their magic," Shimmer explained. "We have the spiral in the void. They have the Dreamworld." Shimmer gave a small sigh. "Shall I fetch Sedgan?" she asked her master.

"I do not intend to bother with invitations," Master Kitable said. "I will bring him here momentarily."

While the master wizard began his spell, Shimmer pushed her hair from her face. "I'll get dressed," she said to no one.

She had her dress back on over her slip by the time the cacophony of magic had resolved, and a bald man appeared in the center of the room.

Sedgan Firewalker had aged more than Kitable had expected. The first thing Kitable noticed was the celebrant's receding hairline. Only a sliver of hair remained around the celebrant's ears now. His long nose had become wider. He had the thick wrinkles of a man who spent too much time outside, and he smelled like a campfire. Dressed in bright red robes accented with golden flames, he was as ornate as a showman. The symbol of Inac was embossed on his robes, but Kitable noted sourly the man covered his chest where a brand of Inac had once been on display.

"What is the meaning of..." The celebrant let his words trail off as he examined his unexpected surroundings. Shimmer flashed the man a smile, waving coyly at him.

The celebrant flushed red but held his tongue when he recognized Kitable. "Wisavi," Sedgan straightened himself pompously, ignoring Shimmer, "you could have asked!"

"That would take too much time," Kitable replied, preferring not to reveal how little energy he had. Moving a person was complicated enough. Having to communicate with the person beforehand would have worn him out further.

"Oh," the celebrant replied, sounding hurt. His eyes narrowed on Tamort. "Is that...?"

The older celebrant squinted, making Kitable think Sedgan needed to invest in glasses.

Shimmer slid away from Celebrant Tamort, clearing a path for Sedgan to approach. Somehow, she did not even limp. But then, she had always been graceful and well balanced. "Yep, your old friend," Shimmer said. She was smiling at the celebrant too brightly. Kitable had not thought his apprentice and the celebrant of Inac were acquainted beyond their minimal interactions in the Manor of Wayburn where Sedgan was the Celebrant of Galanth for King Tohmas. Not only did she seem to know the man, but

Shimmer also seemed to enjoy being overly sweet to him and watching him cringe.

A question for another day.

"Celebrant Tamort," Kitable explained as Sedgan came forward, "is under our control because he has tried to kill me."

Sedgan's eyes went wide. When the celebrant looked again at his acolyte, Kitable thought he was checking if the man was breathing. Kitable usually would not have hesitated to kill a threat like Tamort. "Unfortunately, he has indicated he has the information we need. I need to get it. He's untouchable."

Kitable waited as Sedgan put the statements together.

"Why does this involve me?" he asked. "Tamort was once my acolyte, but as a full celebrant, he is independent. Even if I did once command him, he left the Province of Galanth. He is outside my influence."

"We have no intention of having you command him," Kitable said. "I have no intention of even waking him. He blames me for Loni's death," Kitable saw Sedgan flinch at the mention of the name, "and seeks justice."

"Misguided justice," Sedgan grumbled.

From his place in the corner, Cole snorted. "Does everyone *except* Tamort know who killed this Loni?" he demanded.

Sedgan's glare, perfected over decades of training acolytes, was potent. When it landed upon him, Cole darted back like a boy struck by a cane.

While Sedgan himself gave nothing by way of explanation, Shimmer was less reserved. "Sedgan knows because he was involved."

Kitable expected another glare, but Sedgan's expression became shameful instead. He did not look at Shimmer.

That was suspicious.

Cole cocked his head. "How involved?" he asked.

"I recommended it," Sedgan confessed, lifting his chin in false confidence. He briefly set his eyes on Shimmer but could not hold her gaze.

They had shared something, Kitable realized. A secret was held between Sedgan and Shimmer. Something she knew could damn the man, and she was flaunting it. Sedgan, a man who ruled over all the holiest people of the Princedom of Galanth, was cowed and shamed. He was anticipating her betrayal.

What secret does she know?

"You recommended it, the king commanded it, and the prime protector performed it," Cole said, shaking his head. "Basically, everyone *except* Kitable was responsible."

"And yet, I am the one he blames. That is enough, Cole," Kitable said, drawing Sedgan's attention back from his half-brother. He had hoped Sedgan would ignore the two other people in the room. Until this series of events, no one had known about Kitable's family. He had been hoping to return to that.

Yet how could he now? Shimmer knew. But she would not tell anyone, would she?

More questions for another day, he decided. They had to act now to get Tamort's information.

"Sedgan, you have walked in dreams," Kitable said. "I want you to get into his."

The celebrant shifted his feet. One hand went to his chest where Kitable knew the brand of Inac had been burned into his flesh. Since learning gods and goddesses were things of myths, Kitable had discovered that the "miraculous" brand had been set into Sedgan's skin by Loni herself, not by Inac as the legend professed. He had never told the man that, of course. Sedgan had been unconscious for the event.

Sedgan stared down at Tamort for a long while, studying. At length, he asked, "What information does he have?"

Kitable had prepared a suitably vague reply, but Shimmer interrupted. "You ass," she accused Sedgan. "You can't do it, and you weren't going to admit it."

The celebrant glowered at Kitable's apprentice. "These things are finicky," he replied.

Shimmer cocked her head. "Seen the goddess recently?" she asked.

Sedgan's face went bright red. "Seeing Inac" often meant having sex. Even Kitable was grateful his illusion would hide his flush of irritation. Shimmer was out of line.

Kitable pushed himself to his feet. "Weaver," he snapped, "get out if you are not going to be helpful. I can see there is far more going on in this conversation than words, and I do not have the patience for it."

She clenched her jaw, cutting off her sharp reply because of the presence of others. Had they been in private, she would never have hesitated to give him her full opinion.

But had they been in private, she would have explained this too, something she seemed unable to do.

Then again, would she have explained? Or would she have kept whatever she and Sedgan had done buried in her past with everything else she had never told him?

Since she said nothing, Kitable accepted that she would behave and turned back to Sedgan.

"Your faith can grant you the powers you need," he informed the celebrant. "Do whatever you need to do. Go pray or something."

Sedgan sneered at him, looking like a cross turtle. "You don't even believe gods exist," he rightly pointed out.

"I don't have to believe. You do."

They paused there, their stares locked, and said nothing for a long moment.

For the first time that morning, Marionna rose. She had slept in her clothing, but the garments appeared accustomed to such. She collected a sack of cloth and declared, "It's too nice to be sitting inside. Celebrant, perhaps the light of Inac can inspire you?" She held out a hand, and bewildered, Sedgan took it. He glanced at Kitable, asking who the woman was with his stare.

Kitable did not answer him. He let his mother lead the celebrant outside.

Once Sedgan and Marionna were outside, Kitable again looked at his apprentice. The presence of Cole in the corner was not enough to hold her tongue now.

"He *is* a hypocritical ass," she insisted.

Biting back another outburst, Kitable thought back to their last discussion on religion.

"You once told me you had lost your faith in celebrants some time back," he said. "Does he have something to do with that?"

The ire on Shimmer's face faded. "I thought you didn't want to know."

The idea of knowing Shimmer's past in any great detail terrified him. He thought Shimmer was an amazing pupil, bright and creative. Her wit was quick, her heart sweet, and her intelligence unmatched. He did not want to mar that with the life she had left behind. She had been a dancer.

"I fear knowing about your past will cause me to judge you for it."

"Judge me?" Shimmer snapped. "How can you *ignore* the rest of my life? How can you *not* care about it?"

He sensed that question was not the one Shimmer had wanted to ask but was unsure why she had not voiced the other one. "You aren't who you were," he replied. "You aren't Seraph or Radiance or..." He trailed off when he recognized he had offended her.

"Or Bliss?" Cole joined in, his voice light and cheery. Startled by the reminder of an audience, Kitable stopped another outburst. He had forgotten about his half-brother and was now feeling his face flush with anger. Shimmer usually was more controlled than this, particularly around company. She knew better.

"Bliss?" Kitable echoed instead, looking at Shimmer. He knew his stare was accusatory, and he could not correct it.

She did not wilt away but lifted her chin. "I will always be who I was," Shimmer replied, her voice uncommonly flat. "That demure little housemaid I was in the manor was the act." She gestured at herself, drawing attention to her layered skirts and many-pocketed frock. "This is what I am! Apothecary, wizard, dancer, and all of that is built on who I was, who I still am when the damn courts of Espar aren't watching."

Kitable opened his mouth to reply but stopped. Nothing he thought of would be appropriate with Cole present.

"So," Shimmer finished into his silence, her expression set, "do you still not want to know?"

"Unless it concerns our current situation, I do not want to know."

"Well," Shimmer said, her smile vindictive, "it may have something to do with our current situation, seeing as that man is drugged from his bald top to the bottom of his feet."

"Drugged?" Kitable asked, shaken from his convictions. "Drugged with what?"

Shimmer shrugged. "He's on frozen freedom," she said, "again. And I don't feel like helping him get off it this time."

"Again?" Cole asked, grinning. "Done it before, has he? So this ain't a poisoning."

"Nope," Shimmer replied. "Voluntary, I expect." She fixed her stare on Kitable. "Won't make him helpful, though. You sure you want to deal with him?"

The only thing he was certain of was that he did not want to carry on this conversation.

"We'll see," Kitable grumbled and headed out into the light of the day.

Celebrant Sedgan was the pillar of strength for Inac, and she had destroyed him with a sentence. Shimmer felt vindictively pleased.

Kitable followed the celebrant outside. He did not ask the questions he should have, leaving Shimmer abandoned. For all their time together, the cleft between them persisted.

Shimmer took a seat beside Tamort. Someone had to watch the unconscious celebrant. It would all be for naught if he died.

She was tempted, not for the first time, to make a deliberate mistake. It was complicated getting these drugs right. She could overdose him. Then Tamort would never wake, and the threat would be over.

She mixed her own medications first to give her mind time to settle. Then, once she was sure she would be calm and careful, she measured Tamort's to safe volumes.

Cole came to sit beside her once more. "On frozen freedom, eh?" he said. "How'd you know?"

Shimmer smiled sadly. "It messes with people's eyes, and they get twitchy. I knew him when he was on and off it. It was obvious to me."

Cole nodded solemnly, looking like he was mimicking Kitable. Kitable's was more impressive. "I've tried that stuff before." He glanced at Shimmer. "You ever done freedom?"

Shimmer shook her head. "I saw enough of it."

"So did I," Cole said, "but I knew this boy. He said that freedom could open your mind so wide, it'd let magic in. I was a kid. I'd always been able to hear magic, but I couldn't cast. I wanted to be a wizard, so I tried it."

The problem with frozen freedom was that the high it generated required increasing doses of the drug over time. It was easy for a single try to turn into a lifetime of increasing amounts. Those lifetimes were notoriously short.

"How deep did you go?" she asked delicately.

Unlike his brother, who would never have answered her, Cole shrugged and admitted, "I did five grains once."

"I haven't seen you reach for it," she said.

"After the boy I knew died, I had a … let's call him a friend, or I guess a mentor, who stepped in. He locked me in a dead-end tunnel. He'd toss in water and food but never any freedom. Once I was through the shakes, he told me I was worth something to him, so he wouldn't let me kill myself. That was it. If I touch the stuff, I figure he'll lock me in that tunnel again and won't come back to open it."

Shimmer smiled sadly. Weaning off frozen freedom was terrible. There were softer ways of doing it, but they were not always available. "A bit rough," she said.

"Saved my life," Cole replied. "You met the fellow last night."

"Black," Shimmer said in understanding. She thought over what she had seen of the man and decided, "I can see that. He'd do what he needed to for an asset. I guess he's got more invested in you now." She thought for another moment. "But he didn't teach you magic," she said. "You didn't even know he was a caster."

Cole's face fell. "I didn't. I've never so much as heard a rumor that he's a wizard. I know he has a ton of trinkets. Are you sure that isn't what you sensed? Enchanted items. He collects them, studies them."

Shimmer shook her head. "I know how to recognize an active spell."

Cole watched the low-burning fire momentarily before saying, "So do you think you could dress up again and scare Celebrant Sedgan into having an inspired moment?"

Shimmer smiled. "I doubt he'd believe it. He didn't trust Loni."

"You could try," Cole suggested. She eyed him until he shrugged. "I liked that costume."

"Cole!" she snapped, punching him on the shoulder.

He flinched as if being dealt a much harder blow. "What? You're beautiful, Shimmer. I'm not saying it as an insult! It's true."

Despite herself, Shimmer smiled. It was nice to be complimented.

"And smart," Cole added when he got no other reply. "Scary smart. Smarter than me anyway, and that's pretty smart."

He gave her a coy smile.

Shimmer laughed. It felt good.

10

Kitable sat outside the cottage, lacking the will to approach the celebrant. The low garden fence had crumbled since he had been a boy, and he had grown too tall to dangle his feet from its edge, but it provided a place to sit nonetheless. Seeing Marionna in conversation with Sedgan, he let them be. If Sedgan was going to be unhelpful, Kitable would have to find another solution, and the sun's warmth helped him think.

Like wizard magic, untouchable magic was power channeled through a person. They came from a different place, but the power itself was similar. For wizards, the source of magic was the great light in the darkness. For untouchables, the power came from dreams.

He was less confident of that. He knew dreams and the untouchable powers came from the same place—the Dreamworld—but was unsure if the dreams themselves were the power. He knew that dreaming would dispel a wizard and that wizards tended not to dream, so there had to be a connection.

Could he coach Sedgan into dreaming? Meditation was common for wizards, but it was designed to bring the mind out of the body and into the great void. From there, a wizard could see the spiral of light and command it. Would meditation lead Sedgan to the Dreamworld or into the wizard's light?

Kitable woke again, having drifted off in the warm sunlight. He had trouble focusing his eyes as he opened them, seeing spots and feeling like his head was wrapped in wool. Every action he took was heavy and slow, worn out by pain. The pain pills did not seem to be working anymore.

Opening his eyes, he saw his mother staring down at him.

"You hurt," she said softly, taking up a place next to him.

"Of course I do," he replied.

Sedgan had moved away and was pacing in the field outside the cottage, looking indecisive and leaving Kitable and Marionna alone.

It occurred to Kitable that this was the first moment they had shared alone since all of this had begun. He searched his thoughts for a suitable thing to say but found nothing. They had not spoken in close to twenty years. He would have written letters, but she could not read. Having not intended to return in person, Kitable had never planned their conversation. Nothing he said could make up for decades of absence.

"I'm sorry," he blurted out. "I'm sorry you got dragged into this."

Her smile brought so many painful memories into Kitable's mind that he flinched. He had been sent away at the age of ten and still remembered her in the haze of childhood fondness.

She was his mother.

He tried to focus, but she wrapped her arms around his shoulders, and he felt like a child again. Saying nothing, Kitable savored the gentle touch of his mother, not felt in twenty years. She even smelled as he remembered. He was grateful he'd lacked the strength to cast the Moulded Shield this time and could feel her touch.

At length, she gave a small sigh and pulled away. Kitable met her eyes, seeking approval. He saw it in her adoring gaze. His load lightened.

"I know you would never have brought this upon us should you have had a choice," she said. In a sentence, he was absolved. "I'm sorry I sent you away." Her eyes filled with tears. "I thought I was doing right by you. I thought…"

It was his turn. It hurt his stitches, but Kitable wrapped his arms around his mother.

"You did what was right at the time," Kitable insisted. "Despite Master Sylas, I did become a wizard. I have everything I need provided for me, and I'll keep providing for you. I can send more," he added, "since you have a son to worry about."

She straightened and glanced back at the cottage where Cole and Shimmer had stayed behind.

Kitable tried to pull his mind away from that thought. Something about leaving Shimmer alone with Cole made his stomach turn. He knew Shimmer could handle herself. Cole would be blasted to the far side of the mountains if he stepped a toe out of line, yet it still troubled Kitable. It wasn't that he thought she couldn't set Cole straight. It was that she might not want to.

Cole was closer to her age. Shimmer seemed more relaxed with him than she ever did with Kitable. And that irked Kitable further.

Marionna sighed. "I had a chance to speak to Sedgan there," she said.

"Oh?" Kitable asked. "Should I be apologizing for carting him off to the far side of the world without his permission?"

Marionna gave him a motherly smile. "He's not angry about that," she explained. "He'd like to help, but he's angry he can't."

Kitable rubbed his temples, a headache coming back now. "I cannot make him untouchable. I assumed *he* would know how to do it."

Marionna cocked her head. "I think he needs a reason, Kaylin," she said.

No one had called him that in decades. He didn't even think of himself as "Kaylin" anymore and hadn't since coming into the employ of the first Prince of Galanth. He was Kitable. That was the only life he let himself remember.

But with a word, he remembered being helpless, beaten, and forgotten. He remembered seeing the magic light in his mind and failing to reach it. The frustration of that had driven him into the darkest part of his life.

Sedgan was going through the same.

Letting out a breath, Kitable pushed himself up. Marionna nodded. Somehow, mothers knew these things.

Leaving her at the cottage, Kitable joined Sedgan beside the road.

Sedgan glanced at his approach, then faced away. "I'm trying to figure out which way is home," he said, looking pointedly left, then right. The road between the houses had no signage.

Marionna was right. Had he wanted to go, Sedgan would have. He may have been a celebrant, but he was not stupid.

Sensing this was his opportunity, Kitable stated, "SoulBurner is killing King Tohmas."

Although he briefly let his eyes go wide, Sedgan recovered his nonchalant demeanor in a blink. "The enchanted sword the goddess gifted him?" he asked, his tone as if they were discussing weather patterns. "Unfortunate."

"It's draining his soul," Kitable agreed. "Because of it, he's going mad. I have been charged with finding a cure. Tamort claimed he knew something about it."

Sedgan pursed his lips. He had always been old, but the last two years had made him look ancient. His body seemed strong and stout still—Celebrants of Inac had to maintain physical form for fighting—but his skin looked a size too big now. He'd lost weight, and his leathered skin had crinkled like a tortoise's.

Kitable blamed the frozen freedom for the transformation but had to admit there could have been other factors. Perhaps the strain on his conscience?

"He might, seeing as he was one of Loni's favorites, and Loni created SoulBurner," Sedgan said.

"If I tell him the truth about Loni's death, he will turn this rage against the king," Kitable said.

"Probably will think this is Inac's punishment on the king for killing her chosen one," Sedgan agreed. He still had not decided on a direction.

"Is that what you think it was?" Kitable asked.

At last, Sedgan met Kitable's eyes. He squinted through the light, cynical. "I fear every day that Inac has a punishment planned for the ones who killed her chosen one." The words were heavy with meaning.

"Hence the frozen freedom."

"Among other things," Sedgan confessed. "The drugs brought me closer to her for a while. I've been there, in the golden light, walking between dreams. But the drugs don't help now. The doses I'd need..." He trailed off. For the first time, he glanced back at the cottage.

An idea formed in Kitable's mind. "Would you do the freedom to enter the Dreamworld if you had it?"

Sedgan frowned, and his wrinkles followed it. And yet Kitable sensed he was not the target of the glower; it was Sedgan's disappointment in himself he found so distasteful. "It'd kill me," Sedgan replied.

If he has no faith, perhaps guilt will be sufficient motivation.

Kitable thought of Shimmer and her traveling bag. She knew these drugs better than anyone he had ever met. "What if there was a way not to kill you?" Kitable asked. "Would you do it then?"

Although his eyes were bright, Sedgan's voice was hollow when he said, "Without hesitation."

Nodding, Kitable headed for the cottage.

Shimmer finished checking on Tamort and leaned away. Cole had been helping her but moved away when her Kitable entered the cottage as if afraid of being caught. Her leg did not throb if she did not move. Even the dull ache had subsided since she had applied an ointment of menthe to it and taken remedies for bruising. When sitting, she propped it up to help further reduce the swelling.

Without delay, Kitable asked, "Have you got more frozen freedom in your bag?"

Shimmer lifted an eyebrow at him, lowering her leg slowly. "Of course. Why?"

Kitable's expression was pensive, but instead of pacing, he sat down on the floor. Shimmer assumed he lacked the energy to stand. She dove into her sack, looking for an additional pain pill for him.

"It might be able to inspire Sedgan," he suggested.

Finding the pill she was seeking, she passed it over. "For your pain," she told him, troubled when her master did not object to taking it. "So are we inspiring him into dreams," she asked, "or into seeing Inac up close for a final time?"

"Can you counter it? Let him get into a bliss state, but not let it kill him?"

Shimmer reviewed the effects of frozen freedom in her mind. Each individual symptom could be blocked or supported, but the impact on the brain was unique.

She shook her head. "Not entirely. I might be able to keep the heart stable, but it'll still fry the brain. Only thing that cures it is a Sweep."

Kitable grimaced. "If it works, you won't be able to Sweep."

"What's a Sweep?" Cole chirped.

"A spell I..." She trailed off, awkward.

"Invented," Kitable finished, looking perplexed that she had dropped the sentence. "But it's magic, so it wouldn't work if he's untouchable. And the whole point is to make him untouchable." Kitable's eyes narrowed, glancing between Cole and Shimmer, but the wizard still seemed confused.

He would not understand. Inventing spells was second nature to Kitable. His name was in books used for teaching magic now and had been for a decade. But for her, the creation of spells was still a private affair. No wizard wanted their code to be public. Once it was known, it could be criticized and manipulated.

But Kitable had given away his code so many times before that it didn't seem to bother him at all anymore. Admitting she could create spells made Shimmer stand out more than she wanted.

Sure enough, Cole's eyes went wide. "Wow," he muttered, but it didn't sound as sarcastic as she expected. His awe seemed strangely genuine.

Shimmer tried to find an alternative but shook her head. "Whether a dose is fatal depends on a few things, but mostly what dose he's on now," she said. "If it's low enough, we can get the effect without death…"

"I'm up to four grains," Sedgan interrupted, entering through the lit doorway.

"And you're still flying," Shimmer added. She didn't have to think hard about the answer.

"So no, it can't be done. He'll need five grains, and that's into lethal doses."

Sedgan's look was incredulous. "And that's objectionable to you?" He moved slowly into the cottage.

She could tell his drugs were wearing low. His hands were trembling instead of twitching.

Feeling her face flush, Shimmer steeled herself proudly. "Despite your poor opinion of me and my family, I won't give you something that will kill you, even if I think you're a pompous buffoon with an inflated ego."

Sedgan sat on the bed, his expression no longer sour. She had expected him to be incensed, but he looked only defeated. She'd last seen that expression when she'd revealed Loni had been poisoning him, getting him hooked on the frozen freedom to make him dependent. Shimmer and her father had broken Loni's hold by weaning Sedgan off during the conquest of Espar, but it clearly had not provided the long-term results they had expected.

"What if I want to?" he asked in a tiny voice.

Shimmer glared at Kitable. "By the hells, what did you say to him?"

Kitable shrugged. "I told him the truth." He tilted his head toward the celebrant, his eyes narrowed again in thought. "You are carrying even more guilt than I expected, Celebrant," he added.

Sedgan sighed, his hands clenched to keep the trembling still. "It's my fault," he said softly.

Baffled, Shimmer looked at Kitable, then, not knowing what else to do, she glanced at Cole. Cole at least acknowledged her: he shrugged and frowned dramatically. Knowing she was not the only one confused made her smile.

"A *lot* more guilt than I expected," Kitable said cynically. "Before I condone this, will you explain how you have anything to be guilty about regarding the king being driven mad by his sword?"

Cole's eyes went wide as doorknobs. "What?"

Kitable grimaced. "Damn, I'd forgotten you were there." The master wizard gave his half-brother a long, stern stare. "Do not repeat any of that, ever. If you start spreading the word of this, I will make your life very short."

Cole bristled. Shimmer could not tell if Cole believed the threat or if Kitable meant it. "Don't let Mother hear you," Cole shot back.

Now Sedgan's eyes went wide. "Mother?" he asked, fixing his gaze on Kitable. "Your mother?"

Kitable put his fingers to his temples, his eyes squinted shut in pain. "Do not repeat any of that either," he said to Sedgan. He was slow in correcting his posture, dragging himself back into a straight-backed position. "Can we please focus? In what way is this situation your fault, Celebrant Sedgan?"

Reminded of the topic, Sedgan's face fell. No one spoke, giving the man time to bring his thoughts and words together. At length, Sedgan said, "I sent her to get the sword."

"So what?" Shimmer asked when Kitable did not answer. "Did you make it? Did you give it soul-stealing powers?"

Sedgan shook his head. "You do not understand. I made it up. I put the idea into her head." The celebrant took a long, slow breath. The shaking of his hands worsened, but he pressed on. "After we last met, Miss Weaver, I knew I had to be rid of Loni. I told her I had a vision. I invented the sword, trying to lure her away."

Shimmer had always known it had been Loni in the guise of the Goddess Inac who had presented the sword to King Tohmas during the Northlander war. Once they had learned more about the untouchable powers, it had stood to reason that Loni had enchanted the blade with her powers. Shimmer, like Kitable, had been blaming Loni.

"You sent her to get the sword?" Kitable asked.

"Worse. I entirely made it up," Sedgan replied. "Sent her on a fake mission. But she found it anyway. Willed it into existence, I suppose."

"I guess asking you to believe in your goddess is out of the question," Shimmer said. "You've disproven your own faith."

Sedgan put a hand onto his sternum where a brand had appeared on his chest years ago. He smiled ironically. "Even figured this out," he said.

"Powdered grans on wax," Shimmer agreed. She ignored that she had lost Cole. "She puts it on your skin. You wash in the morning, and a burn miraculously appears. Doesn't require a holy visitation at all."

Sedgan nodded miserably. "But the golden world, what you call the Dreamworld, isn't dependent on Inac," he said, his voice gaining strength. She hadn't noticed how quiet he had become until his usual celebrant voice came through. "I've seen it without Inac. I have walked in dreams without her. So I'll do it again." He looked down at Shimmer, his expression blank. "I'll need your help."

Shimmer swallowed hard but nodded. She pulled the frozen freedom out of her bag, then found her scale and weights. "At least give me a moment to get the dose right," she said. "I'll be damned if I let you end up dead because some dealer cut this with something."

As she worked, Cole placed a hand on her shoulder in support. It rested atop her Moulded Shield spell.

Kitable didn't bother to watch Sedgan fall into delirium but sat back and sent his mind into the darkness in readiness. Cole had taken on monitoring Tamort. Shimmer would do whatever she could to keep Sedgan stable and perform the Sweep spell to remove the frozen freedom when he stopped being untouchable. He was in good hands. Stubborn hands but good ones.

Taking his mind out of his body was a blessing. The aches of Kitable's stitches and the pulsing pain of his head were gone as his awareness moved into the black nothingness near the spiral of magic. After enough visits, Kitable knew where the cliffs were even when he could not see them. He kept back from the spiral. Its presence warmed the air around him, but he was not here for it this time.

Time in the darkness did not pass at a regular rate. Kitable had seen moments pass like candles and days pass as mere flickers of time. He waited, wondering how long it would take for Sedgan to find him, assuming the man could do as he claimed.

Kitable had been brought from this darkness into the golden light of the Dreamworld twice by a dreamer, Elder

Tril. Of course, each time that happened, Kitable had been dispelled. Twice, that had saved him from an enemy wizard's control.

Kitable couldn't help but smile. It had taken a long time for him to trust Tril, but Tril and Shimmer remained the only wizards who had never betrayed him. Kitable had killed over fifty wizards, and every last one was a troublesome memory. Some of them had been, like Cole, barely budding, and others had been masters. He had offered alternatives to many of the earlier ones but had given up on that strategy over time. It was surprisingly difficult for wizards to get along.

He missed Tril now. The Northlander Elder, bound to a wolf's soul, somehow walked between wizard and untouchable magic. Kitable was certain he could have solved this. But Tril had come to Kitable in a dream at the end of the conquest of Espar to tell him that he was leaving to help others and to hopefully save his sanity from the uncontrolled visions. Kitable had not heard from him since. He assumed the man was somewhere in the Dreamworld, but he could not find him. He wondered if he saw him, if it would be the wolf or the man. While he was musing, a golden light reached out into the darkness. Within it, Sedgan appeared, looking twenty years younger with considerably more hair to show for it. He'd been a redhead before age had tinted his hair to gray, Kitable noted. His green eyes were speckled in gold, a phenomenon of the Dreamworld, no doubt. Now moving without the ages' wear, the celebrant strode purposefully up to Kitable and tried to speak.

The darkness did not allow sound. While Kitable knew it was possible to use thought magic to communicate, Kitable doubted the compatibility of his thought magic and Sedgan's.

After several more attempts, Sedgan furrowed his brow, shrugged, and motioned for Kitable to follow him.

Within a few steps, Kitable stood in an expanse of golden mist. Sedgan's appearance changed instantly, becoming a clear incarnation of Inac's power. The man's skin now flickered like fading embers. He wore no robes, and the scar on his chest was two open fissures, lava visible in their depth. His flaming red hair was long enough that the curls waved on an unfelt wind. His eyes held their golden-flecked surface.

Tril had looked like a wolf-man in the Dreamworld when Kitable had seen him. *Perhaps this is a manifestation of the soul?*

Kitable checked himself but found no change. He wore the same clothes he had upon leaving the cottage, although his wounds were missing.

"You look surprisingly sane," Kitable said once they were in the golden light and could speak.

Sedgan looked back at him with his flickering eyes. His voice crackled like flames when he replied, "Here is the soul. I left my mind behind. It continues to spin in hysteria." The green eyes narrowed on Kitable, eyeing him from top to bottom. "Your soul and mind came together," the celebrant said.

"I only had to leave my body," Kitable confirmed. "But at least it doesn't hurt."

"Hurt?" Sedgan asked, his brow raised. Kitable had not noticed it, but the celebrant's incarnation lacked eyebrows. Burned off?

"You couldn't see through the illusion; I was badly wounded. Thankfully, the effect was wholly physical. My mind is fine," Kitable replied.

Sedgan's aspect nodded with reverence. "I wonder what your soul would look like if your mind let it go."

"I am not interested in finding out," Kitable replied, looking into the mists. Golden dancing flecks of light flashed into the distance in all directions, the darkness left behind. For a moment, he thought he saw a wolf moving in the flicking light, but it vanished before he could be sure.

"This way," Sedgan called, turning away and beginning to walk. A golden tether followed the man, reaching behind him like an endless tail.

Kitable checked behind himself and found a tether as well.

"It's your connection to your body," Sedgan explained, traversing the mist. The golden light broke abruptly, and they crossed an open field, reminding Kitable of the rolling hills of the north where he had once waged war. Within two steps, the grassy hill vanished, and the gold returned.

A dream, Kitable thought. *Just passing through...*

"You can always find your way back by following that tail you have," Sedgan continued. He paused briefly, letting a small man with white hair go by. Although the traveler walked without a limp, his leg was bent at a strange angle, a deformity from childhood managed by a thicker, stronger opposite limb. His long hair was tied back.

"He doesn't have a tether," Kitable commented as the man vanished into the haze of light again.

"Dead," Sedgan replied with a shrug. "That is a soul without a body to return to."

Within another two steps, Kitable and Sedgan appeared in someone's house but again left it behind a blink later. Kitable had time to notice that the walls were smooth white stone and not wizard-stone. It looked like nothing he had ever seen in Espar.

They passed through another dozen such dreams, always leaving before the dreamer noticed them. As much as Kitable was curious about what would happen should they be seen, he dared not lose his guide.

At length, Sedgan paused again in the golden light. "I found Tamort's dreams. You should be able to speak to him in the dream, but even I cannot make him cooperative."

Kitable nodded, taking a slow breath. "Will he be able to harm me here?"

Sedgan cocked his head. "You are already dispelled," he said. "Even he lacks the power to destroy a soul. But your mind? A mind does not belong in the Dreamworld. I do not know what will happen. Perhaps."

"My mind is well protected," Kitable replied, his confidence returning. Any wizard worth a copper leg knew to defend their mind using the force of will. His mental defenses, especially since his dealings with casters proficient in thought magic, did not require magic.

"Then good luck," Sedgan said, gesturing forward grandly. "Here, I leave you."

"What will you do?" Kitable asked before the celebrant could move away.

Sedgan shrugged, but his smile had fire within it. "Return to the body and mind that are trying to destroy themselves. Try to bring passion back into them. If I cannot, I will leave them."

"You'll die?" Kitable asked, trying to make sense of the soul's claims.

The fire flashed in the eyes as if the fire within was contained by a shell of flesh that grew increasingly thin. "I won't," he said. "They will."

The celebrant backed up a step and vanished.

Kitable now stood in an army camp at the center of a circle of Temple waggons. The central fire pit burned low, the remnants of a celebratory meal scattered around the benches that bridged the waggons. The four Temple waggons, each with the hallmarks of their gods carved on the outside and hanging in the doorways, faced the fire. Kitable had seen dozens of such setups over the years of the war.

Tamort sat on the steps to the Temple waggon of Inac, his robes the most extravagant Kitable had ever seen. Gold-and-red weave covered him. The mark of Inac glittered from the center of the robe like Sedgan's scar.

He is waiting for someone, Kitable thought. This appeared to be an ordainment, the confirmation of an acolyte to celebrant. The way he was dressed, Kitable guessed Tamort was the one being ordained.

Was he waiting for his celebrant? Would a dream version of Sedgan appear, or had Tamort been confirmed by Loni herself? Although he had been traveling with the army, Kitable had not paid attention to the changes in the Temple waggons then.

Unsure if he would be seen, Kitable entered the fire circle.

Tamort's head lifted. The man's eyes were golden, as if looking through the Dreamworld mist even now, but he otherwise seemed very normal, not containing the powers of a goddess like Sedgan. He was plain by comparison.

"So you come to join me, Master Wizard," Tamort said, rising to his feet like a fighter entering a ring.

Kitable strengthened his mind, bringing his thoughts safely together. Wandering thoughts could be manipulated. There would be no opportunities. His mind was secure.

"You said you knew something about SoulBurner," Kitable said, stopping opposite Tamort and keeping the campfire between them. The flames danced on the wind, looking more like tossed leaves than flickering fire. The embers glowed not with red light but with the golden sparkles of the Dreamworld.

Tamort's smile was bitter. "She told me about it," he said.

Loni, Kitable assumed. Reminding Tamort of Loni seemed likely to end in one place: an attack on Kitable's life. But it had been a distant hope to avoid mention of the crazed celebrant for this conversation.

Yet Tamort was not yet showing signs of rage. He seemed strangely composed.

Loni had been, by all accounts, mad. She had been branded as insane before Kitable had met her and had continued to prove how much the brand suited her throughout the war. Sedgan had somewhat kept her in line, but he had never managed to truly control her. Kitable had a scar between his shoulder blades from one of Loni's enraged assaults.

He could not imagine how the woman would have known enough of her magic to understand SoulBurner. As far as Kitable knew, Loni had not recognized she was untouchable. She had obliviously bumped into spells and wizards, dispelling them time and time again, without acknowledging the power she wielded.

"How much did she know?" Kitable asked gently.

Tamort shook his head. "Not much. She never knew what she did. Her mind was full of blank moments—fits. But I could see it," he said, his golden eyes sparking. "As I learned about the untouchable powers, the powers you tried to prevent us from recognizing, I saw what SoulBurner was."

Kitable wanted to argue that he had never tried to keep them from discovering their powers. Yes, he had avoided Loni because she was unpredictable, but he had spent countless hours with Celebrant Calanor and his wife, exploring the reach of untouchable magic. He had been seeking its limitations, but in the process, he had learned more about this dreamer magic than any other had before.

Instead of antagonizing Tamort, Kitable said, "So what is SoulBurner?"

The celebrant's smile was large enough for two men, his teeth bared in a near-feral snarl. "A prison," he said.

When Tamort moved a step toward him, Kitable kept his distance. Step-by-step, they began circling the fire. Once, years ago, Kitable had used fire to keep Loni away from him. Then, she had been enraged and deaf to his pleas. He had dropped her into a pit to end the confrontation.

He had spared her life, making the pit only deep enough to keep her at bay. Unlike Tamort, Loni had never known enough of her powers to manifest them. Sedgan had come to her rescue then.

Tamort was different. He knew his powers and how to use them against Kitable. This was also not the real world. This was Tamort's dream, and even Kitable did not know how much that would affect what he and Tamort could do.

He had to avoid conflict. He needed words, answers to the many questions about the enchanted sword gifted by a madwoman pretending to be a goddess. If he could keep Tamort talking...

"A prison for whom?" Kitable asked.

"Not for you," Tamort replied. The voice had become taught, annoyance reaching through his otherwise calm exterior.

"Then who?"

Tamort stopped, allowing Kitable to do the same. They had swapped places. Kitable now stood at the base of the stairs to the Temple waggon of Fire while Tamort was backed by the Temple of Totho. A wind gusted from behind him, tossing his golden robes.

"For your king," Tamort replied. "For your kingdom."

Kitable felt a cold stone form in the bottom of his stomach. There was more in those words. He kept his voice level. "So you know what it does."

"More than that," Tamort said. "I know why."

Not wanting to give anything away, all Kitable dared say was, "So why?"

He felt heat rising against his back, most concentrated between his shoulder blades where Loni had once stabbed him. He fought the urge to look over his shoulder, trying to focus on Tamort. The dreamer was there. It was a dream. Surely nothing could harm him.

But his confidence wavered. Tamort's smile was still broad and knowing.

"Because he's a murderer too," Tamort said.

The pain in Kitable's back flared, making him flinch. He steeled his mind again, reminding himself that this was a dream. Nothing here was real except for the soul across from him.

"The king waged war against many—"

Tamort stepped toward him again, passing through the fire as if it was only smoke. Kitable tried to move but found himself fixed. The pain from his scar reached across his back, wrapping around him like a grapple and holding him fast.

"No, no," Tamort said, his face now a hand's breadth from Kitable's. "Not war. Not justice. Murder. The murder of my lady."

The cold stone in Kitable's stomach grew heavy. The secret was known. His king was no longer safe.

Kitable pushed back, both in body and in mind, trying to free himself from the grip behind him. To his shock, nothing moved. The powers grew hot along his shoulders and arms when a voice behind him whispered, "A prison for my killer."

Her voice was alto and hoarse, but he recognized it.

Loni was dead. Carsh had slain her. She could not be here.

But Sedgan had shown that souls walked this Dreamworld. Could the body be dead and the soul still wander?

Wizards could not affect the soul. In this, Kitable was helpless.

Tamort's eyes glowed brighter still. "Thank you, Kitable," he said, placing a single finger on Kitable's sternum. "Now I have a way into the king's court."

Two burning fire lines lashed down Kitable's chest, perfectly duplicating the scars Sedgan wore in homage to his goddess. The double lines were seared through the shirt he wore and into his flesh, burning pain following their every turn.

Kitable struggled again, but the powers holding him intensified. He felt his sides, held under the embrace, burnt to blisters. His mind lost concentration as pain struck again.

"Mine," Tamort whispered. "The perfect disguise." The smile lost joviality and became sinister. "And you killed Sedgan on your way here. So convenient."

The celebrant laughed.

Kitable tried to tell himself it was no worse than other pain he had felt. He had spent his early life in a state of perpetual Spell Burn. He had lived through a cascade of magic that had seared his body from within. He had even survived Tamort's pitiful attempt at torture. He knew pain.

But this pain was different. He could not distance his mind from his body and push the pain away. The pain was in his mind, in his very soul.

And there was no welcome reprieve of unconsciousness.

Shimmer could not watch them all. She knew Tamort was a threat, but Sedgan was in danger. The dose of frozen freedom he took would be fatal to most. With some degree of tolerance, he might survive it, but it remained perilous and uncertain.

But it worked. The man slipped into delirium. As he was sent into dreams, Shimmer now felt the slip of untouchable powers over him. She was careful to stay back at first, getting Cole to check him, but Sedgan's breathing was slowing, dangerously so.

Shimmer checked on Kitable but found no help. Her master was in meditation. He was dispelled, implying that he was dreaming, but that was all the evidence she had that their efforts were being rewarded.

Leaving Tamort's care to Marionna, Shimmer went to Sedgan's side.

In touching him, she felt a wave of cold run over her, stealing her magic. Worst of them all was the sudden weakness in her leg, where the force magic making a splint had vanished. The bone ached sharply, warning her it had shifted.

She made a point of not moving the leg again. She would replace the spell, she told herself, when she had a moment.

Sedgan was deep asleep now, too deep. From his ranting madness, he had slipped away. When she checked his eyes, they were rolled, and the pupils were small.

"Get his pulse," she snapped at Cole, tossing the timing glass to him before rummaging in her bag. She had a dark root somewhere in the sack. While it was a poison in and of itself, it could counteract some of the slowing heartbeat and breathing.

"Forty?" Cole said after a count.

Shimmer cursed.

She pulled out the dark root, checking first that its wrappings were intact. It would be no good if she poisoned herself through a hangnail. It had to get into the bloodstream, and any entrance would do. Poisons were indiscriminate.

If she increased his heart rate, would that harm him? Was the slow pace because of the freedom? She knew the heart would change for many reasons. Was this the only way to increase it? Did it need to increase, or was it low to protect itself?

"Shimmer?" Cole asked. "Thirty-five. And he's not breathing."

She unwrapped the dark root, trying to calm her shaking hands. She hated that she even carried the lethal poison. Using it had never been the plan. She did not know if it would help or make things worse.

He overdosed, she told herself. It was the frozen freedom slowing his heart. His muscles were lax. He was in too deep. She could not undo that, but dark root could overrule it, at least for the body. A small enough dose might not send Sedgan's heart and lungs into a frenzy.

"Thirty," Cole said. "Didn't you say anything less than fifty was a problem?" he asked.

"Oh, demon piss," Shimmer grumbled. Certain her fingers had no wounds, she made a small cut on the inside of the celebrant's mouth and placed a tiny sliver of dark root against it.

Sedgan's body sharply inhaled.

Shimmer re-wrapped the poison and put it back into her sack. Her leg throbbed again. As she retrieved bandage material from her bag, she called over her shoulder, "How's Tamort?"

"Seems a little agitated," Marionna called back. "His breathing is slightly faster. He's acting like he's dreaming." When Shimmer glanced over her shoulder, she saw the celebrant's eyes moving behind his closed lids. He twitched his head on occasion.

"He's dreaming," she agreed, hiking up her skirt and wrapping her injured leg with practiced ease. Marionna tossed her a pair of knitting needles which she could tie into the bandage for extra rigidity. "I think that's a good thing. So long as he's not becoming conscious, we'll be fine."

She faced Sedgan again, pleased he was breathing every few flickers as she tightened the bandage on her leg. She anticipated having to touch Sedgan again. The weaker dressing would have to do.

"Thirty-five... Forty... No—woah...!" Cole paused, concentrating. Shimmer held her breath, waiting for what she hoped was good news. "A hundred now," Cole said, to Shimmer's joy. "It jumped!"

"Here's hoping it doesn't jump too high," she muttered. She rechecked his eyes and found them still rolled, but the pupils were now dilated.

She sat back on her heels, racking her brain for something that would rebalance the celebrant's mind. Giving him anything stimulating would send his heart flying, risking it burning out.

He was unconscious and likely would stay that way for some time.

"Hundred and twenty, but not going any higher," Cole reported.

He was only in this position because he felt guilty about everything he had done in the Northlander wars, Shimmer reasoned. He had known Loni was manipulating him, even poisoning him, yet he blamed himself for her actions. Sedgan had never been far from Loni through the war after that, becoming her keeper. Had that not been enough? Was his guilt so immense?

On a whim, Shimmer pulled out mountain chain flower dust. When consumed, it boosted mood and was used to treat profound depression, such as that which could affect a person without light, after a long illness, or during grieving.

Maybe...

Before she could decide, Shimmer felt the greasy feeling of nearby untouchable powers lift off Sedgan. He had stopped dreaming.

She dropped the dust and placed her hands on the man. No untouchable powers.

"Heart's dropping again," Cole reports.

"To the hells with this," she said, taking a deep breath. "He's not untouchable now. I can Sweep him."

She glanced at Cole, who shrugged. Of course, he would have no idea what she was talking about. Kitable knew the spell. But when she checked on her master again, he was still cross-legged beside Tamort. His eyes moved as if in dreams as well.

"Fine," she said. Drawing in the powers from the distant spiral of magic, Shimmer formed the Double Sweep spell. She would not know what was dark root and what was frozen freedom. She would have to remove both.

As she worked the spell through Sedgan's body, collecting the poisons together for removal, she directed Cole to get a knife and be prepared to cut open a vessel. Knowing Cole had little experience stopping a bleed, she opted to use a small vessel on the ankle instead of risking having the boy cut a major vein and accidentally make the celebrant bleed out. Marionna seemed to understand what was planned better than her son did and dropped off some leftover bandages for him.

Before long, she gathered the poisons and directed Cole to open the wound. The drugs flowed out with the blood. Shimmer showed Cole how to wrap the ankle.

Only a little winded from the spell, a spell that had once been beyond her capacity, Shimmer took another long breath and reassessed the room.

Tamort was twitching in dreams. Kitable sat stoically next to the man. Both radiated untouchable powers. Instinctually, Shimmer wanted to keep her distance from that power, yet she worried about Kitable. His wounds were apparent now, his illusion gone. He was pushing himself too hard. After being whipped, he should be resting.

But then, they all should be.

She was tempted again to make a mistake and poison Tamort.

For Kitable, she did not. Instead, she checked Marionna's monitoring and started making up Tamort's next dose.

Between making her herbs into the pill, she re-cast the spell for her leg.

Kitable opened his eyes wide and jerked himself upright. His vision was instantly present. Spotting Tamort, Kitable yanked the knife free from his belt and slammed the blade through Tamort's sternum.

Marionna leaped away, screaming in surprise. Cole jumped to his feet, a knife in his hand.

Tamort's body shot up from his sedated rest, but Shimmer knew it was a reflex. The man was already dead. That blow had been straight to the heart.

Sure enough, the body slumped down in the next flicker.

"Gods above!" Cole snapped. "What is going on? I thought we wanted him alive."

Shimmer did not move, trusting her master.

Kitable's voice was strangely hollow when he replied, "There's nothing more to be gained there."

Shimmer cocked her head at him. He sounded worn. "So Tamort knew nothing?" she asked.

When Kitable's gray eyes met hers, the stare was cold. "Nothing to know," Kitable said. "There is nothing we can do. There is no way around SoulBurner." Despite his apparent fatigue, Kitable stood up. "I am done here."

Shimmer shoved her herbs back into her bag and came to her feet. She glanced at Sedgan, for a moment confused. Why was he not yet awake? She had taken out the frozen freedom. He should be going into severe withdrawal. He should be conscious.

But with Kitable moving for the door, she scrambled to follow. She snatched up the staff from beside the door.

"Now?" she asked. "Are we—?"

"*We* are not going anywhere, Weaver," Kitable replied, and the use of her last name made her cringe. What had *she* done? "You are finished."

"Finished what?" she asked. She checked the room, balancing on one foot. They had few supplies now, and her life was already in her bag. She could Relocate right now if she had to. She had expected Kitable to spend more time here. His secret was known anyway. Would he not wish to get to know his half-brother? Spend time with his mother? There was no rush, was there?

"Apprenticeship."

Shimmer forgot about the cottage and the people watching them. Her heart fell into her ankles.

"Finished?" she choked out. "I'm—" Words left her. If she was no longer an apprentice, she was a master wizard. And while she had wanted to become a true wizard since she had been old enough to know the word, the thought of ending her apprenticeship now filled her with terror.

If he were not her master, then they would part ways. There would be no Kitable.

Kitable turned and made to leave the cottage.

Shimmer hobbled into his path. "I'm done? That's it? Just, 'you are finished'?"

"What more do you want?" he snapped. "There are no ceremonies, no fine feasts or bestowing of diadems. You are finished. Call yourself a wizard, Weaver. I have no need of you, Radiance, Bliss, or any of your incarnations."

The final sentence struck her like a blow. Shimmer staggered back.

She wanted to scream at him that he had never needed her. It had never been about need. But then, what *had* it been about? He had never taught out of altruistic tendencies. But she had thought he had enjoyed their conversations. Wasn't there something else here?

But her words would not come. Tears in her eyes, she watched him push out the door and vanish into the light.

She felt sick and dizzy, and her heart ached. Everything seemed to close in around her, leaving her struggling to breathe.

The smell of blood hit her, bringing her attention to the dead body in the room and the two other people watching her.

Marionna seemed to see everything: she came forward and embraced Shimmer as she struggled to keep her tears at bay. She had worked for this. She was a wizard. This was what she had wanted.

But he was gone. He did not need her. Worst still, he did not want her.

It had always been a possibility. She had known that from the first day she had met Kitable. Her father had described him as unattainable. She had never believed it, but it seemed her papa had been correct after all.

Still, she had expected a more formal goodbye. Surely he had seen what he meant to her, even if it was not reciprocated.

Perhaps not.

"Give it time," Marionna whispered before pulling away. Shimmer couldn't tell if she meant giving it time for Kitable to return or for Shimmer to stop feeling so miserable.

And she did. Her insides felt worn out. Holding back tears took more energy out of her than the Double Sweep spell had.

Cole gave her a weak smile when his mother pulled away. "Hey, you're a wizard," he said. "Fully fledged!"

Shimmer's eyes were drawn to the man still lying at Cole's feet. Squaring her shoulders, she hefted her bag.

"Whatever that means," she said, moving to Sedgan's side and trying to focus on something real, something that didn't tear at her. "Sedgan should be awake by now."

Cole knelt across from her. "Can I get you a congratulatory drink later?" he asked.

"After I figure out what's going on with Sedgan and after you get that body out of here," she replied. Sedgan needed her. That kept the tears from her eyes for now.

Cole's smile reached from ear to ear. Even the idea of hauling a corpse did not take the enthusiasm from his grin. He skipped up and grabbed Tamort by both feet, dragging him out, blanket and all. The blanket was covered in blood anyway.

But when Shimmer met Marionna's stare, she saw Kitable's gray eyes. Marionna knew Sedgan was being used to push aside her pain.

She had wanted to be a wizard, but she had wanted to be *his* more.

To avoid thinking about Kitable, Shimmer spent her time watching Sedgan. Cole buried Tamort's body outside of town and returned after dark to get cleaned up. That night, Marionna fed them both in sullen silence. She made no mention of the murder she had witnessed.

Shimmer tried to wake Sedgan between spells and eating, but he remained unconscious. Stimulants did not help, nor did putting sniffer salts under his nose. No matter what she did, he lay flaccid. His breathing and heart rate stabilized, and the cut on his ankle no longer bled, but it could not be sleep if he could not be roused. This was a coma.

While his body recovered from the drugs, his mind remained distant and broken.

Around midnight, in desperation, Shimmer gave him the mountain chain flower dust she had contemplated earlier in the day. If he could not take water in soon, he would die anyway. The mountain chain flower would not hurt him now. She would seize any hope.

Unable to sleep, Shimmer sat by the wall, staring at Sedgan. They had placed him in the bed, although he probably did not appreciate the comfort like Cole would have. Instead, Cole fell asleep by the fire, curled up like a dog.

Kitable's words kept repeating in Shimmer's mind, and her stomach refused to let go of the knot tangled within it. Sometimes a tear would fall, but she wiped them away. She had never needed him either, but she had not expected a dismissal. Her power had grown, and the end of her apprenticeship had not been far away for cycles now. But to be dismissed? She had expected more. She did not know what, but somehow more.

During the deepest part of the night, Marionna rose from her bed in the corner once more and came to sit beside Shimmer.

"I'm sure he did not mean to hurt you," she said.

Aware that another tear had fallen, Shimmer cleared her face. "He was always a bit temperamental," she said. "But I could usually get through it. I was the only person he'd listen to, no matter what."

"Have you seen him kill before?"

Suddenly aware that Marionna needed consoling more than she did, Shimmer looked up at the woman. Her gray eyes were cloudy in the firelight.

Dealing with dangers to the kingdom had been part of their job. She had watched Kitable kill Master Terant of Barlaby and the Double Blades leader Tostig. Shimmer herself had been caught up in Kitable's battle with the wizards from Wanter in vengeance for his killing one of their members. The knife wound on her back reminded her of the constant perils of his duties.

Kitable's loyalty was to Espar and the king. He would not allow anyone, fellow wizard or not, to endanger them. He held a particular place of resentment for wizards. All too often, they were in conflict with him.

But that had made their relationship even more impressive. After years of having nothing but deadly encounters, he had somehow found a reason to trust Shimmer. Even Elder Tril, the only other caster friend Kitable had ever had, had left. Shimmer alone had remained.

And now she had been sent away.

"Yes, I've seen him kill," Shimmer replied. "He's done it dozens of times. He has to defend the kingdom and himself." She thought back to the stab of the knife, straight and true, that had ended Tamort's life. "He always makes it quick, painless if he can. It's a last resort, but he'll not shy from it."

Marionna turned her gaze aside, preferring to look into the embers of the fire.

"He's the wisavi," Shimmer explained. "Since he invented the hovering spell, wizards worldwide have tried to best him. He had to kill them first."

"I understand why," Marionna replied, "but it grieves me. I sent him to learn magic because I thought it was his best hope for a good life. But it seems I damned his soul."

Shimmer laid a hand on Marionna's arm in support. "You created someone unafraid to do what is right," she said. "Can you imagine the world without Kitable? The peace of King Tohmas would never have come to pass without your son. Not to mention the Wanter casters! Kitable rescued Tril from them! Oh, Marionna, you cannot begin to understand the many wonderful things he has done."

The mother glanced back at Shimmer, her undone hair casting shadows over her eyes. Unlike formal attire of the court, where the custom was to wear hair up in braid at all times, here the tangled locks were left limp. "Your eyes shine when you talk about him," she said.

Shimmer sat back abruptly, feeling like the ground had shifted under her.

"You will miss him."

"More than anything," Shimmer admitted, finally feeling her emotions settle. Yes, she would miss him. "Didn't sound like he wants me around now."

"Shimmer, I know you want to make him happy. You'd abide by his wishes. But maybe this time you shouldn't. He needs—"

On the bed, Sedgan groaned, interrupting Marionna. Shimmer rushed to the bed, her leg stiff from sitting. She muttered a spell, creating a small light over the corner to better see.

His eyes were open, although they stared blankly ahead.

"Sedgan? Celebrant? Can you hear me?" she called.

The eyes focused on Shimmer, but Sedgan's expression remained neutral. With the frozen freedom out of his body, Shimmer had expected the celebrant to rage against her, seeking someone to blame. But instead, the face under the blue light was blank. Not even recognition stirred.

He said nothing but slowly sat up.

"Celebrant?" Shimmer called again. "How is your foot?"

The celebrant sat on the edge of the bed, bare legs and bandaged ankle dangling. He said nothing.

"Here," Marionna said, handing Sedgan a cup. "Drink."

The celebrant drank from the cup obediently. Once done, he replaced his hands on his lap.

"I can take that," Marionna offered. Sedgan gave her the cup, then stared at her, eyes narrowed in thought for a moment more. At length, he seemed to determine that something was amiss and glanced up into Shimmer's light.

"Just a wizard's light," Shimmer said.

Sedgan continued to stare.

"Don't think he can hear you," Cole's voice said, coming from behind Shimmer. She jumped, not having heard him rise. "Sorry," he said. "Didn't mean to scare you. I heard you cast."

Shimmer smiled weakly, accepting the apology and letting Cole step up before the celebrant. He waved his hand in front of Sedgan's face. The celebrant's eyes tracked the movement, but his expression did not change.

"I've seen frozen freedom do something like this before," Cole said. "We call them scorched. The brain's baked. Nothing left." He glanced back at Shimmer. "Sometimes they come back from this. Other times, they don't."

Shimmer nodded miserably. "I've seen a few scorched myself." She reassessed the man before her, seeing the stereotypical signs. He could hear—his gaze moved to a speaker— but he could not understand anything. His eyes saw, but his mind did not interpret anything he saw or decide to act. His basic functions were there, but his ability to reason was gone. "Someone has to tell them what to eat, when to stand, where to go. They don't function by themselves. One cutter hypothesized that it was a survival instinct. The brain shuts down to avoid the withdrawal of the drug, re-emerging when the trauma is over."

Marionna sat down beside the man, placing a hand on his arm. Sedgan looked at her, no emotions stirring at the contact. "How long does it last?" she asked.

"Days to years," Shimmer replied, her gut tensing. "He may be like this forever if the damage to his mind is too great."

"It's not your fault," Marionna interrupted.

"Yes, it is," Shimmer replied. "I handed him the drug."

"He chose this, knowing the risks," Cole argued.

"But I made it possible," Shimmer said. Reaching out, she directed Sedgan's face to hers, taking his attention away from the light. "You need to rest more. Eat some food, then go to sleep."

Moving like a toddler, the man took the food from Marionna, ate it, then lay back down. He was asleep, for once looking peaceful instead of panicked.

"At least he can remember a list of two," Shimmer commented, adjusting the blanket on him.

Once Sedgan was asleep, the three other people in the cottage faced each other.

"He can stay however long he needs," Marionna offered. "You too, Shimmer."

"I am grateful. Why is it your son never inherited your empathetic senses, Marionna?" Shimmer asked.

"Sure I did," Cole said. He cracked a bigger grin, cocking his head. "I know what to say. I simply choose not to."

Shimmer did not have the heart to point out she had been referring to Marionna's other son. Cole knew as much, she thought. But his jest lightened her heart a little.

"I'll stay to help for a bit," Cole said, "but I've got to get back soon."

"Report in to Black?" Shimmer asked.

Cole shrugged. "He'll need to know what happened to our original contract." Pulling out a heavy pouch, Cole tossed it in the air twice. "He needs his cut anyway."

The irony struck Shimmer: Cole had been paid to help Tamort. Despite having then turned on him, Kitable's younger brother had still come out with a pouch full of coins and a job well done.

She shook her head and went to find somewhere to sleep, too numb to think anymore.

Kitable watched the entire conversation from the back of his mind. He wanted to shout, to tear at Tamort's soul and throw it from his mind, but he could do nothing. Bound by the burning dreamer magic, he remained in the golden world, viewing the world out of his own eyes but unable to command his body.

Refusing to give Tamort the satisfaction of seeing him struggle, Kitable said nothing. He had already tested his strength against the powers holding him, but neither force nor mental will released it. The pain of the fiery touch came and went, sometimes sending his mind into a scattered panic. This was dreamer magic, control of the soul, and it was beyond him. In between searing agony, he felt cold, missing the familiar hum of magic. Those powers could not reach him through the golden mist.

Without Tamort's attention to the realm, the campfire and Temple waggon circle faded away. Kitable was left in the golden expanse, wrapped by writhing fire-filled chains. When Tamort willed it, the mist would form up like a Scry, allowing Kitable to see through his own eyes, hear through his ears, and so knew what his body was doing.

He felt his hand moving when his body stabbed the knife through Tamort's heart. He felt the heat of the blood against his hand. The chains around Kitable's mind cackled with Loni's familiar laughter.

There was no going back. With Tamort's body dead, the soul of the celebrant had nowhere to go. Kitable's body was Tamort's now, a ghost possessing the living.

Shimmer was a problem, one solved with a few pointed words, and that hurt Kitable more than all the lashes in his life. Although she said nothing when dismissed, Kitable saw the hurt in her eyes. She stubbornly denied tears and instead tried words until the words left her. Then she was left with nothing, and Kitable walked away.

Kitable's chest hurt. They should have left together to continue research, to work together as they had for the last two years. He would never have dismissed her.

Notice, Kitable thought. *I'm not wearing spells. You know me better than anyone else, Shimmer. I'd never go without them.*

His heart lurched. *I'd never go without you...*

But she did not notice, too shaken by the events. And then she was gone, and Tamort could return to the Manor of Trulinar in Kitable's body.

Tamort set out, Kitable's body walking down the roads of Woodcutter's Retreat on its way south. It attracted surprised gazes, his wounds no longer concealed, but no one seemed to have the courage to approach him.

The specter of Tamort reappeared in the golden light, standing with Kitable's mind to watch the scenery of the village as his body walked on. The roads were distantly familiar from a childhood long since dismissed.

"Without a horse, it will take you a cycle to reach..." Kitable stopped, realizing the celebrant had indicated he was heading for Wayburn. King Tohmas was not in Wayburn. He was at the Manor of Trulinar and would be for another cycle at least. "To reach your goal," he corrected. "Even with a horse, it will take a halfcycle."

"Assuming I cannot learn what I need to perform a Relocation spell from you," Tamort answered, his smile a sneer.

The chains around Kitable tightened, squeezing the air from his lungs and digging fire into his arms.

"No untouchable has ever figured that out," Kitable replied, trying to keep his voice even despite the crushing embrace of the magic around him. "And you know I will fight you," Kitable added, tension in his voice now. He took one final deep breath, the air like steam. "If my knowledge may help you, I will deny you access."

While untouchable powers differed from wizard magic, Kitable had seen similarities when studying with Celebrant Calanor. The powers of the untouchables had always been limited. They did not train each other or write down what they had learned. Every spontaneous caster had to start anew. Wizard magic had been structured over hundreds of years while untouchable magic remained in its infancy.

But Kitable had shown Elder Tril and Calanor ways of using their magic like wizard magic, allowing them to Scry, create anchors, and use longer-lasting spells. Knowing more about wizard magic might allow Tamort to create spells he would never otherwise figure out.

Tamort reached out, placing a finger on the center of Kitable's chest, and the pressure of the chain released. The burning lines of Inac's symbol on his chest throbbed instead.

"I can take it from you," Tamort said. "I will find a way to target things I cannot see."

He was missing a descriptor, Kitable recognized through his pain. A wizard's ability to target something from a distance was based on uniquely defining the object or person. The level of detail required was extensive for things or places and worse for people. Wizards had trained their minds to think like magic, to better define something in the manner the magic would understand. Untouchables lacked that training.

He could not let Tamort understand that. He could not help the man form a definition, especially not one of the manor.

Kitable steeled his mind, imagining a cage of iron surrounding his thoughts. He had used brute force of will to keep out magic intrusions before.

The world around them instantly shifted; the Temple waggons vanished, the fire out in a snuff. The gold of the Dreamworld overwhelmed the space, flashing bright enough to blind him.

Although he could not see, Kitable felt Tamort's push of power, and the thought of the cage pushed back. The heat against his back throbbed for a moment, making Kitable wince as his eyes shut.

The pressure broke.

When he reopened his eyes, Kitable blinked twice, seeing green shimmering bars around him as he stood in a bright space of golden light. He was no longer in a dream; he was between them. The chains and the terrible laughing voice were gone. He was free to move, although he was surrounded by what appeared to be a wizard's Force Cage.

Tamort paced outside the cage like a mountain cat, the golden light swirling around him like a disturbed pond of water. He now wore simple acolyte robes. "Fascinating," he said. He tapped against the cage, and the light of the barrier pulsed. "But how long can you hold it?"

This was not magic, Kitable knew, but pure force of will. He had spent his life making his mind sharp, but he had no idea how much the training for wizardry would translate into this kind of exercise.

"Long as I have to," Kitable answered. If he failed and Tamort learned what he needed, or worse, learned where the king was, he would kill the king. Losing Tohmas early in his reign would destabilize everything Kitable had helped build.

But worse still, if Kitable failed, Kitable would never get to ask Shimmer for her forgiveness.

He would hold that cage for years if that was what it took to regain Shimmer's favor.

For three days, Cole watched Shimmer follow Sedgan around. While Cole's mother cared for the celebrant's needs, Shimmer offered different remedies. Cole listened in, watching the Woodcutter's Retreat village and listening for news about Kitable. Part of him wanted to find the wisavi coming back for Shimmer. The other part of him was happy to have his older brother gone and Shimmer left behind.

But it hurt her. When she wasn't doting on Sedgan, trying to find a combination of drugs that would wake his blanked mind, Cole saw Shimmer fighting back tears or staring off into the distance. It was as if a family member had died, and she was beset by grief. She left her master's staff in the corner of the room and would not look at it.

Cole did what he could to bring her out of it, telling her stories over dinner to make her laugh and ensuring anything she needed was available. At the end of the three days, though, the lucky rabbit's foot rattled, indicating a message for him.

Cole left the cottage and went to the forest. He tried to ignore the scorch marks on the trees and how he felt the storm rising in memory as he walked through the trees. He had grown up in these woods, and now they looked different, darker. Every chipped piece of bark reminded him of the magic he had witnessed.

Once far enough from the cottage, Cole sat on a log and pulled out his pendant. "I'm here," he said.

<I was starting to get worried,> Black's voice said into Cole's mind.

"Been busy," Cole replied.

The pause on the other end of the communication made Cole nervous.

<With what?> Black asked.

He didn't have to tell Black about helping Shimmer free her master or Tamort's later decision to attack Kitable. He certainly didn't have to discuss that he had discovered his brother was the Wisavi of Espar.

But he knew Black well enough to know his cadre leader knew at least half of that and may be offended if Cole didn't admit he knew too.

"Tamort's dead," Cole said.

The pause lingered again. It was followed at length by, *<This have something to do with that girl you were with in StonePeak?>*

"Yeah," Cole said. "You still want to meet her?"

<Vehemently,> Black replied. *<We clearly have to discuss more than payment. My hall, tomorrow evening.>*

Cole looked around at the forest again, disappointed that he could not stay longer. But sitting around Woodcutter's Retreat was not useful. At this point, Sedgan was the walking dead, and Cole could do nothing about it.

"I'll start walking now," he said. Refusal was not an option anyway.

<*Bring her,*> Black said.

"I'll do what I can, but she's not the kind you order around."

This time, Cole heard a smile in Black's voice. <*I figured.*>

The connection to Black's stone terminated. The twittering of magic was replaced by the buzz of the daylight forest.

Cole sat for a moment more, wondering if he should have said something else. Dinner would be interesting. Should he confront Black about the use of magic beyond trinkets, hidden from him all these years? And what of Black's involvement with Tamort? He had endangered Cole's mother and Cole himself. What if Kitable had not surrendered himself when Tamort had threatened them? Had Black known?

Pushing himself up, Cole headed back to the cottage.

Shimmer sat on the outside wall, her wounded leg propped up. They had found new clothing for her in town, easily adjusted by Marionna. She still favored brightly colored skirts and layers of ribbons and had cut her blouse short to leave her midriff exposed. Cole had already seen how her appearance had affected the local merchants. He'd never seen such low prices.

Shimmer's expression was thoughtful. He assumed she was working on another herbal mix to try on Sedgan.

"I've got to get back to StonePeak," Cole said, sitting beside her.

She cocked her head at him. "Your master call?"

"He's not my master," Cole corrected. He thought to ask if she knew about the link in the rabbit's foot but decided against it. If she did not know, then the question would give it away.

"You are going to ask him about that?" she asked.

Cole shook his head. Black had not told him about his ability to cast for a reason. "Probably not. It's his secret to keep. Not my business."

He sensed his answer disappointed her, but she looked away instead of pressing the matter.

Swallowing hard, Cole offered, "You want to come?"

Her eyes narrowed in thought, but her stare remained distant for a moment longer. Cole was pleased she did not refuse instantly.

At length, she shook her head. Her red hair was down, a tiny braid down the back of her head keeping the shorter strands out of her face. The tassels and beads she had woven into the hair rattled like charms. "I should be here with Sedgan."

"Not much else you can do with him," Cole said. "We all know the mountain flower—"

"Mountain chain flower," she corrected.

"—mountain chain flower dust is what's keeping him conscious. Nothing else you've done makes a difference. He needs time."

Shimmer pressed her lips in a pout Cole thought adorable. How she did it without creating wrinkles astounded him. Everyone else looked ugly when they were annoyed.

"And that's where it doesn't make sense," she said. "It's an anti-depressant."

Cole shrugged. "Pretty obvious he was depressed. Everyone I know who's been on frozen freedom is running away from something."

Shimmer cocked her head at him again. "Including you?" she asked, her voice gentle.

Cole smiled. "I was running from being normal. Clearly, no danger of that now." He skipped off the wall, stirring a host of childhood memories. He extended his hand to her.

"Come on. Take a break. Your mind can work on this while you relax."

At last, she cracked a small smile. "You sound like Kitable," she said.

Cole did his best to look offended. "No need for name-calling!"

This won him a laugh, although it was short. Once it had passed, her eyes became distant again, but this time, Cole was confident her mind was filled with memories of the wisavi.

"Kitable had a theory," Shimmer said, "that we cannot consciously access all parts of our minds. One part works while we sleep, solving puzzles we were unaware of."

"Sounds good to me," Cole said, taking her hand from where it rested on the wall. She did not pull it away, a victory to Cole, although he noted that her spells prevented him from touching her skin at all. The Moulded Shield spell kept a barrier of a finger's breadth between them. "Shall we go?"

Shimmer nodded, coming to her feet with care. "Best tell Marionna," she said. "I'll leave her some pills and a way to contact me." She looked down at her injured leg. "And I had better bring the staff. It will be a while before I can walk easily. But then, yes, we can go."

"Tomorrow, then?" Cole asked eagerly.

"Very well."

•••••••••••

"Weak!" Tamort cursed, pacing outside the cage that continued to protect Kitable in the golden light. The man had come back again from wandering the Dreamworld and was in a fouler mood than before. He had resumed his ornate appearance from his ordainment and seemed taller and stronger than he had in life. His eyes glowed golden.

Every time Tamort visited over the days of imprisonment, his demeanor worsened. At first, Kitable believed it was fatigue, but as the days wore on and it deepened, he optimistically thought maybe he was the cause of the upset.

He had denied Tamort the knowledge he required to create a Relocation spell and still held his cage of will against the celebrant. Now, the man was stuck walking the distance to the king. Even stealing a horse had failed to cheer the celebrant.

Better still, Tamort appeared to be heading to Wayburn. The celebrant had no way of knowing that the king was not in residence there, and Kitable had no intention of telling him.

Instead, Kitable kept his thoughts present and controlled. Loni's spirit had not injured him. Nothing remained to remind him of the pain.

"Your body is pathetic, Wisavi," Tamort accused. "Hardly a candle worth of travel, and it's unable to stand!"

Trying not to think about the damage Tamort's forced march was having on his stitches and bruises, Kitable replied, "Maybe you should not have beaten me, then."

Tamort glowered so profoundly, his eyebrows became one. "If you had been closer to Inac, I would not have had to."

"Meaning closer to the Dreamworld? Capable of dreaming?" Kitable thought back to the lashes. "Was *that* what you were trying to do?" Given that wizards rarely dreamt, Tamort's strategy had been a reasonable one. Trauma and stress tended to generate dreams, that much Kitable had learned from Celebrant Calanor. But wizards' souls stayed far from the Dreamworld. Even when he had wanted to come here, he had required a guide.

Tamort, indignant, turned away.

Kitable took that to mean he was right. "Well, if you don't like the body, you could give it back," Kitable called after him.

"Inac's glory requires physical fitness," Tamort shot back.

"My 'fitness' was fine until you got involved," he replied. "And what are you going to do about it anyway? I can rebuild a bone, but skin isn't the same, and bruising requires nothing except time. Even wizards can't—"

"I am no wizard!" Tamort snapped. His eyes flashed bright. Kitable felt the pressure against his cage when the rage slammed into it.

Drawing his thoughts in, Kitable strengthened his resolve methodically. Inac's power was in passion and anger. The more Tamort ranted, the stronger he became. Kitable's last defense was his barrier, held by calm concentration. Under Inac's hot push, Kitable's mind sent cool strength.

The pressure eased off. Tamort looked spent, and his words were calmer when he next met Kitable's eyes.

"How much longer can you hold it?" he asked. He asked that question daily.

Kitable glanced at his cage. It looked, to him, like a Force Cage made of glowing green force magic. But he knew he had no Spell Sight active, and a Force Cage would not have been visible without enchanted vision. He had assumed its presentation was his mind's interpretation of the concept.

"I've not had to sleep yet."

"Your mind must rest," Tamort insisted.

"But my soul doesn't."

How he had generated the "spell" in front of him still confused Kitable. He knew that Tril had balanced dreamer and wizard powers, but Kitable had never manifested dreamer magic before. Still, the spell seemed anchored in his mind, the part of him close to wizard magic. He still had no control of the golden Dreamworld around him outside of the manifestation of the cage.

"You will tire," Tamort declared.

"Haven't so far," Kitable replied. He knew it had been days. Tamort went away when he had to manage Kitable's body and returned when they slept. That was proof that the soul never required sleep; it was either working or dreaming.

"We will reach the Manor of Trulinar soon enough," Tamort decided, taking a seat on a throne that appeared for him out of the golden mist, a snippet of a dream he called to him when all else was blank gold. He sat back grandly, sneering at Kitable in anticipation.

Kitable's heart lurched. He was heading in the right direction, after all. Wayburn was far to the south while the Manor of Trulinar was due east, and Tamort knew it. How had the celebrant known where to find the king?

Kitable buried his surprise, keeping his mind on the calm control of the cage. Was it possible Tamort was seeing his thoughts after all? He would have to be more careful. But he could give nothing away.

"And then what?" Kitable asked, unwilling to confirm or deny anything Tamort said for fear of aiding the celebrant. But he needed conversation to give him more information. The more Kitable knew, the more he could plan. There had to be a way out of the golden mist.

But he wasn't sure if he dared try. Leaving the cage would give Tamort an advantage, would it not? Even if he escaped from here, what if the celebrant could read his mind while he hid nearby? And how could Kitable reclaim his body at all?

It was like dealing with thought magic, he decided. If his thoughts could be read, he had to ensure only the thoughts he wanted shared were available. Others would have to wait at the back of his mind. There would be an opportunity. Only then would he act and act quickly.

"You will see," was all Tamort said, settling back to watch Kitable with his unblinking golden eyes. The stare reminded Kitable of a man holding a Scry. Tamort's attention was divided, but some of it was still here.

Kitable went back to trying to redefine the cage, to move it without weakening it to Tamort.

The balancing act failed him.

13

The next afternoon, Shimmer and Cole left for StonePeak, and Marionna watched them go. As she returned to her cottage, she noted a young man was sitting by the road. He looked about fourteen and had a broad build with ears that were still too big for his half-grown face. She did not recognize him.

In the morning, the boy was replaced by another boy, and then, in the afternoon, by another. Come evening, the first had returned. They tried to pass as villagers, but Marionna knew all the kids of the small village. Further, these boys each had the bearing of an older, richer type out of place in such a country location.

The following day, Marionna left Sedgan eating his breakfast and walked up to her current observer. It was raining that morning, and the boy had not brought a coat. His shoes were not worn, but neither were they well suited for prolonged walking or candles of standing.

When she approached, Marionna noticed that the boy had the mark of Inac—a pair of long waves—on his forearm. He seemed to be trying to turn his arm to hide the stained mark on his skin, which was fading.

"If you are going to spy on me, at least come in and get a cup of warm tea," she invited. "You'll catch a chill otherwise. And for goodness sake, let me get you one of Cole's coats. Come on." She pivoted and headed back to the cottage.

After a dozen flickers, the boy followed. She had the tea ready for him when he meekly ducked into the cottage.

Marionna pointed to the bed where she had placed Cole's coat. "I can hem the sleeves if you require," she said. "Of course, if you're planning to keep an eye on me, then you might as well do it from here, where it's dry."

She sat back down and prompted Sedgan to drink another cup of water. Shimmer had warned that the man would require a lot of fluids to help his body overcome the frozen freedom's impact, but he needed constant support, doing nothing spontaneously.

When she looked back up, the boy was still standing in the doorway, dripping water and looking awkward.

Marionna stood up and guided the boy, who was a few years younger than Cole, to a seat by the fire.

"Why?" he asked as she put the tea into his hand.

"Because I don't care who sent you or why you are here," Marionna told him. "You're a child, and whoever sent you is clearly not taking care of you. So I will. Drink. Then take off your shoes and put them by the fire. That'll dry them by the time the shift changes at noon."

The boy hesitantly sipped the tea. He shivered, although he seemed to be fighting it, and curled himself close to the fire. Even in the mid-summer heat, the rain could chill.

She waited. After a few sips, the boy took off his shoes as directed and put them on the drying rack by the fire. He sat down, staring into the fire with uncommon focus while Sedgan finished his breakfast and Marionna took him outside to relieve himself.

Once she returned, she helped the celebrant wash his face and hands. The boy watched, perplexed. His eyes were on the scar on the man's chest, which matched the mark on the boy's arm.

"You have a name, I presume," Marionna asked.

"Benn," the boy stammered.

"Well, Benn, it is rude to stare."

The boy averted his gaze but kept glancing back at the celebrant she was assisting. "Was that his robe outside?" Benn asked at last. His accent was from the north, almost Northlander. The boy was built big for his age, which is why Marionna thought he could fit Cole's coat despite being years younger.

"It was," Marionna said. "He has been injured. I am now his caretaker until the goddess grants him back his sanity."

The boy considered the words as if she was speaking a different language. When he spoke, his words were small. "Did you see another celebrant?" he asked.

The boy and his mark of Inac made sudden sense. Of course, Tamort would have had acolytes, Marionna thought. Shimmer and Cole had mentioned them in passing, knowing he had left them behind. Acolytes were commonly younger than twenty. Some could be as young as five. This boy had been, until recently, provided for, and now he and his friends were missing their parents.

Marionna faced Benn, leaving Sedgan sitting by himself on the bed for a moment. The celebrant did not seem to notice. "Yes," she said. "Celebrant Tamort came here, and he died. I'm sorry, but if that was what you were looking for, then you wasted your time. You should have asked. Tamort is dead."

Benn looked one part grieved and one part relieved.

Marionna sighed, looking back at the blank expression on Celebrant Sedgan's face. Would he not have helped these boys? An acolyte needed a celebrant. Some would have families to return to, but others would be orphans with no recourse. Until they could reach a temple, they would be on their own. And even if they reached the nearest temple in StonePeak, the celebrants may not take them in.

"Fetch the rest of the acolytes," Marionna told Benn. "We've enough here to provide for you." Hoping the Goddess of Justice was listening, Marionna added, "And you can help with the care of the celebrant for a change. Once he's recovered, he can decide what to do with you."

Benn stared at her.

"Am I wrong?" she asked. "Are you not an acolyte of Inac? Is this not a celebrant?" She pointed at Sedgan. "Go on, fetch the others."

Benn took a step toward the door, but Marionna stopped him. "Don't go out without shoes, Benn. Take these boots. And how many boys am I expecting? Any girls?"

Benn shook his head. "No girls. Just five of us left. The others..."

"The others could go home, I take it," Marionna said, and Benn managed a nod. "Well, I'll not have five boys going hungry while I have the means to prevent it. And your aid with this celebrant would be a service to Inac, would it not? It'll do for now."

She handed him a pair of boots.

Benn held them momentarily, his face as blank as Sedgan's. Once he had gathered his courage, he looked up and asked, "Fair lady, how did Celebrant Tamort die?"

She would not lie to the boy. He was old enough to know the truth and deal with it. Yet Marionna was loathed to bring Kitable's name into the crime. If Tamort had sought vengeance because Kitable had slain Loni, would this not be a circle about to continue?

"A man called Kaylin killed him," Marionna said, every word truth. "Celebrant Tamort did many terrible things, and justice found him. Kaylin killed your celebrant to save the lives of his family. Is that sufficient?"

Benn nodded, donning the boots.

"Good," Marionna said. "Now make sure you and your friends bring whatever supplies you have with you. We'll need the extra blankets. Anything you don't have, I'll get at the shop. Thank goodness my son sends me coin. Hurry back. I'll need your help the next time Celebrant Sedgan needs to get dressed."

Benn glanced back. "Sedgan?" he said.

Marionna lifted her chin; a mother questioned. "And what of it?"

"He was our master's master," Benn said, finally smiling like the child he was. He straightened. "Glad we will be to aid him. I'll bring the others."

The boy dashed off into the rain, the borrowed coat draped over his back and warm tea in his belly.

Marionna went back to Sedgan and finished his washing.

"Inac is either paying too little attention," she told the mute celebrant, "or is playing us all for fools."

He didn't seem to know which it was either.

They arrived in Thieves Hide Square, lit by natural light in the dusk. The sunset reached through an opening above, followed by a drizzle of rain, and shone like gold and silver where the water and light mixed.

Shimmer followed Cole out, wondering if she should ask for the market again. She knew herbs better than anyone she had met in StonePeak. If she needed a place to stay and a job, she could help Trank. That was familiar enough work.

After so long as an apprentice, she wasn't sure what else to do. Wizards usually took patrons who would pay for their lodgings and supplies, like King Tohmas for Kitable. How did a wizard find a patron? And did she want one? The idea of having to appease someone else to maintain her lifestyle did not sit well with Shimmer. She could do as her father had done and set up a mobile shop. Now that she was free of obligations to Kitable, she could even go back to Dust and the Match and Mixer. They could travel again.

Every idea failed to inspire her. All she knew, for now, was that she did not want to return to Wayburn or the Manor of Trulinar. In fact, she'd have to avoid most of the north. Everything reminded her of Kitable, and that thought made her ache. The one place that did not seem to hold Kitable's ghost at every turn was StonePeak.

Cole paused at the mouth of a tunnel. "You can conjure a light if you want," he said, bringing her back to the moment. His smile broadened when she glanced up at him. "Or you can use it how it's meant to be used." He put out his hand. "Not afraid of the dark, are you?"

Shimmer's father always said a town was best experienced, not looked at. Having a local guide meant she would get to know StonePeak better now than on any previous visit. She took his hand and let him guide her down the corridor into the dark, following the markings on the wall. He again paused to let her check the symbols, juggling the staff and holding his hand.

"Where are we going?" she asked once they were surrounded by darkness.

"Stop in at my place," he told her, "but then dinner with Black if you want to join."

"And I didn't bring anything to wear," she said, following Cole down a side corridor. The floor became rougher as if fewer feet had passed this way.

"You already look great," Cole said, and the factualness of the statement caught Shimmer off guard. "Besides, it's nothing formal."

"You sure you want me there? You'll probably be talking about things I shouldn't hear."

"I'm sure," Cole said. "Black wants to talk to you."

He stopped in the dark but drew his hand to his side, pulling her up to him. Her shields prevented direct contact, but she felt him close like a pickpocket in a crowd. "But you don't have to if you don't want to," Cole said, his voice coming from a hand's breadth ahead of her.

Shimmer's stomach knotted. Was he saying he would lie to Black for her? If she said she didn't want to come, would Cole be penalized?

His voice sounded like Kitable's. Perhaps even StonePeak was not safe from memories.

Shimmer eased back from Cole, suddenly needing to keep her distance. Some of her objected to the movement, having preferred to stay close. That frightened her most of all.

"I'll go," Shimmer said, keeping her voice even against her emotions, "but if you expect me to be a perfect guest, you don't know me well. I may have spent time in the king's courts, but no one took me to fancy dinners. I don't suffer fools."

She could hear a smile in Cole's voice. "No, I expect that, around you, the fools are the ones who suffer."

He led her on.

At length, they exited the dark corridors and into a sunlit cavern. Far above, openings brought down the evening sun to cast red light over the stones. Like an inn, the cavern had multiple rooms built into the stone walls, each set with a lock. Cole entered one. He did not bother to light a lamp but left the door open for illumination.

His home was a bed, a chest, and a bookcase. Shimmer made a point of not entering the room.

Quickly swapping out a few trinkets and tools, Cole reemerged a moment later.

"You look the same," Shimmer pointed out. He was dressed in black again, his thicker vest acting as rough armor. It would not do much in close conflict, but it might delay a knife under the right circumstance.

Cole shrugged. "Told you," he said. "It's not formal."

Retaking her hand, Cole led Shimmer back into the tunnels.

After navigating two dozen dark corridors, they passed through a small concealed doorway and stepped into a manor-sized home, coming in as if through a servant's entrance. Light streamed through the windows, which were glass works depicting mountains, each pane made of hundreds of smaller, irregular glass pieces. The floor was smooth stone, like wizard-stone but the wrong color. Shimmer recognized it. Someone had used earth destruction spells to make this room.

Cole winked at her and then led her deeper into the building.

Once outside the receiving room, they were in a more traditional manor. The walls were stacked stones, plastered smooth. The windows were still stained glass, but some were clear glass casting the light toward the vaulted ceilings and illuminating the trim of the ceiling and doors. Thick oak doors hung on solid iron hinges, each the weight of Shimmer and Cole combined. It was built like a fortress, reminding Shimmer of the Manor of Trulinar. While ornate and beautiful, it was still ready to repel attackers. She saw no additional signs of wizardly construction; here, the stone had been built up or carved by tools and muscles.

The windows looked over parts of the city of StonePeak. As far as Shimmer could tell, the manor faced the city but backed onto the mountains, the servant's entrance connecting to the maze of stone tunnels and all they contained.

Yet, for all its size, no guards or servants were present in the immense manor, putting Shimmer on edge.

Cole found his way with practiced ease, passing through sitting rooms and grand halls better suited to a prince's home. As they walked, he chatted about the furnishings, filling the silence with empty words.

At length, they arrived at a dining hall where Black was waiting. Black and Cole were attired identically in wraps of clothing that could be subtle in concealing their outlines while being silent if required. The long knife was gone from his hip, but Black still wore the brooch and ring Shimmer had detected earlier, the feel of him potently magical.

Shimmer immediately became aware that she was still holding Cole's hand. She dropped it, standing before Cole's master with her mask of confidence in place once more. Her hand tightened on the staff. Knowing she was meant to be a guest, Shimmer did not activate Spell Sight. She already had defenses and reminded herself that the staff was still enchanted. She was safe, her hovering spells only a word away.

Black stood by the room's fireplace, a hand on the mantle as if he had been resting after a long walk. It seemed deceptive. Although he was twice her age, Black showed no sign of age or wear. She had no doubt he was as fit as Kitable or Sedgan, albeit for a different reason.

He approached them, clasped hands with Cole, then bowed his head over Shimmer's hand in greeting. He stopped short of kissing the back of her hand, a fact she appreciated. Should he attempt it, his lips would fail to contact her skin, making the entire gesture odd. "I am delighted you joined us, Bliss," Black said. "Please, come have a seat, both of you."

Shimmer checked with Cole, but her guide smiled comfortably and offered her the closest chair. She propped her staff by the door but dropped her bag by her feet and placed the strap over her knee protectively. Her leg still ached despite her pain pills, but sitting helped.

She sat straight backed, surrounded by the guise of Bliss. Bliss was confident and needed no one; she made that as apparent as she could.

Black took his chair, lounging in his seat at the head of the table. The other two places had been set close to his, near the fireplace.

Before taking his seat, Cole placed a pouch of coins on the table beside Black's hand.

"Contract completed?" Black asked as Cole circled behind him and found his seat across from Shimmer.

"And settled," Cole said as he sat down.

"But the celebrant is dead?"

Shimmer expected more of a reaction from the two men. Shouldn't Black have been upset that the man Black had assigned Cole to assist was now dead? Did he know Cole had played a role?

Cole was the one who poured wine from a jug at the center of the table, handing each cup to the recipient in turn. Black slid the pouch of coins under the table as he took his cup from Cole. Had it not been for Shimmer's experience with her father's shows and his sleight of hands, she would have missed it.

"He had the misfortune of offending the Wisavi of Espar," Cole reported. "So yes, dead. Tends to happen when people cross Wisavi Kitable."

The mention of Kitable, so casual from Cole, struck Shimmer in her gut. She buried the sensation, keeping her mask of Bliss perfect. She still felt sick.

"I hope you have managed to avoid that fate, my dear Bliss," Black said. "You show considerable skill. Show too much, and you may attract the wisavi's attention. Wouldn't that be a shame."

"Power doesn't have to be ostentatious," Shimmer replied. She took her drink from Cole politely and sipped it, thinking about the wine instead of the man who had left her behind. She knew nothing about vintage or grapes except for grapeseed as a remedy. This wine was too weak, like fruit extracts with little alcohol. Likely northern, she decided.

As Black answered, he gestured to the meal before them as invitation. Cole did not delay in taking a helping of stew and a chunk of bread, then sitting back. The dinner smelled good, although Black lacked Marionna's sense for spices, and the stew was bland. At least the bread was crusty.

"Wisavi Kitable does have a way of keeping wizards in check, though," Black said with a shrug. "It's simple: if any wizard offends him, he kills them. Is it any wonder that wizards have become more subtle in their magics?"

Shimmer wanted to defend Kitable, but doing so may reveal her ties to the wisavi. Kitable's actions had always

been in favor of peace and justice. True, other wizards had died because they opposed him. Most had been trying to kill him. He had been defending himself or the king.

But Black was right, at least in part. Shimmer had seen fewer wizards over the last few years since King Tohmas took over Espar. Were they going into hiding?

Perhaps that had been the point of the contract with Tamort all along. Had Black been trying to kill Kitable so he would not be the next one the wisavi targeted? Or had Black accepted the job for the coin like any other job? As a hidden wizard, Black stood to gain if Kitable was dead, especially as the wisavi was responsible for wizards who operated outside of the laws. Who else would keep justice for the wizards?

But had Black known about Kitable's family, or had that been Tamort's doing? Shimmer's mind spun.

"Perhaps it is the finesse of magic developing," Shimmer said, unwilling to reveal more and trying to keep her mind on the conversation. "Are you trying to warn me, Black? Are you going to tell me this for my own protection? Poor, vulnerable me?" Bliss needed no one's protection.

Black put out his hands in surrender. "Dear girl, I speak because you remind me of a friend, and I would have his child protected."

Shimmer narrowed her eyes on Black. She could assume much from that statement. The man excelled at committing to nothing. She put down her spoon and leaned toward him, her words short. "Stop speaking in half-truths," she said. "I'm tired of games and shadows. If you got something to say, say it directly."

Cole choked on his stew, but he grinned from ear to ear. Shimmer thought she saw admiration in his eyes.

Kitable had looked at her like that sometimes.

Black laughed as well but had the benefit of not being in the process of chewing when he did. "Bliss, you are a woman of marvels! Imagine! A woman who speaks her mind! No subtle hints we are meant to decipher or brewing thoughts hiding in the depths where we mere men cannot see!" He went back to his wine for a sip. "I can only return the favor," he added. "I knew a man named Dust Weaver years ago. He was a clever man and knew more about alchemy than any other the world over. But he left StonePeak nearly twenty years ago. He left our less-than-legal world entirely, bowing out of contracts and dealings with tact. I found out later he had sired a daughter and was now devoted to her. I never did find out her name, of course. Those things Dust kept secret." Black fixed Shimmer with a curious look, the first genuine expression she had seen him wear. "Are you Dust's daughter?"

"My father's in Wayburn if you want to ask him about my name," Shimmer said, "but yes, I am she."

Black sat back, satisfaction on his face as he held the goblet atop his moderate belly. "I suspected so strongly! You have his bearing, not to mention his hair! And your brilliance with herbs made it obvious." He brought a hand to his chin, where the day's stubble was progressing. "But he was a minor caster. Not like you, Bliss. You've surpassed him. Are you a wizard?"

Memories of Kitable's dismissal flooded into Shimmer, and she winced. She had been enjoying the conversation, but this reminder of Kitable wounded her.

"Does it matter?" she asked, delving into the food to avoid having to say more.

Black leaned forward, folding his hands atop the table. "Perhaps it does. Could you teach Cole?"

Shimmer met Cole's stare across the table. Through his apparent shock, he still wore a grin. "I could," she said. "I am a master wizard, after all." The words sounded strange, coming from her throat. Master wizard… She had wanted to be the apprentice, but she had never considered the time beyond that. All apprenticeships had to end.

"Then I offer you my employ," Black declared, his voice formal. "As you can see," he said, gesturing to the surrounding hall and manor, "I have room enough to offer you a wing all your own. I will provide all you require and a hefty retainer. Once Cole's training is done, I hope you would be open to training others, but I'll not require it. But I'd like you as part of my team."

She had wondered how to find a patron. Apparently, going to dinner was one way of doing it.

Shimmer sat back, leaving her meal and her drink. She activated an invisible Spell Sight and saw no sign that Black had detected it. Cole tilted his head, catching the sound of magic but unable to narrow in on the spell, no doubt.

This time, Shimmer openly assessed Black from the top of his head down. With a critical eye, she took stock of his hovering spells and broke down the elements and domains of every single one. She further dissected his magic items, finding them to be of good quality and clever construction.

"You tell me why you hide your magic from your allies," she said, "and I'll consider it."

His hands tensed along the knuckles. His expression did not change, but she felt his energy flex as if to intimidate her.

"It's simple, Black," she informed him. "I'll not be set up as a patsy, ready to take the blame when something magical is caught up in scandal."

His eyes fixed on hers. Bliss was there, staring back, unwilling to give even a hand's breadth. They would be equals in this, or there would be no relationship.

At length, he dropped his stare to his goblet. "I hide it, young lady, because it's safer."

"You've been doing it longer than the wisavi's reign," Shimmer pointed out. "This has nothing to do with Wisavi Kitable."

To her satisfaction, he nodded. "When I'm attacked," he said soberly, "they don't expect magic. This secret is my finest defense." He met her stare again. "Ask Cole," he added. "There have been no strange magical happenings. It is an asset I keep to myself."

Cole glanced at his mentor, then away.

"At least I had," Black finished, "until you, Bliss."

A silence filled the room, Shimmer unsure if she should rise to the indirect compliment.

"Why'd you never train me?" Cole asked into the pause, his voice small.

"It would have given things away," Black said. "Cole, I have survived this long by being hard to track, hard to know. But if Miss Weaver here wishes to join—"

"Do *not* call me that," Shimmer corrected harsher than she had intended. It sounded too much like Kitable. That was a reminder she did not need.

Black cocked his head, clearly recognizing she would say no more and accepting it. "If you wish, Bliss, I am—"

The doors of the hall burst wide. Cole and Shimmer shot to their feet, Black moving slower than they did by a flicker. A young man in a celebrant's robe sprinted into the dining room. Shimmer registered few of his features except for one simple fact: he was brandishing a knife.

She snapped an activation word, instantly closing a Force Cage around the boy. Driven by apparent fury, the boy slammed into the wall of his cage at full run, bounced off, and clattered to the ground within the spell, stunned. The knife fell from his grasp and skidded between the bars of the invisible cage to stop at Black's feet.

Cole slowly lowered his arm from a throwing position. He kept his knife in hand. "Who by the hells is that?" he asked.

Black's composure seemed forced. Shimmer detected a tremble in his voice.

"An attacker." He glanced at Shimmer, then at the fallen intruder. "Force Cage?"

"It was handy," she replied.

"Your aim is impressive," Black commended. "He was at a run."

Black moved up to the cage, activating a spell. Since he stopped outside the enclosure without running into it, Shimmer assumed he had Spell Sight active now. His eyes were unchanged, making her believe he, too, had a concealed version of the spell.

Comparing the codes for the two versions would be fascinating.

Once he had assessed the spell, he turned his attention to the boy lying on the floor within it. "An acolyte of Inac," he said.

Shimmer looked over the boy, not recognizing his face from Tamort's camp but recognizing the robes. The boy even had the mark of Inac on his forearm, although it had smudged against the robes and was hard to make out.

"Best leave him to me," Black said. "Perhaps Tamort's followers do not understand contracts. I will have to teach him."

"The dead don't learn well," Shimmer warned.

"Words of wisdom," Black agreed. "He's also no good at sharing his revelations if he's dead. No, you can rest assured he'll be released with a whole new outlook."

"We should go, I assume," Cole said, coming to Shimmer's side and handing her the staff. He then took her hand, and she was too confused about her thoughts on the gesture to pull away, even if it did sit against her Moulded Shield and not her skin.

"My apologies for such an ending to our meal," Black said, bowing his head like a courtier. "Please make use of one of the rooms here for the evening. Cole can show you the way. You are welcome to stay until you get your feet under you in StonePeak." He set his stare on Shimmer, and his smile returned. "And please consider my offer. In light of this evening's events, I am even more interested in procuring your services, Bliss."

"We'll see," Shimmer replied. Following Cole's lead, she headed back toward the exit. She thought about telling Black when the spell holding the acolyte would end but then realized he was more than capable of dispelling it at his leisure.

As they returned through the empty manor, two things kept nagging Shimmer.

Firstly, where were Black's defenders? He was a known power here. He had to have bodyguards.

Secondly, why did she not recognize the acolyte from Tamort's camp?

Unable to accept Black's offer of a room, Shimmer asked Cole to take her to an inn. He seemed hurt but found a middle-grade inn outside the underground portions of the city and left her for the night.

Black had given her something to work on, at the least, and she thought a life in StonePeak was a real possibility. It kept her far from the king and his wisavi, and for now, that was for the best.

But once all the excitement had passed and she was alone, her heart hurt again. She fell into fitful sleep, forbidden tears burning behind her eyes.

Sedgan walked.

At first, he walked through dreams. He stumbled into dreamers, upsetting memories and changing their dreams. He confused a dancer into falling from the stage and had a child excitedly toss stones at him. He heard the pleas of a drowning man and watched a woman wander through endless poppy fields. He stood by the ocean and watched the birds dive at hidden crabs, then watched the crabs soar through the air, chasing the birds.

They did not have what he needed.

In between dreams, the endless expanse of golden mist stretched. Sometimes he passed people without a tether, but they did not notice him, leaving him lonely. Once, the golden mists formed into the shape of a dog, but it did not solidify. He tried to make it into other shapes, but it remained empty. It did not have what he needed.

But words reached him through the mist.

"Time to eat. Good job. Now drink. You must be thirsty."

The voice was distant but familiar enough for him to recognize it. It was a woman he had met. He knew she was a mother. He could hear that much in her voice.

"Give me that back. Sit here. Not too close."

Each direction was simple, as if for a child. A routine emerged as days passed in the world outside the golden light.

Wake, eat, wash, walk, eat, wash, sleep…

And while those flickers of life provided the rhythm in his mind, Sedgan walked the golden Dreamworld, seeking something more.

He saw purple grasses under a green sky and watched a man climbing the waves of the ocean. He joined a woman and her horse as they rode through the undergrowth of a distant land, snow falling in clumps from the branches. Her hair was dark brown, and the black paint on her face silhouetted her eyes.

"Put out your hand. Time for a wash. How you get so dirty, I will never understand."

When there were no dreams, he followed the tracks of the Dreamworld. They led him deeper into the gold, but then he could not hear her voice.

He retraced his steps.

"Right foot, then left. There. Now we can go for our walk. Come along."

That was important. He wanted to hear her voice.

The dreams came and went. He stood on cliffs over an ocean of purple and was chased by butterflies when he tried to leave. He walked between quarreling lovers, leaving them as they fell into each other's arms.

"Lovely bright day. Probably won't rain for another few days."

The words only came when he walked in the golden mist, so Sedgan avoided dreams, wanting to hear her speaking to him.

"Put out the lamp, would you? Careful with the fire."

Although he did not leave the golden world, he remembered putting out the lamp as his caretaker had asked.

He walked on.

He waded in the river, watching a child chase minnows. He felt the chill of mountain air prickle his cheeks until his breath became crystals and his hands were blue.

And one day, he came across a man in a cage of green light. He was an odd man who did not exist within a dream but stood in the mist, pacing the cage he believed in, unable to gather his thoughts sufficiently to escape it.

"Hold on, the boys are coming too. Right foot, then left. There. Now we can go for our walk."

When Sedgan walked on from the man in the cage, he sensed he was walking along a village's dirt road. Cleared fields banked the footpath, but a forest rose on the horizon, the edges of it still whittled at by tree fellers. He had company for a while, a woman and a gang of five younger boys. He knew none of their names, but the woman's voice was familiar.

"Oh look, a snake!" one boy exclaimed.

"Don't touch it," the woman warned. "That's an adder. See its thin tail?"

Sedgan fell back into the golden light. He had stumbled into a dream but quickly retreated from it, not wanting to lose the walk on the path he had been sharing.

But it was gone.

He walked on.

* * *

At first, Kitable saw swells in the golden light beyond his cage of green bars, like a fog bank over a ditch disrupted by a hidden hare. These flares of currents within the mist were present only when the celebrant was not. He counted them but found no pattern with Tamort's passing, time of day, or what Kitable's body, controlled by the celebrant, was doing.

But as time—what Kitable suspected was days—passed, the swells came in higher frequency and took more certain forms.

On a day like every other, Kitable still trapped in his cage of green light, one such swell took sudden substance, and a wolf's face appeared. It vanished in the next blink.

Thinking of Tril, who had appeared to him as a wolf-man when they had last entered the Dreamworld together, Kitable sought evidence of the Northlander elder. But where he had hoped to find the wolf, Tamort arrived. Kitable pushed the thought out of his mind lest it be spotted.

The celebrant grinned petulantly at Kitable, his robes disheveled once more. New lines had formed on the man's face, but his eyes were sharply gold. The golden mist behind him slithered forward, taking the form of a snake two strides long. It flickered with strange fire as it climbed up Tamort's leg and wrapped around his shoulders.

He did not seem to notice the fire of the serpent. "Look what I found!" he exclaimed.

He extended his arm, and the snake coiled down its length, then launched itself to the ground. Where it landed, a fire burst into life, and from the flames, a woman formed.

Kitable expected Loni, thinking the snake had to be her wandering, broken soul, but a curvaceous woman appeared instead of Loni's frail shape. Long golden curls fell lusciously down her back, and her smile was coy. Her attire flattered her yet was simple. Like Shimmer, her blouse was low cut, and her skirt had a high slit allegedly for dancing, although Kitable had never seen Maybel dance.

She was beautiful. Kitable had never denied that. But she had relied on that beauty, never becoming more. Complacent and simplistic, Maybel had never interested Kitable.

But seeing her put a stone in Kitable's stomach. Maybel had been useless, but her companion had been a talented enchanter and Kitable's enemy. Tostig had used Maybel against Kitable, something Kitable had no desire to revisit.

"You remember her," Tamort said. "What was the spell? Heart's Desire?"

Without thought magic defenses, Kitable had been fooled by the spell. Fooled and poisoned.

The image of Maybel shifted, and suddenly, Shimmer stood outside his cage.

He had never told Shimmer about that encounter with Maybel, yet now he knew she had been involved in recovering him from the poison. Had she wondered how he had been poisoned by a Good Night Kiss?

He heard his own voice: "I thought she was you."

Tamort grinned wider still as the memory struck Kitable.

When beaten and bleeding, Kitable had uttered those words in confession. Shimmer knew that he had kissed Maybel, believing, thanks to Tostig's magic, that she was Shimmer.

She had not mentioned it. Was she hoping to forget? He was older than her by more than a decade. She preferred a life of wandering the kingdom, trading herbs by day and dancing once the sun set. Having endeared herself to the king and queen, she could now choose any suitor in the kingdom and expect approval. Kitable had told Cole as much. Everyone from paupers to kingsmen had proposed to her. Surely she did not need him, a sour wizard with little time for frivolities like romance.

Kitable glared at Tamort, burying the pain he felt at seeing her. He had wronged her. She had left him, and rightly so. He had been doing her a disservice in keeping her with him. She deserved a real life, and now she had it.

He still felt himself extending his hand, wanting with all his heart to somehow reach her. He wanted to explain, beg forgiveness, and set it right. He needed to.

He let his hand fall. The specter impersonating Shimmer stood wrong, he thought, just a bit hunched. And her smile wasn't genuine, too flat. Shimmer owned no black skirt like that, favoring brighter colors.

It was not her.

The illusion lost power as he recognized this was not stolen from his mind but a fresh creation of Tamort's. He had to assume even the emotions contorting his mind were illusions of the celebrant. His cage might have cracked, but it had kept the celebrant out.

"Doesn't matter," Kitable said, taking a long breath. He placed his resolve into his cage, sealing any openings in his mind. "So she knows. Doesn't matter. And you slipped up, Tamort," he added. His smile twisted. "Now I know my cage is working." He nodded toward the depiction of Shimmer. "That's not from my head. I wouldn't have gotten her so wrong."

Tamort's face scrunched into a scowl, and the image of Shimmer dissolved into falling embers. The snake reappeared in the ashes, hissed, and slithered back to its master.

"No matter indeed," Tamort said. "So stay in your petty cage, Wisavi. Hide away! I will do what must be done!"

Tamort sauntered away, leaving Kitable again in the golden, empty world.

He thought he saw the flash of eyes in the gold once the celebrant was gone, but soon, all was still once more, and Kitable was left with his grief.

After walking through a dream filled with shipwrecks and friendly eels, Sedgan paused in the middle of a dream forest. The trees were conifers, and the air was crisp with incoming snow. The colors were deep greens, the sun low in autumn shades.

He had arrived in this dream at the center of a grove. A perfect ring of cedar trees surrounded him, their canopies dimming the light.

Despite the darkness, Sedgan spotted the dreamer sitting at the base of the largest cedar, her legs folded under her and her eyes shut.

Sedgan squinted into the low light. The woman seemed to have a soft golden glow around her, not unlike the golden light of the Dreamworld he had left behind. Yet she had an evident tether coming from behind her.

"Why don't we go by the baker? It's a bit of a longer way, but the exercise will do us a world of good. I need more bread anyway."

The familiar woman's voice echoed in the grove, the first time Sedgan had heard her while in a dream. The suggestion was quickly followed by, "Mind the roots here. The path is tight."

One after another, the calm instructions arrived on the forest air.

"The day is too wet to go far. Let's turn back at the corner."

"Right foot, then left. Don't forget your coat."

"I'll have to sit a moment. These old legs don't manage the hills like they used to."

While the grove was dark and damp, the voice brought Sedgan surprising joy.

He did not want to move for fear of losing the voice. The dreamer did not seem to notice him. He could stay here, close to Marionna, until the dreamer woke, and he doubted he would be a bother.

Marionna, he realized. He had remembered her name.

Sedgan did not move, but he saw the stranger in the grove open her eyes. To his surprise, her sapphire stare looked right at him with calm confidence.

"Your soul comes alive when you walk with her," the dreamer said.

While Sedgan was sure the words were not Esparan, he understood them. Self-conscious, Sedgan shrugged. "She is kind," he replied.

The woman came to her feet, and Sedgan realized he knew her name too: Messenger. And as surely as he knew her name, he knew that it was not her name but that her name was too sacred to be given to strangers. That she had given him something to call her was still a profound compliment.

Sedgan stepped away, his confidence waning. He did not know this woman. Despite being the height of a child of ten years, she was fully grown. Her hair was a chestnut brown, darker than any Esparan's. Her eyes were brilliant blue and sparkled with golden flecks moving in a mist.

Her eyes led into the Dreamworld.

He wanted to ask who she was but knew in his soul it would offend her. Instead, he asked, "Why are you here?"

Her robe—a simple long smock of undyed wool—fell around her shapelessly as she stood.

"I am waiting for you," Messenger replied. Her innocent smile was childlike, yet an arctic wolf appeared behind her. It sat down on the edge of the trees, its gold eyes watching passively, and its body relaxed.

He thought the wolf was significant but could not remember why. Like Marionna's name, it felt like it should be obvious and yet evaded him.

He knew the wolf meant him no harm, but Sedgan still heard his voice shake. "You are a dreamer?"

"I am," Messenger said, turning around enough to show the golden thread that extended from her back. "This thread binds me to my body as yours binds you. But I am different," she added, opening her hands wide. Her tanned skin was tattooed extensively, tiny dots making a flowery pattern over her hands and arms to her elbows. The robe had ties to hold the sleeves back, much like a healer's garb. "I am a guide."

"Watch your head!" Marionna's voice said in the air around him. Sedgan ducked obediently, a moment later glancing about and expecting the matronly woman beside him. She felt close, but he could not reach her.

"Goodness, you are far too tall for my cottage!"

Realization followed. Messenger was the dreamer here. She was bringing the voice to him.

As he acknowledged the stranger, Sedgan's mind woke. He realized he had been walking in the dreams of others with the golden light between. In his travels, he had seen

Kitable in a cage made of Kitable's own desperation. He had found the wisavi trapped and done nothing.

He searched and found he did not care enough even to feel guilty. But Marionna's voice brought him joy. The feeling was fleeting, and that pained him.

"Why torment me?" he asked the woman before him. "Why bring me here and let me understand these things when I cannot do anything about them? I cannot go back!"

The body was still there, walking, eating, drinking, existing. But Sedgan had no love for life now. It was a lie born of fear of retribution. He was a celebrant of a goddess he knew did not exist. Every word he spoke was hypocrisy. He could no longer live like that.

"I do not come to torment," Messenger said, "but to give you a choice. I am a guide. I will show you the way out of here. Will you follow?"

He wanted the dreams and the confusion to end. He wanted peace. "Yes, I will follow," Sedgan answered.

Turning, Messenger patted the wolf's cheek as she passed. The wolf's stare did not leave Sedgan.

Once Messenger's foot stepped beyond the ring of trees, the forest vanished, and Sedgan stood once more in the golden light of the Dreamworld.

The wolf followed Messenger out. Curious, Sedgan did the same.

For the first time in years, Shimmer dreamt.

She dreamt she was walking through a field of grains. Some branches were barley, others wheat, and the scent was poppyseed. The mountains in the distance were covered in snow like the Crescent Mountain range, but she recognized none of the peaks. She was a long way from any landmarks or familiar roads.

The field was broken in two by a river. Ice floated on the surface, at odds with the ready harvest she walked through.

By the water, she found a raven. The bird skipped on one leg, going around in circles. Although it had no obvious wound, it continued to hop and did not fly away. Despite her efforts, she could not catch it.

But as she followed the bird down the stream, she noticed another animal. On a broken branch hanging low over the water was a white snowy owl, the kind found in the upper reaches of the Crescent Mountain or the far northern provinces. She had only seen feathers from the animals before. Seeing one in the wild was meant to predict a hot summer.

Its massive talons, a testament to its role as supreme hunter, were tangled in a thin twine, tying the bird. It flapped uselessly, unable to break either the branch or the string. Giving up on the raven, Shimmer stopped to help the owl. She had no sooner touched the tree trunk, ready to climb up over the water, when she awoke.

Cold flooded over her. Her spells were gone, and the splint support of her leg had been dispelled.

She winced and, in the darkness behind her eyes, saw a hawk lunging at her.

Startled, Shimmer rolled out of the bed, catching up with herself in the middle of the room. While she felt no spells tethered to her, all her belongings appeared unchanged, and she still could sense her defenses radiating from the walls and entrance. Her leg screamed in pain as she moved without supports on it, but Kitable's repair of the bone held.

She had been dispelled, but spells not attached to her had been spared. There was no threat. She had merely been dreaming.

Steadying her heartbeat, Shimmer sat on the bed and drew a slow breath. Retrieving her bag, she bandaged her lower leg once more, supporting it without magic.

She tried to remember the dream, wondering about its significance. Before becoming the apprentice, she had dabbled in tarot cards and other superstitions. Dreams were meant to be views into one's soul.

The last time she'd seen a raven in a dream, it'd been a series of thought manipulations. Did the raven mean magic?

The owl was new. And a mixed field? No one planted mixed seeds. The other details were fading, except for the final vision of a hawk diving at her.

She decided she would have to research the symbolism of birds in dreams, then lay back onto the bed. Morning was coming. She did not bother trying to sleep; she rose and cast her spells.

Resolving not to try to solve all her life in one day, Shimmer decided to keep to what she knew well: being an apothecary. After finding the tools to create a proper splint for her leg, she sought out the Mountain Market, where she found Bale and Trank at their booth. Bale was sleeping, his feet dangling from under the bench.

Trank was a mountain man. His long beard never seemed to have been trimmed, and his hair was a cowl around his head. His teeth were broken like a dog's after chewing too many bones. He seemed to use mint and bicarbonate for his teeth, but the bicarbonate concentration was too high, staining his teeth in spots.

After introducing herself, still using Bliss, Shimmer said, "I was here the other night, and you weren't. It turns out I'm

in the area for a while, so I figured I'd make you an offer: I'll cover any time you don't want to work in exchange for half of the profits."

The bushy man lifted a skeptical eyebrow. She wondered if he was Northlander. He reminded her of the northern men she had fought beside at King Tohmas' command.

"Half?" Trank said, frowning.

Bliss shrugged. "Just half of the profits, not the sales," she clarified. "And it's money you would not be making otherwise. Bale's useless at herbs."

The grizzled older man scowled, his chapped lips out in pout. "True," he begrudgingly said. After consideration, he pointed at the cart where the wares were drying. "Name it," he challenged.

"Franx flower. Powerful in women, causes abortion. In men, it feminizes them, so it's used as a joke by self-righteous juveniles." She eyed the display on the cart. "You have it center, so it's a high-seller. Probably to women, which is a shame since I know a mix that works more often and doesn't make them sick."

Trank cocked his head. "Arrogant," he said.

"No, just very good," Shimmer retorted. "I'll prove it to you."

He pointed at another herb.

"Fennal. Used in mixes. Dampens the senses. Miners like it because it makes their work less menial and helps reduce the annoyance of the clanging. Better than wax in the ears, but side effects include making bad decisions. Salespeople love giving out free samples. Also is a mild laxative."

Trank blinked at her. She assumed that meant he had not known that fact.

"Grotu root is better," she admitted, "but you can combine the two." She leaned over the makeshift counter. "Why don't you watch me work for a day? I'll be good for business."

He conceded.

Shimmer talked the first person out of dried bodrin and into green powder instead, twice the price but three times as good. The second person was one of the women seeking franx flower. Shimmer took her aside, found out when she suspected she might have become pregnant, determined it was recent enough for another mix, and prepared that instead. It was two copper legs more expensive than the franx flower, but the woman accepted Shimmer's recommendation and paid the extra.

"She'll be telling everyone about it," Shimmer told Trank. "You men have no idea what you ask of a woman when you give her franx flower. This mix is milder and far more likely to work." She winked at the merchant. "I can get you the recipe if we're going to do business together."

Trank's selection was good, although not exhaustive. After selling a double dose of old lady's slippers to a man having trouble sleeping, she suggested Trank also get in the smaller cousin, fair lady's slippers, for the wealthy who could afford to avoid the side effect of the old lady's slippers.

By the end of the day, she had lured Trank into conversation. While he lacked formal training, Trank knew herbs well, particularly the northern ones. He was less familiar with southern herbs, which led to them sharing ideas about other things he might consider sourcing.

While it was fun to be exchanging ideas again, it made Shimmer miss Kitable.

At the end of the day, when the lamps were extinguished, and only the small lanterns on the individual sales carts remained, Shimmer spotted a final person approaching. He was no customer.

"Here," Trank grumbled, interrupting her assessment of the new arrival. He handed Shimmer a pair of silver shard coins. Although they had the anvil of Lour on them, they were familiar weight. "You did well," he said.

She smiled at Trank. "We got a deal?"

"Yep," he said. He extended his hand, and Shimmer knocked her fist against it. "Be back at midnight, and I'll let you take over for the morning shift with Bale."

Shimmer pocketed her new coins. Thinking a quick rest and some food would be in order, she retrieved her staff and made her way out from behind the counter.

"Hold," the person moving between the other waggons called.

Standing tall, Shimmer faced the man. He was dressed in wrapped cloth like Cole, but in maroon, not black. Leather armor held the fabric down over his shoulders and calves, and the weapon on his belt was a well-used Lourite short sword.

He put out his hand. "Pay dues."

"Dues to whom?" she asked. She understood dues to the kingsman would be required eventually. Her life on the road had dodged that, but the Match and Mixer had been subjected to tolls for crossing out of provinces in lieu.

Trank pulled a coin from his pouch and handed it over. It was a whole disc coin, double what he had given Shimmer.

"To Rancer," the man said, putting Trank's coin away.

"I'm new here," Shimmer said, her voice still light and conversational. "Who's Rancer?"

The thug's shoulders tensed. *Not accustomed to being questioned,* Shimmer thought. But as Bliss, Shimmer had no fear. No one gave her orders.

"Rancer's the one who keeps you safe," the man replied.

"Protection?" Shimmer said. "You're not working for any official power. You're running a racket. Should I fail to pay Rancer, you're saying something bad will happen?"

The man put a hand on his sword. "Something bad always happens to people who don't pay."

She considered appeasing the man, but she needed the coins, and eventually, this would wear her out. She decided to get it out of the way.

Shimmer reviewed the man's path in her mind. "Not everyone in here pays Rancer," she said. "About a third do. Who do the others do business with?"

The thug's face changed color. He peered over Shimmer's shoulder. Perhaps he thought he should try someone else if she could not be intimidated. "Rancer won't be happy if you leave us, Trank," he said.

Trank had backed away and was now out of the sword's reach.

"Keep him out of this," Shimmer snapped, stepping between the thug and the apothecary. "I'm independent. He can do what he wants." She ensured the thug met her stare when she added, "The other two-thirds pay someone else, I assume. The way you've got it set, nobody goes without protection. It'd be asking for a problem from both sides."

She thought back to how Bale reacted when Black showed up at his waggon. "Black's the other one," she concluded, and the man's face darkened further, making him look like a disgruntled toad.

"You got an association with Black?" the man demanded.

"No," Shimmer said, "no matter what the rumors say about dinner last night." She left him wondering about that, lifted her chin, and added, "You can go. Until there is a benefit to Rancer's association, I'll not pay him a single copper leg."

The brute glanced at Trank, then slowly took in the other onlookers. At least one shopper and two vendors had stopped what they were doing and were watching the exchange. Shimmer already knew the man would not leave. The loss of authority was too significant.

At least the matter would be settled quickly.

Leaving his sword, the man puffed himself up and stepped forward to grab Shimmer's arm. She didn't move, letting him wrap his hand around her Moulded Shield. "Look, girl, you're new here. You can't expect—"

His brow furrowed, and his words fell off when his skin failed to contact her or her sleeve. He looked down at her arm, his expression puzzled.

He wasn't wearing gloves, Shimmer noted.

"Bad idea," she softly warned. With the next word, she activated a Heat Shield. It was her version, which meant the heat rose much faster than the traditional spell.

The bully stared at her, his face now crimson in building rage.

"I'll show you what—" Before he could finish the sentence, the heat had risen under his hand. She saw him debate holding on further. Knowing the spell would burn to the bone if required, she hoped he would be stubborn.

He pulled his hand, his teeth clenched to keep from crying out. She was pleased with how far he withdrew, now giving her a respectful space as he cradled his blistering hand.

"I suggest picking up some cak cream from Trank," Shimmer said cooly. "Helps with burns."

"Bitch!" the man snapped.

"Definitely not the worst thing I have been called," Shimmer replied, waving him away. "Go get your boss and buddies. And tell him to bring anyone else who wants to discuss matters with me. Let's get it over with." When he did not move, Shimmer stepped toward him, satisfied when the thug scrambled away. She confidently met his gaze and enunciated every word: "I belong to no one."

The man left at a brisk jog.

Letting out a short breath, Shimmer turned back to face Trank, who had paled. For a man who lived in a cave, she had not thought that possible.

"Need some dried bodril, Trank?" she asked. "You're not going to faint on me, are you?"

The apothecary cleared his throat and re-centered himself. He smiled weakly.

She glanced over her shoulder, making sure the thug was on his way. "I'll stay away from you until this is settled," she promised. "We can deal once I sort that fool out." Sensing a familiar set of hovering spells nearby, she smiled as she checked to her left, finding Cole settling into a position outside the market proper. He had chosen a wall to lean against but could not have been there long. She would have sensed his magic.

"You can invite Black too," Shimmer called to Cole, drawing the attention of the onlookers to him. They may not have seen him, but she had.

Cole shrugged. "Black's already given you leave, Bliss. Do what you want. I'm here to enjoy the show."

And he *was* going to enjoy it, Shimmer sensed. His smile was profoundly satisfied.

◦ ◦ ◦ ◦ ◉ ◦ ◉ ◦ ◦ ◦ • •

Keeping well back, Sedgan followed Messenger in the mist. He thought to turn around more than once, yet his feet kept

moving forward. He rarely heard Marionna's voice now, and that gnawed at him. He wanted to walk with her.

Messenger's promise of a way out of the Dreamworld enticed him.

They came to a place without dreams, yet souls walked. Around him, all manner of people traveled in the golden light, none with a golden tread following them.

At length, Messenger and her wolf came to a stop. Sedgan hesitantly joined them.

Another hundred paces ahead loomed a colossal gate. The craftsmanship was superb, yet it was of no style Sedgan had ever seen. It was wrought iron, gleaming black in an ocean of gold. It stood closed.

"Behold," Messenger said, gesturing, "the Gate."

One by one, the souls Sedgan had been walking with approached the Gate. Some went straight to the construct, touching the black metal and vanishing. Others milled about as if working up their courage to approach. Those who did not go up paced and wailed, the sounds audible if they passed close but otherwise muffled.

"Where does it lead?" Sedgan asked.

"It is obvious," Messenger replied, eyeing him like a disappointed mother.

None of the souls around him now had a tether to their bodies. These were the loose souls of the dead, passing through the Gate, one by one.

"To death," Sedgan concluded.

Messenger cocked her head, and the wolf matched her. "Yes and no," she replied. "These are the dead. Moving through the Gate is the release. Some say it is the reward of your gods while others claim the hells lie beyond. I believe they are all correct. That which you expect on the other side will be there. But there you are, Sedgan. You are free. Cut your thread, and you may pass through. Wander no more."

It was the simple solution. He had thought about it before, even attempted it. His willingness to take frozen freedom had been suicide. He had wondered if it would work but had been indifferent to that hope. He had no desire to return to his body or to his life.

He had come to Inac's service seeking vengeance once when he had been young and full of hatred. Training to be a celebrant had taken too long for that vengeance, and he had come to consider that Inac's blessing. After all, was he not a champion of Inac's justice? Hunting down his mother's killer would not have been just.

Once sworn in, he had carried Inac's blessing with him in every action. He had been confident of his fate.

Loni had shaken that confidence into rubble. She had convinced him that he had been wrong all along, that Inac's purpose was more than guiding a gathering through prayers and providing homage at the temples. For a while, he had joined in her fanaticism.

Shimmer had destroyed it in a single afternoon, stripping away all his conviction. She had recognized the drugs Loni used on him and cleared his mind with a Sweep spell.

Purpose had never returned. Inac's blessing still evaded him, and Loni could not provide a substitute. Sedgan had followed Loni still, dedicated to keeping her from drawing others into her thrall as she had him. He had controlled her insanity as best he could and, in the end, been the voice condemning her to death. He had known that day that his soul was damned, yet even now he did not think he could have done differently. He had helped her kill others when not in his right mind. Allowing her to do that again would have damned him further. In having her executed, Sedgan had at least chosen his sin.

He moved toward the Gate.

What awaited him was one of the five hells: of that he was sure. But walking in the golden light, without purpose and without companion, seemed like the first hell anyway. Here, he knew hope still. Hope had become torture.

"Right foot, then left," Marionna's voice said from the back of his mind. "There. Now we can go for our walk."

Sedgan stopped. Marionna would not be on the other side of the Gate.

"There will be no hope there," he said, unsurprised that Messenger had come up beside him in anticipation of his question.

"True."

"Is there hope here?" he asked, looking down at the small woman.

"Always," Messenger replied. "But you must decide."

Sedgan took a step back. "I will think on it."

He thought Messenger sounded disappointed when she replied, "Don't take too long. You will miss the moment."

"What moment?" he asked.

She smiled, her smile sad but optimistic. "You'll know it."

Following a sharp gesture of her tattooed hands, a wind rushed at Sedgan, sweeping him back. The Gate vanished into the mist, the golden light soaring past him like a meteor shower. In a blink, Sedgan was back in the cedar grove, and Messenger was again sitting by the giant cedar, her eyes shut, and her wolf crouched behind her.

He let out a short breath, still feeling the Gate in his mind like a lodestone in his pocket.

He knew she would say nothing else and knew that, should he want her guidance again, he had but to call out her name, and she would know.

And he knew her true name.

"Watch your step," he heard Marionna's voice say. "It's farther up than you'd expect."

Putting a hand on his golden tether, Sedgan left the grove behind and followed his own thread to his body.

The boys made themselves useful. When Marionna requested it, they carried laundry, washed dishes, or tidied the house. She insisted they went for a walk at least once a day, and they took turns walking beside Sedgan. Some of the acolytes would lead a prayer. Others talked to the celebrant about their life as an acolyte. One dared talk about life before being sworn in, which earned him suspicious glares from the others.

Benn explained it when they returned: "Once you become an acolyte, life before that doesn't matter. There are no judgments." He glanced at the boy who had told Sedgan about his missing mother. The boy was Grant, the youngest at ten years old. Marionna assumed the boy didn't have anything else to talk about. "We'll do a lesson," Benn decided. He, as the eldest, had been assigned their leader. "We'll teach him better."

Benn was a gentle soul, so at odds with his devotion to Inac, Goddess of Fire, Passion, War, and Lust, Marionna felt she had to ask, "What brought you into this gathering, Benn?"

The boy frowned. "It suited me."

She handed him a dozen potatoes, and the boy immediately began to peel them. He used the knife he, like the others, carried. This blade had a second edge on the tip, making it useful for stabbing. It was both a weapon and a tool.

"I do not see that," she told him.

"It suited me at the time," Benn admitted.

"That I believe," Marionna replied.

Once the dinner was done, Sedgan had been washed, and one of the boys had taken him to the outhouse. Marionna settled in her chair by the fire to do some knitting. Grant had put another hole through his stockings, prompting Marionna to make him a new set. After a point, the material itself could not hold any more darning.

Sedgan returned and was put to bed. Soon enough, the others were asleep, all piled next to each other on the floor. She had offered them Cole's bed, even if they used it in rotation, but they insisted she slept there. Sedgan still had the main bed.

The coals of the fire left little light, but Marionna could knit with her eyes closed if she had to, and she had seen the rain clouds approaching. Grant would need a new set of stockings tomorrow. His current ones were going to get wet.

She had begun to drift to the sounds of the gentle breathing of the boys when a quiet voice cut through the sounds of the night.

"Why should I wake?"

Marionna glanced up at the bed where Celebrant Sedgan lay under her patchwork quilt.

"Why should I wake?" the voice said again.

His mouth moved, but his eyes remained shut. Having seen far too much magic, she shook her head and wondered if it was the man who spoke or another. Deciding she would answer regardless, she said, "These boys could use guidance." She kept her voice soft, hoping not to wake the acolytes, as she continued her knitting.

"False goddess," Sedgan replied. He did not move, lying flat on his back, his eyes closed in sleep.

Marionna sighed, lowering her work to her lap. "Then wake to show them that," she replied. "If you want to get Inac back, teach them something else."

There was a long pause. She thought the voice in the sleeping celebrant had gone, but when she returned to her knitting, the voice interrupted.

"It's real—the power, the dreams. It's not the goddess's. I don't understand it," it said.

Marionna yawned, realizing the stocking was done. She tied it off. "Sedgan, you have two options," she said. "Dead, you can no longer do anything about anything. You can't change the fate of these boys or anyone else. You can't atone. You can't make a difference. If you seek that release, let go of this shell."

She waited, watching the breathing of the man on the bed. His chest rose and fell in deep slumber. She expected it to release in final breath, but after each breath came another.

"On the other hand, if you want to be something of worth, then wake up and get started," Marionna said.

She waited again, wondering if he had heard her at all. She wasn't sure if she was talking to the man's ghost even now. Would he open his eyes?

Nothing happened for long moments more. Marionna yawned again, sleep tugging at her mind. Deciding that she had done what she could, she set the new stockings at Grant's feet, then crawled into her bed.

Once she had settled into the straw mattress, the voice came again from the darkness. "Will you walk with me still?"

"If you want," Marionna agreed.

The body took a long hollow sigh. "I like our walks."

Marionna smiled, nestling into the pillow. "So do I," she told the insane man.

"But you would not like me if you knew," Sedgan's voice said.

"Knew what?"

"I saw your son in danger and did nothing," he said.

Marionna's breath caught, but she did not move from her bed. She was not sure she was speaking to the man at all. Was his mind too far gone? Could it be trusted?

"My son is always in danger," she said, knowing the words were true and wishing they were not. Many years ago, Cole's arrival had brought her attention away from Kaylin. With a new baby to care for, she had been able to cope with losing her older child. She had known, eventually, that he lived, but the fact that he never returned to her made her believe he was in danger.

But then Cole had gone to live in StonePeak, working with thieves and thugs. It seemed her sons were fated to remain only a step away from death's door.

"I do not want you to be sad," the celebrant said.

Marionna could not find her voice.

"I will go," Sedgan added, his voice solemn. Then, with a brightness like a smile, he finished, "But return so that we can go on our walks."

She drifted off into silence that was followed by happy dreams despite the fear knotted in her stomach for her sons.

Days of waiting passed in the golden light, protected by the Force Cage. Tamort had left Lour now and was traversing the province of Solta toward the Manor of Trulinar. There, Tamort had made it clear, Kitable would kill Carsh, make evident the limitations of the king's insane mind, and tear down the entire fledgling kingdom. And there remained nothing Kitable could do about it.

Kitable sought the wolf, but his mind played tricks on him. He saw the face of the wolf, the movement of a paw, or the wisp of a tail without cease. It took effort for him to keep the wolf out of his mind while Tamort visited. He did not want the celebrant to see the little hope the glimpses brought him.

Tamort had found a way to infuse Kitable's body with untouchable magic, healing some of his wounds and giving him the energy to continue his trek. They were only a few days from the Manor of Trulinar when, after another long lecture from Tamort about the doom of the kingdom Kitable had helped forge, Kitable saw the wolf again.

It hid behind the celebrant and his snake, pacing the clearing in the mist like circling a treed prey. Kitable did not goad Tamort on this time but let the man wear himself out. Without reactions from Kitable, the celebrant lost interest and stormed away.

Once the celebrant was gone, Kitable glimpsed the wolf again.

"Don't you dare go sneaking away!" Kitable shouted from his cage. It could be a trick from Tamort, but if it was, it was one he was tired of. He needed to know, one way or another.

Where he had seen the golden-touched wolf snout, the face materialized once more. It cocked its head at him like a dog heeding his master's call.

"You heard me!" Kitable snapped. "Get out here!"

Paw-by-paw, the wolf came out of the mist. Its black eyes scanned the small clearing around the cage, the only region Kitable could see in the haze of golden light.

"He's gone for now," Kitable offered, thinking it was checking for Tamort. "He'll be back when they rest in a few candles." Tamort's schedule was predictable now that he was on the final stretch to the manor. He pushed himself hard enough to maximize the distance without breaking the body he was using. He was less gentle with the horses. Kitable could not tell if they were run to exhaustion or burned by untouchable forces, but the results were the same. More than one horse had died along this harried trek.

The wolf slunk forward as if shy of discovery but came to the cage. There it sat, its flat eyes staring up at him, questions on its bristled face.

"Tril?" he asked.

"Can you think of another wolf that patrols the Dreamworld, Kitable?" the wolf replied, although its mouth did not move.

Kitable let out an uneasy sigh. "No."

"Of course," the wolf said, "I could be a dream."

"I do not—" Kitable cut himself off. He did not usually dream, but standing in the Dreamworld had distanced him from his magic. Perhaps he could dream now.

But why would Tril make that suggestion?

"But does that not make it real?" he asked, his mind hurting. "I'm in the Dreamworld. Isn't a dream of you the same as the real thing?"

The wolf cocked its head again. "Probably not," it answered. "If I'm a dream, I'm *your* dream. I only know what you know."

Kitable leaned back, resting against the cage around him and putting his hand to his temples. "Why would I use a wolf?"

"Probably because it's the only familiar thing you've seen in the Dreamworld. Besides," it said, "Tril was a wolf-man when you last saw him. And he is an arctic wolf. This is a timber wolf."

"He's probably got control of his appearance," Kitable argued. "Could be anything."

"I know," the wolf replied, "so why be the wrong wolf?"

Kitable thought about that point for a moment. "Am I arguing with myself?"

"Yes," the wolf replied. "Although, for what it's worth, you'll win."

Kitable shook his head. "So I dream now, of all times." He looked at the bars again. Was it safe? No, not yet. What if Tamort was heading back? If he was caught…

"With how close we are to the Manor of Trulinar, it doesn't much matter, does it?" the wolf said.

Kitable felt his head ache again. "What do you mean?"

The wolf somehow managed to look like an irritated parent. "Think about it! You are in there to hide from Tamort. You were keeping information from him. But that information doesn't matter once he reaches Trulinar."

Despite his headache, that much made sense. "I should drop it?" Kitable asked.

"Can you?" the wolf answered.

If it was a Force Cage, he could dispel it. No, that wasn't right. It wasn't magic, not his magic. Did that mean it had to be deactivated? He had no way of knowing. He wasn't used to untouchable magic.

"Of course, you aren't," the wolf chided. "You're a wizard, remember?"

Kitable saw the pale green light of the bars glowing. The glow was steady, and that suddenly seemed odd. Only alteration magic was smooth.

"Creation magic is cloudy," Kitable said. "This isn't."

"Oh dear," the wolf said, smiling a snarl of teeth, "you might be onto something."

Kitable reached out to a "bar" and felt it under his hand, tingling like magic but not right. "Magic or not, if I built it, I modeled it on the Force Cage. I know those auras. I would have made it cloudy like creation."

"So..." the wolf prompted.

Kitable remembered the image of Shimmer he had seen: close, but not quite right, built from someone else's memories. Realization, like the cold sweep of arctic air over exposed skin, fell over him.

"I did not create this," Kitable said.

"No, you did not," Tamort's voice said. The wolf was gone in a blink, and Celebrant Tamort walked out from the mist across from Kitable. He had the snake of fire curling itself around his arm, then shoulder. From the fire, the woman's laughter echoed out.

The haze of Kitable's mind was clear for a moment more, enough to recognize that his fear of Tamort accessing his mind and using it to further his gains was not real either.

"A thought..." Kitable muttered, struggling to bring his mind into enough focus to follow the conclusion. "This cage! You made a thought illusion."

"Easier than making a cage for you here," Tamort replied, taking up his customary place in front of Kitable. A campfire appeared between them, like the Temple waggon fire but without smoke. The stones of the fire glowed with images that Kitable often studied but never remembered.

Force creation was a basic spell for a wizard. Thought illusion was considered impossible.

"The cage is your illusion," Kitable realized. He followed the logic, feeling each conclusion push back a mist, one he had not even recognized until now, from his mind. "The thought made me accept it, even think it was my doing, that it was for my protection."

Tamort smiled a mirthless smile.

Kitable thought of the wolf. "My soul has been trying to warn me." He settled his thoughts, bringing them in around him like armor. He would use logic. The celebrant had used Kitable's fear and his pride to manipulate him. But reason was impossible to subvert. It made sense, or it did not.

The argument felt hollow. He had been fooled already once using that defense. And the cage, whether illusion or not, felt solid. He did not know how to escape it.

Tamort shrugged. "Too little, too late," he said, chuckling. The sound was echoed by the laughing voice of Celebrant Loni. "Tomorrow, we arrive. The likes of you cannot undo that cage."

Kitable felt the sheen of untouchable magic reaching through the bars this time, seeking purchase in his mind. He waved his hand, batting it aside, and was surprised when that was sufficient. *That makes some sense,* he thought. Thought magic could always be resisted. Untouchable thought magic appeared to be following the same rules. If he knew what he was resisting, he could fight it. He had to be more careful.

"You blunted my mind," Kitable replied. "You made these thoughts to keep me from trying to leave. If I could not break this cage, then you would not have bothered; you would have exalted in my struggle against the impossible." Calm in his logic, Kitable met Tamort's gold-filled gaze firmly. "You know you have something to fear from me," he concluded. "I will find the weakness."

Keeping his thoughts close and controlled, Kitable designed an experiment. He would test each bar, physically and mentally. He would try any combination of—

Tamort's smirk settled in. He lifted his arm, the fire snake slithering off him. It climbed into the air, moving over the golden mist like solid ground, the female voice it embodied laughing.

"No, no, you won't," Tamort said.

The snake slithered through the cage, and Kitable did not bother trying to retreat from it. It reared back, the fangs barred, and Kitable steeled his mind, ready for more manipulations, whatever their form.

With a hiss, the snake struck.

Kitable's mind filled with pain. When he opened his eyes, he stood atop a city's wall, a battle raging on either side below. He had a handful of spells active around him, limited by time and unable to cast more. He had insufficient defenses. Master Terant of Barlaby, a wizard of supreme strength, hit him with a Black Agony spell. Kitable fell to his knees.

The scene played out, requiring nothing from him. He fought through the torment of the spell, choking out syllable after syllable to cast, desperation driving him, knowing that failure would kill him.

His spell took Terant across the throat, pinning and strangling him.

But the last spell from the master wizard atop the wall of Arcott took Kitable's voice from him. He was left muted and locked by the pain of spasmed muscles. He was vulnerable to any other passing soldier, unable to cast, and unable to move. Helplessness, followed by despair, flowed through him.

It was only the first of the aching memories Kitable's soul was dragged through.

•••••••••••••

The first thing Rancer did was send another thug. That one left with fertility issues after his groin was the target of a reduction spell. He conveyed a message to Rancer: *Come yourself, or I will come to you.*

Days passed, broken by nights in the inn and dreams she remembered in part. Shimmer never freed the owl, although she often found herself in the same open field with the single three-branched tree by the river. She located a scholar who did not know her and discussed the symbolism of birds. The man tried to convince her she was fighting to free herself from shackles.

One night she managed to get up the tree but could not release the twine. It was one long tangled piece, without knot or end.

She bought a tarot deck, but it did not seem to like her. She gave it away the next day.

After a quartercycle, she sent a message to Marionna, who reported Sedgan was unchanged. Shimmer sent another supply of the mountain chain flower dust, unsure what else to do. The deeper part of her mind had still not solved the problem.

And each morning, she awoke dispelled. She invested in a proper splint for her leg, which she wore constantly. The bone had been knit, leaving her with the pain of bruises to contend with, although she dared not put too much weight on the repair yet.

Although the other elements of her dream changed, the owl showed up repeatedly, always caught in a cage or by a tether. It never seemed willing to accept either state.

Shimmer made trades in the market, abiding by her promise to keep clear of Trank and Bale until things settled with the protection racket. She was surprised when the other dealers happily accepted her business. At length, so did Trank and Bale.

After some investigation, Shimmer discovered that they had allied themselves with Black, who had endorsed her publicly.

But it was known that she paid protection funds to neither thug. The issue hovered over every conversation she had in the market. She set out to discover what she could about both sides of the rackets, learning more about Black in the process. His word appeared to be good. She found no connection to anything remotely magic. He dealt in illegal sales of coliron, a blend of iron and carbon that was nearly indestructible and expectably good for enchanting. His "legitimate" business front was slaves, which he traded across provinces.

Shimmer knew that would have to change. King Tohmas was in the process of changing the laws around slavery to reflect those of Galanth, which would give the slaves rights. It had been the king's mother's doing.

As days passed, it became clear that one of them would have to act to settle the Mountain Market, and Rancer was the most pressed. He was losing face. If he did not confront her, he risked losing all credibility and, with it, business.

While she stayed at different inns as the mood struck her, Shimmer prepared daily for a duel, with a small batch held apart overnight. Even if she dreamt, that package of spells was present when she awoke dispelled.

A day after her conversation with Marionna, Shimmer sensed something amiss at lunch in her inn. Fewer people entered than usual, and those that came in were hurried and uncomfortable. Knowing she was threatening established thugs, Shimmer used a short Scry to view the area outside the inn and spotted Rancer and his gang.

They had attracted a crowd, which meant they had no fear of witnesses. Making the point, two of StonePeak's local wardens were approaching the inn, wearing their uniforms and weapons. She assumed Rancer had utilized his influence among the official lines of the city.

Beyond the crowd, Shimmer spotted magic auras and found Cole. He had located another wall to lean on, positioned well into the shadows of a house to allow most of the crowd to walk by him without noticing his presence.

The two wardens reached the inn door, and Shimmer felt the crowd hush in anticipation.

Anticipation of what? she wondered. *Will they expect fire and lightning?*

Shimmer sat back and decided to finish her drink before venturing out. A private word with the wardens was prudent. She didn't need huge displays, not yet. The wardens were two short men armed with bludgeoning weapons. She had become accustomed to weapons of war—maces, swords, spears—but these men carried saps and clubs, better suited to subduing, not killing. She thought the two men were not just brothers, but likely twins. They moved together in stride with the same stiff posture. Their helms were open, and both had mustaches that reminded her of Northlanders. Each wore the outdated shards of rank on their chests.

King Tohmas had replaced the ranking system in all princedoms with his own: companions, wardens, and guardians. In Lour, the eight-tiered system of rank based on skill in battle had been removed. True to form, these men wore the tabard of their province, gray with gold and a blue rank rope over their right shoulders. But what she found interesting was that these two had the old shards indicating ranks of five and six. They were far beyond the usual warden skill level, yet they carried a low rank in the new system. Without being companions, called to action only during war, these men were the lowest rank they could be.

They had offended someone, Shimmer thought, or their skill with people was well below their skill with their weapons. Without a war, their skills were not of use. She decided one would be called Sap and the other Club since the only way to tell the two apart was the weapon they carried.

"Bliss…" the first man said as the two arrived at her table. He paused awkwardly as if leaving a space for a last name, "may I see your merchant's seal?"

Shimmer bat her lashes. "I got no goods," she pointed out. "I don't need a seal. I was on hire for another licensed merchant when I sold things. All else has been trade items, which are exempt since no money was exchanged. But in case you are worried, I have applied for a license. You can ask at the City Hall if you want."

She waited for them to process the information. They had no crime to act upon. Would that be enough?

Club came to a decision first. "Where are your documents?" he asked. With her sitting, they towered over her, probably one of the few times that ever happened to them. Even Kitable's mother would have looked down on these two. Shimmer only had to stand up if she wanted to add weight to her assertions.

Shimmer's smile grew, sure they were not expecting her to produce them. The concept of formalized identifications was new, and few people had bothered having any made.

But she had traveled with a servant of the king. Shimmer had been one of the first.

They were not going to like what it said.

"That," she said in the same honeyed tone, "is a wildcat of a topic. But if you *really* want them, then here." She pulled her bag into her lap and produced the slim vellum from the hidden pocket.

Club, ignoring her warning, opened the folded sheet. He read it for a moment, then scowled. "No listed mother," he said curtly.

"Lady Loria Darmac," Shimmer replied. "We never wrote it down. Gets awkward."

Club frowned at her. "You cannot claim to be official when there is no—"

Shimmer held up a hand, stopping the man short. "Wait for it," she said, pointing at Sap. "He's figuring it out."

Club turned toward his twin, whose face was contorted. She thought the expression would hurt if held much longer.

"Lady Loria *Darmac*?" the man stuttered.

"Yep," Shimmer answered.

Sap leaned over to check the vellum, his eyes wide.

"Father's not Carltric Darmac if you were wondering," Shimmer offered.

Club's expression went blank.

"There you go," Shimmer said brightly. "So here's the thing: I can vanish whenever I want. I've spent the last two decades doing it." She teased the vellum from the hands of the two wardens. In their confusion, they released it. "I'll let you two decide if you want to say anything to anyone about this. Personally, I'd not want to be the messenger on this one."

Slinging her bag over her shoulder, Shimmer stood up, gathered her staff, and smiled again at the two men. "I'll talk to Rancer now if you'll excuse me."

They were still by her table, standing side by side, by the time she left the inn.

Telling the kingsman's sister that her bastard daughter was in town was not a task anyone volunteered for.

Shimmer paused in the doorway, assessing the crowds again and activating Spell Sight to better interpret the magic auras she felt in the area. She used the version of the spell visible as colors drifting over her eyes.

She had a good sense of who were Rancer's men by their dark red attire but was having trouble figuring out which was Rancer himself. He was probably surrounded by his people, but that didn't narrow it down enough.

Instead of shouting, Shimmer paused, letting them all assess her and draw their conclusions.

Bright loose clothes: a dancer.

Herb bag: an apothecary.

Flickering lights over her eyes: a wizard.

She waited until one of the groups of Rancer's men approached, then met them in the center of the empty street. With her splint hidden by her long dress, the slow, calm walk suited her.

Bliss was blunt. "Which one's Rancer?" she asked, certain the man would have to identify himself. Hiding behind someone else implied he feared her, and wasn't the entire point of this conversation to disprove that?

Rancer stepped up. He was not, as she had expected, the man in the middle. She had overlooked him because of his appearance.

He was perfectly formed, the kind of fitness one could only be born with. His blond hair was short curls, sweet enough to be childlike but luscious enough to be handsome. He had the perfect shaved cleft chin and stunning sapphire eyes. He could have made a fortune as a performer.

Bliss did not care. Shimmer's alter ego had no interest in men or women romantically. She was practical and always direct. This man's appearance may have made most people gawk, but not Bliss.

Shimmer fixed her eyes on him, analyzing the auras. He had two magic items on him, a rarity. One was a strong attack, but not one that would get through her defenses. The other, interestingly, was a Fear Ward she was barely outside the range of.

She focused on the ward and found the minor alterations protecting the nearer thugs from its effect.

Leaning on her good leg, Shimmer raised her eyebrow. "You're Rancer?"

"Surprised?" the man asked, his voice angelic. He probably had an incredible singing voice too. Dust would have loved to sit up with him overnight and exchange stories, maybe share a show and split the profits.

"Not really," Shimmer replied. "It works, I guess. You walk into the room, and all the girls stop paying attention to anything else." She swept her eyes over the crowd, seeing the younger women flushed with secret thoughts. "The men start watching the girls and get all defensive and stupid." After assessing the nearest men and woman, all wearing the crimson loose cloth of the cadre, she added, "Or if they're not, they're swooning at you too!"

His cadre comprised of adoring people—some lovers, others lusting. It was different than the usual fear and intimidation, but it was still manipulation.

And he wasn't smart enough for her. Looks or not, he was uninteresting.

"To each their own," Rancer said, his hands open as he advanced toward Shimmer. In doing so, he put her into the range of the Fear Ward.

The Fear Ward lashed out, but Shimmer did not flinch, having anticipated it. Her Deflector buffeted most aside. Her remaining thought defenses erased the remnants.

"It's sobering to have someone unwilling to judge me by my appearance," the man said as if finishing the thought.

Shimmer laughed falsely. "Pretty words and a pretty face, trying to hide that you just attacked me."

Rancer shrugged. "Whatever do you mean?"

She assessed the spell again. Sensing an opportunity, Shimmer shifted her weight back, putting her outside the range again.

"Oh, I assume you know about it since you choose targets," she said. Shimmer leaned forward, allowing the ward to attack her again. She ensured it would bounce off her Deflector, halving its potency. *Can't have them dying of fright.*

Kitable had once had a more complicated name for the spell she activated, but he had agreed to use the Rydan word for revenge instead: *Turnabot.* The spell had a set number of variables required, and once they were met, it used a complicated alteration to take control of the spell from the caster, then returned it along its trajectory.

It turned the attack against its owner.

Rancer leaped backward, grabbed a nearby cadre member, and ducked behind the man.

Shimmer pressed her lips, trying not to laugh. The confrontation could yet become dangerous. Kitable would never have approved of her mirth. But seeing the handsome man scramble for cover was profoundly satisfying.

The effect lasted a blink. The man immediately sobered when the next natural thought replaced the artificial one of terror.

"What...?" Rancer muttered, his poise lost. The man he had hidden behind glared at the cadre leader, no doubt wondering why he was considered so expendable as to be used as a human shield. "You bewitched me!" Rancer accused.

"Bewitched?" Shimmer said, chuckling. "How outdated! I did not bewitch you. I bounced *your* spell off a defense, meaning you attacked first." Shimmer stepped up, and they, every last one, flinched. But she let her regular defenses deal with the ward this time.

"You, Rancer," she said, "have gotten too big for your britches."

The man stiffened, his perfectly proportioned shoulders square in denial. "I will not—"

"Yes, you will," Shimmer interrupted. "You made a mistake when your goon confronted me in the market, but instead of thinking about it, you sent another. Then you showed up to save your image without for a moment assessing your target. I've been expecting a tail. I've been hoping for a Scry or a spy. Send a plant! But you have assumed I am exactly as I appear, to your detriment."

She leaned in, not caring that he was taller than her. She held her defenses between them. "Who am I?"

He cleared his throat. "Dust's daughter," he said.

That surprised her, but she did not let it show. This man was too young to have worked with Dust. Someone had told him.

But it did not matter. She was more than her father's reputation now.

"And?" she prompted.

"Apothecary, dancer, whore." He said the last word with a leer.

She matched his smile, which stole the confidence from his grin. "And?" she asked again.

He glanced away, right at the shadow where Cole had propped himself.

"No, look at me," she warned him, and he brought his glorious eyes to hers. He soon looked away. "What do my eyes tell you?" she asked.

"Wizard," he said, the word chocked.

"Master wizard," Shimmer corrected, and the words sounded better to her ear than they had before. "Now, it's clear to me you've been given just enough information to have you bash on, running headlong into me when you should have run away. That's not my problem; it's yours. All I want is to be left alone. Stay out of my affairs. Got it?"

"You start throwing magic around, Wisavi Kitable might have something to say about it," the man answered, but his voice was already weaker.

Her stomach flipped to hear his name, her wounded heart still fresh enough to cry. But she buried it again, giving nothing away to Rancer.

Before she could answer, a cold wave ran through Shimmer like a crash of a mountain river. She heard someone whisper, "Shimmer."

Her spells dropped, not destroyed, but gone. She felt like her legs had given up after a panicked run. Exhausted, the energy surrendered to oblivion. Her items were untouched, except for the two that had been active. She was vulnerable as if she had been dreaming.

A knot of panic clutched at her gut, but Shimmer dared not show it. She'd been a performer all her life. She could not allow them to see her sudden vulnerability.

Steeling her voice, Shimmer ran a hand through her hair in a mock flirt. The movement allowed her to activate a bead woven into her hair, which immediately replaced two of her most vital defenses, Moulded Shield and Anchor Block.

"Oh please," she said, "tell Master Kitable where to find me. I'd *love* to see him." She stared at the man, ignoring the beautiful glint of his blue eyes. He was oblivious. Clearly, he had not been the source of her sudden dispel. For it to have missed her other magic items, it could not have been an Eight-layered Dispel. She had no idea what had struck her, but it seemed to have stopped for now.

Rancer turned his gaze aside first.

"Glad we have an understanding," Shimmer said with a laugh. Tossing her head, she turned away, heading toward the cavern openings to enter the tunnels behind and around the city. With her splint, she continued her slow, calm stroll, staff in hand. Her license would not be valid for days more, but trade was open. She had collected a treasury of gems and jewelry worth expanding, anticipating the day she could sell them for outright coin.

She knew it was not over. Rancer would try something with less of an audience next. She needed a quiet place to re-cast her spells and rearm herself.

Rancer did not follow, but when Shimmer was within the soft shadows of the cave, Cole arrived at her side.

"Your boss is an ass," Shimmer told him, allowing him to join her.

"Yes, but good at his job," Cole replied. He waited a half-dozen steps before adding, "Any particular reason he's an ass at this time?"

"He set up Rancer," Shimmer said. "Rancer knew enough about my father to make some dangerous conclusions. Damn near got himself killed."

She glanced over. Cole's expression lacked his usual joyfulness. "I can't say I knew about that," Cole said, "but he did ask me to keep an eye on you." For a moment, Cole's face brightened. "That's been a nice job." In the next blink, the smile was gone. "You going to tell me what happened back there?"

"What part?" Shimmer turned down the corridor. The lights were maintained here until sunset, although the traffic was sparse. She would head for the market, then try to send Cole away.

He caught her hand gently, leading her to a halt. "The part where you lost your spells," he said, his voice soft.

Hearing his concern, Shimmer allowed him to hold her shielded hand in the dim hallway.

She had no answer. She did not know why that had happened.

"You all right?" he asked.

"I'll be fine once I get the spells back up," Shimmer replied. Worried about hurting him, she squeezed his hand. "I need to find a private place to cast."

His gray eyes glinted as if metallic in the firelight. "You can use my place. I promise not to eavesdrop. I know how personal casting is."

She let him lead her.

His mind made up, Sedgan let go of the body he had briefly reclaimed and returned to the Dreamworld. Once back in the golden light, he shouted out Messenger's name.

The little woman appeared out of the mist a dozen moments later. The wolf was conspicuously absent.

"Are you ready?" she asked in that language that was not Esparan but still made perfect sense.

"No," Sedgan replied. "In fact, I don't want to go. I want to go back and help Marionna. That means helping Kitable and his brother. And I guess the king."

Messenger tilted her head, but she was smiling.

"You win a wager?" Sedgan asked.

"Something like that," she replied. "But if you do not wish to go to the Gate, why call me?"

"I don't know how to defeat Tamort. I don't believe in Inac now. I can't call down…" He trailed off, his eyes narrowing. Messenger was not Esparan. She did not appear to be a follower of Inac, and she was here, walking with souls in the Dreamworld. And Celebrant Calanor had faith in Totho to guide him. "Is this power, this place, from a god?"

"No," Messenger replied, her smile growing larger still. "No, this is the power we all possess in our souls. Our gods may help us focus it, but you do not require Inac for this, Sedgan."

"How can I stop Tamort?" he asked.

"Believe that you can," she said, shrugging again. "His soul is already detached, walking lost."

Around them, the Dreamworld changed to show the interior of Marionna's little cottage. Sedgan saw his body lying on the floor next to Tamort as Shimmer worked over him with magic, trying to save him. Suddenly, Kitable sat forward and stabbed Tamort's body. The man was dead instantly.

But Sedgan could see Tamort still, overlying Kitable's body. The soul was there, hiding in the wisavi.

He knew that it had been no dream but a memory. He assumed it was Marionna's, amplified with the power of the Dreamworld.

"So his body is dead," Sedgan realized as the scene faded back into the golden mist. "Can you guide his soul to the Gate?"

Messenger's smile lessened, then was lost. "He knows where the Gate is. All dead are drawn there. But he will not follow where I go," she said, like a child denied a playmate. Her eyes were bright when she looked up at Sedgan once more. "You will need powers of the Dreamworld to even wound him. But first, you must separate him from your ally."

"From Kitable? How?" Sedgan asked. "He is a soul."

"Even souls can be burned," Messenger replied. "But your time is passing, Sedgan. It will be too late if you wait. Tamort has Kitable's body and is approaching the Manor of Trulinar."

For a moment, the golden light of the Dreamworld coalesced into a healing waggon. Among the many cots lay a man Sedgan remembered all too well. He had become old and lay dying of disease, his skin already graying. He lacked the strength to do harm now. He would never beat another woman. He would never kill again.

Killing him would shorten his suffering. In his memory, Sedgan turned and walked away, leaving the man to his pain and death. He walked away from exacting revenge as he had intended, accepting that Inac's path was not always that of violence.

He had let that moment pass.

"How do I find my way to Kitable?" Sedgan asked.

Messenger beamed at him like a mother with a child taking their first step. "The same way you find anyone. You will it to be."

Sedgan closed his eyes. "Kitable," he said, "you will owe me one."

He focused on the wisavi and the cage of green light he had seen. He remembered the master wizard in detail. He told his mind that he needed to find that.

He felt the wind of the Dreamworld rush around him. When he next opened his eyes, Messenger was gone. He heard voices.

He recognized Tamort's voice. Peeking forward, he saw the same cage and clearing he had before. He was pretty sure Kitable spotted him. As he retreated, he sent one pleasant thought to Marionna's son.

There is hope.

He would bide his time until Tamort left, then aid Kitable. In the meantime, he had to get the others organized. Shimmer needed to know what was going on. The king had to be defended.

He closed his eyes again and willed himself to find Cole.

• • • • • • • • • • • • •

After the walls of Arcott, Kitable was taken back to child-hood, falling from a tower window and careening from ice to stone. He relived his days on the streets, hiding in terror of discovery. He was a thief, a murderer, and a fugitive. Hunger gnawed at him. The cold of the city threatened to eat his fingers and toes. Every day was fear and uncertainty.

When he rested, almost feeling safe, his muscles burned. Magic teased at the corners of his mind, always far enough out of reach to keep him helpless in face of his hunters. He slept, fearing he would not wake.

Before he could escape the cycle of pain and desperation, Kitable was brought to another memory, standing atop a riverside cliff surrounded by hostile Northlanders. Elder Tril and Ela set their magic against him, and Ela's thought magic scrambled his mind. Tril could see through his illusions, easily attacking through Kitable's defenses. He was defeated. The fear lasted an eternity.

Into that panic, another memory attacked him. King Tohmas' voice told Kitable that Shimmer Weaver had been stabbed and lay near death in a Healing waggon. His heart reeled, rage and guilt flooding over him. He was responsible. Her association with him would cost her her life, and it was his fault.

The thought of Shimmer brought Kitable a moment of clarity.

She wasn't dead. She had survived that. She was still out there.

Before his mind coalesced, Kitable was thrown back into memories. Tostig died, and a flurry of spells was released.

The inn exploded around Kitable, sealed by a spell even he did not recognize. His hovering spells were altered beyond recognition. He no longer knew the words to call for them, and without them, he would be immolated.

Next came the Full Reversal spell while defending HillTop during the Northlander war. Every hovering spell he wore was taken from him, turned around, and undone. The magic filled him. His body was scalded, and his mind was driven into the darkness by the magic spiral. His consciousness was dragged toward the light. He was unable to stop his speeding route to the cliff and oblivion.

Shimmer had saved him then, hiding him from his enemy when Seria had come to kill him. He had never thanked her for that.

Shimmer, he thought. Part of him reached out, seeking, needing to speak to her. He connected for an instant, catching a glimpse of her standing in a strange street, facing unsavory thugs dressed in maroon...

A hiss in his ear scattered the thought. He was brought to his duel with Master Clarin, faced with a spell he had later replicated: an expanding wall of destruction that would, in moments, destroy every element of his body. He sat on the floor, setting his Scry and alteration spells against Clarin's, but the magic bit into his foot...

Shimmer had been outside when he had left that vardo. No matter how much he had told her off, her curiosity brought her back. That beautiful mind...

In memory, Kitable lay beside her, a hand over her waist, pretending to be sleeping as Cole's Scry passed over them. The soft scent of her perfume eased the tension in his chest, and he felt, for a moment, euphoric.

A woman shrieked, and Kitable found himself suddenly back in the golden light of the Dreamworld, his cage gone.

The fire snake recoiled from him, screeching as it retreated to Tamort.

Focusing slowly, Kitable spotted another shape behind Tamort. Even at the distance, Sedgan's form had changed. The scars on his chest were no longer open burning rivers of lava but were sealed over like new scabs. His eyes glittered in gold, as did the celebrant's entire form. Sedgan's soul was smug, and Kitable had a strong suspicion he knew where the pleasant memory had come from.

But before Kitable could call out to the man, Sedgan backed up, disappearing into the gold mist. Instead, Kitable had to face Tamort, who was crimson in anger.

"How did you do that?" the celebrant shouted.

Kitable tested his movement. Nothing held him now. All the burns, lashes, and stitches he had endured both in the Dreamworld and in memory were gone.

"I doubt I did," Kitable answered.

He thought of Shimmer again. His memories of her clarified his mind through the chaos of Tamort's influence.

A focus, Kitable realized. All this time, he had thought a focus was the pinnacle of mental control of wizard magic, but it was the opposite; it was a manifestation of untouchable powers. That was why anyone with a focus couldn't be targeted with magic. Shimmer had been right.

He had tried for a lifetime to create one. In Shimmer, Kitable had a moment of innocent peace that no manipulation could twist. He knew her better than he knew himself. She was, to these casters, unreachable. And when untouchable magic meant untouchable, they were even.

"On second thought," Kitable said, taking a slow, deep breath, "maybe I did."

Tamort snarled. The snake of fire returned to his shoulder, twisting over his neck and limbs as the man paced. "Don't expect *her* to save you," Tamort grumbled. "She's abandoned you."

But the memory of the smell of her, his cheeks tickled by her hair and knowing he still did not want to move away, stayed with him. No rage remained.

"I do not believe that," Kitable said.

Tamort waved his arm, and the mist formed as before. Instead of looking through his own eyes, Kitable was looking through someone else's.

Shimmer walked along a dark hallway in her bright traveling clothes before the observer. She held Cole's hand as Kitable's brother told a funny story. Her laughter was light but genuine.

"See! Into the arms of another! She doesn't care," Tamort declared.

"She doesn't know," Kitable corrected. He wondered if he could reach her through the spell Tamort had made. Clearly, she had not heard Tamort's voice. She walked on with Cole, her steps balanced and smooth. She was always a moment away from dancing.

But Kitable could only watch helplessly as the person he was looking through approached. Glancing down, he saw that he held a knife.

Unseen by Cole or Shimmer, the person approached. When close enough, he lunged, the knife set to dig into her back.

Kitable's heart stopped in his chest. "Shimmer!" he shouted in warning, knowing it was useless. He felt something in him shift, like a part of his soul tripping.

Tamort gestured sharply. The Scry snapped away. The celebrant burst into crackling laughter.

"Wonderful!" he cried between breaths. "I could not have done it better! You! You dispelled her!"

Kitable's stomach sank. "Dispelled?"

Tamort bent double, roaring with laughter. "Perfect! Dispelled by the power of an untouchable! You reached her, and you dispelled her!"

The knife had been coming in from behind. She had not seen it and neither had Cole. Without her defenses, it could be her death.

"I think we'll wait," Tamort said, finally finding enough calm to speak coherently. His eyes glittered malevolently. "Then let's check again."

The moments crawled back, the silence of the Dreamworld mocking Kitable.

Shimmer found herself sitting on Cole's simple bed, the door closed and locked from the inside. Cole had excused himself, willing to wait outside for her privacy. She had scanned the room for magic and, unsurprisingly, found none. She had seen Cole's limited ability to cast wards when in his mother's home.

Once she was out of the public places, the full weight of the day's events settled on her. She trembled as she recalled the chill of the magic leaving her. It was worse than being naked before strangers. She had been defenseless.

But why? No one had gotten through her spells. There had been no dispel. She would have sensed that. No, only untouchable powers did that.

But no one had touched her. And she felt the passage of untouchable magic like a wave of greasy air. This had come all at once and only affected her. Cole hadn't noticed anything either, untouchable or wizard.

The whispered voice in her ear echoed again in memory, too hoarse to be recognized except as a distant, desperate whisper.

Wrapping her arms around her knees, Shimmer waited for her shaking to stop. She had so many questions and no one to ask.

She missed Kitable. Cole was sweet, but he did not know enough to prompt her. Precious few times in her life had she been alone. Bringing her mind back under control, Shimmer focused on casting. She could not sit here, pining for better days, and expect that to help. She *was* alone. If she didn't like it, she could Relocate back to Wayburn in a blink. Her father would be pleased to see her.

But that wasn't what a master wizard did. She was stronger than this.

One by one, Shimmer replaced her spells for the day. She cast the tethered cloud of spells again, ready for another untouchable attack. Should she be dispelled, at least the spells would remain in the area. It would no longer follow her after a dispel, but neither would it be lost.

The weight of the extensive casting left her worn out, like after a long hike, but she felt safe by the end. Her leg, while still needing support, had whinged when the magic dropped, but it was not bothering her now. The bruises were purple and yellow, and the ache had become familiar.

Untouchable powers had come to her in dreams, Shimmer thought. *Was I dreaming somehow?*

Cole met her once she was done, his wry smile eager. "Better?" he asked.

She tried to match the smile but lacked the energy. "Much," she said.

"Any idea what happened?" he asked.

"Untouchable powers," she replied. "No idea how, though."

Cole's face fell for a blink. "I thought you knew all the untouchables in Espar," he said.

Shimmer shrugged. "They are rare, and rarer still are those who can manifest the powers. I don't know, Cole, but that's what it felt like."

When she glanced up, Cole was grinning. "Need a place to think?" he suggested. "There's a cave in the deeper tunnels that is just..."

Shimmer cocked her head skeptically at him.

Cole raised his hands in defense. "Not like that!"

"It's a bit of a suspicious pickup line," Shimmer told him. "Does it work?"

"It's not—" Cole cut himself off sheepishly, momentarily dancing from foot to foot. "Well, yes, it has worked before, but it's the most beautiful place in StonePeak. I thought you'd like it. It's peaceful."

"Peaceful is not something I get often," Shimmer admitted, "largely my own doing. I've been picking fights."

But Kitable would have never allowed someone like Rancer to get away with their crime either. Somehow, even as she avoided him and everyone he associated himself with, Shimmer was still followed by her master.

Cole extended his hand, and Shimmer hesitantly accepted it. His genuine joy brought a smile to her lips despite herself. Although his hand wrapped over the force magic of the Moulded Shield she wore, he was not dissuaded.

"Maybe it will clear my head. Not too far, I hope," she warned. "My leg isn't all healed yet."

"Not too far," Cole replied. "Just far enough."

Cracking a mischievous grin, Cole pulled her from the main housing area and into the shadows.

They walked silently for a hundred paces along the mountain's paths. Soon, he led her off the lit roads. He still followed the markings on the walls, his free hand holding hers.

After a dozen intersections, Shimmer dismissed her Moulded Shield, and Cole's hand fell into hers. He had warm skin, but his palm was callused from constantly playing with his knives. It vastly differed from any courtiers who would take her hand to bow over it, seeking favor.

He stopped, startled by the sudden contact. After waiting in the darkness for a reaction, Cole cleared his throat as if to speak, but he managed only a confused sound. Shimmer sensed him shake his head, and he led her forward once more.

Was it that he reminded her of Kitable? His eyes were the same gray, his voice much like his brother's. His joy was similar, although it had been a long time since Kitable had shown happiness.

She thought that was her fault. Something had changed when she had come to be his apprentice. She'd worked hard to bring him out of his shell and, as she had once told her father, see him dance. There'd been joy for a bit, but of late, the more she tried to make him smile, the more sour he became. She had never understood why.

Light appeared ahead, a soft glow unlike any natural light Shimmer had seen before. It reminded her of a phoslight, alchemical in origin, but did not flash or flicker. The sound of dripping water reached her ear.

But as they reached the end of the tunnel, a voice shouted, and Shimmer again felt her magic tremble.

"Shimmer!"

Kitable's voice, so clearly him, hit her. As it left, all her hovering spells and active defenses were swept away.

She ducked, heeding the warning in his voice.

A blade cut across her back.

Memories cascaded over her. A stab from a supposed friend had once punctured her chest through that very place and flooded her lungs with blood. Death had come so close her father had been forced to beat it off with a large stick.

Her back stung, but this attack was shallow, barely enough to cut the skin. Her sudden move had dodged most of the blade.

"Shimmer?"

Cole's voice was tense but not panicked. All he knew was that she had abruptly shifted her weight. She felt him turn toward her, his outline haloed by the light they headed toward.

He could be seen.

Lunging up, Shimmer crashed into Cole, knocking him prone. As she fell, she activated a bracelet, filling the area with a blinding light. Knowing it was coming, Shimmer squeezed her eyes shut.

Once she landed, Shimmer rolled off Cole and grabbed the bead in her hair once more, reactivating her two most vital spells. The moment she opened her eyes, a knife struck at her face, deflected by the Moulded Shield she had replaced. Although the blade did not cut through the spell, the force hit like a punch. It was followed by the weight of someone landing atop her. She had not even managed to get to her feet.

Shimmer's head knocked into the stone behind her, the impact blunted but not by much. She briefly saw stars.

But the weight atop her stirred an instinctual reaction. She struck with her fist, then grabbed and pulled while bringing up her knee to throw the person off her. The Moulded Shield encircling her fist made the impact all the more brutal.

Her back flared in pain, but she ignored it, rolling into a crouch. She choked out an activation word, realized the spell was gone, and reached for her bag, which had stayed with her throughout the tumbling. Before the assailant could gain his feet, she had retrieved a phoslight from her bag and broken it open to the air. She kept it away from her face to avoid burning her eyes.

The attacker wore maroon cloth. A mask prevented her from recognizing him, but it was one of Rancer's men.

The moment the light hit him, he shielded his eyes. He flicked another knife into his hand and threw it. Sensing no magic on it, Shimmer held her ground and let it bounce off her shield.

Remembering she had a cloud of spells following her, Shimmer shouted an activation word and pointed damningly.

The conjured stone launched itself at the attacker, although the narrow space of the corridor made it miss. It crashed against the tunnel's walls, shattering and lashing out at the man with rubble.

What was visible of the man's face blanched. Without another blink, he returned the way he had come and fled at a sprint.

The phoslight had another ten flickers left in it, but it was long enough for Shimmer to seek out Cole. She spotted him lying on the ground where she had knocked him.

Throwing the phoslight down the tunnel in anticipation of others, Shimmer grabbed Cole's collar and dragged him into the cave they had been heading to. There she checked him over.

The cavern was lit by a blue-green glow emanating from the plants along the damp walls. Lichens had taken up phosphorescence and glittered with every drip of water that flowed over them. A small pool had formed at the center of the cave, each drop that struck its surface making the waters glisten in light. It was surprisingly warm.

She had a moment to admire the beautiful place before pushing it from her mind and reciting the code for a light. Using the familiar yellow glow of fake fire, she checked Cole over.

He had cracked his head, and a knife had cut across his left forearm through his shirt sleeve. She checked him for poison with another hastily recited spell and found none. Belatedly, she realized she was at the same risk and repeated the spell on herself. But the attacker had expected the knife to do the work, not requiring poison, and she found none.

Leaving the light hovering over her, Shimmer rummaged in her bag until she found pain pills, stimulants to help Cole regain consciousness, and braun salts to stop any swelling in his head. She debated something to stop bleeding, but the wound on his skull had almost stopped oozing, and she could find no fracture, so she settled for a bandage. She then placed a second one, coated with poultice, on his wounded arm.

Cole stirred as she finished the second bandage.

He said little but took water when she told him to and listened to her explanations. His posture went tight when she revealed the person who had attacked them had dressed like a cadre member.

"Not that anyone couldn't dress like that," she concluded.

"Worth a few questions," Cole said, a hand on his wounded arm. "The cadres know better than to attack each other. If Rancer's man hit me, it'll be war." He tested the movement in his hand. As she had expected, he moved well but winced. The tendons were fine. The muscles had been wounded and would hurt.

"Agreed," Shimmer said, "but it may have to wait."

She was relieved that when Cole glanced at her, his face was dark with guilt. He had led her here, putting her at risk. But the only reason he would feel guilty was if he, at the least, had not known about the danger. She had feared a trap and now was certain there had been none.

"Wait for what?" he asked.

"I believe Kitable is in trouble," Shimmer said.

Cole brought his hand to his face and winced again. "My head is a bit jumbled," he admitted, "but ... why do you think that? What'd I miss?"

Coming forward, Shimmer peered at his eyes, bringing the light down to better check him for concussion. He made to bat aside the light, but she slapped his hand, and he tolerated her investigations.

"Because before the first knife struck, I heard his voice."

Unsatisfied with his mental state, Shimmer handed him another braun salt for his head, then another drink of water. He took it all without question, then leaned back.

She waited as her words gained meaning for him. He sat up straighter. "You're dispelled," he realized.

"Which is why I'm worried about Kitable. His voice dispelled me."

Thoughts came slowly through Cole's hazy mind. "Why would he do that?"

Shimmer shook her head. She knew Kitable. "He was trying to warn me."

Cole took a short, exasperated breath and leaned against the wet cave wall. Doing so put pressure on his wound, and he pulled away. One hand went to his head, where he discovered her bandage. "I'm lost again." He gingerly explored the bandage and his head wound. "Warned you by dispelling you?"

"Warned me from the Dreamworld," Shimmer said.

Cole stared at her, blinking for a few moments more. "No wonder you think he's in trouble," he said.

"You able to stand?" she asked. "Travel?"

Cole nodded but then took a moment to refocus. "Kind of. Where are we going?"

Shimmer put a shoulder under his arm and helped him up. "You are going home. I'm going to go to Kitable."

Cole steadied himself against the wall, squinting at her in disbelief. "You can define him?" he asked. "Anchor him?"

She had never admitted it to herself or Kitable, but she could. It was a wizard's greatest defense to be undefinable. Kitable's outer appearance varied, as did his belongings and attire. He wore illusions in public, even conjuring false scars or the appearance of consistencies designed to confound any anchor.

But she knew him.

"Yes," Shimmer realized. "I can find him. Maybe not bind him, though. He'll be protected. But..."

Before she could begin to cast the Relocation spell to take them to Marionna's, she felt magic burst around her. Cole winced, having also detected the spell.

Having no trinket to bring Spell Sight to bear, she started reciting the code for it. She paused when she heard a voice say, "Don't bother. It's a Seal."

Backed by the last dying light of the phoslight down the tunnel, Black stepped into the cavern.

Cole squinted, staring at the man as if unable to recognize him. "Wha—?"

Black activated another spell. Shimmer felt her heart sink.

"It's a pity you didn't attach yourself to Cole, Shimmer," Black said. He lifted a hand, tossing the spell at her. With only her Moulded Shield and an Anchor Block active, the spell wrapped her in force magic, pinning her hands at her sides. "We're too close to let you go now."

Behind Black came two others, one of which Shimmer recognized as the earlier assailant. He wore the crimson wraps but was too at ease to be anything other than Black's man.

Kitable was not the only person in danger, Shimmer realized. Now she was dispelled, facing another master wizard, with Cole too concussed to help.

She had shared multiple hopeless situations with Kitable, but this one seemed likely to be her last.

s Black entered the glowing cavern, all Cole could think about was his head.

He was seeing a haze. He believed Kitable was in trouble—Shimmer had said that, and he trusted her—but now Black was here and was stopping them. He had heard the spells. He knew it was a Seal. She couldn't Relocate without dispelling it.

He couldn't Relocate at all. That was beyond him.

Why is Black involved? Where is Kitable?

His thoughts could not settle, tossed by the throbbing in his head, but he recognized that he was holding the lucky rabbit's foot in his hand. Black had given it to him years ago, a promise of allegiance. He had made himself useful. He had been rewarded.

Shimmer was dispelled and bound with rope, and Cole could not decide whether to object. She tolerated it; he presumed to buy time until she could act.

She wouldn't stay bound, would she?

Cole came to his feet with effort, his hand still on the rabbit's foot. Shimmer, in a soft buzz, was casting from within the confines of the spell holding her. He recognized the musical sounds: a Relocation.

A Seal trapped her. No Relocation could get through that. But if he could get her outside the Seal...

Black advanced, a hunter ready to examine his trophy kill. He did not seem to hear her whispers.

Cole stepped between them.

"What by the hells is going on, Black?" he demanded, trying to make his voice sound stronger than it was. "One of your goons either has bad aim or *really* bad aim, depending on what he *was* trying to hit!" He held up his arm to draw attention to his wounded arm and away from Shimmer.

"Collateral damage," Black replied. "You'll be fine, boy. She's the prize!"

Black nudged past Cole, and Cole let him, knowing he was too unstable to stop the man physically. But his mind was clearing, probably thanks to the pills Shimmer had given him. As an advantage, Black had his back to Cole now.

But Cole knew Black wore enchanted items. He had no spells that could get through those constant defenses.

He looked down at the rabbit's foot, bound to one Black carried at all times for communication. He could target the trinket. Without doing anything, Cole had a binding already in place that connected them.

"You didn't have to hurt her," Cole objected, keeping his voice light. He had seen Shimmer cast while carrying a conversation, but he doubted his ability to do that. He had to focus, and doing that through a headache was hard enough.

Shimmer glared up at them, her green eyes glimmering in her magic light. She had either finished or paused her spell, for she had stopped casting. Cole could hear the magic nearby turning over with bouncing notes, not building but not ending either.

Black bent low, grinning in a manner even Cole had never seen.

Although Black's main enterprises were smuggling coliron and coercion, Cole knew his patron had diverse holdings in StonePeak. Cole had been a messenger, assassin, and bodyguard. He had helped merchants leave the city unnoticed, their waggons stuffed with slaves for the market. That smile was the same one Cole had seen a slave trader give one of his beautiful charges.

But instead of cowering, Shimmer fumed. Had she been a hound, Cole knew she would be raising her hackles and baring her teeth.

"You've been eyeing her since she appeared, my boy," Black smugly said. "I've made her available. Do me proud, and I'll let you have her."

Cole swallowed hard, a stone forming in his chest. He wasn't sure who terrified him more: Black or Shimmer.

He mumbled the first words he needed for his spell, then stopped and choked out, "That's a prize I'm willing to work for." Speaking the words made him nauseous.

Black snorted and rose. Cole struggled to keep the spell half formed in his mind.

"Good lad," Black said, clapping him on his shoulder and making his head swim. When he regained his balance, Cole was surprised to find his spell still waiting.

He whispered the following few words, drawing in power as Black boasted, "Drag her out to my house. I've got a special place for people like her."

Black looked back at him, and Cole stopped his spell.

"So, can I have her?" he asked, not recognizing his own voice.

"For a while," Black agreed, turning back to the tunnel and the other cadre members. Cole finished his spell, holding the last word in readiness. "But she's not one you leave alive, Cole. Too dangerous this one. Little viper."

Cole bent down, lifting Shimmer to her feet. Her hands remained bound at her sides, but the spell swung around her. She was ready to Relocate if only she could get through the Seal.

Seals stopped magic, not people.

He wasn't sure why she didn't fight him as he hooked her over a shoulder into a deadman's carry, but she didn't. She even seemed to jump a bit to make it easier. She said nothing, something that struck Cole as decidedly uncharacteristic. Did she know he was lying to Black? And if she knew, did Black know?

Taking a deep breath and bracing himself, Cole said the last word of his spell, dug his heels in, and took off at a sprint.

His spells chimed, bypassing all of Black's defenses by using the binding between the rabbit foot trinkets. A burst of fire took hold in Black's pocket. The cadre leader yelped and flailed to extinguish it. The attention of the other cadre members turned to the sound and light.

Between them, Cole bolted at top speed, Shimmer slung over his shoulder. He traversed the dozen paces needed to get clear of the Seal before the cadre and the master wizard could put out the flames and follow Cole's sudden departure.

When Black figured out what he had done, Cole would end up dead without a doubt. But he knew Shimmer would be able to Relocate to somewhere safe, even if he could not. It terrified him, but it was the right thing to do.

"Cole!" Black's cry followed him, and Cole winced, not hearing magic approaching but expecting it soon.

The twittering sound of the Seal passed over them.

Before any more magic could catch them, Shimmer completed her spell and, with Cole, Relocated away.

The two of them landed on a mattress in a cluttered room.

* * *

When Tamort did not immediately bring Kitable back to the tunnel where Shimmer had been attacked, Kitable's spirits lifted.

"You missed her," he told Tamort's soul. "Dispelled and all, and you *missed* her!"

Tamort puffed himself up indignantly. "She's dead soon enough," he said. "She's offended Black of StonePeak." He smirked victoriously at Kitable's confusion. "You wouldn't know him. Not your kind of person."

Kitable went back through his memories, trying to remember anyone called "Black." He had recognized the tunnels of StonePeak, a place he had once known well. But in his apprenticeship, he had been kept far from the affairs of thieves.

The golden mist drifted into the clearing Tamort had summoned once more, and Kitable thought, for a moment, he saw the tower of Master Sylas in its shadows, answering his memories.

"Black's a master wizard," Tamort interrupted, and the golden light drifted back, allowing the Temple waggon circle to take over again. "Easily a match for your little sprite."

Memories of Shimmer lying on the floor of a Healing waggon during the Northlander War struck Kitable. She had been pale then, close to death. A knife had pierced her lungs. The healers had saved her, but it had been cycles before she had danced again.

Anger flooded over him once more. His thoughts were scattered.

He had seen her dance again. In dancing, she was unsurpassed. The memory snapped out of existence, and the pain of loss lifted. Kitable was immediately face-to-face with Tamort once again.

The celebrant's expression was pure fury. "Stop that!" he cried. The anger had been created, imposed on him to distract him. Shimmer's memory had chased it out once more.

Calm certainty was Kitable's now. "We call it a focus," Kitable told Tamort. "It defines and protects thoughts. You've been playing through my memories and manipulating my emotions, intensifying them. Now you can't."

"Little good it will do you," Tamort replied. "We have reached the Manor of Trulinar. You and Carsh will die. Tohmas' empire will crumble! I will tear it down in her name!"

"We'll see," Kitable said.

Squaring his shoulders, Kitable turned away. The vast expanse of the Dreamworld spread before him. He did not know where he was going, but he was no longer forced to remain where he was. Somewhere else may have new opportunities.

"Get back here!" Tamort cried, a slight twist of panic sneaking into his voice.

"No," Kitable replied. "No, you cannot hold me now."

In a step, he left the campfire circle and the celebrant's voice behind. He kept his memories of Shimmer in his mind to defend against the celebrant and his thought magic.

Tamort did not follow, but the fire snake did. When it approached, Kitable thought of Shimmer, and the snake recoiled away. Kitable put his back to it, trying to leave it behind.

He tried to envision the blankness of the familiar void. He wanted the great black, the gap by the spiral, and the light that cast no shadows. He needed the perfect silence of his magic, not the ongoing chaos of dreams. In that place, he was the master. He could find his way home from there.

Despite his best efforts, the world did not change, except from dream to dream. He had no control over the golden mist.

The dreams went from stone homes to wooden huts, well-worn paths to absolute wilderness, and vast libraries to sea caves. He searched, never sure what he was looking for but knowing it was out there. He kept Shimmer in his mind through it all, and the snake followed him.

He sought through all the visions for the edge of the golden light and the blackness where he would find the magic spiral, but the golden mist never ended.

He walked on.

Marionna sat beside Sedgan's body as the acolytes moistened the man's lips again. She could already see the hue of the skin changing. Another acolyte had run for StonePeak to bring Shimmer or a healer back, but she feared they would be too late to save the man. Nothing she did roused him.

She wept for him.

Benn placed a hand on her shoulder, and she leaned into it. "What else can I do?" she asked.

The acolyte knelt beside her, holding her tear-covered face in the cup of his hand. "There are things beyond us all," he said. "But we are acolytes. Pray with us," he offered.

Despite her reservations, Marionna nodded and joined the boys in the prayer to Inac.

In her heart, Marionna doubted the prayers would be heard. And even if they were, how would she know if Inac was interested in the celebrant who had forsaken her?

When the prayer ended, she started it anew. Even if it was fruitless, it was the only thing she could do.

18

Once in the Manor of Trulinar, having anchored a familiar spot, it took Shimmer a handful of words to get out of the spells Black had tied her with. She tested her leg, pleased that the splint still stabilized it despite the lack of other force magic. By the time she was ready to get up, Cole still had not moved from where they had landed on the mattress.

Tossing her head, Shimmer rose, and Cole followed. When she smiled at him, he shrugged. "A Two-Person Relocation? Didn't realize you'd been casting that."

"It's excessively complicated," she warned. "But I had a good teacher." She offered him a hand to his feet.

"What is this place?" Cole asked, warily accepting her help. His eyes were clear as he stood, the concussion fading.

Kitable's room was filled with books and trinkets. The fireplace was cold but had wood stacked on hand and the kettle still hung. One of the spell codes she had been working on was still on the table, and Kitable's teacup had grown a strong-smelling mold. The room was lit already, like the rest of the manor he had built for King Tohmas, responding to the presence of someone. The enchanting blue light was never too bright and would dim for sleep. For some reason, it had to be blue.

"The wisavi's room," Shimmer replied. She thought to explain how the master wizard had a unique pattern engraved under the mattress to act as an anchor, but he had shared that secret with only Shimmer. Her Relocation spell also had been built around the other defenses of the room, making it likely anyone attempting to follow would end up dead. She did not want Cole to try it.

"You have access to his room?" Cole asked, taking a long look around the lit chamber.

"I was his apprentice, remember?" she replied, putting her bag by the table. "Now sit down," she prompted. "I need to recheck your head. The braun salts are wearing off."

Cole pointed at her instead. "You've got blood on you."

Shimmer checked herself, hiking up her skirt to inspect her splinted leg, but found nothing.

"Your back," Cole said.

"Demons," Shimmer said. "I'd forgotten. You'll have to check it."

Cole's face went crimson.

"Knock it off," she said. "Kit has defenses all over this place. I doubt Black will be able to find us for a while, but we can't spend all day in here. If Kitable's in the Dreamworld, then he's in trouble. I need to find him." She removed her vest. Her blouse had a drawstring, allowing it to be adjusted off her shoulders, a favorite trick of hers for dancing. "To do that, I must leave this room and its defenses. It would be best if you were undefinable in short order. I don't think I need stitches, but having you look is easier than a Scry right now. I'll need my energy for casting my hovering spells for the *third* time today."

She turned around and dropped her blouse from her shoulders to expose her back.

Cole stepped forward but still kept a distance. "Scratch only. It... It's stopped bleeding now. You want a bandage?" he asked.

"Not worth it," she said. "Just put this on it," she directed, pulling a vial from her bag. "Treo oil. It'll keep it clean. I'll grab a new shirt. You'll have to change too. Scratch across any tattoo you have. Make a scar bigger, fresh. Don't keep anything you had on you before arriving here. It'll get us a little reprieve." As she spoke, Shimmer checked Cole's wounded head, then his eyes. She had not done up her vest but pulled the blouse back into place. "You seem to have your wits about you. The braun salts did their duty."

She pointed to a large armoire beside the mattress. "Kit's clothes are in there." She crossed the room into the side room where her cot and chest were. She retrieved a new shirt and hastily swapped it out. Thankfully, the scratch didn't hurt much, and the treo oil soothed the dull burning sensation. Ironically, even if Black had known about the scar between her shoulder blades, the scratch had distorted that unique feature.

Giving Cole time, she traded her used hair beads for new ones out of the chest. She debated a few other items but didn't want anything that would be active inherently, as that would be open for dispel should another untouchable power reach her. She then sat down and Scryed.

Her Scry failed, and the knot in her stomach tightened.

Kitable was a powerful wizard. He could shield himself to a great extent, but she knew him and his defenses intimately. She should have been able to find him or at least

identify where the defenses had blocked the spell. He could stop her from anchoring him, but he should not have been able to avoid detection.

Only an untouchable would be invisible to magic.

Her hands shook when she tried to guide herself through another casting set. Giving up when she felt the magic slipping through her mind instead of settling for use, Shimmer located a rejuv pill from her bag and swallowed it. The herbal mix was her father's design and highly effective at staving off enervation. A Rejuvenation spell may have given her enough energy to run back to StonePeak by noon, but it would knock her out for a day afterward, and she was not confident things would be resolved by then. The pill version would last a few candles but did not have the same side effects as the magic version.

While she waited for the pill to take effect, Shimmer cast the force spell around her leg once more, ready should she have to move quickly. Soon enough, the herbs took effect: her stomach warmed, her head cleared, and her fatigue lifted.

But she still did not know what to cast. Untouchable powers had reached out to her, so the tethered set made sense, but Black had shown his intentions now. He was a caster with defenses she would have to work around.

Which threat was more significant?

Her feeling of urgency rose. Kitable was in trouble. She would have to do both.

Settling back down, Shimmer cast a mix of hovering spells. She reduced her tethered package of spells to a handful, knowing that a drawn-out confrontation would be deadly, so she went for quick and powerful. She focused on the spells that would defend her against a wizard, then tied them to a separate rope in case she met an untouchable and then had to duel, and hoped she wouldn't have to move around much.

She paused there, breathing slowly. While she had tried to cover the most dangerous series of events, she had weakened herself should the wizard come at her first. But she was at a loss. What else could she do?

Confident she'd given Cole sufficient time, Shimmer headed back into the main room.

The robe was too large for him, but the shoes fit. He looked like a child dressing up for the summer festival, except for the fresh wound on his face where he had altered his scar.

"I was scared to touch anything else," Cole said when Shimmer approached. "This place sounds like a full choir and orchestra. But I'm pleased to say my head doesn't hurt as much."

She scanned the room, suddenly recognizing how odd the place was to an outsider. The shelves were stacked with assorted and unusual magic items, mostly Kitable's but some from other sources. Bookcases lined four out of five walls. The floor was no longer level, the table was scratched and dented spectacularly, and she still did not know what the two green lines on the ceiling were from.

"You still think Kitable's in trouble?" Cole asked, not following her as she went to the shelves to pick out trinkets that might be useful. Most would be useless against an untouchable, but at least if Black came in to join the party, she'd have a surprise for him.

"I tried to locate him," she said, "and I couldn't."

"He's no doubt defended," Cole argued.

Shimmer threw four wands into her bag, then, a thought occurring to her, pulled a piece of chalk from her bag, picked up another wand, and labeled it. "I'm not anchoring him," she explained. "I'm defining him. Right now, according to magic, he does not exist."

While she finished writing on the wand, Shimmer headed over to where Cole stood by the armoire. "I can't figure out why," she finished.

"I can help," a voice said.

The wand she had in hand contained a penetrating destruction spell. Shimmer brandished it as she spun to face the male voice that had joined them.

The specter of Sedgan looked like a younger, fitter version of the man but partially transparent. He glittered in golden light, his eyes solid orbs of gold that stared unblinkingly. He did not stand but hovered without tension in any muscle, not even to form an expression on his face. His robes had lost their holy symbols, although the golden light was broken by the two long waving scars on his chest that had once been the sign of Inac.

"Sedgan?" she snapped, cutting off her activation word for the wand and lowering the trinket instead. She blinked a few more times. "Or an illusion?"

"I cannot focus on this for long," the celebrant said, "but I dared not dispel you by speaking to you directly."

"I appreciate that," Shimmer admitted. "You're in the Dreamworld, I assume."

"My soul is. My mind... Well, it is still insane, and so is sleeping."

"If..." Cole cleared his throat, pausing to form the thought. "If he's untouchable, did he dispel the wards on this room?"

Shimmer activated Spell Sight and spun in place, assessing the familiar lights and patterns of the wards she had lived under for two years.

There was a hole in the magic under Sedgan. "You touched the floor," she said. "Yep, dispelled." She scanned it further. "Huh, Kitable made it so it would be maintained everywhere else... Impressive."

Cole winced. "Does that mean Black can find us?"

"Probably," Shimmer admitted. She finished writing the instructions on the wand and handed it to Cole. She then selected another from her bag and labeled it for his use. It was surprisingly hard to find room on the wand for useless chalk markings through the runes that she knew better than to disrupt.

"We've not got much time," he said.

"Sedgan," Shimmer said, not looking up from her work on the wand, "neither of us apparently have time. If you got something to say, say it."

Without a hint of the irritation that Shimmer would have expected the celebrant to have, Sedgan's soul replied, "Tamort is in control of Kitable's body. They are approaching the west gates to the Manor of Trulinar, intending to kill Carsh for his role in Loni's demise."

Shimmer cocked her head. "Not killing King Tohmas?" she asked.

Sedgan shrugged, his action again slow, as if tired. "Once Carsh is dead by Kitable's hand, the king's support is dissolved. Whether Tamort kills Kitable or uses him for further destruction is unknown. Either way, the king's madness will become plain, and his kingdom will fall. That is far better by way of revenge."

After completing the second wand, Shimmer handed it to Cole. "Not sure what use conjuring up that much water will do, but okay," he said absently after reading the text.

"We have to stop him," Shimmer said, ignoring Cole's comment.

"Sure," Cole commented dryly, finding another pocket to put the wand in. "But how exactly do you kill a soul?"

Shimmer looked at Sedgan for the reply. She dreaded his following words, but they had to be said. "Kill the body?" she guessed. She labeled another wand for Cole, burying the anxiety she had caused by suggesting killing Kitable.

Sedgan's soul eased its head to one side, cocking it in curiosity like Shimmer. "Killing Kitable will not help us," Sedgan said.

"Oh, thank—"

"Don't say 'gods,'" Cole interrupted.

Shimmer cut short a smile. "Fair point. I wasn't sure I could kill him, to be honest."

"I believe I will be able to remove Tamort from Kitable's body," Sedgan offered. "It will then take a visible form. Tamort's soul will have to be distracted when I try."

"What good is that?" Cole replied. He drew a knife, eyeing the spirit before them. "Pretty sure my knife won't do anything against you or him."

"Of course not," Sedgan replied. "But there is a blade that may."

"SoulBurner?" Shimmer said, her voice sharper than she had intended. She offered Cole another wand, but he did not seem to notice.

"The king's sword?!" Cole was even less restrained; he shouted the exclamation. Shimmer felt him check with her, his eyes wide. "I'm a half-decent thief," he said, "but I do *not* have enough time to organize something of *that* caliber."

"Don't have to," Shimmer said, her mind turning over. "I can ask for it."

"Ask?" Cole exclaimed, reminding Shimmer again that he was in over his head. She missed Kitable's calm.

Enough of missing him, she thought. *I am going to get him back.*

"If we can kill Tamort's soul with SoulBurner, he dies?" she asked Sedgan, figuring she would explain details to Cole later.

"We believe so," Sedgan replied.

"We?" Shimmer asked.

"I am not the only wandering soul in here, Shimmer," Sedgan replied. "Kitable and Tamort will be at the manor shortly. It would be best to keep this outside."

"You sure you can kick him out? Give me Kitable back?"

"I believe so. If his attention is in this world, not in the Dreamworld where I will confront him, it should work."

Finally, Cole took the third offered wand. Shimmer let her sack drop over her shoulder. "Then let's go. Anything else?"

The soul of Sedgan squinted in thought. "Nothing I can think of, but then, I did leave my mind behind."

"A fine excuse," Cole grated. "Hey! Wait up!"

Deactivating the wards on the door, Shimmer was already on her way into the corridor, by habit skipping to spare her injured leg. Black would not be far behind them, although Cole had made himself considerably less definable since they had arrived in the manor. But if Kitable reached the Manor of Trulinar's gate, he would bring the battle into contact with other innocents, which hindered Shimmer and favored Tamort.

She had to stop him before he reached the Manor of Trulinar.

As they left the wisavi's room, Cole threw his rabbit's foot down the corridor in the opposite direction. Shimmer raised an eyebrow at him. Fearing he had insufficient time to explain, he said, "It's definable."

She resumed her run, quickly darting up a set of stairs. Sedgan had vanished.

Cole was shocked to find the rooms they passed through were made of smooth wizard-stone, although the floors were textured to help avoid falls. Thinking back, he recognized the room had been wizard-stone too. He had failed to notice it because of the many bookcases hiding the walls. But the presence of the magically constructed stone explained why the chime of magic was audible in every direction.

A light had appeared around them in pale blue, lighting their way without torches or lamps. He glanced back, seeing a dark spot in the blue light behind them, and assumed it was Sedgan. As a specter, the man was a draw on the Dreamworld, and that would block wizard magic.

Shimmer stopped at the top of the stairs, hopping on her good leg. Two soldiers dressed in green tabards with a silver tree crest on their chest were on guard around the next open doorway. Neither tensed as Shimmer arrived, clearly recognizing her.

"Protector!" she said, pausing. "Where is the king?"

"Main hall, Shimmer," the protector replied. "Kingsman Sol is visiting."

"Thanks!" she called, turning around and taking off through a series of short rooms arranged end to end. The furnishings were Lourite in origin, made of iron and accented with precious metals, but Shimmer passed through too fast for Cole to get a chance to see more.

"How do they know where he is?" Cole called forward, worried that magic communications could be cut if Tamort managed to infiltrate. Would it be worth warning them?

"I have never figured that out," Shimmer replied, not pausing. Having left the wing of the wisavi, Cole and Shimmer were now weaving between other denizens of the manor. More than one protector paid clear attention to her, but none moved to intervene. "It's not magic if that is what you are thinking."

Cole ducked under a platter of bread and dodged a courtier. The protectors turned toward him.

"He's with me!" Shimmer shouted at the next doorway. The protectors cleared the entrance, letting her through. She slipped on the turn but recovered immediately. He was impressed by the pressure she was putting on her bad leg but had to remind himself that she had always put force magic around it.

Breathless, they arrived at a huge black wood door. A layer of wizard-stone made the pattern of the silver tree across its front, each leaf ornamentally depicted down to the veins.

Four protectors stepped into Shimmer's path.

"It's urgent," she told them, flipping a leather token to one of the men. The protector lifted the token to the eye slits of his helmet.

"Wisavi's," he said. He backed out of the doorway, clearing the way for them. The others followed him.

"And Cole's with me," Shimmer added, ducking between the armored bodyguards.

Cole tried to stay calm as he passed within reaching distance of four of the best warriors in Espar.

While it was not barred at the time, Cole noted the door was set to be sealed if required. He felt the magic of it pass around him and hoped Sedgan would not follow them here. The king seemed prepared to repel an invasion if needed, and dispelling it would probably not be helpful.

Cole could not figure out who he was protecting himself against. The Manor of Trulinar had been built this year as a retreat for the royal couple. The closest village was half a day away and was a tiny hamlet barely able to sustain itself. Cole had not even known the manor was ready yet.

The hall went quiet as Shimmer slowed her run to a brisk walk.

The king was indeed in conference with a kingsman. The two had set their seats at a table, where a pair of swords held down a large map. Tokens were stacked around the map, similar to that which Shimmer had used to identify herself to the protectors outside.

The king was dressed in his green tabard, like a protector, but wore a silver rank braid on his right arm and a silver circlet over his brow. The man he was speaking to had worn his province's colors of red and blue and the black rank braid of a kingsman. He was older, like Black, while the king was maybe a few years Cole's senior. The sight of the man, his beard short and young, made Cole feel guilty about his lack of accomplishments to date. This man was running the world.

Behind the pair of leaders, a lithe Rydan paced, recognizable by his tall frame, slicked-back hair, and grass bracelets. He had two blades out and was fiddling with them like a juggler. His movement was like the hunters Cole had met in StonePeak selling skins of mountain cats and bears. His green eyes narrowed first on Shimmer, then on Cole. One blade was briefly sheathed but soon returned to its owner's grip. Since the Rydan had no sleeve, he'd tied his rank rope around the arm hole of his vest, which was in turn draped by a pair of baldrics filled with knives. It was the green rope of a protector, but with a black thread in it to denote that the man was none other than Prime Protector Carsh.

The queen, a slight woman dwarfed by everyone in the room except Shimmer, lowered herself from the stool where she had been watching the conversation between the king and kingsman. She had tiny white flowers wrapped in her golden braid and wore a pure, simple green dress.

"Sorry to interrupt," Shimmer said.

"You are always welcome, Shimmer," the queen said, her voice soft as suede. Her voice seemed deceptive to Cole. She sounded sweet, but Cole thought the woman was likely tougher than her husband.

Shimmer gave a quick smile and bow. Cole echoed the gesture a beat later, feeling forgotten.

"Can I borrow SoulBurner?" Shimmer asked.

Cole had not been sure what to expect from the question. Incredulousness had seemed most likely. Suspicion had been the next. Affront had been third. Whatever the reaction, they would need a lot of explanations to convince the king to part with the goddess-gifted sword that represented his kingship.

But the king merely lifted an eyebrow at Shimmer as he released the sword knot on his belt with the ease of having performed the gesture a thousand times. He soon held the sheathed blade in hand. "If you need it," he said, offering the sword.

When Shimmer first gestured to him, Cole failed to translate it—he was too stunned by the complete trust of the man surrounded by guards, enchanted walls, and reinforced doors. But Shimmer repeated the gesture, and Cole realized she was asking him to take the sword.

It made sense. Shimmer risked being dispelled by handling the untouchable weapon. Cole, having no hovering spells left, would be unaffected unless he chose to cast.

Shaking, Cole inched forward. The king's eyes were mischievous, like the man might pull away in jest, but he allowed Cole to wrap his hands around the embossed sheath of silver and emerald.

Cole retreated to Shimmer's side, mutely holding the sword in front of himself. It didn't feel special. He could not hear any magic. The handle and sheath were heavy and cold.

Cole jumped when the king spoke. "You need help with something?" he asked.

Shimmer checked the surroundings, pensive. Her gaze paused on the Rydan. "No," she said. "As much as I'd like Carsh's help, I need him here in case I fail."

The king nodded and leaned back over his map.

The queen came forward in the pause. "What are you expecting?"

Shimmer had to take a steadying breath before speaking. "Kitable's body has been possessed," she said, her voice breaking. "We're going to stop it, but if I fail..."

She looked back at the door and the four protectors on duty.

"Kitable doesn't have tokens on him," she said, speaking to the king, then the queen in turn. She avoided looking at the Rydan again. "If he doesn't have one, it's not Kitable. Do what you have to. He's here to destroy the kingdom."

"Have a good time," the king said.

Cole knew the king was renowned for his unflappable confidence, but that seemed excessive. Kitable had been willing to die to protect the king. How could he risk his life for someone who cared so little for his well-being!?

But the queen frowned, her eyes on her husband, and Cole had the distinct sense he was missing something.

Something to do with how SoulBurner is driving the king mad? he wondered.

"Be safe," the queen said so sincerely Cole's heart skipped.

Shimmer nodded, pivoted, and took off once more. Cole took a final assessment of the main hall, the likes of which he had never seen before and would never again, and followed her. In his hand, he held the enchanted sword of the king.

They made their way out of the manor at the same run and were soon in the countryside.

Shimmer passed through the gate using a token of Kitable's again, Cole on her tail with the king's blade wrapped in his coat. She warned the soldiers there not to admit Kitable himself without a token, although she doubted they would have the gall to stop the wisavi if he objected strongly enough. He had, after all, built the Manor of Trulinar itself. She was surprised that the protectors appeared to miss that Cole carried SoulBurner, but it was a welcome oversight.

Outside the manor, the sun beat down, offset by the clouds in passing. Sedgan's voice came from her right. "I can't find him."

Shimmer slowed her sprint. "What do you mean you can't find him?" Shimmer asked. She couldn't see Sedgan yet, but he had to be nearby.

The specter appeared, hard to make out in the light of the day, but the glow of gold was still present around him in a faint haze.

"I can't find Kitable," the ghost said.

"I thought he was ahead on the road," Cole said, his eyes flickering up the road. They had turned a bend, and the manor was no longer visible behind them, lost in the trees. The smoke from it was still tracing lines over the clouds above. The road was a dirt path, wide enough to allow for a waggon. With the manor's remote location, no one was expected on the road except Tamort.

"Not the body," Sedgan corrected. "I can't find his mind or soul. They left."

The bottom dropped out of Shimmer's stomach. "Left? Meaning what?" She wanted to put words to her greatest fear, but her voice failed her. The possibility was too painful.

"Maybe dead," Sedgan said, making Shimmer want to strike him. This was the life of Wisavi Kitable, the Master Wizard of Espar and her mentor. Most importantly, it was her friend. Even if Sedgan did not care, Kitable's death should not be considered so causally. He added, "Maybe not," in the same monotone.

"If not dead, then what?" she asked, glancing ahead. She had to keep Tamort away from the manor. If he could see the towers, he may be able to Relocate to it or even within. Untouchables were limited by their inability to Scry or define things from a distance, but if something was visible, then nothing was stopping him. The manor was defended from wizard magic, which was useless against untouchables, and the longer they delayed, the closer Tamort came.

"Wandering," Sedgan answered. "I will go looking."

"In the Dreamworld, I assume," Cole added helpfully. "What are we supposed to do in the meantime?"

Sedgan shrugged with the same indifference. "Delay Tamort," he said. The apparition faded into the sunlight, leaving an empty road.

"How by the hells are we supposed to do that?" Cole demanded too late to get an answer. Cole searched the area as if expecting Sedgan had camouflaged into the trees. Finding nothing, his eyes fell onto the sword in his hand. He shook his head. "Don't expect me to fight him! Swords are not my thing."

Shimmer let out a long breath. "I guess I'll do what I always do: argue with him."

She resumed her travel, racking her mind for what she would say. Would Tamort pretend to be Kitable, or would he suspect she knew? She knew Kitable; she could have distracted him easily. She could ask him to explain temporal spells and why they continued to elude him. Or ask him why he never let Lady Elanis into his rooms. The kingsman's daughter had been chasing him since she had come to live in the manor in Wayburn and was a point of constant irritation. Sometimes Shimmer thought Kitable had made the Manor of Trulinar so *he* could escape. She could get him ranting about that.

But Tamort? She knew nothing about the man besides outdated rumors from days in Fixer City, following King Tohmas' march to conquer Espar. Then, Tamort had been Sedgan's acolyte. He'd been among the first to accept Loni as a celebrant, but masquerading as Loni would not work twice.

Did Tamort know Kitable's mind? Would he know their usual discourses, or would he only know Kitable's public personae? Kitable acted differently when they were alone.

Shimmer was still trying to devise a spell that could delay Tamort despite his untouchable powers when she turned the bend in the road and saw him a dozen paces away.

Choosing one of her ideas at random, Shimmer began a performance.

She brightened, turning her brisk walk into a trot to approach Kitable. She knew coming into contact with him would dispel her, but she was ready.

Cole had to follow along, SoulBurner wrapped and held loosely at his side.

"Wisavi!" she called, waving her arm. "Wisavi Kitable!"

He stopped on the road, and his eyes narrowed on her. He paused for a blink, taking a moment to recognize her.

He did not smile. His usual trimmed beard was shaggy with neglect, and he had not bothered to wash his hands in the fourteen days since she had last seen him. His wounds were healed, but many stitches had not been removed, and the lines were still stark against his tanned skin. His robes were dusty and tattered, a far cry from his usual proper attire. She was not sure whose shoes he was wearing. Painfully obvious was the lack of wizard magic around him. Even if she had not known that another mind lurked within the body before her, she would have recognized in a blink that something was profoundly wrong.

Once she was within a reasonable speaking distance, he answered, "What do you want, Miss Weaver?"

By using the "Miss Weaver" title, he was defaulting to the public personae they adopted when being observed by others. That gave her a role to play. She needed Tamort distracted. For that, she needed a confrontation. One thing she had never done was fight with Kitable in public.

She stopped a stride from him, dramatically putting her hands on her hips. They were no longer master and apprentice, and she was a slighted woman.

"Master Weaver now," she corrected. "If my apprenticeship is over, then I am a master wizard, as good as you."

The mannerisms were all wrong. Instead of tensing into a straighter posture and glaring down at her as Kitable did when annoyed, this version of her mentor sank into a fighter's stance. Shimmer had seen many soldiers position themselves like that when bracing for combat. With his training, she expected Tamort to be versed in fighting. One of Inac's many manifestations was the Warrior Queen, after all.

His voice was tight. "So be it, Master Weaver," he said. "What do you want?"

"A wizard is breaking the law in StonePeak," Shimmer told him. "I may be a fine wizard, but this is no longer my duty. Your problem."

To her satisfaction, Kitable eased out of the fighter's stance, and she assumed that meant he was less suspicious. "I will investigate it once I have finished my current duty," he replied. He then made as if to walk past her and Cole.

Shimmer stepped into his path, mocking anger. "Don't you dare brush me off again," she snapped. "Black is a threat to you and the king. Whatever you plan to do in the Manor of Trulinar cannot be more important than the king's life."

It took Tamort a moment to respond. He analyzed her, almost as if assessing her with Spell Sight, seeking an explanation.

"My purpose at the manor is as urgent," he replied, his sneer unfamiliar despite the well-known features.

"I know what you are doing," she said, waving her finger at him, keeping the momentum going. "Avoiding me! I should have known that night in Woodcutter's Retreat was you leading me on! You've been trying to get under my skirts since we met!"

She saw the expression change, first to confusion, then to wide-eyed shock. For a moment, Kitable's mouth hung open.

"Come on, Shimmer," Cole gently said from her right. "We've got things lined up."

Thinking that meant Sedgan had told Cole he was ready, Shimmer attacked one last time. Pushed too hard, Tamort would lash out. She needed him too confused to react for a moment more.

"How dare you dismiss me! How dare you pretend I am nothing to you!"

Beside her, Cole looked aghast, but Tamort's expression blanked. His mind seemed to stop functioning for a moment.

Shimmer was a trained actress, and she felt her performance was authentic. It seemed too much so, for her eyes were cloudy. Even if it was a lie, the frustration at being pushed aside was real.

Kitable was right here, but he was not. She was so close to having him back and yet would never have him, not even if he escaped Tamort now. Even if the words had been Tamort's, they had said the thing neither of them had wanted to admit. Her time with him was over. She could not pretend to be the apprentice anymore. That ruse was done.

But so help her, Shimmer would kick Tamort's soul into the third hell before she accepted that inevitability.

"Damn it!" she shouted. "Kitable, I'm in love with you."

After another span of empty mist, lost in the Dreamworld, Kitable came upon a river in an open field. For the first time, no dreamer was evident. He paused.

The trail in the field was deep, as if many feet had followed the parting of the grains down to the straggled tree by the small river. He followed it down, watching wrens dart across his path. The broken, barren tree had three branches, the lowest reaching above the water. The wood was sun-bleached and brittle when he placed his hand against the trunk.

Rustling in the grass upstream, an asp slithered into view. Its eyes flickered with fire. But it stopped atop the exposed root of the tree, curling into a circle and raising its head to watch him.

His eye caught movement: a mangled piece of twine was tangled around the branch over the water. It felt familiar and important.

The snake hissed, and Kitable glanced back at it. Its head slid over a curl of the body, inching toward him threateningly. Stubbornly, Kitable held his ground. The beast wanted him to move on. Whatever that monster wanted, he would deny it.

"Good choice," a voice said.

A white wolf bounded up to his side. Hackles raised, the wolf snarled at the snake, and the asp drew its head back uncertainly.

"Be gone," Kitable said with confidence now. "This is my realm. You are not welcome here." As he spoke the words, he realized they were true. He was the dreamer here. This was his world now.

The wolf growled and stalked forward another step in support. The asp curled back, its head swaying, considering the wolf's approach.

Kitable cracked the branch off the tree, hefting it like a club and joining the wolf in the attack. "Begone, spirit!"

As he lifted the branch to strike, the asp slithered away, disappearing into the tall barley and wheat of the field. The wolf bounced after it with a sharp bark.

Kitable waited another moment to ensure it was gone, then lowered the branch. Again, his eyes were drawn to the twine on the branch he now held. A wren, the tiny songbird holding a bit of twine in its beak, landed on the branch and peered at him with black eyes. It felt of vital importance, yet he did not know why.

The arctic wolf left the pursuit of the asp and trotted back to sit at Kitable's side. "She was here," the wolf said.

Kitable looked out over the river, remembering other such fields, a march across the world, battles, and duels, all to form the Kingdom of Espar.

"Has it always been so obvious?" he muttered.

"To the rest of us," the wolf replied, "yes."

He knew it now. Shimmer was his focus, but it was certainly more than that. A focus came from something so powerful that it engaged the soul.

"I've been in love with her since Arcott," Kitable said, the words tightening the feeling in his heart with certainty. It was pure truth, something even Tamort had been unable to twist. That was his focus. "She showed up soaking wet, having summoned most of a lake to save her father and herself from Master Terant. She was so damn cheery about having failed a duel but lived. I fell in love with her." His eyes went back to the wren, wondering about its significance. "Yet now I cannot reach her. I cannot find my way back." The wren took flight, and Kitable's attention returned to the twine.

The wolf snorted. "Of course you can," it said. "You have the wrong destination."

Still unable to determine why the twine seemed important, he looked down at the wolf. This wolf was pure white, shining unnaturally in golden light. The eyes sparkled gold, making it hard to meet its stare.

"You look different," Kitable remarked.

The wolf tilted its head, then changed. The form shifted, stretching out into a bipedal form. It retained the long muzzle and fur coat but gained a near-human shape. It was exactly the creature he had last seen in the Dreamworld when Tril had aided him.

"Tril?" Kitable exclaimed.

The wolf-man smiled wide, his long teeth bared. "Who else?"

"But it wasn't you last time! You... How could..." Kitable finally caught up to himself. "Where have you been?"

"Busy," the Northlander elder replied. "Espar is but a corner of a large world, Kitable."

"Then why appear now?" Kitable asked. "I am dispelled, as I was the last time you came to me, but what difference does this make? Tohmas' life is in danger. I spent two years creating peace, and it will be brought down! And you appear now? At the last?"

Tril shrugged his thick white shoulders. "I cannot fix the world," he said. "I am here because you had a question."

Kitable racked his mind. He did not have *a* question; he had hundreds. He did not yet know how to stop Tamort, even if he could gain control of himself again. What would happen to the soul should Kitable return? If it was not destroyed, was there a way to destroy it after? Where was Shimmer? Had the attack wounded her? Did she need his help?

Would she forgive him?

As he ran the questions through his mind, seeking the one question Tril seemed to believe mattered most, Kitable's eyes went to the twine around the branch on the tree.

The answer struck him. "Why am I drawn to that piece of twine?" he asked.

Tril's feral grin grew. "Because the tether you seek needs a beginning and an end, and this one has neither," he said. "All other questions are answered down that path."

Kitable looked at the twine and recognized that Tril was right. The string was a perfect circle.

"You've been searching in all the wrong places, Kitable," Tril added.

Kitable reviewed the places he had visited in his walking. He had looked in forests and mountains, in homes and on hills. He had checked oceans and ice flows. He had searched everywhere.

Everywhere except behind him.

The snake had been there, always on the edge of his vision, keeping his attention away from the one direction he should have been looking.

Turning, Kitable found the golden tether bound like a tail behind him.

"It leads to the physical world," Kitable remembered. "I had been looking for the darkness."

"But your body is where you need to be," Tril answered. As if hearing a voice, the wolf-man tilted his head, his eyes fixed on a distant location. "Good luck."

"Tril, but what—"

"You two work well together," the wolf-man replied, disappearing with a bound into the wheat. "You always have."

The clearing around the tree was immediately silent. Even the birds had gone still.

Kitable turned around, touching the golden thread attached to him. He kept one hand on it, following it back.

The field vanished. He had taken two steps into the golden Dreamworld when, out of the mist ahead, Sedgan appeared.

"About time! How did you get so far—never mind! Got everything ready for you," the celebrant said, falling into step with him.

"Everything?" Kitable wondered. "I can take back my body?"

Sedgan's soul shrugged. "Maybe. But I suggest we take a running start."

Kitable looked at the specter, confused. "What does the speed have to do with—"

He was too late. Sedgan had sprinted off like a runner with a message for the king himself. Kitable rushed to keep up.

They came crashing into the same waggon circle Kitable had been desperate to escape. Kitable entered as Sedgan tackled Tamort's spirit. When the pair fell back, they vanished into the golden mist, and Kitable suddenly could see through his own eyes.

For a blink only, the body of Kitable blurred. Shimmer was not certain it had not been the tears in her eyes, but when next she could focus, Tamort, a shadow of partial color and diluted substance, stumbled out of Kitable.

Kitable collapsed.

"Cole!" Shimmer shouted, lunging to slow Kitable's fall. Cole dropped the coat off the sword and thrust the sword forward but miscalculated Tamort's stumble and grazed the celebrant's shoulder.

Tamort's spirit shrieked, retreating from Cole and clutching at his wounded shoulder. Golden blood flooded over his hand, his eyes filling with fury. He stopped at the edge of the dirt road, his back to thick undergrowth.

Cole squared himself between the celebrant and Shimmer, the sword positioned to keep Tamort at bay. Shimmer didn't know if it was to defend her or Kitable but didn't care at the moment. Kitable was breathing. To her delight, he opened his eyes and squinted into the bright daylight.

"What *is* that?" Tamort hissed, his voice echoing as if from the back of a cavern, but his eyes fixed on the king's blade when Shimmer looked over. "SoulBurner?" he exclaimed, no doubt recognizing it from the conquest of Espar.

"Sharp enough to cut even you," Cole taunted, waving the sword back and forth.

"What happened?" Kitable's voice croaked.

Shimmer's heart swelled to bursting. She choked back tears, trying to find the proper order of words to explain. "Tamort... He... Sedgan told us..."

Kitable's eyes went wide. "Tamort!" he snapped, unsteadily rolling away from her and to his feet. She caught him, assisting until he stabilized. He seemed to be relearning where his feet were.

Shimmer joined him in searching the area. Tamort had not moved but finished assessing his wounded shoulder.

"You are out of your league, boy," Tamort said with a sneer as he paced along the length of the road, Cole mirroring to shield Shimmer and Kitable still. "You've got no aura to defend you," he pointed out.

Sure enough, SoulBurner rested inertly in Cole's hand. The legendary red aura that could stop dragon fire was absent.

"Course there ain't. Do I look like the king?" Cole snapped, following Tamort's pacing with SoulBurner, uncertainty in every step. The tip of the sword dipped slowly lower despite his double-handed grip. This was no knife, Shimmer realized. She had treated many soldiers for wrist pain after battles. Seeing the weight of the blade pull on Cole made it clear why. "But it still cuts, don't it?" he added.

Tamort lowered his hand from his shoulder. Instead of blood, golden light and flickering fire poured down his arm. Where it touched the ground, embers appeared in the road's dust.

"But you are no swordsman either," the celebrant said, his scowl shifting in realization.

As Tamort reached out his hand, the light and fire coalesced into a blade of his own. It was longer than SoulBurner by a hand and glittered with embers along its length. Serpents of fire made the cross guard, slithering around the base of the blade and Tamort's hands.

Cole blanched but held his ground. Shimmer was impressed.

Before Shimmer could activate one of her tethered spells, Sedgan's voice entered the road.

"He may not be, but I am," he said.

The specter of Sedgan appeared beside Cole, taking on a brighter form in the shadows of the forest canopy. He stepped through Cole, his hand out. When he slid out the other side, he had a sword in hand, a ghost of SoulBurner. In contrast to the fine but bland blade in Cole's grip, SoulBurner in Sedgan's hand glowed in its traditional fire aura. The Celebrant of Galanth squared himself before Tamort.

Tamort hesitated. This was his celebrant, the man who had taught him. And all Celebrants of Inac were trained in battle.

Realizing she had not acted, Shimmer hefted her bag.

"Take these," Shimmer handed Kitable a selection of trinkets out of her bag. Among them were his magic items left behind at Marionna's house, including his crystal pendant. "At least if one of us gets dispelled…"

Tamort gave a cry of rage and slashed at Sedgan. The older celebrant adjusted his footing subtly, parrying the strike. Despite neither blade having actual substance, they rattled like coliron on stone. Embers rained down onto the dry earth, smoldering.

Cole inched around, getting into a better position to strike Tamort once more. Before long, he had entered the edge of the woods, using the trees to conceal his approach.

Taking her eyes from the battle since Sedgan seemed to have Tamort's undivided attention for the moment, Shimmer was pleased to see Kitable analyzing each item as he pocketed them. He now wore his usual crystal pendant and had activated one of her beads, providing basic defenses.

"Tethered spells?" he asked, keeping one wary gray eye on the exchange between the celebrants. Tamort spotted Cole and spun to lunge at him. Sedgan intervened, sparing Cole, and Kitable's brother ducked back into the cover of the forest, SoulBurner in hand.

"I've an assortment," she confirmed.

His smile was filled with something Shimmer did not recognize, but it warmed her. "Can you keep him busy? I—"

"Another thunderstorm?" she asked, her fear of Tamort gone. With Kitable at her side, she could defeat anyone.

"Something like that. These items won't hurt him. I need time—"

A flash of magic, felt by them both, interrupted. Shimmer glanced behind her but then spun to face the new arrival. Her heart sank when she heard the familiar voice.

"Out in the open," Black said, appearing on the bend in the road, a wand in his hand. "I had expected better of you."

Even without Spell Sight yet active, Shimmer could feel the magic around the man pulsing. He had taken time to build up his array of trinkets. In addition to the usual magic items, Shimmer sensed a dozen more.

He had armed himself. Even at her full power, Shimmer was not confident she could match him. Shimmer was worn within a hand's breadth of enervation, and Kitable was still without hovering spells.

Tamort cackled in laughter. Glancing over her shoulder, she saw Sedgan's spirit knocked prone.

She knew every word in a magic duel should be used. Kitable had survived despite the opposition because he never wasted a single syllable and had taught her to do the same.

And yet Shimmer cursed.

Words did not matter. They were undone.

·●·●·●·●·●·●·●·

Sedgan felt alive.

He had not held a sword in decades. As a full celebrant, he had left the more violent obligations to the fragments of the Warrior Queen. In the conquest of Espar, his duties had been religious. Loni had reminded him how to use a knife, but the sword had remained forgotten until he gripped the hilt of SoulBurner.

The blade remained with Cole, but something of the sword's spirit came with Sedgan. It flared with fire as he brought it into Tamort's path.

Dream swords clashed. Tamort was faster, but Sedgan had experience on his side.

They ignored the trees, moving through them. The swords clashed, passing through stone and wood as if neither existed. When either blade cut onto the soul opposing it, it burned.

Sedgan had been branded before. He ignored the sensation. This was not a body; this was his soul. The pain was not permanent.

Tamort grew impatient, lunging beyond Sedgan to strike at Cole, who was standing guard with SoulBurner. The thief dodged away, but it was close. Sedgan ensured he was again in Tamort's path.

"Inac's favor is with me," Tamort boasted. He landed a blow onto Sedgan's left wrist.

The bitter truth of that made Sedgan grimace. He had walked through dreams for a lifetime and failed to find his goddess. Kitable had called it faith, and Sedgan now understood it. While he no longer believed in a goddess, he knew—he believed—that his purpose was here, setting right his mistakes. Loni's influence in Espar had been his fault. He had believed in her. He could not allow his error to destroy the peace of Espar.

"Inac's favor is a thing of the past," Sedgan replied. He thought of the times Loni had appeared as the goddess, fooling even King Tohmas. "Inac is a farce."

Although it was not his intention, his words drove Tamort into a rage. The soul began to flicker with Dreamworld gold as he lashed out at Sedgan. It kept him from targeting Cole, at least.

"Lies!" Tamort snapped. "You are the one who has fallen! You have lost sight of the glory of our—"

The words reminded Sedgan of Loni. He felt his rage rising.

He pushed it down and spoke calmly. "All you have done, you have done by your soul's strength. Inac has not aided you. Inac does not exist."

Filled with fury, Tamort let loose another battle cry, and he struck at Sedgan. Sedgan brought SoulBurner above in a firm block, angling the blade to let the other sword slide off it. The moment the weight of the celebrant was against the edge, Sedgan dropped the tip of his sword. Tamort fell forward. Fast as a striking snake, Sedgan stepped, turned, and brought SoulBurner down in flawless chop into the base of Tamort's neck. He kept his balance perfect, halting the blade as it passed through the shoulder to keep his guard centered.

He thought his duty done.

Tamort did not fall but slowly straightened, fire flowing freely from the cleft in his shoulder and through his neck. His burning eyes were no less bright.

"Inac preserves me," he said, raising his sword backhand to strike at Sedgan's front.

Sedgan stepped back, his sword already positioned to deflect the strike. Some things, he found, were never forgotten.

And as he went forward, Cole came in from behind, stabbing two-handed through Tamort's back until SoulBurner's tip appeared through his navel.

Tamort paused long enough to look down at the sword. Then, with a shrug, he turned on the blade, slashing open his abdomen and cutting toward Cole.

"Whoa!" Cole shouted, scrambling away but remembering to take his sword with him. "I ain't taking that chance!"

Sedgan came around to meet Cole, positioning himself between Tamort and the thief. It made sense that the soul could not be harmed in this battle—it was a thing of energy and dreams. But Cole's soul was connected to body and mind. Would a blow from the ghost's sword do him injury?

"If we can't chop him up, what are we doing?" Cole demanded, following Sedgan as he parried Tamort once more. When he could, he used the trees themselves as a blind.

Knowing that he, too, could not be slain by his opponent's blade, Sedgan traded a slice across his leg for the opportunity to push Tamort back.

The injury did not even hurt anymore.

He was vaguely aware that someone else had arrived on the road, but Sedgan dared not take his attention from Tamort long enough to investigate. He had to get Tamort into the Dreamworld, that much he knew. Only in the Dreamworld could the soul be contained. The Gate was there, waiting for him. Tamort had no body, no tether. Perhaps the souls of the Dreamworld could drag...

But the souls he had met in the Dreamworld would not leave the golden light; that much had been clear. Sedgan himself did not know the way to the Gate, and the thought of seeing it again sent a shiver through his soul. When he saw those great black gates next, he would face his own death.

In that, Sedgan had his answer.

He led with his open hand, ignoring the pierce of Tamort's blade into his chest. He hooked his left hand onto Tamort's arm, then shoulder. Once confident he had a strong enough hold, Sedgan swung his blade behind his back.

In severing the golden thread connecting him to his body, Sedgan knew he was ending his life, but it also gave him the information Messenger had promised: he knew exactly where the Gate now stood. Better still, he felt the pull of the Gate.

And Tamort, held firmly, was dragged into the Dreamworld with him.

●●●●●●●●●●●●

The man who appeared on the road bend was older than Kitable by several decades but had aged well. Despite the garb of perfect black and the loss of his beard, he was still recognizable to Kitable. He arrived with a large flash of magic that lingered in the air, feeling like a Seal to Kitable.

Kitable's crystal pendant had just become useless. If he had not changed the enchantment, he could have at least moved within the Seal, but he had keyed it to return him to the Manor of Trulinar. That destination was inaccessible now.

"Out in the open," Black said, "I had expected better of you."

Several things made sense in succession.

"That's Black?" Kitable exclaimed, pointing. "That?"

Tamort's source for information about Kitable's family became obvious. The celebrant may have been searching for vengeance against King Tohmas, but he had stumbled upon an ally willing to help take down Kitable.

Kitable met the eyes of the wizard on the road, seeing every wrinkle on the familiar face. When he had last seen the man, nearly twenty years before, Black had been a young master wizard. The years had worn out the wizard's skin like a dried-out riverbed. His scowl had become permanent, but he felt like a mountain of magic was behind him, ready to come crashing down.

"Yep," Shimmer said, sighing. While the sound could have been exasperation or frustration, with Shimmer, it was pure resolve setting in. "Black!" she called. "This ain't a good time. We won't have time to talk, just fight, and that won't go well for you."

Like him, Shimmer was weakened. She was trying to bluff to buy time, time to allow for casting.

Kitable took quick stock. He had no hovering spells. His defenses were basic and would keep him from being anchored, at least until Black decided to dispel the shield.

Kitable activated one of the trinkets Shimmer had given him as a starting point, gaining Spell Sight. The auras around Black blinded him. Many were illusions, tricks to confound him, but sorting through them would take time he did not have.

"Oh, Bliss," Black teased, "I can't leave now. I'm sure Kitable will understand."

"Sylas, you bastard!" Kitable exclaimed, using words to buy time as Shimmer had. But he knew he could not keep Black talking. He would have to recruit another distraction. "If you are going to frame me for your murder, at least have the decency to be dead!" he accused.

Sylas Colean's smile was a leer full of confidence, enough to make Kitable's mind snap back to two decades before when he had been thirteen and Sylas had controlled every aspect of his life.

But he was no longer the scared child. He had fought against his master then. It seemed he would have to do it again.

"You were convenient," Sylas replied, lifting his wand.

Kitable read the auras of the trinket. No anchor. No way to be bound. He prepared to dodge.

Cole stepped between Kitable and Sylas, SoulBurner held low at his side. Kitable glanced to the side, seeking the dueling celebrants. He did not see them at all and hoped that meant they were at least too occupied to become an issue in this conflict.

"Sylas Colean," Cole said slowly, his voice tight as a bowstring. "*You* are Sylas Colean?"

Beside Kitable, Shimmer started casting. She cast one part, then paused, waiting for the wizard on the road to dismiss the rise of magic. She tiptoed down her spell like sneaking in to steal from a bedside table.

Casting without being obvious was tricky. Kitable had once managed to cast while holding a different conversation, but it was a unique skill. Sylas was unlikely to suspect it.

Leaving Shimmer's side, he joined Cole on the road.

"That means he is your father," Kitable added, starting his casting. The conclusion did not perturb Master Sylas as Kitable would have liked, but he could see the words sink into Cole.

"Of course I am," Master Sylas replied. "Why else would I have taken you in, Cole? I have provided for you since you set foot in StonePeak. I have been there more than your half-brother has. Did he tell you the truth about his departure from my service? About the notes he stole? About killing my associates?"

Kitable's chest tightened. The nightmares of his youth had been silenced by decades of deliberate disregard, but they were still hiding at the back of his mind. No one had known his name. No one knew where he had come from. There had been nothing to remind him.

Except for Sylas. Now that the master wizard stood before Kitable once more, he felt like a thirteen-year-old hiding in the cupboard, praying for the magic to come to him and grant him escape. Desperation gnawed at him.

Cole's head turned toward him, his stare accusatory, and Kitable acutely realized he had stepped up beside the man holding SoulBurner.

"Cole," he said, "I didn't know you existed." Between words, Kitable tried to remember what spell he had been planning and why he thought it would succeed. SoulBurner had only to touch him. The greasy feeling of untouchable magic tainted the air beside him.

"That's because you never visited mother," Cole snapped. "It would have been obvious if you had visited her even once."

Kitable was taken aback. He had expected Cole to want explanations from Black. He had not expected to be defending himself against his half-brother.

Black activated his wand. The spell attacked Shimmer.

Cole started, following the sound of the spell as it streaked by them, but too far away to intervene. Without thinking, Kitable stepped into the path of the spell. It was a complicated dispel, and it destroyed his Moulded Shield, but in hitting Kitable, it failed to reach Shimmer.

She had enough time: in quick succession, Shimmer released three spells. Two broke down shields. The last one went in for a direct blow to the heart. She had identified the weakest elements, targeted them for dispels, and made the attack.

Black brought up an item. Her strike failed.

"So much for discussion," Black commented dryly, retrieving another wand from within his coat. Kitable did the same, activating the wand to set a sizeable impenetrable shield around himself in time to block Black's force magic. Shimmer cast an illusion next, splitting herself into a dozen simulacrums and sprinting away in different directions.

"Kitable," Cole pleaded, putting his back to Black but retreating away from Kitable, "he's my father. Leave him alone!"

Kitable shook his head. "He has been hiding for decades," he replied, creating a spell within the spaces between words. "This is not about me, at least not only me." He glared at Black but saw the man's eyes flickering away, tracking Shimmer's movements. Her illusions were superb. Even an amplified Spell Sight would fail against them—at least Kitable's would. If Black got a strike through her defenses, Kitable still would not have a chance to apologize. "Think about it! He's not hiding anymore. He let you know who he was."

Black and Cole were now side-by-side, but Cole was watching Kitable. Black's burst spell flooded over the area.

It was stopped by the shields around Kitable but destroyed all of Shimmer's illusions in one swoop.

The words completing the spell flowed from Kitable's lips, the final syllable held. Black had been hiding for too many years. He had not marched with King Tohmas. He would not know the Lady Skirt's spell.

But Kitable hesitated. The spell was indiscriminate. It could eat through all types of defenses but ultimately was designed to destroy a person. Cole was too close. He would be killed.

Planning to tether the spell, Kitable held it at the ready. But, out of the corner of his eye, he saw movement. Shimmer stumbled into view.

She had a hand on her side. Blood seeped between her fingers. Her tanned face was ashen, and she staggered.

Rage struck Kitable bluntly. Cole was allying himself against them. He did not matter. Shimmer was hurt.

Kitable released the spell, and the bright auras erupted before him. He expanded it with a thought, driving it toward Master Sylas and knocking aside each shield as he came across them. The spell was built to protect it from all dispels and alterations now. It was indestructible.

But Black did not seek to block or destroy it. With a word, he vanished within his own Seal and appeared a dozen paces to the side, next to Shimmer.

Kitable dropped the Lady Skirt's spell, sparing Cole.

But when Kitable spun to face Black, the master wizard grabbed Shimmer's wrist and pulled her hand away, revealing a branch impaling her at the waist. His direct contact with her wrist proved that she had been dispelled to a level Kitable had not realized. She was vulnerable.

"Foolish girl," Master Sylas said. He looked back at Kitable, his eyes full of hatred.

He knew Kitable was helpless. Even his fastest spell would never be fast enough. Sylas still had defenses up. He would do better to be throwing rocks at the man.

Master Sylas used an activation word, and Kitable watched Shimmer jerk, then collapse in dead weight.

From the cover of the forest, a dozen paces away from Black, Shimmer saw the old thief's face as he activated a deadly destruction spell and shot it into the illusionary Shimmer he had by the wrist. The magic shot through the image of her. Shimmer willed the body to collapse.

Her illusion responded perfectly, but Black's expression was suspicious. "Too easy," he muttered, looking at his hand, then down at the crumpled illusion of her at his feet.

Perhaps her skin had been too warm, or the passage of light over her hair was inconsistent with the forest shadows. Shimmer had accounted for hundreds of details, but another dozen could have evaded her in her haste to create the spell. And Black was clever.

But even if Black sensed something amiss, he had fallen for it and was well within Shimmer's reach. She no longer had to contend with his outermost shields at all. Only a dozen remained between them.

She took one step, leaving the trees to better position herself, and she saw realization strike him. He pulled back, reaching for a trinket on his wrist.

Activating another three spells quickly, Shimmer blasted apart his remaining four shields and slammed a force spell into his sternum. Even if it struck a Moulded Shield, the force was sufficient to crush ribs into the heart.

To her dismay, he managed to activate the trinket, and a burst spell intercepted her final spell, triggering the impact too soon and blasting the master wizard from his feet. Kitable had to move aside to avoid being hit.

It was then that Shimmer finally noticed Kitable's face. He looked pained but elated, as if every stitch he had had burst open, then promptly closed again. Although her blow to Black had failed, Kitable was bursting with pride.

Black landed back where he had started—at Cole's side. Kitable had dropped his spell but was raising a new trinket, an orb Shimmer had named "Dragon's breath."

The tiger's eye orb contained a burst spell of pure, concentrated fire sufficient to bring down a building. A body caught in it would be immolated, but the spread of the magic was aggressive and would spread from Kitable by a dozen paces. It would easily catch Cole, and Black still had at least two shields against fire that would minimize the spell's damage.

But it would still hurt.

"Need a cage," Kitable shouted to Shimmer.

Black scrambled to his feet.

He intended to throw the orb, Shimmer realized. A Force Cage, when closed off with Kitable's variant of it, would seal the magic around their target, sparing others.

He was prompting her to protect Cole, Shimmer realized. Although she did not wish Cole harm, she was shocked

Kitable didn't either. He was usually too logical to be sentimental and had known his brother for too short a time. When Cole joined Black, Shimmer expected Kitable would be willing to kill him.

"Sure, but he's defended," Shimmer shouted back, casting anyway. She would have to pick a nearby target, something close enough but unprotected. Black's shields still protected the surrounding area and would prevent the spell from locking onto the man himself.

Black spun to face Kitable and Shimmer. He pulled a wand out, and Shimmer was acutely aware that Kitable had no decent defenses remaining. Still, her master did not lower the orb to seek out a protective spell. His hand drifted to his crystal pendant briefly, but he lowered it. The Seal was still in place. Even if he could get through that, the pendant would take him to the Manor of Trulinar, abandoning Shimmer.

But before Black could activate the wand, Cole leaned over and tapped his father on the back of his knee with SoulBurner. He could have attacked had he been seeking to kill the man, but the gesture was more of a swat, no more than tossing a hand to deflect an insect.

The effect was instantaneous: Black's defenses were dispelled by the untouchable powers of the sword. Whether the wand died, Shimmer was unsure, but the sudden loss of magic pulled Black's attention from Kitable or Shimmer.

Incredulous, Black glowered at his son.

Cole shrugged and hopped back a step. "You sold Mom and me out to Tamort, you bastard. Burn."

Her spell completed, Shimmer released the Force Cage. With no magic to protect him, it locked onto Black. Kitable threw the orb, relying on no magic to guide it. Black had to shield his head to avoid being hit in the forehead.

But as the orb bounced off Black's arm, Shimmer spoke the second activation word of the Force Cage and closed the bars of force into solid walls. The orb bounced off the inside walls of the Force Cage and landed at Black's feet.

An infernal hurricane exploded out, momentarily appearing to be solid light and heat. Cole scrambled farther back, shielding his eyes from the blinding glare but not looking away. Held by the walls of the spells, it formed a perfect cube.

Like Kitable, Shimmer kept casting. They each had another two hovering spells in place by the time the spells ended and the fire vanished.

The earth was a black sheet of glass in a perfect square where the Force Cage had been. To her surprise, a body lay within.

"Drop the cage!" Kitable called, rushing forward.

"If he is still alive, that will free him!" Shimmer argued. The Force Cage would protect them from most magic if somehow Black had protected himself from the fire and lived. It could contain him if they needed it to.

Kitable was already at the edge of the Force Cage, peering down at the crumbled form within it.

"Looks like he's dead," Cole said, coming up beside Kitable.

Kitable paced, peering at the body. "And that's familiar," Kitable replied. He glanced over his shoulder at Shimmer. "Drop it. If he's alive, this is a bluff."

Trusting in her master's assessment, Shimmer dismissed the Force Cage, allowing Kitable to approach the body.

He put a hand down on the black cloth. His hand passed through.

"Not even a good illusion," Shimmer cursed, seeing it. "Mine was better."

"Fooled me!" Cole admitted. "Didn't hear it."

"You couldn't have heard it over the raging fire, Cole," Kitable corrected, searching nearby. At the base of the illusion, hidden under the fake corpse, he pulled out a small spoon.

Shimmer had seen something similar before she had come to work with Kitable. One of Kitable's enemies had used an elaborate illusion to fake his death, and the trinket he had enchanted had been a similar spoon.

"Now I know where Tostig got that spell from," Shimmer said, recognizing it.

Kitable was already on his feet. "So, where did he go?" He briefly turned around as if expecting his rival to step out from the forest as Shimmer had done. "Where did Tamort and Sedgan go?"

"StonePeak is the safe place for Black," Cole guessed. "But the celebrants?" Cole scanned the area. "Sedgan tackled Tamort, then they both vanished." He shrugged. "I have no idea beyond that."

Shimmer activated a part of her remaining spells, searching for anchors. She saw none, even when she layered divination on top of it. Black's spell was beyond her ability to find, and the celebrants had left no trail. She had to assume they were in the Dreamworld. She hoped Sedgan was in control.

"But why would he leave StonePeak in the first place?" Kitable said, frustration in his voice. "That man has been living under a false identity for two decades. The threat of discovery by me was minimal until recently. Why stay there? Why come here? Why now?"

"Because his corner of the world was invaded," Shimmer answered, sorting through everything she had learned in StonePeak in the last fourteen days.

Kitable faced her. For the first time since regaining control, he met her eyes.

She fought to keep on track despite the way her stomach tossed. "He had created a kingdom of his own in—"

Kitable lunged at her, scooping her up in his arms. Cut off by Kitable's crushing embrace, Shimmer squeaked. With her hands pinned at her side, she could not return the gesture, but she felt the tears in her eyes.

It was him, back as if from the dead. He had wrapped his arms around her and buried his face in her hair, closer now than ever. She had been moving from task to task since spotting Tamort on the path, but it all fell apart when Kitable touched her.

Nearby, Cole raised an eyebrow and gave Shimmer a little shrug. She smiled at him, surprised by Kitable's affection but delighted.

After a moment, Kitable released, and Shimmer could breathe. He seemed confused again and looked away but said, "Thank you for coming after me."

"Course," she said.

He faced Cole. "Put the sword down, please," he said.

Nervous, Cole placed the king's sword on the ground. "You are not going to hug me, are you? You know I was lying, right? About being mad? I had to get closer."

"You are not upset that we tried to kill your father?" Kitable asked frankly.

"If he'd been my father, I would be, but Black was never a father. He was a boss. And he set me up while endangering my mother. So no, I'm not upset you tried to kill him. I shouldn't have pulled my punches."

Kitable studied Cole, and Shimmer knew what he was thinking.

"I trust him," she offered, coming to stand beside the boy.

Kitable sighed, and his stance softened. "Then I do, too," he said. "What were you saying about Black's little kingdom, Shim?"

Her heart fluttered. She liked the sound of the nickname in his voice.

"I was saying," she restarted, "that Black made a little kingdom for himself. He may have been proficient at smuggling, but his main enterprise is the slave trade."

Kitable nodded. "I'll check the manor," he said, launching into a Scry immediately.

Cole cocked his head, peering at Shimmer. She assumed he did not want to watch as Kitable searched afield by magic since Kitable had a way of doing it that left half an eye watching his surroundings. It was unsettling until a person got used to it.

"So what if Black sells slaves?" he asked. "Slavery is not illegal."

"That's the point," Shimmer explained. "King Tohmas is about to make it illegal. That happens, and Black will lose his one legal venture. Won't be easy for Kingsman Loritat to ignore him then."

She looked back at Kitable, her stomach tensing again. She blamed the adrenaline of the recent duels. Still, something about his disheveled appearance was giving her terribly inappropriate thoughts, and they were all more driven by the memory of his embrace.

"Besides," she added, "Black could not expand while Kitable was on duty with King Tohmas. He knew Kitable would recognize him. I wonder how many others would love to know Master Sylas Colean is alive."

Cole drew a breath through clenched teeth. His expression hardened.

"A lot?" she guessed.

"Master Sylas had enemies," Cole agreed. "Among the survivors in StonePeak, it's called the 'Purge.' One night and the local wardens took out over half the cadres with the rest wiping each other out. Black survived. He always said he happened to be out of town at the time and not important enough for the wardens to know about."

"No, he set them up," Kitable interrupted, his stare present suddenly. "He gave the wardens the information and turned the others against each other by faking his death. Seems he is not happy with the small corner of the world he claimed as his own." He met Shimmer's stare again. "He's heading for the Manor of Trulinar."

"King Tohmas?" Shimmer guessed.

"I assume he doesn't like that law," Kitable answered.

"That, and killing the king means you lose face," Cole added.

It made sense. The kingsmen would assume the worst of Kitable if the king died during his first stay at the enchanted home Kitable had built. At best, they would believe he was incompetent. At worst, a traitor. And should Master Sylas offer his aid, would they be brought to doubt Kitable's loyalty?

Kitable glanced at his brother, then back at Shimmer, concern on his face.

They would have to face Black again, and this time the man would not be fooled by Cole's lies. Going up against the master wizard would put Cole in danger.

Shimmer held open her bag to Cole. "SoulBurner in here," she directed.

While Cole retrieved the sword, Kitable cast a Relocation. Cole paused, tilting his head to listen. Shimmer heard the words defining the location and understood Kitable's idea.

"We're going to send you back to your mother," Shimmer explained. Before Cole could object, Shimmer explained, "Sedgan might need support, assuming he's alive and your mother is still a target. If we succeed in chasing Black off, he may yet go after her. He won't expect you there. We need you to protect her."

His objections fell off, and he dropped the sword into the bag.

"I don't get a hug, Bliss?" he asked.

Letting the bag fall against her awkwardly, Shimmer gave Cole a hug. "Be safe," she said.

"You too," he said, stepping away to stand before his brother. The long robes he had borrowed narrowly missed tripping him.

Kitable held the last word of his spell for an extra moment.

"Thank you, Cole," he said. Shocking Shimmer, he then reached out and embraced his brother. "Take care of Mother. I will see you when we are done."

"You'd better," Cole replied. "Now get me out of here so you can go after that bastard."

Nodding, Kitable finished his spell, and Cole was Relocated away.

Worried Kitable's mood would foul at the mention of her alter egos, Shimmer glanced at her master. "How are you doing?" she asked.

"I feel like I am second place in a foot race," he replied, smiling at her still, "but I am not enervated if that is what you are worried about." Concern washed over his face as he reached a hand out to her. She accepted it, the contact strange against her skin. "You nearly are, Shimmer." Catching her eye, he smirked. "Bliss, Radiance, Seraph ... whatever you want to call yourself, you are enervated."

"We don't have time to worry about that," she warned, her heart lifted by his ongoing playfulness. "Black's probably—"

"He can't Relocate into the manor," Kitable interrupted, squeezing her hand. "Can't Relocate anywhere near it. We can."

The Two-Person Relocation spell was one Shimmer had learned late in her apprenticeship, as it was unexpectedly complicated. Kitable performed it as if he had been doing it since childhood, and they reappeared in his room.

"That's cheating," she said. "Hardly a way to race."

Kitable's gray eyes were mischievous. "You can't cheat in duels," he said. "There are no rules."

Her heart soared. He indeed was back.

Once the thread was released, Sedgan felt a pull. Not fighting it, he clung to Tamort's soul and rushed after the sensation. He dragged Tamort with him, flying through the Dreamworld's golden expanse at a sprint.

He ignored Tamort's cursing and struggling and held on. Wounds and pain did not matter, not to his soul. Tamort conjured fire, which scorched Sedgan's arms, but the flames were too quickly left behind. He bit and flailed, but Sedgan did not release.

Other souls appeared around them, just as they had when Sedgan had followed Messenger. These souls walked outside the dreams, and no golden thread followed them. These were the dead. The Gate was near.

Sedgan did not slow, even when Tamort's struggles became frantic. He called out for Loni, but Sedgan kept running, dragging the celebrant with him.

The Gate came into view. The nearby souls milled about, talking to each other or pacing outside the valley where the gate loomed.

Finding the pulling sensation released, Sedgan took aim for the Gate and continued his run.

"You can't do this!" Tamort cried.

"Watch me," Sedgan said. "I'm dead, and so are you. I'm moving on, and so are you!"

A snake reared before him, a colossal serpent made of pure fire. It coiled before the Gate, its maw opened wide in a hiss, showing off the fangs of light and flame.

Sedgan ignored it, plowing forward even as it struck at him. He felt the puncture of fangs, and the burn of poison flooded into his veins, but it did not matter. The Gate was there. It, of everything in this realm, was the only real thing. What could this beast do to his soul? He was nothing but energy and thoughts. He could not be killed again.

Sure enough, the bite stung but did nothing else. When he ducked his head, tightened his hold on Tamort, and trudged on, he passed through the beast and reached the Gate beyond it.

As he approached, he realized he had been wrong: the Gate was not made of metal but black glass, imposing yet fragile simultaneously. It now loomed above him, tall and wide enough to admit dragons, should they find their way through dreams.

Sedgan hooked a hand onto Tamort's collar, holding him as he placed his other on the Gate. He dared not step back unless it was necessary. Tamort was still struggling.

He placed his hand on the glass, the surface chill against his skin through the blisters from the fires. He felt no pain. The glass faded away before him, opening a path.

The pulling sensation returned, stronger. Sedgan could not have retreated even with all his strength, and neither could Tamort. Both were yanked forward into the blackness beyond.

Yet as he crossed the threshold, Tamort screaming curses carried past him, Sedgan felt a tug on his belt. His advance into the shadows halted. Tamort was hauled from Sedgan's grip, vanishing into the distant dark.

The pull on Sedgan's belt intensified. He staggered back. The pressure before him did not give, making him feel like a tug-of-war rope between giants. Step-by-step, he was pulled back, the great darkness growing distant.

The black glass reappeared. The tug of the darkness beyond released. He fell back, landing in the golden light of the Dreamworld at the feet of a woman in red.

He scrambled to his feet.

She was perfect. The woman was tall as a Northlander and beautifully proportioned with long legs, broad shoulders, and generous breasts. Her long ruby hair was braided down her back, a band of gold and red wrapping her brow. Her dress reached to the floor but had a slit to the hip and chain mail accents layered over her bosom and hips. She had a sheathed sword on her belt, the hilt ruby and gold like SoulBurner.

Sedgan fell to his knees instinctually.

He had once seen Loni impersonate the goddess Inac and promised to never again fall for her ploys. This was not the same. The way the woman breathed proved she was a goddess, and none could question it.

At a loss, Sedgan spoke the prayer to Inac. When he finished, he glanced up, finding the goddess's gaze still unwaveringly upon him.

For the first time, he saw she was not alone. Kneeling behind her, Sedgan could make out faint silhouettes of people. They appeared to be acolytes of Inac, their robes neglected but proudly worn. Each existed like ghosts in the realm, their colors faint and their forms partially transparent, yet each had a clear thread connecting them to the image of Inac.

And one of the group was an older woman without any holy markings.

Inac sneered down at Sedgan.

"I reattach your soul, and this is my thanks?" she said, her voice a rich alto. "A muttered prayer? Hasty and… dare I say, insincere?" Inac looked over her shoulder. The heads of the acolytes were bowed in prayer, their eyes averted.

The woman among them glanced up, her eyes finding Sedgan. She smiled wide, small crow's-feet showing at the corners of her eyes.

"She prays for you, not to me," Inac grumbled as she faced Sedgan once more. "But so be it. Prayers have formed this thread. It is yours."

He checked behind himself and found a robust golden thread. He put a hand to it and felt the pull of his own body. *A cord of life,* Sedgan realized, *created and maintained by the power of prayer.*

Sedgan stared up at Inac, unsure. Was a goddess formed by the faith of others any less than a goddess who existed in her own right?

"I know what you are," he said.

Inac smiled, showing her teeth as if ready for battle. "I know," she said with a shrug. "The more important question becomes: do you believe?"

He nodded.

"Then go," she said, turning away, her red braid tossed over her shoulder. "Get out of my sight, Sedgan Firewalker."

Sedgan took his anchored tether in his hand and followed it back.

• • • • • • • • • • • • •

Shimmer and Kitable reappeared in his room, standing atop the mattress. He held onto her hand until they had stepped onto the firm footing of the floor.

He knew she was a skilled dancer. She would not have fallen, but it was a good excuse.

"Here," Shimmer called after him as he approached the door. She handed him a handful of his tokens.

"Why?" he asked, throwing them into a pouch, then going to the bookcases and sorting through the nearest trinkets. He wasn't sure what he was looking for but was confident he could figure something out. Master Sylas would not be far.

"Just give one to anyone who doesn't seem convinced you are who you are," she said sheepishly.

Kitable looked down at her, smiling. "You readied them in case I remained possessed."

Shimmer shrugged, but he knew she could hear the pride in his voice. "Do we have a plan yet?" she asked.

"Not—" His eyes fell onto the wands used to remodel the manor during construction, and his words fell off.

Shimmer followed his gaze, and her eyes brightened. "Wizard-stone," she said.

The wizard-stone that made up the manor had lingering magic within it. While it was natural stone, it contained various forms of force and binding magics. It had earth within it and yet was not earth.

Sylas' defenses would be useless against it. Wizard-stone could not be dispelled, and it could not be summoned away. Normal defenses would target the wrong element combination.

Kitable handed her one wand and took another for his pocket. "A mix of earth, binding, and force, unlike anything in the world," he agreed.

"None of his defenses were aimed against that combination," Shimmer replied.

"Chance of a hidden one?" he asked.

"Low," Shimmer said, walking at his side, stride for stride, matching him. "He has things concealed, but not against our Spell Sight. We'll have to let him into the manor to use wizard-stone, though." She thought for a moment. "I've never attacked anyone with wizard-stone before."

Wizard-stone itself was peculiar in that it was resistant to wizard magic. It could not be created quickly or easily.

"He's had a chance to recast," Kitable warned.

"You're aiming an unusual spell. He's not likely to bulk that up. I opened him to fire and light elements. He'll have to cover those first."

"Glad we agree."

Now in the hallway, they passed a pair of protectors. The two men tilted their heads curiously but said nothing. Kitable thought about the token, wondering what he could expect from the protectors, but Shimmer placed a hand on his arm when he reached for them and explained, "I ran this way a short while ago, and I didn't come back in."

Her touch made his heart skip.

"Wizards," the protector muttered. "You do that kind of thing."

Stepping up, Shimmer opened her bag to the protector. SoulBurner's hilt stuck out. "Could you return this to King Tohmas? At a run, please. He'll need it if we screw up."

Kitable almost stopped her but then realized she was right. They could not use the enchanted blade without dispelling themselves, and neither of them was trained with a sword. And if they failed, the king would do well to have the sword. Unlike them, Tohmas could bring out the magic-nullifying aura, and he had Carsh still.

Even with that, Kitable did not dare count on either SoulBurner or Carsh. If Master Sylas was that close to success, he was too close. Kitable had worked too hard to build this peace to have it ruined.

The protector's eyes went wide. "How by the hells did..." He trailed off, sighing. "Never mind. Damn wizards."

Taking up the blade with reverence, the protector left his post briskly. Kitable and Shimmer took a different turn than he did after the first intersection, but by the time they left the corridor, a new protector had arrived to replace the one who had left.

"Get him into the manor," Shimmer said once they were on the move again. "Shall I draw him on?"

"You think too much like me," Kitable warned. Still, he could not help but smile. "You are not in a position to duel him," he pointed out. "Use what spells you have, but do not push yourself. You are too close to enervation."

"I'll manage what—"

Kitable caught her hand and pulled Shimmer to a stop at his side. "Please, Shim," he said. "I don't want you exhausted."

The words that came out were not what he wanted to say. He wanted to tell her that seeing her wounded, even as an illusion, had terrified him, and the thought of her death made him sick. His imprisonment in the Dreamworld had made him realize how dangerous their lives were. Losing her would destroy him.

But those words were too complicated. He had to deal with Master Sylas first.

"I know I'm not useful collapsed on the floor," she replied. "I'll be careful."

It was the closest he was going to get to agreement. He nodded and turned down the hall, Shimmer following at his side.

"You want to rebuild a room again?" she teased.

He chuckled. Every wall in the manor had taken him a dozen tries to get perfect. Wizard-stone was an involved process, one she knew he had come to resent. "I've gotten good at that," he replied. "As a result," he added, "I happen to know how to break wizard-stone."

She squeezed his hand, and he was surprised to realize he had not released it since their pause. Even in recognizing it, he still did not let her hand drop.

"Then let's bring down the house," she said, holding the destruction wand ready.

As she kept pace with Kitable, Shimmer felt her leg throbbing. It had mostly healed, but she had been careful to stay off it whenever possible, making the day's constant rushing exhausting for the injury. Thankfully, the run from Kitable's wing to the main entrance was short. She still arrived breathless.

"Protectors, pull back to the dining hall," Kitable commanded once they reached the main entrance. The dining hall was the room beyond the narrowed door and would allow plenty of room for them to be ready.

The six protectors at the open outer gate gave Kitable a stubborn stare and did not move a muscle.

With a sigh, he handed one a token. The man scrutinized it, then declared, "Real."

They paused a moment more, then began moving toward the dining hall, abandoning the entrance.

"Is there a problem, Shimmer?" a voice called from behind.

Spinning on her sore leg, Shimmer found Queen Arnika standing in the doorway just within the dining hall. "We're doing pretty well," Shimmer said. She smiled at the queen. "I got Kit back!"

The demure queen tilted her head. "Yet you are preparing for an assault?" she asked.

"Master Sylas Colean of StonePeak," Kitable explained. "It's a long story, but suffice it to say, he's powerful and bent on killing the king. We are the best hope at stopping him, but if we fail..." Kitable looked at Shimmer meaningfully. The queen clearly had more trust in her right now.

"If we fail," she said, "the next room protectors can wear him out. He cannot Relocate within the Manor. By the time he reaches the king, he'll be full casting and slowed down or using trinkets. Carsh will be there, as will SoulBurner."

She felt the queen's stare delving into her. "So you wish to pull the protectors away from the gate?" she asked.

Phrased that way, it did sound unbelievable. After telling them that Kitable could not be trusted, she understood their doubt.

"Yes," Shimmer said. "We're going to be a bit messy. Better they be back, ready to interfere if we fail."

She checked with Kitable to find him smiling at her broadly. She could not remember such a grin in years.

"Very well," the queen said, casting a final sweeping gaze over the entrance hall. "Protectors, pull back to the dining hall."

None of the six hesitated this time, marching through the inner doors without looking back.

The queen lingered for a moment more, her stare on Kitable. "Keep my husband safe," she said. It was the perfect command.

As she left them alone in the hall, Shimmer saw Kitable shiver. She cocked her head, asking him if he was all right.

His smile returned. "I have stood before hundreds of casters," he said. "I have been scrutinized by more than a dozen variations of alteration and divination spells. I have had my hovering spells dissected by strangers down to individual codes. And yet, I feel like that woman saw more in that glance than any of those who tried to analyze me."

"A woman's intuition," Shimmer said. "Where—"

Before she could ask about the specifics of their plan, she felt a surge of magic behind her and had to turn. Her leg throbbed again.

The outer gate trembled, vibrating finely and creating an audible chime.

Shimmer knew the spells on the gate would prevent destructive magic, but Black appeared to be taking a different approach.

"We need him in here," Kitable reminded her. "He'll come after me. Stand—"

The gate shattered, metal shards bursting out. Shimmer stepped forward, knowing her defenses were stronger than Kitable's despite their harried casting. The metal, down to the tiniest sliver, was deflected away.

Kitable activated a wand instantly, cloaking himself with the advanced alteration of a Concealment. She felt him move away from her.

Knowing Black would see through that spell, Shimmer draped a yellow light around herself, creating the type of aura Spell Sight would identify as an illusion. With one aura, she made her true self appear to be illusionary.

Black stepped through the exploded gate, the metal remnants clinking against the stone floor under his feet. He scanned the room, an obvious form of Spell Sight draped over his eyes, giving his stare a scintillating hue.

His gaze landed on Kitable as the wisavi slid back toward the far door to the dining hall.

"I see you, Wisavi," he said, pointing a damning finger. He was ignoring Shimmer, believing in her fake illusion.

Kitable had known that Black would recognize his concealment. He was hiding in plain sight, drawing Black in. Sure enough, Black advanced through the entrance.

Improvising, Shimmer pretended to cast as if trying to draw his attention, but Black ignored her still, except to throw a basic dispel of light at her.

She activated an illusion in response, one masked from Spell Sight like before. This time, she made it an illusion of nothing, pretending to vanish as if she, the illusion, had been "dispelled."

Her head was foggy as she tried to sort out what "nothing" would look like under the circumstances. She made it look like the wall behind her, which was plain white. She drew a shadow where she thought the floor and wall would meet from Black's point of view.

It seemed to be close enough. Ignoring her, Black stepped into the room to cast at Kitable, who deflected the spell, then dropped the concealment to retaliate.

Her illusion protected her from being seen as she moved from the corner of his eye to behind Black.

The door was the issue now. With the gate broken, Black had an escape. Kitable's and her enchantments would stop any Relocation, but if he threw his anchor behind him through the door, he could get away.

Shimmer cast quietly, counting on Kitable's flashing duel to hide the magic. She created an impenetrable Seal for the doorway, all the while inching toward the exit herself.

Once she was outside, she could seal it. Kitable had a way out: he had designed his pendant to bypass the enchantments of the manor. Within the crystal lay a One-Person Relocation that would take him back to his room.

She had reached the doorway when, with a flick of his hand behind him, Black tossed a spell at her.

She was so shocked her spell failed, a mistake she had not made in two years. Black glanced over his shoulder, catching her eye, and Shimmer realized the illusion had never fooled him. Moving closer to get around him, she had put Black between layers of her defenses, allowing him to strike without bypassing at least half of her shield.

The spell struck true, and the confusing array of dispels cut through her other defenses. It was much like Kitable's Uncover spell, but the auras were twisted differently.

She was dispelled instantly, and with finality, an Eight-layered Dispel burst around her. In a flicker, she was stripped of all hovering spells. Her trinkets, including the wand to destroy the wizard-stone, went dead. This was no untouchable magic able only to dispel that which touched her. This expanded, tearing apart every magic item she had down to the beads in her hair.

Her splint was dispelled, and her leg failed, the muscles too tired to move.

With her leg injured, Shimmer knew she could not get clear of the entrance hall before Black killed her with his next spell. With no other option, she rattled off a basic creation spell and aimed it at the door, blocking it and trapping Black with her in the entranceway.

Black scoffed, and he tossed another spell at her. It would take him a few more moments to destroy the wall of regular stone she had made over the door, and he had Kitable at a disadvantage. His spell was aimed to kill.

She winced, knowing she had nothing left to protect her. She did not even have Spell Sight to reveal what spell was going to kill her.

But the attack crashed into Kitable, who appeared between her and Black. His shields blocked the spell. His expression was stern as he stared down his previous master.

Black's face changed from elation to frustration. "Never learn, do you, Kaylin?" he snapped.

But Kitable did not answer—words were too precious now. Instead, he pointed his wand up and activated it.

The stone above them cracked, drawing Black's attention. He scrambled for another trinket. It did not matter. He could not stop the enchanted rock.

But neither could Shimmer. She, like Black, was to be crushed.

Kitable spun in place, his wand dropping to the floor. He held his pendant in his right hand, wrapped his other arm around Shimmer's waist, pulled her against him, and crushed the crystal into his palm.

A crack shot out along the ceiling in a blink. The stone buckled and crashed down like an avalanche.

Shimmer was shocked to feel magic wrap around her, whisking her away from the crush of the falling ceiling.

* * *

Cole appeared in the cottage, standing at the center of an unexpected circle of praying acolytes.

He searched the dim home but found nothing amiss yet. He heard no magic, and Sedgan was still lying on the bed, his face a dangerous shade of gray. Marionna was still kneeling at his side. He thought he heard her voice joining in the prayers.

"Sorry to interrupt," Cole said when the bowed heads of the acolytes lifted to stare at him. "Carry on," he added. He gingerly made his way out of their circle. They were each in their red robes of Inac, but none were marked as celebrants, confusing him.

He began to recognize them as followers of Tamort and held ready a spell to keep them from his mother, but Marionna did not seem distressed, and if he could believe his ears, these acolytes were praying *for* Sedgan, not against him.

Carefully, Cole knelt beside his mother, placing a hand on her shoulder.

"I cannot wake him," she told him, her eyes sad but tearless. No tears remained. She held the celebrant's hand in hers, his ashen against her tanned, callused one.

"It's not your fault," Cole consoled. "He came to us, helped us. But Tamort..."

Cole let his words fall as the faint glow of gold rose from the celebrant. Behind him, the prayers dropped off. Cole felt the stares of the acolytes lifting, although some glanced at him in accusation.

He retreated from the body of the celebrant, guiding his mother to follow him.

The glow of gold intensified. He had seen this gold once before when Tamort had used the flow of his golden blood to forge a sword, and it was not something he trusted. He could hear no magic, and this felt like untouchable powers. Something from the Dreamworld was reaching out.

Sedgan's body arched, and a golden fire snake shot into the single-room cottage. It collided with the ceiling, spinning off a rafter before landing on the floor amidst the acolytes. It formed into a viper the length of a tall man. Its eyes glowed in gold, its body flickering in fire.

Fire caught in the rafter where it had passed. Through Sedgan's mouth, speaking over the crackle of flames, a woman's voice said, "Behold the serpent, the traitor to us! Kill the serpent, my acolytes."

The acolytes answered, arming themselves with anything they could. The eldest of them blocked the doorway, a fire poker in hand, stabbing at the snake as it hissed. Another snatched up a blanket and moved in as if to extinguish it like a brush fire. Another grabbed the rush broom to bludgeon the writhing creature.

The broom caught fire, as did the nearby chair when the startled boy dropped it. The little fire in the rafters sent embers into the thrush, and Cole saw smoke.

The snake circled once, trailing fire, and struck at an acolyte. The boy fell, fire-filled puncture marks on his thigh. Flames oozed down his robes like venom, and he screamed in agony.

The snake then lunged at the exit, seeking escape, but the eldest acolyte stabbed at it once more with the fire poker and took it in the eye. It flailed and slithered back.

Should it escape the room, there would be no chance to kill it. The fire would spread to the forest and all of Woodcutter's Retreat.

But this was untouchable magic. Even if he had known a spell to defeat it, it would fail. Cole's magic was useless.

He shoved his mother toward the door, content when the acolyte eased himself aside to allow Marionna to escape. She fought him, turning as he tried to shove her into the fresh air outside.

"We can't leave the boys!" she cried, holding onto the doorframe to prevent him from pushing her out.

"Boys?" Cole answered, looking back as another acolyte took a bite to his chest, the snake jumping upon him with its total weight. The fire of its scales caught on the robes. The other acolytes moved to help, pulling their companion free and stripping him of his ignited robes while the other batted the snake back with the blanket.

Where the blanket struck, the snake appeared extinguished. Its renewed motion restarted the flames.

"Did you adopt them all?" he snapped.

"Please, Cole," his mother begged, frantically clinging to Cole's arm. "They are innocent."

"Innocent but useless!" Cole replied. "It's not like acolytes of a Goddess of Fire can do much here! We need water or..."

Cole's mind skipped, and he remembered the wands Shimmer had given him. Perhaps he did have a use for quite so much created water.

Pulling the wand from his coat, Cole stepped back into the fray, the air already thick with smoke. The snake had coiled at the center of the room, its head swaying to line up another strike, this one at the acolyte blocking the doorway.

Cole aimed the wand and looked at the short stick, seeking the activation word. She had written it there. He had seen...

It had smudged on his coat and was gone.

The snake lunged at the acolyte, and the boy smashed it to the side with a fighter's skill. He turned and stabbed down, but the snake was too fast. It rolled and struck again, catching the boy in his arm. The acolyte screamed, the poker falling from his hand.

Cole closed his eyes, remembering Kitable's room. He envisioned the moment Shimmer had handed him the wand. He had read the word. He had to remember...

The snake began to slither over the fallen acolyte, heading out of the smoke and through the door.

"Oh no, you don't, you bitch," Cole heard his mother say.

Cole's eyes snapped wide. Marionna now stood in the doorway, a wood plank held like a longsword in front of her. "I will not allow you to escape!"

Cole's heart stopped.

He remembered the word.

"*Ocenan!*"

Water crashed down, an instant downpour over the entire interior of the cottage. The torrent pelted like a rockslide on his back, launching him forward. He lunged for his mother. They were both tossed out of the house and off their feet.

Cole lay on the ground for a moment more, listening. He no longer heard the hiss of the snake, only the sizzle of a doused fire.

He rolled over cautiously, looking back toward the house. The roof steamed, and the inside was white with mist. He saw no light.

Sputtering, an acolyte lurched out of the home. He was soaked as if having fallen into a river, his feet squishing when he stepped out and pushed his sopping hair out of his eyes.

Cole smiled sheepishly. "Did it work?" he asked. The wind cut through the wet back of his shirt now, and the cottage looked like one of Leviathan's hot bath houses for all the steam.

The acolyte tumbled but was nodding. "I think so," he said. "I couldn't see any fire remaining."

Another acolyte emerged and gave a similar report. The needs of the wounded acolytes being carried from the home took priority. The acolytes were assisting in placing the wounded out in the sun. Those bitten by the snake seemed to be stirring, although they shivered.

A runner was sent to the neighbors, requesting to borrow some clothes.

As they all went about tending their injuries, Cole remained staring at the door, knowing someone would have to check for the snake. *It's got to be me*, he realized. At least he was armed. Shimmer had not said if the wand had more than one charge on it, but he assumed it would. If he had to, he could flood the home once more.

But if the first attempt had not worked, it was unlikely the second or third would either...

"I'll check it out," Cole told his mother, using the bravest voice he could. "See if it's safe to start cleaning up."

She smiled at him, and it was different. She had always been supportive and devoted to him, her smile filled with maternal love. It had been a doting smile, one that had not changed from the time he had been a young boy.

This smile had pride in it. He had never seen that before.

With her confidence bolstering him, Cole strode into the single-room home alone. The ground sloshed under his feet. Several hot days would be required to dry out the dirt floor now.

He searched the area behind the curtain and the fireplace and found nothing. He started back, keeping to the back wall to ensure he had checked everywhere. He was not sure what effect the water would have on the walls, being stone, but if it had hit the underside of the roof, the thrush would need replacing before—

A figure rocked into view, and Cole started crying out. He brandished the wand, but the creature was not made of fire, and the water creation spell seemed unlikely to be useful. He reached for his knives, then paused.

"Celebrant Sedgan?" he asked.

"My name is Sedgan, yes," the man replied. In the mist, he squinted in thought. "I am less confident of the celebrant part." Sedgan waved his hands before him as if to push away the fog, but the moisture did not stir. "Where is the door, boy?"

Cole pointed, then realized the man could not see the gesture. "This way," he said. Once the man was within reach, he hooked his arm around the celebrant to help him walk.

"How long was I unconscious?" Sedgan asked in a quiet voice.

Cole counted back through the last quartercycles. "Fourteen days of insanity," Cole answered, guiding the man into the sunshine. Like the acolytes, the celebrant was soaked. He thought it probably good that the celebrant was not wearing his robe. With the extra weight, Cole doubted the man would be able to move. "No idea about being unconscious, though. You were conscious when I was last here."

Once out in the sunshine, Sedgan took steps on his own. Cole saw his mother notice the man, leave the stirring acolytes, and rush across the path to stand before him.

Sedgan paused, his stare no longer vacant and childish. They stood in worthwhile silence for long moments, neither one moving.

"Madam," Sedgan said at length, "I think I need to go for a walk."

Marionna smiled once more, this smile even more foreign to Cole. This smile was not pride or motherly love but pure joy.

"I would be pleased to walk with you," she said, her voice filled with cheer as she extended her arm.

"I would be honored by your company," Sedgan replied. He still staggered with every few steps, but her presence stabilized him. Still wet enough to be collecting the mud of the road on his bare feet, the two walked, arm in arm, down the path.

Cole knew better than to follow. He returned to the acolytes, pleased to find that the puncture wounds from the snake were nothing but red marks on the skin now, and the affected acolytes were already back on their feet.

He lay back, closed his eyes, and lay in the sun, waiting to dry off.

•○○○○○○○○○○•○•

They landed atop each other on the mattress in Kitable's room.

Shimmer lay stunned for a moment longer than her master, who bounced back onto his feet.

He had carried the crystal pendant since before she had come into his life. With his permission, she had analyzed it once and knew it to be thoroughly enchanted to prevent Scrys or divination that may reveal it to his enemies. Previous incarnations of the pendant had been designed to break through Seals or generate random anchors to avoid predictability.

Shimmer had never realized he had changed the enchantment to include a second person.

"Shimmer?" Kitable's voice was worried. "You all right?" he asked, kneeling beside the mattress once he realized she had not risen to join him. He reached for her but seemed to withdraw at the last moment as if afraid of coming into contact with her now.

Nodding, Shimmer pushed herself up. Her leg ached, slowing her rise.

"Just wondering when you changed the enchantments on your pendant to a Two-Person Relocation," she said, trying to keep her voice light. "That was risky." Had he been alone, the crystal pendant, his final resort, would have been useless. The spell worked by having two targets. Without someone else, it would have failed.

Seeing her discomfort, Kitable had her drop her legs off the edge of the mattress and coaxed her to remain seated. "Nonsense," he replied. "When would you not be at my side?" He quickly cast the splint spell again, supporting her break, and the pain disappeared.

She could not think for the moment it took for him to bring her to her feet.

Once she showed she was ready to move, Kitable led her back through the manor until they were again at the dining hall. They entered through the same door as before, but instead of long tables and empty chairs, they found the gate protectors in ready positions. Despite the obvious irritation of the protectors, the queen was still in the room.

A familiar voice exclaimed: "Damn wizards!"

She had to smile. Kitable and Shimmer had not, according to the protectors, left the entrance hall, and yet here they were, re-entering it!

"All good," Kitable shouted to the queen.

"Just making sure!" Shimmer added.

They opened the door to the entrance and peered in. The roof was open to the sky in several places, and stones littered the floor. The stones had maintained their shape, not cracking or splintering beyond what Kitable had caused. Large chunks of the rock had fallen, enough to crush a man.

Getting out a new wand, Kitable made short work of putting the stone back roughly, revealing the crushed wizard beneath it. Shimmer and Kitable both sought magic but found none remaining except his trinkets. After exhausting every possible avenue for escape or deception, Kitable finally sat down on the re-made bench by the exit and declared Black dead.

Shimmer sat beside him, the entire day catching up with her. The weight of her recent brushes with death landed on her. She shivered.

Kitable immediately faced her. "I'll check in with Cole, then finish cleaning this up," he promised, placing a hand on her knee. "Go rest. Use the bed in my wing. It's best protected."

Feeling the danger was finally over, Shimmer nodded. As she walked back to the basement where Kitable made his home, she was surprised to realize how closely he had understood her. She did need to feel safe now. There had been too many changes to adapt to. The familiar wizard-stone and wards on the walls made sleep inevitable.

She awoke to a loud crash. Without taking time to dress, Shimmer rushed from her room and into the living space wearing her slip and blouse. By the time she had found the source, a strange noise was cackling through the room.

Kitable lay sprawled on the floor beside a crumpled chair, laughing hysterically. The chair, the one she had been pestering him to repair for so long, had shattered. He had landed next to the Scrying circle, the same one they had used the day before leaving for Woodcutter's Retreat, and the pillows there.

He continued to laugh as he got up and spotted her standing stunned, words for a spell on the tip of her tongue.

"I escape untouchables, survive another duel with a master wizard, and save the king from assassination, yet am defeated by a chair!" he declared between ongoing chuckles. "And I missed the pillows!" he added. "There is a veritable field of them, yet I missed every single one! Gods above,

Shimmer, is it so wrong that I am pleased to fall on my face? Anything real!"

He sobered slowly. His grin was still broad when he finally could say, "I'm sorry to have woken you. How are you feeling?"

Shimmer came forward to the table near Kitable and, in moving, had the answer to his question. "Better," she confirmed. Nothing hurt. She had no enervation remaining. The spell on her leg was holding.

And she was home. Everything felt right.

"Are Marionna and Cole all right?" she asked, finding a seat at the table.

"Perfectly. I helped dry out the house. Cole decided to stay in Woodcutter's Retreat for a bit. He says he wants to avoid inheriting anything, so he will not go to StonePeak." Kitable pulled out a chair across from her and cautiously tested his weight before perching on its edge.

"Dry out the house?" Shimmer asked, bewildered.

"He fended off a denizen of the Dreamworld, it seems," Kitable explained. "Not bad for a dabbler. Mother is fine, and Sedgan is awake, too, by the way. He may or may not ever put on a celebrant's robe again, but he's awake."

He leaned forward and placed a hand on her knee, an echo of the gesture he had made at the entrance. Her heart skipped. They had so rarely been around each other without defenses set between them; she had come in direct contact with him only a handful of times. "He's alive because of you, Shimmer. I am... Your devotion and care humble me. You have done amazingly during this."

Shimmer relaxed into a sincere smile.

Clearing his throat, Kitable added, "For all the things that Tamort did, the one thing he got right was releasing you from apprenticeship," he said, seeming to have to force the words out. "You are phenomenal, Shimmer. Your mind, your skills, your memory, your power, your ability—all of it. You deserve to be called a master wizard more than any other wizard I have met, and I kept that from you. I am sorry for that." His words gained speed and confidence. "I was being selfish. I didn't want you to go. I couldn't imagine this place without you."

Shimmer found all hints of fatigue gone, her heart doubling in speed. Her skin tingled where his hand still rested on her skirt.

"So I release you, Shimmer," he continued. "Apprenticeship over. You're a master wizard." He gestured as if ending a grand play and pulled her to her feet. She rose uncertainly, distracted by the touch of his hand on hers. He was beaming at her, and she felt her face flush. "As such, you are free to do as you please!" he said, ranting at a comfortable pace. "Seek patronage or don't; travel again or settle down. Kingsmen all over Espar will try to hire you. Your services will be sought by the stupid and the wise, and the stupid will become wiser for it while the wise will be humbled. You could stay here, of course. I'd rather you stay. You understand magic, the language, the dance of it. I would never have taken you on if that had not been the case, but you've proven it a hundred times. Seeing you duel Sylas made that obvious! You were brilliant!"

Too stunned to move, Shimmer stood with her mouth agape as Kitable spun in place. When done, he cupped her face with both hands, holding her gaze, and her stomach felt as though it had been tossed from a mountaintop.

"Better than brilliant!" he continued, his face alight. "Amazing! Your illusion was flawless beyond anything I have ever seen, including my own. You have such an attention to detail. Such a beautiful, marvelous..."

His rant trailed off for a heartbeat. In the next blink, he added, "Oh, to the hells with it!"

She opened her mouth to ask what he meant, only to find her mouth covered by his in a kiss.

Shimmer forgot to breathe. The world spun.

He pulled away but did not let go of her. The pause lingered between them. His throat flashed in the nervous swallow. "Please tell me if I should be readying defensive spells," Kitable said, his voice instantly sober. "I've seen that targeted alteration you do, and it's nasty."

Her mouth dry, Shimmer failed to find words. She saw his pain as he waited. Whatever she said now would seal or damn them. This was her chance.

She took a long, slow breath to give her head time to settle. Then, ready, she smiled. "If you do not kiss me again," she said, her throat loosening, "I will do worse than that."

His smile grew, and she felt the fear in him evaporate. "Truly?" he asked, easing himself forward.

"I may tear out the fourth page of every book you have," she threatened. "Or I'll swap the tea leaves for dried dragon weed. Or..."

He laughed, his smile too broad to be widened further. "I had better kiss you again," he said and did. It was from a slight distance and remained awkward.

Shimmer let out a sigh of ecstasy. "I have been waiting for that for nearly three years," she told him, pressing herself against his front to close the distance between them. His arms fell around her, resting on her waist, and it felt perfect. He was no longer afraid. This tension was anticipation.

"Why did you never say anything?" he whispered, his chin tucked against her temple.

Shimmer pressed her cheek against his collar, savoring the sensation of skin on skin. "Because you were my master," she replied. "Wouldn't have been appropriate." Her heart fluttering, Shimmer ran her fingers over his shoulder, then down the drawstring of his shirt. Before she could do more than fiddle with it, he had adjusted his hold of her and kissed her forehead.

"That I understand," he said.

"You're not going to wake up in a few days and lose this new lease on life, are you?" she asked timidly. "Near-death experiences can change—"

He cut her off with a kiss. He tasted heavenly. "I have been in love with you for three years," he said, his gray eyes burning into hers. "I am not going to wake up and forget that."

"Why did *you* never say anything?" she teased, poking at his chest.

"Wouldn't have been appropriate," he replied. "But now? Now..." She teased the drawstring once more, prompting him. He gave her a nervous smile. "I have never done anything like this before," he warned, but he leaned into her touch at his neck. "That said, whatever you want, Shim, I will do."

"I am fairly certain that whatever *you* want to do will please me immensely," Shimmer said, deliberately placing his hand on her hip so that his fingers rested below the small of her back.

Pulling her forward, Kitable covered her mouth with his once more. Lust stole any further words.

The End.

Book Club Questions

1. If you could Relocate anywhere, where would you go? What would you do with that kind of magic?

2. Shimmer uses different personae when necessary. Which seemed the most authentic? Which was your favorite and why? Does everyone have different personae to draw on?

3. What does the book's title refer to? What would you have called it?

4. Why did Kitable consider the queen the power behind the throne? Is this kind of arrangement common in leadership?

5. What were the most significant moments in Cole's character development? How did they change him?

6. Sedgan experiences a religious event despite having lost faith. What role does the power of faith have in the story? How did his faith evolve?

7. Did you want Shimmer to end up with Kitable, Cole, or neither? Which had a better relationship? Why?

8. Was the ending satisfactory? Why or why not?

9. What surprised you in the story or about the characters? Why did that stand out?

10. What do you think happened after the end?

Author Bio

At a young age, Deborah's rampant imagination kept her up, lending great detail to all the terrible things lurking in the night. In desperation, her mother suggested she invent her own stories to distract her brain. She has been doing that since, channeling her ideas into sword and sorcery-style fantasy novels and shorts.

In her other life, Deborah is a veterinarian. She lives in Sooke with her husband of 15+ years, their two sons, and three demanding felines.

Follow for news on other Tales of Espar
or the new series "The Falling City"

If you enjoyed this book, hop over to your favorite platform and leave a review, such as on Goodreads or Amazon.

Get special updates and deals by signing up to the Newsletter! Start with a FREE EXCLUSIVE short story series of four books of Espar, including the short "To Dream"!

Discover more at
4HorsemenPublications.com

10% off using HORSEMEN10